STEVEN DANIELS

Blood Drive

Dear Readers,

Jac and Billy: Blood Drive is a young adult, supernatural novel about vampire siblings who suffer life-altering events, must flee their home, and fight for survival. The story contains language and violence often found in films labeled as viewable for ages 13 and above. Consider the following content list to determine if the book is right for you or the intended reader.

- Some coarse language
- Death of a parent
- Violence and death
- Suicidal thoughts

I feel it is also important to mention that Jac and Billy: Blood Drive is about the strong bond between siblings, resiliency, friendship, and learning there is love and beauty in the world.

My best,
Steven Daniels, Author

First edition: January 2024

Edited by R. Ramey Guerrero

Cover designed by MiblArt

CONTENTS

FOR THOSE WHO REFUSE TO SURRENDER.

GONE AND GONE

Mom had left written instructions in case something happened to her. Something did.

Jac's mom had been missing for three days when Sunny stopped by the apartment. He brought a piece of lined paper folded in thirds. The paper felt inconsequential in Jac's hands, but the reveal was substantial. The letter inked in her mom's horrible handwriting, "Hieroglyphics," is what Jac called it, read like a final message. It was part apologetic, part to-do list, and part goodbye. Ignoring the painful details, Sunny called the letter "unconditional orders."

Mom's instructions were for Jac to take her brother Billy to San Diego to stay with the Castillo brothers—family friends. Which was no simple task with California on the other side of the country from her home in Philadelphia. Mom would reunite with them if she could make it. With Dad gone too, Jac and Billy had no one to help ... aside from Sunny.

Sunny sat across from Jac at the circular family dinner table for four. The table had thin or missing varnish in some areas, with grooves and nicks showing its age and wear. The smell of burned pizza, over-baked for 25 minutes instead of 18, filled the air.

The quick shower Jac had intended took longer than expected once her mind wandered to sad and anxious places. As the shampoo rinsed from her hair and flowed down the drain, she thought of her dad. Three weeks had passed since he was … murdered.

The day Dad didn't come home, he had planned to take her to a Phillies game against the 'damn Mets'—one of his not-so-endearing names for them. It would have been a rare occasion when she got to go anywhere other than the local spots—the grocery store, the park, and the library.

Dad got tickets in what he called the 'nose-bleed' section. Considering her family's proclivity, she thought he was being funny, but he did not coin the term. Sitting in the nose-bleed seats meant they would likely and purposely have a good amount of space between them and any other person. The day of soda, popcorn, hotdogs—the big Italian sausage kind—and cheering for hits and strikeouts never happened. Dad didn't come home from work that day and never would.

Cold water, like ice razors, shooting from the shower head, and Billy yelling that Sunny was at the door brought her to reality.

Jac sat with her head lowered, peaking at Sunny through her still-damp black bangs. His elegantly manicured fingers slid a photo ID and short stacks of cash across the kitchen table. Sunny always resembled one of those perfectly dressed and groomed middle-aged men in the suit-store commercials. He carried himself with a level of composure that made her want to scream for him to show some passion, some anger, some ... something. He trained his bright blue eyes on her.

Jac picked up the ID—a Philadelphia, government-issued driver's license. On the ID's left was her photo, and in the middle, her fictional date of birth had her age as eighteen. Her pretend name was Sarah Dwyer.

"What do you expect me to do, Sunny?" Jac flipped the ID onto the table.

"Take it," Sunny said with the slightest of shrugs.

Jac pressed her lips. Never having seen that much money, she didn't know if she should be impressed, grateful, or worried about where or from whom it came.

"Take it, and go as your mother asked, as she instructed."

She shot him a fierce look. "Don't talk about my mother."

"Jacqueline, she was my friend—"

"I said,"—she raised her voice and her head to glare at him—"*don't* talk about her. Especially as if she's dead." Her daggered eyes pointed at him. "Or maybe she is, and you know it."

Sunny looked over her shoulder to Billy, sitting on the couch. Headphones plugged into his tablet hung half off his head.

Billy stared at them with blue eyes and a slight frown. He, the epitome of a "momma's boy," had suffered more than Jac at Mom's disappearance. Dad's death had upset him, of course. He had a right to be devastated. When Dad was gone, he still had Mom. Or, he did. She disappeared only three days after Dad's funeral. Mom and Dad were gone within a week, and Billy spent hours in silence, contemplating in that way he did.

Losing their parents thrust Jac into the role of Mom and, in some regard, Dad. She cared for Billy day and night: cooking, cleaning, laundering his clothes, tucking him in at night, and being there when he woke. Still, she had her own sorrow to contend with. Dad's death wrecked her. Days passed before any significant time between bouts of crying and before she cared to eat. Mom and Billy comforted her, and it wasn't until this morning she questioned if they seemed to have taken his death so well because she robbed them of their time to grieve.

"Sorry, Billy, we'll be done really soon," Jac said gently. "I promise."

Billy returned his focus to the tablet and pushed the headphones into place.

"How is he handling this?" Sunny asked.

"Better than I am. Ya know, he's that way."

"You *must* do this for him. It's not safe here for either of you."

"I know."

"He needs you to be the adult."

"I *know*." Jac chewed on her bottom lip and glanced back at her little brother. His headphones sat in place as he rapidly pressed the tablet screen, destroying an opposing army or monster. She leaned in toward Sunny and repeated, hushed but still firm, "*I know*."

Sunny sighed, easing back in his seat. "My dear Jacqueline. What happened to the sweet girl I once knew?"

Her mouth gaped. *Did he really just ask that?* "What happened? My dad is dead, and my mom is gone. I'm seventeen and trying to be a parent to my eight-year-old brother. What the hell do you think happened?"

A slight frown cracked Sunny's ordinarily pencil-straight lips. "Of course. How insensitive of me. I apologize."

"Whatever." She gave a dismissive flick of her hand. "When have you ever known me to be a sweet girl?"

Sunny allowed himself the slightest of smiles. "A time you don't recall. I suppose."

"Must have been a long time ago."

"Yes, well, better days, I'm afraid." He eyed the stacks of bills. "There's enough cash to help you get settled in San Diego. Though I suspect the Castillo brothers will allow you to stay with them as long as you need."

"What about all of our stuff?"

"When you're settled, I'll have the place packed and shipped to you. We'll rent a few storage—"

"All of it."

Sunny studied her a moment, then scrutinized the apartment's contents as if passing judgment on each item that was an accumulation of her and Billy's life.

The apartment had been Jac's one and only home. Everything within it was all she had ever known. She had spent more time within these walls than in any other place. Being an adolescent vampire—subject to sudden and near uncontrollable urges for blood—meant supervised trips to the store, the park, or outside in general. Her control in the presence of humans had improved in the last few years, allowing for unsupervised excursions close to home. But venturing beyond the apartment walls without intending to return and giving up all of her stuff seemed unfathomable.

"*All* of it." She grabbed a single strap of bills and squeezed. "And if you look at our stuff again like it's meaningless crap, I will shove this money up—"

"Of course, all of it," Sunny concluded.

An awkward silence fell upon them—an appreciated opportunity to end the encounter. "Are we done?"

He traced his finger on the table and ended with a tap. "I suppose we are."

The chair's feet scraped across the tiled floor as Sunny pushed away from the table and stood. He straightened his suit and, with a "Goodnight," turned to leave. Looking back as if to speak, his lips parted, but he said nothing and opened the door.

"Sunny," Jac called, removing the bangs from her eyes.

Sunny turned to face her. "Yes, love?"

She wanted to scold him for calling her "love" but set it aside in the things-to-be-mad-at-Sunny-about mental pile and mulled over how to ask what she wanted to. The question she decided upon would sound like an accusation but with a little less bite. "You would tell me if you knew something about my dad and mom, wouldn't you? If Edgar was involved?"

He tilted his head and replied with a semblance of sincerity. "Of course, I would."

She studied his response, looking for truth, looking for honesty. Unable to discern either, she looked away when the eye contact became uncomfortable.

"My driver will arrive in the morning; be ready. The private jet is ours, but there's still a schedule to keep."

She nodded, pretending to care.

"And Jac,"—he paused as if measuring his words—"please do try to remember that girl you once were." Sunny left, taking the air of discomfort with him.

How the hell could Sunny not know something? He was the emissary for Edgar, the Philadelphia Coven leader; one of Sunny's jobs was to know everything and anything important to the coven. He should know if her dad's death and her mother's disappearance were Edgar's doing.

Jac wanted to trust Sunny, to have one friend left in this screwed-up world, but her gut pegged him as a liar and maybe worse. She stared at the closed door, rehashing their conversation and recalling his expression for any hint of a clue when she asked him about Mom. A twitch of the cheek, a falter of his ruler-straight lips. There was neither. Sunny was a vampire and an emissary. Having the ultimate poker face, when needed, came with the combination.

"Jac."

She jumped in her seat and turned to Billy, ogling the stacks of bills. Any time Billy found his voice was a welcome improvement, a step toward him getting better—whatever that meant, based on their circumstances.

"Hey, Billy boy."

"Is all that real?"

She put the cash up to her nose and flipped through the bills. Used, they smelled of sweat, alcohol, smoke, leather, and a myriad of fragrances. She forcibly blew air from her nose and gave it a quick and vigorous rub, expelling the stench. "I think so ... I hope so."

He frowned and leaned into her shoulder.

"What's on your mind?" She placed her hand on his head.

"Do we *really* have to go?"

"Yeah, we do." She hugged him tightly and kissed the top of his head. "But I promise, when we get there, we'll focus on having as much fun as possible."

"And find Mom?"

Her gaze lingered on a family photo on the wall. A few years ago, at a local park, Dad had asked a woman to take their picture in front of a grove of trees. Everyone was dressed in their fall color best, and smiles plastered their faces. Even better, everyone was still alive ... and not missing. *I guess that was one of those better days.*

"And Mom, too," she said, "we'll focus on finding Mom."

HUNGER

T he flight to San Diego Sunny arranged was a scam. How could she have ever called that liar, Uncle? In the apartment, preparing to leave, Jac had overheard the driver, who arrived to take her and Billy to the private plane, talking to Sunny on the phone. The driver repeated instructions on how he would instead bring them to a pre-planned location, hand them over, and then, who knows what. The idiot human driver had no idea she had heard every word from the other side of the apartment door. Jac played along, and she and Billy left with him.

Five minutes into the drive, Jac whispered to Billy to grab his backpack during a red light at a busy intersection. She gripped his hand, and they darted from the car into the great unknown. They left the driver dumb-faced, standing behind his open door with one hand on his head and the other gripping his mobile phone. Sunny's deceit had unceremoniously birthed Jac and Billy into the human world. Alone.

The siblings still had to reach San Diego but had limited travel options. A commercial flight was out of the question. They couldn't risk being stuck in the air with humans. Besides, they wouldn't get past airport security with Jac's less-than-official identification. That left the next best but imperfect option.

Jac had never purchased a bus ticket, much less been on a bus. Within 24 hours of leaving—escaping—home, she sat in the back seat of a bus, traveling across the country. Making the situation exponentially worse, Billy was hungry. Protecting her little brother was her responsibility, but choosing to travel by bus proved to be a tremendous mistake. She had inadvertently trapped the humans with them in the moving metal box. Every second that passed, the bus inched closer to being a mobile slaughterhouse.

"I can't make it to the next stop," Billy said, his voice ragged. He curled up in a shivering ball with his head resting in Jac's lap.

"We're really close to Tulsa, maybe twenty minutes. You can make it." Jac caringly swiped away the tear-soaked hair from Billy's face. She fought back her own tears, needing to be strong for him.

Billy groaned as his muscles tensed to steel, and his hands clenched into fists. Jac massaged his arm and stroked his sweat-laden head. She'd do anything to get him through the next half-hour. Then, they'd be off the bus and could figure it out from there.

After glimpsing her ghostly reflection in the glass, Jac searched for a mile sign in the darkness beyond the bus window. They drove past a line of blurred trees shrouded in the night. The first mile sign she saw soon after the bus left Philadelphia was literally the first she'd ever seen. Miles upon miles of new and unknown territory stretched out behind and ahead.

"I can't make it to Tulsa." Spittle seeped between Billy's gritted teeth, and two prominent canines peeked between his lips. "You hafta make the driver stop the bus. I can ... smell them."

A white-haired woman rose from the seat in front of them and turned to Jac. Gold-framed glasses rested upon the thin nose of her kind face. Like Jac's neighbor, old Ms. Pearl, the woman smelled musty with an undertone of rubbing alcohol. "Is that boy okay, honey?"

Jac smiled, as stiff as dry leather. "He's fine."

Jac had picked the bus's back seats to avoid unwanted attention. As luck would have it, or it being summer and people traveled during summer, the bus was maybe a dozen heartbeats from full.

The woman's eyes narrowed. "He looks like he has a stomachache, somethin' awful."

Jac looked into the crows-footed eyes of someone's mother, someone's grandmother, someone's everything, and the first one within Billy's reach if he were to snap. "He'll be okay. He's ... sick. Probably better if you sit up a few rows if you can. I'm not sure if he's contagious."

"Oh," the woman said with wide eyes. "Well, I sure hope he gets ta feelin' better." She gathered her belongings, offered a parting smile, and shuffled a couple of rows up, where she found an empty seat.

"Jac, it's really bad," Billy said, his voice strained.

"Box the urge, just like Dad showed you. Box it and hide it away for a while."

"I can't." His body wrenched. "I t-tried that. It's too late."

Jac bit her lip, suppressing the urge to cry, to scream. This wasn't supposed to happen. Her parents had not prepared her for this. She shouldn't have been in this position, but she was, with nowhere to hide or anyone to turn to. Besides Billy, she was alone, not only in the coffin of a bus, but in the whole damn world.

Billy was right. They only had one option, and time was running out. She leaned close to his ear and whispered, "I'll talk to the bus driver. I need you to stay here."

Writhing, Billy nodded and made a sound somewhere between a moan and a grunt.

"Stay right here ... don't leave this seat. Do you hear me? *Do not* leave this seat."

He craned his neck to meet her eyes. "H-hurry."

Carefully, she lifted Billy's head from her lap, slid aside, and eased him onto the seat. Leaving Billy alone was a questionable decision, but sitting and waiting for the inevitable was worse, reckless. They were in the calm before a tragedy she desperately had to prevent. Billy and everyone on the bus would pay dearly for her inaction. Sunny's words echoed in her mind—*Be the adult.*

Jac stood, facing the twenty-something rows of seats leading to the front of the bus. Soft blue LED lights lined the walkway's sides. Overhead reading lights illuminated several heads as if the passengers were in the spotlight of a one-person show. Faint sounds filled the bus: Billy's intermittent moans, the steady hum of tires on pavement, snoring passengers, and hushed conversations. It smelled of fast food picked up at the last stop, and too many people a day or two passed needing bathing.

Jac breathed deep, slowly exhaled, and swept her bangs behind her ears. She shook her hands and took the first step. Creeping down the aisle, she counted the rows of seats between her and the driver as she passed each one while stealing peripheral glances at passengers.

Fifteen rows, fourteen rows.

The bespectacled, caring lady who changed seats smiled at her as she passed.

Thirteen, twelve. Jac paused and closed her eyes, placing her hands on the seat tops to her left and right. She inhaled deeply through her nose, held it for a five-count, then slowly exhaled from her mouth and opened her eyes. "B negative," she murmured. A young girl, maybe four, sat in the seat to her right. Her mother slept with her mouth agape and a pillow ring around her neck. The innocent-faced, dimple-cheeked, blonde girl waved at her.

Just over eight years ago, Jac's mom sat her down for "amazing news." Mom said that Jac would be a big sister. She wished for a baby sister each night while lying in bed. Weeks later, her mother broke the news of a brother after a visit to the obstetrician. Heartbroken, Jac resented Billy until he was born. Mom placed him carefully in her arms, and he looked up at her with beautiful baby-blue eyes. Though she still wished for a sister, Jac had adored Billy ever since.

Jac smiled painfully at the girl and turned away. Wincing, she clinched the shirt covering her aching heart. Her hands crept to opposite arms, squeezing and clawing skin through the sleeves as she continued forward. *Please, please don't let her be the only one.*

Whispered words escaped her mouth as she rehearsed a conversation with the bus driver. How could she convince him to stop the bus miles from their destination, on the side of the highway, near midnight, and excuse all passengers from their seats? If he stopped the bus, what then? What if the driver stopped the bus and ushered everyone off? Billy would still be desperate for blood that had to come from one passenger. She shuddered. Could she do what Billy needed? The awful deed that needed to be done? *One step at a time, Jac. One step at a time.*

Ten. My brother is sick. We should stop. Nine. She paused, repeating the deep inhalation and slow exhalation. To her left, a couple—twenty-somethings—slept in row nine. The girl, petite, beautiful, and presumably a wonderful person, rested her head on the boy's welcoming shoulder. He was handsome and, by all accounts, enamored with her. Their clasped hands rested upon his thigh. A brilliant but modest diamond adorned the girl's ring finger. They were probably starting their lives together, just married and on their way to a honeymoon destination. *My God, don't make me do this.*

Jac continued forward. *Eight. Contagious, he's contagious. Seven.* She paused and again breathed deeply. A man slept in the window seat of row six to her left. A baseball cap pulled low, and a bushy brown beard concealed most of his face. He wore a gray T-shirt bearing a sports team logo that covered all but a hairy inch of his bulging belly. She stared at him long enough to pinpoint him as a snorer and a third option. She had no reason to dislike this man but of the choices... He appeared to be in his late forties. Someone who had a chance to experience life, most of it, anyway. Where was he traveling? Was he meeting someone he met online? Maybe visiting a sick or dying parent? He was her best option of the three. Still, that didn't make it right.

With her decision made, she went ahead feeling noticeably lighter, no longer burdened by the dimpled girl's and young couples' lives. Though the lump in her throat and pain in her chest remained.

The bus driver—a large man with plump fingers—acknowledged Jac's approach with an eyebrow raise and a friendly "Hello." He lowered the volume of an upbeat dance track playing from his mobile phone.

"Sorry about that. We can't use headphones while we're driving." His eyes darted between Jac and the road as he spoke. "The music helps me stay awake and focused ... not that I'm tired." He nodded assuredly. "You should be in your seat. What are you doing up here?" He pulled an enormous plastic drink cup from its holder, tongued the red straw, wrangled it between his lips, and took a long sip of what resembled brown soda.

Jac wrung her sweaty hands and skipped pleasantries and an apology for being out of her seat. "I—I need you to stop the bus."

The driver momentarily took his eyes off the road and looked at her incredulously. "Stop the bus, you said?" He returned the cup to its holder and ran the back of his free hand across his lips. "I can't do that, young lady."

"My brother, he's sick." She turned toward the back of the bus, craning her neck, bringing the top of Billy's head into view. "I'm worried he—"

"Then I shouldn't stop." He pointed at the dark highway before them, illuminated by the bus's headlights. "We're about twenty minutes from Tulsa. If he's gonna be sick, take him to the toilet in the back."

The blacktop and darkness ahead could lead to Tulsa or the end of the world; it didn't matter—they wouldn't reach either in time. Only one person needed to die, and she was determined to keep it that way.

A hair-raising, pained moan came from the back. Billy wriggled in his seat and, so far, kept his promise not to leave it. Only yards separated him from her, but it might as well have been a mile if he were to break. She couldn't reach him before he reached someone else.

"No, he's not that kind of sick." She tugged at her shirt. "He's contagious. Everyone will get sick if we don't stop and get them off the bus. *Now.*"

"Listen." The driver pointed a stubby finger toward the rear of the bus, his tone edging on authoritative. "I need you to go back to your seat. We'll reach Tulsa soon, where he can get checked out." He flashed a reassuring smile, looking at her every few words. "Tell ya what. I'll call it ahead and have someone waiting to help."

Jac's hands formed into fists. She shifted her weight from one foot to the other. *Stay calm. Stay calm.* She had to convince him, and anger wouldn't help. "We can't wait." The words came out louder than intended.

A smattering of passengers woke from her voice, including the burly man in row six. Their sleepy eyes surveyed the surroundings before focusing on her.

Billy moaned again, loud enough to bring people sitting in rows close to him to their feet for a closer look. His little hands clamped the edge of his seat.

Get. Away. From. Him. "Get away from him," she muttered through gritted teeth.

Teeth. Jac brought a hand to her mouth. A rush of blood swelled her gums. She slid her tongue across her top row of teeth—smooth, bump, smooth, bump, smooth. *Oh, the Hell.* Heat enveloped her, radiating from her tingling skin. Her heart pounded against her ribs as if furious at them. She wasn't hungry, but stress had caused her canines to descend, and now *she* was on the clock. Would Billy break first, or would she?

HE STAYS

"Fear is a great motivator," Jac had once heard her mother say years ago in a conversation between her parents. "Fear makes people take action, good or bad, right or wrong." Jac wasn't sure of the context, but her mother's claim about the power of fear made sense, and it stuck with her ever since.

Something else her mother once said was relevant at the moment. At just six years old, Mom warned her that biting someone would kill them. It wasn't until her early teens that Jac learned the truth—a vampire bite was not a death sentence. She didn't accuse her mother of perpetuating a lie. Her mother was simply protecting her and everyone she would come in contact with.

Jac understood that, without question, it was a mistake of the utmost magnitude to bite a human. People *can* die from a vampire bite. Being injected with the vampire virus was severe and not for the weak. However, most people lived through the vampiric transition resulting from the bite. And to be clear, vampires were not undead. They were very much alive. Though she believed the world would be a better place if all vampires *were* dead, in the no-longer-conscious and breathing sense.

Fear makes people take action, Jac repeated to herself. If she fostered fear in the passengers, they might help encourage the driver to stop. She stepped closer to the driver and raised her voice, intent on creating a scene. "Stop the bus. *Now!* We can't wait for Tulsa!"

An angry vein bulged in the driver's forehead. "Young lady, this is the last time I'll ask you to return to your seat. You're putting all of us in danger." He snorted. "I *will* report you to the authorities when we get there." He shifted in his seat and nodded in agreement with himself.

"Sit the hell down!" The row six passenger sat up straight and adjusted his hat.

Jac glared at the man momentarily before returning her focus to the driver.

Fear makes people take action. She leaned close to the driver, breathing in the odor of his sweat. "If you don't stop this bus, everyone will die!"

The driver shuffled in his seat away from her, aimlessly grabbing for his phone until his shaking hand found it. "That's it. I'll have the police waiting when we pull up."

Jac's hands turned to rigid claws; her muscles, like tense piano strings, verged on snapping a terrifying chord. The heat on her skin threatened ignition. She ripped the phone from his hand and shattered it against the floor before a word left his lips. Small pieces of plastic and glass scattered across the aisle and into the darkness under the seats.

Passengers murmured concerns, some already collecting their belongings.

Jac braced for the protest that would assuredly come from the driver. Their eyes met, and his face morphed from anger to confusion to, finally, what resembled fear. He fidgeted in his seat and looked around as if he'd jump from the bus if it were a viable option.

Stepping back, Jac gently touched her jawline and cheeks. Her skin stretched thin over her bones, creating unnatural curves and contours. Though she couldn't see their damage, her eyes were assuredly bloodshot. Anger brought her to this regretful state, turning her into the monster she despised.

A pained scream from Billy captured everyone's attention. People who had stood to check on Billy moved closer to him, offering help and supportive words.

"Jac, I need you!" Billy cried.

"Just hold on, Billy. Please!" Jac yelled, her voice tremulous. Hot blood rushed through her shaking body. This was her first test at saving Billy, and she was failing. Failing.

The bus swayed to the left, and the passengers screamed. They braced themselves as the distracted driver pulled the bus back between the lines, narrowly missing a horn-honking car in the adjacent lane.

"Damn it." The row six passenger stood and pointed a meaty hand at her. "I'll take that bitch back to her seat. Over my shoulder, if I have to."

"This kid looks really sick!" yelled a voice.

"Get away from him!" Jac edged toward the back. If Billy snapped, he'd attack people indiscriminately. People would die.

The damn bus had to stop even if she had to yank the driver from his seat and do it herself.

"Stop the bus," someone cried, followed by a chorus of agreement.

Fear makes people take action.

Jac shared a look with the driver; his expression included a level of disgusted curiosity. He grunted as he grabbed his com. "Ladies and gentlemen,"—he paused and grimaced as if his next words would coat his mouth in a bitter film—"we'll be pulling to the roadside. Please remain seated until we come to a stop, and then calmly and orderly exit the bus with all of your belongings. We won't return to our seats; leave nothing behind."

Moans and choice words came from some passengers, while others expressed relief.

Jac also desperately needed relief, and sacrificing the passengers' comfort by forcing them off the bus got her a step closer. She swore she would never take the following unforgivable and necessary action. But she didn't see another viable option. Someone on the bus would be an unwilling sacrifice.

"This is bullshit. We're almost there," the row-six passenger said.

"We have a medical emergency," the driver continued, "and it's not safe for anyone to stay on the bus. I'll have another bus pick us up and finish the drive to Tulsa."

The bus slowed and pulled onto the shoulder, crunching gravel and roadside debris under its tires as it came to a squealing-brake stop.

"You broke my phone." The driver's jaw clenched. He averted his eyes. "How am I supposed to call for another bus?"

Passengers aimed their phones for a better shot of Jac. She turned away, only allowing the driver to see her monster mask of a face. She pointed to them. "Borrow one."

The bus door opened, and, one by one, the passengers exited down the stairs and into the warm night air. Jac caught glances of them glaring at her as they passed. She turned away as some of them maneuvered their phones for a clear shot of her face. Something for them to post on social media for likes and clout, making them and her an internet hot topic, at least for a day.

Jac eyed the man in row six, who she couldn't let leave. She had no plan on how to keep him on the bus while everyone else left, other than by brute force. Be it luck—good for her and bad for him—the man remained firmly ensconced in his seat. *Yes. Stay right there.*

As she passed, the bespectacled old lady who had offered support placed a gentle hand on Jac's arm. Jac wanted to look at her, to say sorry, but her face was an image of horror, something to be feared, something to be hidden. The dimpled-cheeked little girl pointed at Jac, muttering something as she passed by with her disheveled mother.

"Take your time. Exit carefully. I'll get us a backup soon," the driver said, offering encouragement. He lumbered to his feet, pulled up his sagging gray khakis, and peered down the rows of seats.

Everyone had exited the bus except for Billy and the passenger in row six, who glared at her.

The driver thumbed toward the exit. "Let's go, sir."

"I'm not leavin' my seat until the replacement bus shows." He crossed his thick arms.

Jac stared back at him from the darkness, silently supporting the man in his decision.

"I need you off the bus," the driver repeated.

"Not. Happening."

"He's staying," Jac said matter-of-factly, continuing to stare at the man as if they were playing a game of who would blink first.

The driver threw his hands in the air. "But you said everyone has to—"

"He stays." She faced the driver. "But you have to go. Please."

He gave her that look again, the look people gave her on the few occasions when they witnessed her get angry or hungry—the look of surprise, fear, and that something wasn't quite right with her. She never faulted them for looking at her that way. Nor did she fault the bus driver. They were right; something *was* wrong with her. Wrong in an unimaginable way. Wrong in a way that would get them killed if they weren't careful.

"Okay, man. I—I can't force you off; staying is your decision." He gave Jac an uneasy look and trundled down the stairs and off the bus.

"No matter what happens, don't get back on." She closed the door.

Only she, Billy, and the man in row six remained. The quiet accentuated Billy's moans and screams.

She walked the illuminated path to row six, stopped, and stared down at the man. He sat straight with his arms crossed.

Seconds passed before he looked at her, his face defiant, then contorting as if he had eaten something disagreeable. "What the hell is wrong with your face and ... your eyes? Are you on drugs or something?"

"Get up," she said, her tone cold.

"I told you, I'm not gettin' up."

Jac closed her eyes and breathed deeply. To do what was needed, the horrible thing that was needed, she had to erase any sense of her humanity. This was not a person near her; *it* was prey. Her nature was to use *it* for what she needed. But all of that was just words. She had no experience in … killing. Her parents warned her about the dangers of being around humans and what she could inflict on them. They taught her to avoid these situations, not how to perform the dreaded evil deed.

I can do this. I have to do this. She opened her watery eyes and repeated, "Get up."

The man scoffed and shook his head.

A skin-tingling scream of "Jac" came from Billy, and then he fell silent. His limp arm dangled from the seat. He had sacrificed his need for life-giving blood instead of attacking the passengers. Time was up for Billy *and* the man in row six.

"If you don't shut that kid up,"—he motioned to the back—"I'll go back there and do it for you."

Jac's heart thumped a painful rhythm in her chest. A man did not exist in row six, only sustenance for Billy. Billy needed this. She slowly blew out a shaky breath. "Get up … now."

"I'm not leavin'." He folded his arms and eased back into the seat.

Her bottom lip quivered, and she blinked once, hard, sending tears rolling down her cheeks. Her voice cracked. "I'm sorry."

"You can be sorry all you want. I'm not gettin' off this bus."

Like drying clay, Jac's face hardened when the tears reached her chin; her eyes formed a dead stare. Any sense of right and wrong, love and hate, had vacated her. "I know."

Before the man could utter a word of protest, she gripped his arm and shirt with talon-like fingers and dumped him like a sack of sand into the aisle, sending his hat flying a row back. The bulky man's arm gave way, bending in an unnatural direction as he tried to right himself.

"My ... arm!" Rapid, panicked gasps escaped his mouth. His out-of-socket arm flopped uselessly to his side; the bicep, torn from the skin, hung outside a gaping, blood-pouring wound.

Jac kneeled behind him, slipped her slender arm under his chin, gripped the bicep of her other arm, and tightly squeezed. He kicked his feet and shifted his weight, desperately grabbing at her with the hand of his functioning arm. She counted the seconds with her eyes clenched, forcing out the remaining tears from an emotion she no longer felt. Using this man wasn't wrong; it was necessary, natural. A required act for a needed outcome. For Billy.

A commotion outside broke her focus. She peered around the man's mussed hair and down the aisle at the door, still shut. A sense of urgency gnawed at her; refocused, her arms became vices around the man's neck. Gurgles followed a sickening crunch.

Jac stopped counting at three minutes—a full two minutes and 40 seconds after the man stopped moving. His limp body fell to the floor with a thud as she stood. She sprinted to the front and retrieved the driver's plastic drink cup.

"Billy, hold on. I'll be there soon."

Billy didn't reply.

Goosebumps rose on her arms. *I'm too late.* She poured the cup contents onto the driver's seat, shook out the few remaining drops, and ran back to the fallen man. She pulled a long, thin metal chopstick from the side pocket of her brown cargo pants. Before boarding the bus, she had purchased a set at a Chinese restaurant near the station. She needed a weapon to defend herself if a coven member found them, but she couldn't bring a weapon on the bus. Not an actual weapon. Chopsticks, however, were not a weapon but a utensil for eating that was adequate for defense and perfect for what she had to do next.

Hesitating only a moment, she shoved the chopstick deep into the side of the man's neck. Blood splashed across her hand and shirt sleeve. Hysteria-inducing blood dripped from her hand like warm shower water. She shook her head. "This is not for me," she muttered. "It's not even my type."

Content with the damage, Jac pulled the blood-streaked chopstick from the wound. She cleaned it with three swipes across the man's stretched and torn shirt and slipped it back into her pocket. A stream of blood flowed onto the floor, pooling around the dead man's head. She positioned his neck to direct the blood flow into the plastic cup, quickly filling it.

Jac studied the face, frozen in time, of the once loud, foul-mouthed jerk. Guilt crept at the edges of her mind, with her humanity slowly returning. She clasped a hand against her chest. *What have I done?* She had killed a son, brother, husband, or ... father. *Did you have kids? Will anyone miss you? Will someone hate me for what I've done?* Blood overflowed from the cup and trickled down the sides, breaking her trance. She flung blood from her fingers and raced to Billy, who was quiet, too quiet.

Billy sat motionless, his head slumped to the side. He had sunken, dull eyes and chalky pale skin.

"Billy! Billy, wake up!" She righted his head, placed the cup to his cracked, blue lips, and slightly poured. Blood pooled and dripped from the corner of his mouth. "Billy. Drink. Please."

Billy twitched. He grabbed the cup with shaky hands and eagerly drank in large gulps. He paused and ran his tongue across his lips. "It's warm." The color returned to his cheeks like a sunrise, and his dull eyes regained most of their lost brilliance.

Jac breathed a shuddered breath and blinked. She tenderly pushed sweaty bangs from his forehead. "How did you do it?" She asked for herself as much as for Billy. "If it were me, I would have either jumped out of the window or …."

This position was new for both of them. If she had been the one with blood lust, torn bodies would have covered the bus floor like a morbid scene from a horror film. Billy handled his bloodlust like an elder vampire—ready to die before hurting someone and exposing himself to the world. The world wasn't ready for vampires, at least not real ones.

Billy looked up at her with bloodshot eyes and pupils the size of clown shirt buttons. "Thank you, Jac," he said in a weak and scratchy voice. He peered down the aisle at the body of the man whose blood he had just consumed. He smiled grimly. "Sorry."

"Anything for you."

After sharing heavy smiles, Billy slid from the seat, and they quickly gathered and stuffed their belongings into their backpacks.

Jac wanted to give Billy another full cup, another infusion of blood that would last him the trip, but they were out of time. A faint, unmistakable sound came from miles in the distance—the wail of sirens.

ON THE RUN

With their backpacks strapped on, Jac readied their exit from the bus. She gripped the levered door handle and paused. "Billy, listen to me. Do not talk to anyone. Do not look at anyone. We step off the bus and run."

Billy's eyebrows pinched. "Okay, but not too fast. Don't leave me behind."

She scoffed. "Not likely, with that fresh blood in you."

"Oh yeah. I'll leave *you* behind."

"Let's just try to stay together." She pulled the handle, and the bus door folded open. "Ready?"

"Ready."

They bolted down the steps and turned a sharp left. Their feet struck the ground in a sprint. Calls of "look" and "there they go" echoed behind them.

"Hey!" the bus driver yelled.

Jac jerked to a stop and kept her back to the driver as Billy continued into the darkness. "Don't go on the bus. Okay? At least not yet. And ... I'm sorry."

"Sorry about what?" the driver yelled as she sprinted away.

After leaving the bus, the body, and the bystanders' accusatory stares, Jac headed west with Billy at her side. She intended for anyone watching to believe that Tulsa was their destination. Instead, fifty yards later, they crossed the dark highway at a break in traffic and backtracked for an exit ramp the bus passed about a mile back.

They walked briskly beside the highway, weakly illuminated by the half-moon above like a companion or maybe a watcher, tracking their attempted escape. Carefully, they navigated roadside trash and strips of shredded semi-tire while ducking out of sight of every passing car.

Jac walked in silence, battling her emotions. She did the one thing she swore she would never do—kill a human. The horror of it all replayed in her mind: the blood, the look on the bearded man's face, how he fought helplessly for his life, his arms going limp, never again to move. Undeniably, she became the worst version of herself—a murderer.

Though she wanted time to reflect, to acknowledge, again, the horrible thing she had done, it wasn't the time to drown herself in self-hatred. She had to pull herself together and stop selfishly worrying about her well-being and self-worth. Billy should be her one and only concern. The night's events compromised the sheath safeguarding Billy's innocence. A strip of it yanked away. It was Billy who saw his first dead body. It was Billy who had to drink blood from a freaking plastic cup when, in his entire life, he had only consumed prepackaged blood. Mom and Dad kept a fresh supply in the fridge, with the blood type clearly marked, ensuring no one drank from the wrong bag. *A damn plastic cup.*

The exit ramp came into view, and they reached it a minute later. The sirens were close, a half minute from the bus, maybe seconds. They stepped under a towering streetlamp post, illuminating their surroundings, exposing them like a circus's spotlit main attraction. *Ladies and gentlemen, I present to you real-life vampires. Bloodsuckers from these United States. Step right up for a look at their fangs, but don't venture too close. You wouldn't want to lose your life.*

Jac's stomach knotted at the sight of her red-stained hands, arms, and clothes. The blood had coagulated into a sticky paste. The steely-eyed, muted-emotion girl she became to kill had receded to the dark places of her mind, leaving her at the edge of tears. Billy intertwined his fingers with hers without concern for the blood. They shared a look, Billy's conveying understanding and support. His touch and demeanor comforted her like a warm blanket on a chilly night, pulling her back from the edge of despair. She squeezed his hand when he gave her a grin. *Is he okay? He seems okay. Yeah, he always seems okay.*

Billy was built differently, especially from her. His resisting ripping into the passengers added to his burgeoning legend— Billy the Unflappable. He had this emotional intelligence at a ridiculous level for a vampire his age. Mom called it his "calming presence." Dad often reminded Jac that she didn't have the helpful trait ... on any level.

In difficult situations and circumstances, Billy could understand and adequately manage his emotions and the emotions of others. It differed from turning off humanity; he was by no means dead inside. Billy loved to laugh and have fun. He could be disagreeable at times and was prone to grumpy moments. And sad ones as of late. If given a modicum of time, he could snap right out of sadness, anger, and depression. Still, he deserved a chance to grow up and be a kid. He was her sweet little brother, and she wasn't ready to lose that.

Jac imagined the goings-on at the bus: police analyzing the crime scene, asking the passengers questions, and examining videos taken with their phones. Videos of her and Billy. Someone would find the man on the bus, and though his condition should make it obvious, they'd check for a pulse to confirm he was dead. It wouldn't take a genius to conclude he had been murdered and by whom. In the distance behind them, red and blue lights danced in the air to sirens' echoes. She and Billy had escaped for now, but their past was close behind.

The bright lights of a fast-food restaurant came into view. This little town, named whatever, wasn't much, but it was civilization, an improvement over the seemingly endless trees and highway they had traveled.

Jac tugged on Billy's sleeve. "Come on. We have to keep moving."

They broke into a sprint—their backpacks hopping up and down against their backs—running past the fast-food restaurant where patrons filled their stomachs with hot fries and greasy beef patties.

Billy gave a hungry look at the restaurant. "I'm starving ... for food this time."

She was hungry too and desperately wanted to clean up, but they couldn't sneak in unnoticed to the restaurant bathroom with her resembling a bloody zombie girl. "Sorry, Billy. We'll get food soon, but we have to clean up first."

Billy refocused and kept stride with her.

"Follow me ... behind there." She pointed toward an auto shop in the distance with darkened windows, closed bay doors, and an empty parking lot. "No one will see us back there."

Aside from the moonlight, darkness engulfed the rear of the auto shop. Sparsely wooded lots flanked the building's left and right. A grass field stretched out behind the shop, with a row of homes lining the far side.

Gasping deep breaths of the warm, humid air, Jac leaned against the building and slid down to a sit.

Billy squatted, huffing. "What now?"

The auto shop looked much like she expected. Various car parts lay beside and leaned against the red brick wall. A gas can sat atop one of three rusted rims, and a worn green hose connected to the building snaked around a stack of bald tires. *This will work.*

She stood and applied a firm counter-clockwise turn to the rusty water valve. A puff of air escaped the hose, followed by a steady stream of water that smelled of iron and deteriorating plastic.

"Come over here so I can look at you."

Billy plodded over.

Kneeling in front of him, she examined his clothes in the moonlight. "You look pretty good, but you spilled a little blood on your shirt, and there's some on your hands and chin." She scrunched her face. "Gross. Change your shirt and wash your face and hands."

"Hey. Look at me." Billy placed his hands on her cheeks and stared into her eyes. "You're going to be okay. Okay?"

She looked into the too-wise eyes of her eight-year-old brother. He was checking in on her when she should have been checking in on him. Billy did and had been doing this for years—easing his sister back from her breaking point. The corners of her mouth twitched, and the tension in her shoulders slightly eased. She patted his hands. "Okay."

He smiled with red-stained teeth.

"Ew. And rinse out your mouth."

Jac stood, satisfied she'd identified all evidence of the crime. She inspected a rusted metal barrel while Billy dropped his blood-splattered shirt to the ground and washed off in the hose.

"Throw your shirt in this barrel and grab a fresh one from your backpack. You should have a couple." She had planned for a quick escape from the limo, which meant leaving their suitcases and most of their clothes and shoes. Before leaving their apartment for the fake flight, she had instructed Billy to remove his tablet and headphones from his backpack to make room for clothes and essentials. He failed to convince her the tablet was necessary to prevent potentially significant boredom. Losing the argument, he reluctantly agreed to leave it behind.

Billy scampered over to the barrel, his face and hands dripping water.

"And turn around." She twirled her finger. "I need to change."

Jac carefully removed her long-sleeved shirt, keeping the bloody parts from her face. She tossed the shirt into the barrel, using her fingertips as if the clothing were a contagion. She stepped on the heels of her shoes to remove them, slipped off her socks, and stuffed them into the shoes. After emptying the pockets, her bloody cargo pants were next into the barrel. Though not a single eye watched, her hands autonomously moved to cover exposed skin in a fit of modesty. When the day started, she didn't expect she'd end up hiding behind an auto parts shop in her underwear and tank top. Today had been an unfortunate and significant change from internet surfing, watching TV, or playing games with her family. The ordinary stuff that encapsulated nearly all of her nights.

The cold water from the hose soothed her face, steam rose from where it touched her skin. It erased at least the physical evidence of the terrible act she committed. The fresh, long-sleeved shirt smelled of lilac as she pulled it over her head and tank top, and the clean cargo pants fit comfortably around her waist. She slipped into her already-worn socks and cringed from the wet squish when she stepped into her shoes.

Jac pulled a book of matches from a side zipper pocket of her backpack and grabbed the nearly empty gas can from atop the rusty rim. "Stay back a bit." She dowsed the inside of the barrel with what little gas remained and set the can on the ground. With a strike, the match came alive, releasing a whiff of sulfur. She tossed the flaming stick into the barrel, and after an initial ignition of the fumes, orange flames danced and jumped inside.

"Whoa. That was cool." Billy shielded his face and stepped back from the barrel. "Why do you have matches?"

"Dad's candle." She stepped back next to him and gave him a melancholy smile as she pulled at a memory—one both cherished and heart-wrenching.

"Oh, yeah. I wish I brought something of Mom's."

"Maybe I count?"

He leaned into her. "You're my favorite thing of Mom's."

"What a coincidence. I feel the same about you."

It was silent a moment when Billy asked, "What do you think Mom is doing?"

She laid her head atop his. "I don't know. Staying safe, I hope."

"That's what I'll imagine then, Mom being safe."

"Me too."

The flames emitted more light than Jac had expected, and even if they weren't being watched, it felt as if they were. She scanned the surrounding area and focused on the homes across the empty field's expanse. Imagined residents turned on porch lights, suppressing the darkness, questioning if they had heard or seen something. Imagination aside, no one stirred; only darkness stretched out in all directions.

The initial burn-off of gas subsided, leaving a low smoldering flame and remanence of what could be clothing if someone looked close enough. Satisfied the flames destroyed the evidence, Jac doused the fire with water from the hose. Steam rose with the smoke and dissipated like a ghost ascending toward the heavens.

"What now?" Billy asked.

Sirens continued to wail in the distance. They didn't seem closer, but neither were they farther away. Someone could have seen the flames, speeding the police to this very spot.

Jac's amygdala kicked in. "Grab your backpack. We have to go."

WE WEAR OUR SUNGLASSES AT NIGHT

T hough a lie, the flight to San Diego *was* a plan. Though an absolute failure, the bus ride to San Diego *was* a plan. Aimlessly walking through Oklahoma was survival. After another mile of walking in the small-town darkness, where the sky came alive with stars, Jac and Billy came across a gas station with a convenience store. They crouched in the shadows next to the parking lot, where the light gave way to darkness. Jac closely listened to conversations and watched for anything that seemed ... off.

Billy leaned into her and motioned toward the store.

"Yeah, I think we can go in now," Jac whispered. "But you have to stay with me and do everything I say. Got it?"

"Got it."

"First, we hit the bathrooms and then find snacks and drinks." She squinted at Billy. "Come over here, into the light."

She grabbed his hand and pulled him to the edge of the parking lot between the darkness and bright light. "Great, your eyes are still a little bloodshot."

He pointed at her face. "You too."

Jac instinctively reached for her eyes as if she could feel the damage. "Damn ... okay. Tell me you brought your sunglasses."

He frowned. "No. You told me to pack more clothes, and I didn't think I'd need them."

She sighed. "At least I have my sunglasses. We'll buy you a pair in the store."

"Okay."

"But look down and squint your eyes until we get them. Don't look at anyone, not even me."

Jac donned her sunglasses as they walked across the parking lot and into the overhead lights' full illumination. Everyone watched them; she was sure of it, and they were walking into a trap. The people pumping gas and inside the store were waiting for the right moment to apprehend her. And the disheveled man precariously leaning against the store's red brick wall, drinking from something hidden inside a brown bag? He was in on it—especially him.

"Stay close," she reminded Billy.

He intertwined his left hand with her right.

Burdened with the guilt of what she had done, Jac's paranoia intensified. She expected pointing fingers, accusations of murder, and desperate cries for her and Billy to be stopped. With every step toward the store, she scanned the surroundings for escape routes and dark places to hide.

They reached the glass doors to the store. Inside, food, candy, and other on-the-go supplies lined the shelves. There were walls of refrigerated drinks, an ATM, a clerk behind a checkout counter, and a few customers. A door chime announced their entrance, and a blast of cold air welcomed them, striking their sweaty faces. The store clerk glanced their way and returned to helping his customer.

A quick scan revealed a guy at the soda machine, filling a cup much too large for a single person, and an older woman perusing the display of Oklahoma-themed tchotchkes. Jac released a held breath at not seeing people of authority and then focused on the task.

"Come on." She pulled the limited-sighted Billy toward the bathrooms. He staggered behind her. She opened the men's room door and gave an awkward look inside. "It's empty. Okay. Listen. Use the toilet with the door."

"But I don't have to go—"

She huffed. If Billy simply did what she asked, they could get what they needed and leave with as little attention as possible. "I don't care. Use the toilet with the door. I'm going to the girl's room. I'll knock when I'm ready for you to come out."

"Okay," Billy relented.

"I mean it; don't come out until I knock."

The men's room door closed behind Billy, and a punch of anxiety hit Jac for leaving him alone. Hurrying into the girl's room, she stepped into the first empty stall, accidentally slamming the door behind her, rattling it at the hinges. The urgency to relieve herself, suppressed by the night's chaos, returned.

Finishing with a flush, she positioned the sunglasses atop her head and went to wash. Cursing the too-hot water streaming from the sink, she twisted the handle for cold, and the water cooled. After several cleansing splashes to her face, she gripped the sink edge with both hands and leaned in.

Look at it. Look at your reflection.

Her knuckles whitened. Water dripped from the tip of her nose and splashed onto the ceramic sink.

Look *at it.*

The sink groaned under her grip.

Jac gazed into the mirror, past her reflection, hoping to see her face in some other dimension. A dimension where she was an ordinary girl with dreams of a future and making mistakes and memories. A girl out on Friday night with friends, pining for a boy's interest ... instead of his blood.

"Look at it!"

This other world didn't materialize beyond fantasy. The momentary comfort of losing herself in the nothing faded, leaving Jac to focus on her genuine reflection. She shuddered a breath. Bloodshot eyes were the telltale sign of vampire bloodlust or, in her case, damage caused by an overly emotional event, like the act of murdering someone. Tears streaked to her dropped chin. She had seen enough.

The bathroom door opened. Jac cursed under her breath and gritted her teeth as the tchotchke-admiring woman walked in. *Can't I get a few damn minutes of privacy?* She turned away and clumsily put on her sunglasses. The woman may have smiled at her before disappearing behind the stall door, but Jac couldn't be sure.

After a final inspection of her arms and face for any missed blood, Jac wiped away stray tears and audibly exhaled. She froze. Proof of her transgression hid under her hair—a streak of dried blood near her right ear. She pushed up her sunglasses for a better look, and the disgust and guilt returned.

"What have I done?" she murmured. Her eyes fixed on the red smudge. She mindlessly snatched a paper towel from the dispenser, wet it, and erased the blood with a vigorous scrub. As the dispenser buzzed, emitting another sheet, she tossed the evidence into the trash on the way out.

* * *

"Just a sec," Billy responded after Jac knocked on the boy's room door and whispered his name.

"Come on, Billy. Let's go."

There were shuffling steps, and Billy opened the door. Jac shared an awkward glance with a man drying his hands before the door closed behind Billy.

"What took you so long?" Billy asked. "I finished a long time ago."

"Nothing." She grabbed his hand and pulled him along.

"Nothing? What kind of answer is—"

"Hush and think about what you want."

The sunglasses display stood near the store entrance. As the universe would have it, a small gathering of people stood in line near the entrance to complete their purchases. People Jac wanted to avoid. Several others wandered the aisles. She carefully considered each person from behind the seclusion of her sunglasses, fearing one of them would recognize her and know what she had done. She swore the clerk stole glances at her. He knew something; he had to. The walls and people closed in. She tensed, prepared to run from the store with Billy and fight for their freedom, for their lives.

A voice at the store's entrance cracked the tension.

"Hey, Rusty," a young man entering the store said to the clerk, unknowingly breaking Jac's paranoia. "How goes it?"

"Living the dream," Rusty said.

"I've told ya, Rusty. We aren't living the dream; living *is* the dream."

Jac eavesdropped on their conversation while searching the shelves for snacks and candy. Billy kept his head down and eyes slits, opening them only for a quick confirmation of what he clutched in his eager hands.

"Try telling yourself that when you're old, grow a gut, your back goes, and you lose all your hair," Rusty said, followed by an apology to the bald man next in line.

"Sorry, Rusty, but my generation and the ones after won't grow old as fast, scientific advances and all. I'm going to live a long and happy, hairy life."

"Not if you keep downing those energy drinks and eating pizza. You'll have a heart attack at fifty."

"Gotta stay awake to deliver cheesy pies to the public. They need me."

"Go get your fix then," Rusty relented.

Realizing she had stopped breathing, Jac inhaled deeply and released a relieved exhale, thankful they didn't discuss the events surrounding the bus. She and Billy were not yet the news everyone couldn't wait to tell their family, friends, or anyone with a heartbeat. The store turned friendly again. No one was out to get them, nor did anyone know what she had done.

Billy got her attention with a cough to show off his hands full of goodies.

"That's a lot." She raised her eyebrows above the rim of her sunglasses.

"Have to be prepared," he said.

The guy, the Pizza Guy, who spoke to Rusty, walked in their direction toward the drink fridges in the next aisle, the exact place they needed to go to next. He wore a hat high on his head with "Chuck's Pizza" in block letters across it. The hat covered most of his sandy blond hair except for some longer strands sneaking out on the sides and back. He had a carefree smile and a confident stride. The aroma of pizza filled the air as he passed.

Billy looked up at her for approval with another candy bar in hand.

"Nice choice." Jac grabbed a spicy beef stick when someone spoke behind her.

"Whoa, going for the hot one ... I don't recommend it."

"Excuse me?" Jac turned toward the voice.

"The spicy one is a scorcher," Pizza Guy said with a wince, pulling a regular beef stick from the shelf. "Just thought I'd let you know. I took a bite of one of those and threw the rest of it away. They're a waste of money, if you ask me." He flashed a cavalier smile. "Go with the regular."

Behind her sunglasses, Jac stood stoically, concealing her displeasure at being talked to.

Pizza Guy squinted. "Unless ... you're into that kind of stuff."

"Was I talking to you?" She crossed her arms. "Or did I ask for your opinion?"

His mouth opened to answer, then paused. "That was the very definition of rhetorical."

She tilted her head and stared at him.

"What's rhetorical?" Billy asked.

No one answered. Jac and Pizza Guy had a staring contest of sorts, with her having the unfair advantage of sunglasses.

"So, you're wearing sunglasses at night ... *and* inside." Pizza Guy tittered. "You either have sensitive eyes or are way too cool for the rest of us."

Jac continued her silent stare.

Pizza Guy's shoulders slumped ever so slightly as he scratched his cheek. The conversation had clearly become awkward for him as whatever game he had frayed at the edges.

"Walk away."

All evidence of his smile evaporated before Pizza Guy walked away in a slump. "Maybe you *can* handle the spicy ones," he muttered.

"Yeah, I can."

He turned around with a slack mouth. "D-did you hear—"

"Yes, I heard you. Keep walking."

Jac eyed him as he walked toward the back of the store. Confident he wasn't looking her way, she grabbed a regular beef stick while defiantly keeping the spicy one.

* * *

In line to pay, their hands overflowed with food, drinks, and a pair of sunglasses. Billy ogled his haul of goodies. Jac allowed him to pick out whatever he wanted. Happily, or greedily, he took advantage.

"Don't get used to this. We'll eat a proper breakfast tomorrow." Jac remained disappointed she couldn't treat him to a decent meal, at least not yet. Grab-food-and-go was the best course of action based on the circumstances. They would be on the road for a couple of days, and today would be a junk-food holiday. Things could be worse.

Grinning, Billy didn't seem to mind. After what he had endured, his happiness warmed her heart. That was Billy. Instead of breaking down in response to shock or emotional pain, he would act as if nothing was wrong. He would go inside of himself, briefly hide away, then come out on the other side a-okay.

A final person, a tall man, stood in line in front of them. A TV on the wall, above and behind the clerk, showed an infomercial for a wearable blanket. With the summer heat, how did it make sense for anyone to walk or lounge around wearing a freaking blanket?

"Is that your sister?"

That voice, again! Jac turned and glared at Pizza Guy. She shoved a bottled drink in the crook of her arm and pulled Billy close, his head still down and eyes hidden. "Do *not* talk to him."

"Backpacks, handfuls of snacks ... you two are traveling on foot." He crossed his arms and grinned. "You're not local. Most people here are friend ... ly," he said, cringing as if he wanted to regretfully shove the word back into his mouth.

Jac pulled Billy behind her and approached Pizza Guy, veins pulsing in her neck. "Do I need to get rhetorical again?"

He raised his hands in defense, one holding an energy drink and the other a beef stick—mild. "Whoa. No. I'll stop talking—"

"Bothering, you mean."

"Yeah, that too." He raised a finger. "If I could say one more thing."

She widened her stance. "What?"

He pointed behind her. "It's your turn."

Jac glowered at him briefly before turning and approaching the clerk. She placed the bottled drinks on the counter, and Billy dumped two handfuls of snacks and sunglasses from his hands.

"Hello, young lady and lad," Rusty said as he scanned their stuff. He pointed in the direction behind them. "Don't let Devin bother or fool you. He's a nice guy, but doesn't use the off button for his mouth often enough."

Devin cleared his throat. "Thanks, Rusty. I think."

Jac grinned at Rusty. Kindness lived in his brown eyes, though they carried a heaviness of many long nights and life's troubles.

"Cash or card?" Rusty asked.

Jac pulled cash from her pocket, and a crisp bill fell to the floor. Her hand brushed against Devin's as he beat her to pick it up. She snatched the bill from his hand and met his hazel eyes as they straightened. "I can manage. Thank you."

She handed Rusty the hundred-dollar bill. Rusty examined it *and* Jac as if the Benjamin was fake, and she'd crack under the pressure of his glare. He ran a highlighter across the bill and nodded.

Devin's pointing hand reached past Jac. "Hey Rusty, turn up the TV. There's a special news report."

Jac froze.

Rusty grabbed the remote and turned up the volume loud enough for the entire store to hear. The bold letters at the bottom of the screen that read "Special Report" might as well have said "Teenage Killer on the Loose."

Two makeup-caked TV anchors rambled on about an incident just outside of Tulsa. They introduced an on-site reporter standing several yards away from the bus engulfed in red and blue flashing lights. Passengers, some Jac recognized, lingered in the background.

"We have to go. Now," Jac urgently whispered to Billy. She grabbed their bagged goods and Billy's hand and hurried to the exit.

"Oh, sorry, little miss, you forgot your change," Rusty said as she pushed open the door.

"Keep it," she shot back.

"But it's forty-five—"

"Keep it," she abruptly repeated.

"Alright, then. Have a good night. Be careful out there."

"Bye." Devin smiled and waved.

She smiled at Rusty, smirked at Devin, and left with Billy in hand. As the door closed, the on-site reporter revealed at least one fatality on the bus. *Yeah, I know.*

Jac kneeled with Billy on the sidewalk outside the store. They stuffed the snacks and drinks into their backpacks' main compartments and side pouches. She yanked the hanging price tag from the sunglasses and awkwardly placed them onto Billy's face with a shaky hand. "Just until we get away from people."

"Was that news story about us?" Billy pushed the sunglasses into place.

"Yes."

"Does this mean I can't eat my snacks yet?"

"We'll get to the snacks soon, I promise. First, we need to find somewhere to hide for ...." Jac's voice trailed off as a vehicle slowly turned into the parking lot, its headlights blinding. She gasped as it drove past. *This cannot be happening.*

Four spaces away parked the Oklahoma Highway Patrol.

HIDE

"Billy," Jac said, hushed, "grab your backpack and follow me. Stay low."

Billy's eyes widened, mirroring hers. "What's wrong?"

"Cop."

Billy turned on his heels.

"Don't look," Jac urged. "Follow me." She grabbed Billy's hand and pulled him along behind her in a duck walk between two parked cars. She pulled the rear door handle of the car to their right—locked.

"Oh, crap." Jac gripped her shirt just above her rapidly thumping heart. A patrol car passed by on the main street, its high-beam light scanning the darkness like a lighthouse. She leaned against the four-door sedan to her left, pulled Billy beside her, and tried the passenger side handle. "Locked. Damn it." The patrol car passed, continuing its search down a side street. She released a breath. "We gotta hide."

Jac surveyed her surroundings and pulled the rear passenger handle. It opened. She motioned for Billy. "Get as low as you can on the floor behind the driver's seat."

Billy climbed into the car. "But there's junk on the floor."

"Just move it out of the way. Quickly."

"And it smells like—"

"Hush and stay low."

Jac climbed in behind him and closed the door. An assemblage of food wrappers and energy drink cans covered her side of the floor. She indiscriminately tossed the discarded trash onto the back seat. She settled low and recoiled. "You have to be kidding me." The smell was more pronounced than when he first walked by her in the store. Out of all the cars in the lot, she climbed into Pizza Guy's.

Billy tossed a dirty sock in Jac's direction.

"Billy ... gross!" She flung the sock onto the back seat.

With Billy settled, Jac adjusted his backpack over him like a turtle shell.

"Now, be still and say nothing."

She eyed the store entrance from between the seats. The highway patrolman entered the store as Devin exited through the adjacent door with an energy drink and beef stick in hand. He exchanged hellos with the patrolman and walked toward the car.

"He's on his way." Jac hastily shuffled her body as low as it would go, offering gratitude for still being tiny at seventeen. She had always been small. Her parents often remarked on her diminutive stature. Even now, she stood barely taller than Billy, nine years her younger, and maybe weighed a hundred pounds with her hair wet.

Waiting for the sound of the opening door, Jac lowered her head to an inch above the sticky floor that smelled of who knew what and adjusted her backpack atop her back. She blew out her cheeks. "I'll need a shower after this."

With a click, the door opened, and a chime announced Devin's arrival. Jac raised her head to check on Billy. Devin dropped into his seat, slightly shrinking the space Billy occupied. The center console obscured her view of Devin from the chest down. Carbonation escaped an opened can, and Devin tilted his head back, chugging down the drink.

"Man, that girl was *ruthless*. Wearing sunglasses inside *and* at night." Devin removed his hat, ran his hand through his hair a few times, and put it back on. "She was cute, though."

Jac wasn't sure if she wanted to laugh, die of embarrassment, or grab him by the throat and tell him off. She decided hiding was the continued best course of action.

Devin started the car. Speakers blared an angsty nineties rock song—before her time, but timeless—about today being the greatest day. The song certainly did not describe her day so far.

The car reversed and accelerated forward. It slowed again, hit a bump, and accelerated quickly. They were on the road, creating space between them and the cop at the store, who Jac imagined would ask Rusty if he had seen a girl with her younger brother. Rusty didn't know he had just sold snacks and drinks to Oklahoma's new Most Wanted. She and Billy certainly would have their own reward poster hanging on police precinct walls across the country. Would their images be an artist's sketch? A blurry still shot from a store camera? A photo taken by a bus passenger? Or maybe a collage covering all angles and profiles. What's the reward for catching a teenage murderer?

Jac didn't forward think the plan of hiding in Devin's car, so potential next steps ran through her mind. They could ride with Devin until he reached his destination and figure out what to do from there. Maybe he would stop somewhere, giving them a chance to exit the car. They'd give him a quick "thank you" and "goodbye" and disappear into the night. Or was he going home, somewhere remote, leaving them lost? Should she speak up, explain things, and take it from there? She disliked the uncertainty of "take it from there."

She decided, for now, to stay hidden. Not out of fear but because she didn't know precisely what to say. What do you say in this situation? Hi Devin, sorry about hiding in your car. Thanks for the ride. Or, surprise, I'm the girl who was mean to you in the store, sorry. Or, hi Devin, I'm sorry we hid in your car, but we seriously needed the help. And what if he asks what or who they were hiding from? What story, less psychotic than the truth, won't send him running away screaming? She rehearsed the dialogue while trying to tune out Devin, singing embarrassingly horribly to every song. The current song was unfamiliar—a hypnotic tune about a girl who was supposed to go to Mars on a train, missed it, and ended up counting stars instead.

Minutes later, the car slowed and turned. The smooth ride of blacktop turned bumpy. Jac's stomach knotted, fearing they were close to Devin's destination, and she wasn't ready to come out of hiding. She doubted she ever would be. Slowly, she lifted her head, bringing Devin's top half into view; his head bobbed to the music. He spun the wheel to the left, the car slowed, stopped, and he turned off the ignition.

Inside, the car turned coffin-quiet.

Here goes nothing. Mustering the courage to speak, Jac cleared her throat and meekly said, "Devin."

"Holy crap!" Devin flailed about at nothing and fumbled for the door handle.

"Devin, it's me," Jac said softly, hoping her calm manner would influence an equally calm reaction.

It didn't.

The car door flung open, sending Devin stumbling to the ground. His hat slipped from his head as he scrambled to his feet. "Who the … Hell?"

Jac crawled to the seat, opened the door on Billy's side, and stepped out of the car.

"Can I get out too?" Billy asked.

"Not yet, Billy, hold on." She closed the door.

Devin doubled over, fighting for breath; his arm extended toward her in a don't-come-any-closer manner. "What—What are you doing in—"

"Hi Devin, sorry about that." She pushed her hair behind her ears and hugged herself.

They stood on a gravel parkway next to a single-wide trailer that had seen newer and better days. Pink paneling that had faded to peach lined its top and bottom. Vertical dirty white paneling covered the rest of the home, its edges and creases lined by green mildew. Moonlight shone through a network of tree branches above, and lights from the surrounding trailers weakly illuminated the area.

Jac lifted her chin toward the trailer behind him. "Is that your home?"

"What? My what?" He turned toward the trailer and then back to her, tilting his head to the side. "Yeah, but seriously. Why were you in my car?"

"We needed a ride."

"To my house? And who is we?"

Billy opened the back door and peeked his head out.

"Devin, if you get back in the car, I can explain," Jac said.

"Get back in my—" Devin laughed. "You can't tell me to get into my own car. No, you two need to get out. You don't … you don't hide in someone's car without—Oh damn," he grimaced, gripping the hair atop his head as if it would fly off. "You heard me singing and everything I said."

In the limited light and with her sunglasses on, Jac couldn't see the embarrassment on Devin's face, but she felt it radiating from him.

"I'm coming out," Billy announced. "The pizza smell is—"

"Billy, stay in the car," Jac ordered.

"Why?"

"Just do it."

He dropped onto the back seat. "Fine."

"Thank you."

"Wait, why is he staying in my car?"

"So you don't get in and leave us, or lock it and go inside with us stuck out here."

Devin stood momentarily speechless as if analyzing a way out of the predicament she had placed him in. "Damn." He shook his head. "You got a whole lot less cute now that I know you're crazy." He pointed at her face. "And still with the sunglasses? Your brother, too."

She let the "cute" comment tickle her ego for a quick moment before moving on. "I'm not crazy." Knowing the dark would hide her bloodshot eyes, she removed and pocketed her sunglasses, wanting Devin to see the sincerity on her face. "We needed to get away from the store, and, by coincidence"—she chuckled softly —"your car was unlocked."

"There's a thing, you know, called asking? Not that I would have said yes with how you treated me in the store." A flash of understanding covered Devin's face. "Wait, you said, 'get away.' Get away from who?" He scoffed. "Were you getting away from that cop?"

"Yes," Jac answered without hesitation, surprising herself. "We were."

"Serious?" Devin's mouth gaped. "Are you two wanted or something?"

Then Jac recalled an episode of TV about a girl who ran away, practically escaped, from her abusive stepfather. The story could work. She went with it. "We're runaways," she said straight-faced.

Billy, in a whisper, questioned her.

"Our stepdad," she continued, "he ... he's abusive, and we don't want to go back home." She mocked a pained expression and wiped away an imaginary tear. With no previous acting experience, she wasn't sure if she was coming off as believable or making a fool of herself.

Devin swiped twice at a bug flying around him, smacked the side of his neck, and inspected his hand. He refocused on her but only mouthed part of the first word he wanted to say.

"We needed to get away," she continued. "I'm sorry we didn't have time to ask for a ride. Properly."

Devin looked at her sideways. "Why not tell the cop about your stepdad? Let him help you?"

She chewed at her bottom lip. "No one believes us, so we've been on the run."

Devin studied her a moment, turned toward his home, and spoke to himself at a level Jac couldn't quite decipher. He turned back to face her with his lips pressed tight.

"So?"

"Well, you can't stay in my car all night, and you can't stay at my house. My mom is ... she—" Devin scratched his head as he scanned his surroundings. He swiped his hat from the ground, then knocked it free of dirt and leaves with a hit against his leg. "She's home." He slipped on the hat and tucked long strands of hair inside it.

"I understand." Jac slumped her shoulders. "If you could at least point us toward Tulsa, we'll walk there."

"Wait. Walk to Tulsa? Tonight?"

"Yeah. We don't have much of a choice." She laid it on thick now, tugging at strings and hoping to find that Devin had a heart. "We'll figure out what to do when we get there."

"This is insane." Devin gripped his head as if it would settle the world around him. "You are *not* walking to Tulsa." He mumbled something, then sighed. "How about this? I'll take you someplace you can stay for the night."

"Really?" Jac gripped her sunglasses' temples. "You would do that?"

"Yeah. But it's not free. You have a credit card or cash, right?"

"Cash."

"I can't believe I'm doing this," he muttered. "Okay. Get in the car. I know a place."

THE WHITE ROOM

S unny waited in a small, square, white-walled room. Not only were the walls white, but also the floor and ceiling. Two white fabric chairs stood in the room next to a white side table, on which sat a white orchid in a white vase. Other than the orchid's stem and soil, Sunny's navy blue suit, pink tie, and brown shoes were the only colors in the room.

He sat anxiously for nearly a half-hour, spending the time meditating. However, it didn't entirely vanquish the lump in his throat. When informed of Jacqueline and Billy's escape from the driver *he* sent to retrieve and deliver them, he expected a summons to the White Room for a meeting. The kids' escape was his fault, regardless of not being there to control the situation. He had sent the driver, and the driver failed. Fearing association with failure, those in the Coven's inner circle avoided Sunny like a coughing person in a pandemic. As for the driver, he faced an unfortunate fate.

Sunny sat forward. He rubbed his eyes, irritated by the blast of white. If he didn't leave this—Heels struck the tile in the hall. The White Room door opened a moment later. He stood and greeted a heels-taller woman with perfect pale skin and long red hair, straight as a line. Her form-fitting black dress warranted an appreciative look.

"Evening, Ava," Sunny said politely. "You look extraordinary."

"Evening, Sunny, and thank you," Ava said in a silky voice, never taking her emerald eyes off his.

They hugged and kissed cheeks.

"Is he ready for me?" Sunny asked.

"He is." Ava moved from the doorway; her arm extended toward the exit. "After you."

Sunny tucked his shirt, straightened his tie, and smoothed his jacket and pants. He passed Ava and stepped into a long hallway, his shoes striking the tile, creating a lonely echo. Fluorescent lights lined the middle of the ceiling, illuminating the gray-tiled floor and gray-painted brick walls. Doors of various colors to other rooms lined the hall's sides. A black door loomed at the end.

"To the end?" Sunny asked, staring at the dark rectangle.

"Oh, no, certainly not. Yellow."

Sunny figured as much. Still, he couldn't take his eyes off the black door, taunting him with death like a black hole to a deep space traveler.

The Black Room contrasted with White in more ways than color. Devoid of comforts and light, its purpose was to strike fear into its unfortunate occupant, create unease, and wreck their equilibrium. Paradoxically, the darkness offered nowhere to hide, and those who entered never left alive. This room without an exit was the limo driver's destination if he hadn't already paid it a visit.

The yellow door stood before Sunny like a rectangle of sunshine.

"Sorry, Sunny," Ava said, looking the slightest forlorn.

"Free yourself of concern. It's only yellow. I'll see you when I'm out."

He cleared his throat and opened the yellow door. The room's comfort and contents matched the white but in an off-putting, headache-inducing yellow.

A man already inside sat on one of the yellow chairs. He wore a black suit, a white dress shirt, and a yellow tie. He had a thin build and a sharp-featured face. "Hello, Sunny. Thank you for joining me." He spoke with the guile and confidence of a poisonous snake.

Sunny regarded the yellow tie. "Hello, Edgar. I'm here as you requested."

"As I ordered." Edgar raised a corrective eyebrow.

Sunny respectfully bowed his head. "Of course, as you ordered."

Edgar smiled broadly, revealing a mouth full of dazzling white teeth and pink gums. He motioned to a yellow chair like a casket salesman in a funeral home. "Please sit for a bit, won't you?"

Sunny winked at Ava as he closed the door. He unbuttoned his jacket and occupied the chair next to Edgar. He shifted in his seat, searching for comfort.

"Do relax, Sunny. We *are* in the yellow room. Besides, I have blotted out, as a thick cloud, thy transgressions, and, as a cloud, your ... well, let's just call them your miscalculations."

"Apologies. I'm unfamiliar with that verse. I assume it means—"

"It means, Sunny, I'm not here to kill you." Edgar erupted into a laugh, sounding like a mix of hyena and clown.

"Yes. Fortunate and forgiving of you."

Edgar's laughter subsided, and his lips slowly sealed, forming a severe grin. He leaned close to Sunny. "But we must discuss the Kelley children and why they and their mother still breathe."

JENKS MOTEL

The trio sat in Devin's car in a parking lot somewhere in Jenks, Oklahoma, where hotels were three-star at best, and every other place for transitory stay was you-get-what-you-pay-for. Above them, a sign glowed that read "Jenks Motel."

"A motel?" Jac raised an eyebrow. "You've taken us to a motel." She had never stayed in a motel or anywhere other than the family apartment. From what she'd seen on TV, motels were linked to all kinds of illegal stuff, like being a quick hideout for criminals.

"Yeah. You need a place to stay tonight, and this is the place," Devin said matter-of-factly.

Truthfully, a motel with few to no guests was a brilliant idea. She and Billy needed space from people for now and in the foreseeable future, being criminals on the run. Still, the single-story building looked like ten dingy square blocks fused together to form one long, dingy rectangle.

Jac eyed the motel check-in desk. "We can't go inside to pay. We can't be seen."

"Yeah, I figured. Give me twenty-five dollars, and I'll go in."

Jac's eyes narrowed. "That gets us two rooms?"

"No, just one."

She leaned away from Devin. "You are *not* sharing a room with us."

"No ... What?" Devin laughed. "I'm not staying with you. I'm only getting the room, one room. Then I'm going back home."

She softened. "Oh, you're leaving us?"

"Yeah, for the night, but I'll be back in the morning to take you to Tulsa. And then," he shrugged, "you can do whatever you need to. Besides, I can't ask for two rooms; the owner knows me. She'd know something weird was up."

Devin inspected the one-hundred-dollar bill she handed him. "Now, *that's* crisp. Give me five minutes, and I'll take you to the room." He stopped before getting out of the car, gave Jac a suspicious look, and took the keys. "Stay in the car. There are cameras around. I don't want to explain to Dezi who you are."

"Dezi?" Jac asked.

"She's the owner. She works at night because she is usually too hungover to crawl out of bed in the morning."

Devin walked into the motel lobby and out of view.

"I like him," Billy said.

Jac smirked and scoffed. "You like him?"

"Sure. He's helping us."

"I suppose."

Jac appreciated Devin's help, but that didn't mean she trusted him. She was rightfully wary of trusting people. Sunny and the

Coven created that troublesome trait within her. Until recently, she considered herself an excellent judge of people. Could she trust Devin? Or had she misplaced her trust in the first person she met since leaving home? Was his dimpled smile and cute looks part of a ploy? He could be calling the police. They could be on their way.

"Where is he?" Jac leaned over the driver's seat for a better view of the lobby.

"It's only been a couple of minutes."

"Yeah, I know. I just wish he would hurry." *I wish I could trust him.* She brought her favorite fingernail to her mouth and chewed.

"Will Devin take us to San Diego?" Billy asked, breaking Jac from fearful thoughts of Devin betraying them.

"What?"

"Maybe he'll take us to San Diego."

"I heard you the first time. And no, that's crazy. He won't take us to San Diego. Do you understand how far that is?"

"Yes, sort of." Billy sat back and crossed his arms.

"Well, it's a long way."

They sat in silence, Jac mulling over Billy's idea. *Sure, why not ask Devin to take us across half the country? Simple enough.* She *could* pay him; she had enough cash to act as a mobile ATM. Though his car smelled like the inside of a pizza box, it seemed capable of the journey. No. The idea was ridiculous. She barely convinced him to drive to Jenks Motel, five minutes from his home.

The car door opened; Jac jumped in her seat and gasped.

"Whoa, calm down...." Devin plopped into his seat. Looking confused, he pointed to her. "Well, crud. I never asked for your name."

"You didn't?"

"Almost certain I didn't." He handed her the change from the hundred.

"Jac, my name's Jac." She exhaled and leaned back in her seat.

"Jac?" Devin raised an eyebrow.

"Actually, it's Jacqueline," Billy chimed in.

She groaned. "Hush, Billy."

"Well, it's true. I couldn't pronounce Jacqueline when I was a kid. So, I just always called her Jac."

"Oh, I get it. Using Jac makes sense." Devin looked at Billy and then at her. "Billy, that's right. Your sister said your name just after she scared the heck out of me back at my place. And Billy is short for ... William?"

Jac nodded.

"Those are like names of royalty."

She laughed. "Yeah, not even close. We're more like descendants of potato famine survivors."

"Really? I think I remember learning about that in history class. Well, anyway, Jac and Billy. Nice to meet you again, I guess." He nodded once to them individually. "Oh, and don't call me Dev. I hate that. Devin, just Devin."

"The room?" Jac asked, hoping to avoid small talk that would undoubtedly lead to sharing favorite colors.

"Oh yeah, it's near the end. I'll drive us to it. The camera there doesn't work, at least the last time I was here."

"Do you stay here a lot?"

"Yeah, I do," Devin said, his voice trailing off.

She pressed. "Why?"

"Sometimes,"—he turned the ignition—"I need a place to stay when I don't want to be at home."

Earlier, standing outside of Devin's trailer, he said they couldn't go into his home, and he seemed all awkward about it. There was more to the mother situation than he had shared, but Jac pressed no more.

Devin parked in front of a door marked with the number ten. "Grab your bags and let's go. I know these rooms like they're my own bedroom. The AC unit in this room is kinda buggy, so I'll come in and get you settled."

Jac couldn't help but secretly meet with skepticism everything Devin offered to do. Still, she agreed to let him into the room. With the summer heat and humidity, she wasn't interested in staying in a room without cold air blowing from the vents.

Stale and muggy air met them upon entering the motel room. Long maroon drapes covered the front window. Side tables flanked a double bed, the room's centerpiece. A small dining table stood in the corner, with two chairs, and a dresser held a TV bolted to its top.

Devin made enemies with the AC unit against the wall beside the draped window. It rattled to a start after a last kick to its side and blasted cold air into the room. "It's not a four-star accommodation, but I can promise the bed sheets are clean."

Jac internally cringed. She hadn't considered the possibility of dirty bedsheets. She had only ever slept on her own bed and occasionally her parents' bed after a nightmare. How odd and a bit disgusting it would be to lie in a bed where someone else had slept. She decided to be agreeable, grateful even, and didn't mention it. "We've been on the road for hours; this is good ... clean sheets are good."

Billy kicked off his shoes and hopped onto the bed. "This is great," he said as he jumped up and down. The mattress sagged in the middle as if it had endured years of jumpers. He had been through so much heartbreak at such a young age and was only a couple of hours removed from playing witness to a murder and drinking blood from a plastic cup. Though unintentional, he displayed his resiliency, acting like an excitable kid, carefree, and jumping. Jac, however, remained troubled, only allowing the slightest smile to play at her mouth's corners.

"So, I'm going," Devin said, interrupting her few seconds of living in the now. He thumbed toward the door. "I'd take your number, but I haven't seen you glued to a phone; I guess you don't have one."

"No. No phones," Jac said. "We've never needed one, other than the one at home."

"No problem. I have the number to the room, and I'll give you mine." Devin wrote his number on the tablet at the bedside table. "If you need anything, call me."

Jac pocketed her hands. "Thanks."

"You both should get some sleep. No offense ... you look exhausted,"—he pointed to his eyes—"even with the sunglasses on." He nodded to Billy, jumping on the bed. "Well, at least *you* look tired. Billy looks like he could go all night."

Jac tucked her hair behind her ears and looked toward the floor. The disparaging remark hurt a little, but Devin's observation was correct. Her reflection in the store bathroom had disgusted her. How Devin had considered her worthy of flirting with, regardless of how bad he was at it, she couldn't understand. That fact only raised her level of suspicion toward him. He wasn't a vampire; that was easy to discern. Was he something else? A trusted human of the local coven? Though rare, they existed.

"Devin," Billy said, now lying on the bed.

"What's up?"

"Will you take us to San Diego?"

"Take you *where?*" Devin looked at Jac.

Jac laughed uncomfortably, positioning herself between them. "No, ignore him."

"*You* weren't going to ask him," Billy said, sitting up.

"You're right. I *wasn't.*" Her nostrils flared. She mouthed to Billy, "Shut up."

"You're going to San Diego?" Devin asked.

Jac huffed and turned to Devin, her fists clenched at her sides, and answered through gritted teeth. "Yes."

"What's in San Diego ... or who?"

"Family friends," Jac said flatly. She didn't elaborate, unprepared to.

"Good ... that's good. I'm glad you have someone to go to."

Her eyes darted between the floor and Devin.

"Well, there's a bus station in Tulsa. I can take you there tomorrow."

"No," she said too abruptly. *Please don't ask why.*

"Why not?"

Yet another unexpected question.

"We just can't."

"But why can't—"

"Can we leave it at that?" She bit her lower lip.

Devin looked at the floor and traced a shape on the carpet with his foot. "I'd take you if I could. At least, I think I would." He met her sunglasses stare. "San Diego, that's a long drive, and I got stuff, you know, work, home ... stuff."

Jac lowered her head, and her clenched hands relaxed. How could she blame him for saying no? Who were they to expect him, on a whim, to take two strangers across half of the country? However, she couldn't help but feel hurt at his immediate rejection. "It's okay. I already told Billy you wouldn't ... couldn't." She walked to the door, prepared to usher him out like a guest who had overstayed his welcome. "Besides,"—she sighed—"I didn't ask. We're going to get some sleep. We'll see you in the morning." Doubt lingered in her voice at that last part. She watched Devin's reaction for an indication he heard it, too.

"I can't take you to San Diego, but trust me, I *will* be here in the morning."

He *had* heard the doubt.

"Checkout is at 10:00. I'll be here at 9:30."

Jac offered a simple thank you as the door closed behind Devin. She listened for his car pulling away, then pulled the curtain to the side. The parking space was empty. The lot's few cars and the nearby woods drew her attention. No one suspicious lurked in the night, but she wouldn't let her guard down. Someone other than the police was out there looking for them, and they wouldn't stop, not even after reaching San Diego. Hell, she wasn't even confident she could trust the Castillos, but Mom did, and she trusted Mom.

The curtain fell back into place; she locked the door and secured the latch. Jac was far from religious, but to whatever god listened, she prayed no one would find them before morning.

ARE WE MONSTERS?

J ac stood beneath the warm spray of her first shower in days. The water pressure was loads better than at home. She vigorously scrubbed every inch of her body with a small square of vanilla-fragranced soap, wanting to literally and figuratively remove the day's atrocities. However, the memories wouldn't wash away; she could never cleanse herself of them.

Showers had a way of bringing clarity and allowing time for reflection. But Jac pushed away every negative thought or memory that floated to the forefront. After reaching San Diego and ensuring Billy's safety, she would take the time to deal with her emotions. Until then, she'd have to live with feeling like total crap.

She would have loved a longer shower, but her stress accumulated every minute Billy was alone, though only a door away. She shut off the water, stepped out of the shower, and wrapped a bleached white towel around her chest.

"Billy, are you okay?" Jac asked through the door.

"I'm good," came Billy's muffled reply.

"I'll be out in a few minutes."

She wiped the condensation from the small square mirror on the wall, sending down rivulets of water, tracing lines through the fog. Her fingernails were frown-worthy—jagged from too many attacks from her teeth and, even after the shower, still embedded with dirt and dried blood. The blood was *his*, the man she murdered. His memory would live with her, but she needed to erase any physical trace of him. She dug at the dirt and blood with soap and enmity underneath a stream of warm water.

Satisfied her nails were now a wreck and no longer a tragedy, Jac stared into the mirror. Wet black hair clung to her face and hung just past her shoulders. Her cheeks, slightly rosy from the warm water and sunken, contrasted against her porcelain skin. Lips barren and plain, as usual. White straight teeth covered with film. She winced at the state of her eyes—underlined with prominent black circles and marked by remaining broken blood vessels. She resembled someone whose life had fallen apart, or maybe she resembled the murderer she was.

Jac shut her tearful eyes and covered her mouth, muffling a cry. *Why, why, why?* She pounded her forehead with her fist. *I can't do this. I can't do this.*

A moment passed. With tears not yet wiped away, her tremorous hand pulled a toothbrush from her backpack. *Toothpaste. Damn it.* "Billy," she said, her voice cracking. He'd know something was wrong. He'd hear it.

"Yeah. What's wrong?"

Billy's question, though innocently asked, struck at her resolve. She had to remain strong for him. She had to be the adult and see him safely to San Diego, no matter what. There wasn't time for negative emotions.

She pressed her thumb and ring finger against her temples and managed to respond without falling apart. "Nothing's wrong. I just need the toothpaste. It's in your bag."

Billy knocked on the door a minute later. "Got it."

A blast of cold air collided with a puff of warm air when Jac opened the door. "Thanks." She avoided eye contact, grabbed the toothpaste, and closed the door.

After doing what she could to bring herself visually close to normal, Jac sprinted from the bathroom's warmth. She rushed through the bedroom's cold air and hopped under the covers with Billy, wrapping them around her like a cocoon.

"Whatcha watching?" she asked.

"Nothing good is on." He dropped the TV remote onto the blanket next to him. "I wish I had my tablet."

"We should turn off the TV then. We have an early start tomorrow and a long trip in front of us." She kissed his forehead, grabbed the remote, and clicked off the TV. "And we'll buy you a new tablet after we get to San Diego."

Billy slouched. "Okay." He placed a half-eaten bag of chips next to a nearly empty drink bottle on his bedside table. He wiggled until he was on his back and pulled the covers to his neck.

"Stay on your side." Jac drew an imaginary line between them.

"*You* stay on *your* side," Billy retorted.

"Whatever. You're the one who creeps around the bed, flinging your arms and legs in your sleep. And you've fed tonight. I might have to sleep on the floor."

"I don't creep."

"Mm-hmm."

Billy did indeed creep. There were nights he couldn't sleep alone. Jac had pushed him to his side of her bed on more than one occasion over the last couple of weeks. She didn't mind, wanting him to feel safe and loved.

He had revealed his fear of being separated from her or losing her. Still, Jac often felt she needed Billy more than he needed her. She had no doubt Billy understood his role in their remaining family dynamic. She played the part of the muscle and brains of their two-person family, doing whatever was needed and making the tough decisions. While Billy provided emotional support, keeping her from falling off the rails.

Jac turned toward the candle she had placed on her bedside table. The white, vanilla-scented candle was half of its original size. With a strike of a match, the lit wick illuminated the room. With only the slightest wince, she pinched the flame and placed the cooled-off match on the table. The flame flickered and danced.

"Hi, Dad," she whispered. Life with Dad hadn't been perfect, but she loved him. Dad was the strongest person she had known. Invincible. Parents seemed that way. *Her* parents seemed that way. They would have always been around to see her grow and witness her successes.

Her parents would have aged gracefully—three or more centuries for vampires—and died of old age. Before any significant successes on Jac's part, her dad, her Superman, took two bullets to the heart, two to the head, and was gone.

Billy curled up next to her. "I miss Dad."

Jac blew at the flame. Wisps of smoke escaped the wick's ember tip and disappeared into the darkness. She placed her arm around her little brother. "I do, too. I miss him a lot."

"Do you think we'll ever see Mom again?"

Billy had asked that question at least a dozen times. Jac always instantly replied, "Yes," like AI designed to provide answers to questions as quickly as possible. This time, she didn't. Possibilities of what happened to Mom swirled inside her mind. She wanted to believe their mother—someone else on the planet who cared for her and Billy—was alive. She imagined her mother hiding away, keeping herself alive and safe while managing her and Billy's passage to San Diego. Mom was out there watching over their every step. But how could that last part be true? *She* had brought Billy this far, not Mom. If their mother was somewhere, it wasn't here. If the truth were told, she was likely nowhere. But tonight, for Billy, Jac sided with hope.

"Yes, I think we'll see her again."

Billy snuggled into her. "Me too."

Moments passed in silence before Billy spoke again. "Jac … you awake?"

"Yes." She yawned. "What's up?"

"Are we bad?"

Jac paused. The question struck her heart. She could quickly answer the question for everyone except Billy. One answer lived in her heart and soul, which the night's events only reinforced. The row six passenger's expression haunted her; his screams as he lay damaged and bleeding echoed in her mind. She despised the ability to suppress her humanity, which allowed her to choke the life from him. Unequivocally, yes—vampires were bad, and, more to the point, vampires were monsters. Still, for Billy, she avoided her truth and answered from what heart she hoped she had left.

"You aren't bad." She sidled up to him.

"But—"

"No more questions. Go to sleep."

"I'll try, but the sheets smell like bleach."

"So it's not just me?"

"Like, a lot of bleach."

Jac scrunched her nose. "At least we know they're clean. You'll get used to it."

She closed her eyes, pushing her mind toward planning for tomorrow. Still, she couldn't shake the feeling that she had killed someone for the first time. She couldn't pry the self-identifying words out of her head—*I am a monster.*

SAN DIEGO OR DIE

The night for Jac had passed slowly and mostly sleepless. She reacted to every noise, crawling out of bed to peer out the window. She imagined someone waiting in the parking lot, ready to spirit them away to Philadelphia. Or a mass of police cars parked in defensive positions, their lights flashing, with Devin standing in the middle of it all, pointing a betraying finger directly at her.

After a last look through the window and a well-placed kick bringing the A/C to life, Jac's head hit the pillow. She finally allowed herself the needed sleep in the early morning hours. Sleep filled with dreams.

* * *

"Okay. Okay. I *am* awake," Jac screamed in protest, pushing away with her arms as she bolted to a sit in bed. "I'm awake. Please stop!" The image of her dream bled like chalk art in the rain and was gone.

"What the heck, Jac!" Billy yelled from … somewhere.

Jac pressed her eyes closed and shook her head as she stood. She surveyed her surroundings: the bed that was not hers, the drab drapes hanging over the window, and the muted color scheme. "I was just in my bedroom. Damn, dream." She turned in a circle. "Billy?"

"I'm over here." Billy lay crumpled on the floor near the bathroom. He stood gingerly.

"Are you okay? What happened?"

"I tried to wake you up, but you kept yelling stop. Then you woke up and pushed me across the room."

"Oh, Billy, I'm sorry. I was dreaming." She trotted over and pulled him into a hug. "You're okay, tough guy."

"It was kinda fun, like flying for a couple seconds." Billy looked up at her. "What was your dream about?"

Jac closed her eyes, bringing what remained of the dream into focus. "I was in my bedroom with Mom. I … asked her where she was, but she wouldn't answer." She sighed and plopped onto the bed. "It was just like I was there, and she was with me. But I knew it was a dream. It got weird, and I wanted it to end."

"Dad called those Lucy dreams," Billy said.

"Lucy, what?" She laughed. "They're called lucid dreams, silly, not Lucy."

"Anyway, they're like, really, real dreams."

"They aren't real; they just seem like it." She recollected more of the dream. "Mom told me not to trust anyone."

"Stranger danger?"

"For us, that means everyone. We can only trust each other." Jac mussed Billy's hair and kissed his forehead. "We should get ready to go."

"Yeah, that's why I tried to wake you up. It's nine fifteen. Devin will be here soon."

One look at the clock proved Billy right. "You're not kidding. Let's pack our stuff."

Jac's dream of Mom and being in the comfort of her bedroom lingered. She yearned to feel safe and for Mom to assume the caretaking role. Jac wasn't fit for parenting, unable to properly care for herself, much less Billy. She blinked and shook her head. *I need to wake up.* She turned on the bedside lamp and recoiled from the bright light. The room was just as unfamiliar as the night before. She longed for home. A heaviness filled her limbs, but she needed to move. There was a country to travel across, and she hadn't figured out how they would do it.

"I call bathroom," Jac announced.

"You got it. I took my turn while you were sleeping."

Jac stepped around Billy, gathering and packing his things. With a flick of the bathroom light switch, she went straight for the mirror. She rubbed her eyes and studied her reflection, hoping for a better view than the night before. It wasn't much. A few flecks of irritation sprinkled her eyes like peppermint candy. The damage was less than perfect and far from attractive, but thankfully, sunglasses were now an optional accessory.

A few splashes of refreshing cold water brought her closer to fully awake. She dried off with a hand towel and fastened her hair into a ponytail, with wisps of too-short strands tickling the side of her cheeks. The clothes she wore to bed, her last clean set, would have to do. "Okay, let's do this."

A car door closed outside the room. Jac stepped from the bathroom, and a knock rattled the door.

"Don't answer it," Jac whispered to Billy, already two steps toward the door. "Get in the bathroom until I say."

Billy hustled to the bathroom, and she peeked out of the window. Devin stood outside with his hands stuffed in his jeans pockets, nervously looking around and unsuccessfully acting inconspicuously. He parked in the same spot as the night before.

Jac opened the room door, keeping the latch secure. A waft of a woodsy, floral cologne filled the open space.

Devin peered through the door slit with a grin. "Hey, it's me."

"I can see that. Did you come alone?" She scrutinized his response for any signs of deceitfulness.

Devin smirked and glanced over his shoulder. "Uh, yeah. Who would come with me?"

She recognized the that's-a-dumb-question look, but something was off. Wrinkles covered Devin's shirt like he had pulled it from the bottom of a clothes basket, and the back of his hair stood as straight as a peacock's plume. "What happened to your hair?"

Devin felt the back of his head, pressing his hair flat. He shrugged. "I haven't brushed it since waking up." He glanced to his left and leaned forward. "Are you going to let me in? I don't want anyone to see me knocking on the door to the room I'm supposed to be staying in."

Despite Jac's suspicion of everyone else in the world, she edged closer to trusting Devin. He had an honesty to him, whether from true character or stupid youthful ignorance, and something in the manner he spoke and the tone of his voice.

She closed the door, pulled back the latch, and opened the door, letting him in with the morning sun. "Hurry. Get in."

He stepped in and closed the door. "Paranoid today?"

"It's part of staying alive." She turned away and internally cursed her response.

"Staying alive? What does that mean?"

She wrung her hands. "Nothing, never mind."

"Wait. Is your stepfather *that* dangerous?"

"No, it's just … something my mom taught me. You know, the whole 'stranger danger' thing. Everyone is a stranger to me." Lying wasn't her strength, lacking the practice. She didn't know if Devin believed a word she had said. Regardless, he couldn't know the truth. Soon enough, they would part ways, and she could stop with the lies.

"That's timeless parental advice, but I talk to strangers all the time, and most of them aren't that bad. I was a stranger just yesterday, and I turned out to be okay."

"Let's not get ahead of ourselves."

"Besides, I believe that if you're looking for trouble, you'll find it." He tossed his keys into the air, catching them on the way down. "It's better to believe everything will work out and trust that the universe will take care of you."

Jac wanted to respond with, 'What kind of bullshit is that?' Instead, she raised an eyebrow at Devin.

He pointed at her. "I see you have eyes."

"Yeah, they're brown." She reflexively reached for her face. "An exciting reveal."

"I think they're—"

"Hey, Devin," Billy said, stepping from the bathroom.

"Hey, buddy. Good to see you."

"Jac shoved me across the room this morning."

"She did ... what?" Devin looked between her and Billy.

"But she was dreaming, so it was an accident."

Jac tittered. "Never mind him."

"Anyway, I was thinking about San Diego."

She raised both eyebrows. "Why were you thinking about San Diego?"

Billy stepped closer.

"So, I also believe in helping others ... you know." Devin's hands fidgeted. "When you take care of others, they'll ...."

Jac stared at Devin with amusement, witnessing him having trouble finding the words.

"Yeah, so I want to take you and Billy to San Diego."

"Yes!" Billy cheered, his arms raised in a V.

"Wait. Really?" Jac's jaw dropped.

"Yeah, I'm serious. But—"

"But?" She crossed her arms.

"Well, there's gas, food, one or two hotel stays, and I'll miss at least four days of work."

"You want to be paid to take us?"

Devin slipped his hands into his pockets. "Four days of delivery tips is a good chunk of change I would miss out on. I mean, it seems like you could pitch in, at least. I don't even know if you have money."

"You want to be paid," Jac repeated.

"When you say it that way, it's like you're my boss or something."

She raised her hands to her sides. "What word would you like me to use?"

Devin opened his mouth to respond, paused, and nodded. "Yeah, paid works or reimbursed, maybe."

"I mean, it makes sense, paying you."

"So, we're sticking with paid?"

She grinned enough to show a sliver of teeth. "It sounds right to me."

"We have a deal?" Devin extended his hand toward her.

Jac looked at Billy's excited and expectant face and considered the offer. Dragging Devin into their troubles could be the next biggest mistake of her life. However, Devin gave them the best chance of reaching San Diego.

Chewing on the inside of her cheek, she thought better of the deal, then thought some more, teetering between asking Devin to leave and not look back, versus her hopping into his car and giving him the order to drive. *God, I hope I don't regret this.* She smiled at Billy and turned to Devin, giving him a firm handshake. "Deal."

Devin grimaced. He pulled back his hand and flexed his fingers. "Good shake there, Hulk."

Note, ease up on the handshake.

A knock on the door saved Jac from explaining how a girl her size could give a crushing handshake and drained the blood from her already pale face. She didn't hear the car pull up; now, someone was outside their room. Devin had been a distraction.

"Are you expecting anyone?" Devin asked.

"No, you?"

He shook his head.

"Billy, get back in the bathroom," Jac urgently whispered.

Devin peeked out of the window.

"Who is it?" Jac asked.

"It's some clean-cut guy in a suit. And wow."

"Wow, what?"

"There's a nice Benz parked next to my car. It looks like he has a driver and—"

Devin recoiled from the window and made a weird noise as if someone had tried to steal his breath.

"What happened?"

Devin stepped back from the door. "He saw me."

Another knock.

"Get in the bathroom with Billy," Jac ordered. "I'll find out what he wants."

Devin looked at her incredulously. "You? You'll find—"

"I can hear the two of you talking," said a voice from outside.

Jac froze.

Devin mirrored the fear on her face. "What's wrong?"

She said nothing and listened.

"Jac, please open the door so we can speak face to face. You've caused a bit of trouble and a lot of concern."

The voice was familiar. Not the speaker, but the tone and cadence. He spoke all proper, enunciating words as if each sentence were a proclamation. He spoke precisely like Sunny, like an emissary.

"What the hell," Devin whispered. "Did he hear me say your name? Did I even say your name?" He backed farther away from the door and grabbed for her hand. She batted his hand away.

"Jac," came the voice, "Billy can stay in there with your friend. I need only to speak with you."

Jac stepped close to Devin, rose to her toes, and shuddered an inch away from his ear. *Oh my God. You have to be kidding me.* Her legs buckled for a heartbeat, then firmed. She caught her stolen breath, held it, and found the momentary will to whisper into his ear. "Get in the bathroom with Billy and lock the door. If I tell you to call the police, call the police."

"Jac," came the voice again, "do I have to get a room key or have the door knocked in? This discussion is not optional, and you have nowhere to run."

Her heart rate quickened with the stranger's every word, and he wasn't shutting up. She yelled at the door. "Hold on!"

"One minute more, Jac, is all I will offer."

"Let me call the police," Devin pleaded, gripping his phone.

Jac pushed his hand down. "No, I can take care of this."

"You know this guy?"

"Not him exactly, but I think he knows my stepdad. He might want to help us, but I can't be sure until I talk to him."

Devin studied the door. "Let's not take the chance."

"Hey." Jac waved her hand in front of Devin's face and snapped her fingers as if she were gaining a child's attention. "Trust me. Please. Get in there with Billy and keep him safe. I will work this out."

The wrinkles on Devin's forehead smoothed. "Okay, but I have 9-1-1 ready ... just a push away."

"Thank you."

Devin closed the bathroom door, and a confirming click of an engaged lock sounded. A locked door wouldn't save them, nor would calling the police. She and Billy were fugitives—the police were nearly the last people they'd want to see. They were on their own in this mess, and she had to see them out of it.

"Jacqueline," said the voice from behind the door, using her full name for effect.

"I'm coming!" Jac gripped the door handle. She took a deep breath—the first she could since Devin left her side— and exhaled. Wearing her most confident face, she opened the door, knowing her racing heart would betray her attempt at appearing calm.

"Hello, Jac," said the man, staring down at her with bright blue eyes and a broad smile, nearly exposing every brilliant white tooth.

As expected and feared, Jac stood face to teeth with a vampire.

DOES DEVIN KNOW?

"Hello, emissary." Jac pronounced "emissary" as if it were something sticky on the bottom of a shoe.

"Well, aren't you clever?" The emissary smiled wryly. "What gave me away?"

"Everything."

He gave a nod.

"You know my name," Jac said. "I only know your job."

Not short on pride, the corner of the emissary's lip twitched at his highly regarded coven role referred to as "a job."

"My name is Reginald Everleigh. I'm the Emissary for the Oklahoma Coven." He extended his arm toward his car. Its pristine, polished surface reflected the surroundings. "Shall we?"

Emissaries prided themselves on their honesty; they had a "code." Part of the code required all initial contact between emissaries and their mark to be conversational and not confrontational. Code or not, Jac prepared for the worst. She walked out and shut the door.

"Before I get in your car, just know that I'm not going anywhere with you." She jabbed a finger at Reginald and at the ground. "I will fight, and I will die right here, right now."

"Oh no, my dear Jacqueline, there's—"

"It's Jac."

"Of course, Jac." He slightly bowed his head. "But you misconstrue my intentions. I'm merely here for respectful discourse, and the car offers a modicum of privacy. So, you can allay your battle intentions and calm your heart, threatening to beat out of your chest. I do, however, have a single demand of you."

Jac surveyed the car, locking eyes with the driver. He had short black hair, wore a black suit, and had no emotion.

Reginald waved his hand dismissively. "Pay the driver no mind; the brutish appearance comes with the job. He's harmless."

"Looks like it," she said, not hiding the sarcasm.

Dying at the Jenks Motel was not top on Jac's to-do list, but she meant her threat. She would fight. However, Reginald seemed sincere in his disinterest in fighting her. She would see Billy to the safety of San Diego, even if it took getting into the car with the emissary. Nearly anything was better than going back to Philadelphia, back to Edgar.

Jac climbed in the back seat and Reginald behind her. She maneuvered to the other side as he closed the door.

∗ ∗ ∗

Billy huddled with Devin in the bathroom. As Devin instructed, Billy sat in the tub with the curtain drawn, and Devin pressed his ear to the door.

"They must be outside," Devin said. "I can't hear them talking."

Billy slid down the back of the tub and stared at the ceiling. He had heard Jac talking to the emissary, but it got quiet.

"Do you know that guy?" Devin asked.

"I don't know him." Billy wasn't lying; he didn't "know" that guy. But he knew that guy was a vampire and that it was best that Devin didn't.

"I shouldn't have let her go alone. I should be out there."

"No." Billy sat up. "Jac said to stay. You shouldn't go."

"What if she needs help?"

"You really shouldn't." Billy pushed the shower curtain aside and leapfrogged from the tub. "Jac will be super mad if you go out there."

"I don't know." Devin gritted his teeth. "What if they're taking her away?" He wrung his hands as he paced away and back to the bathroom door. He pulled his cell phone from his back pocket and readied a hesitant finger above the screen.

Billy couldn't allow Devin to leave the bathroom. He looked at his hands and then at Devin. He had never tested his strength against an adult human and didn't want to try it now. A kid overpowering him would freak Devin out. Still, he had to keep Devin in the room another way. He reached for Devin's hand when the motel room phone rang.

"Crap." Devin stepped back from the door, clenching his fists.

Billy pulled back his hand. "What's wrong?"

"Crap, crap, crap."

"What's so crappy?"

"I bet that's the front desk." He tapped a knuckle against his lips. "I need to answer the phone."

"You can't go out there." Billy yanked on Devin's shirt, sending him off balance.

"Whoa. Hey." Devin placed his hand on the wall to steady himself and then on Billy's shoulder. "It's just in the other room. If I don't answer it, whoever is at the front desk will come down here. It's probably Frank, and he's nosey as heck. He'll know I rented the room."

Billy's eyebrows pinched. Jac would be upset if she knew Devin had left the room. He had to keep Devin—The phone rang a third time.

"I'm going." Devin opened the door and sprinted for the phone, picking it up on the fourth ring. "Hey."

"Devin?" the caller asked.

"Yeah, this is Devin."

Billy stood in the doorway, watched, and listened. His eyes flashed twice between the door to the motel room and Devin.

"It's Frank. What's going on down there?"

"Uh ... nothing. Why?" Devin pointed to the receiver and mouthed, "Frank."

Billy knew, able to listen in on the conversation.

"There's a fancy black car parked nexta yers, and I just seen a man in a suit get into the back seat with a girl."

"Oh, her." Devin covered the receiver with his hand and winced. He removed his hand and continued, "She's a friend, and that's her ... ride home."

"Devin, ya know we don't allow prostitutes on our property."

"Prosti—What?" He glanced at Billy, then spoke in a hushed tone. "She's not a prostitute. I told you she's a friend."

"Now, I weren't born yesterday. You've been a long-time customer, a good'n, but I won't stand for hookers in our hotel."

"Motel," Devin muttered. "Fine, Frank, no more prostitutes."

"Good. Now, does your momma know about this?"

"*Bye,* Frank." He hung up the phone.

Billy looked at Devin quizzically. Much of the conversation was foreign to him.

"Frank can be a pain in the butt." Devin looked toward the room door. "Stay in the bathroom."

"Where are you going?"

"I'm going to take a peek. I'll be there in a minute."

Billy's head flopped back. He groaned. "Why does no one listen to me?"

* * *

Reginald turned in his seat toward Jac. He wore that emissary expression of superiority, like Jac should be grateful for the opportunity to speak with him. "Typically, I'm asked to welcome guests to the wonderful State of Oklahoma, but it seems out of place with you here uninvited. Not to mention, you've caused quite a problem for us to manage."

Jac's chest tightened. She expected the bus discussion, but didn't care to have it. Several heartbeats thumped before she gathered enough strength to meet the emissary's stare.

Reginald narrowed his eyes at her like an adult scolding a child. "You killed a man and left his tortured body behind for everyone to see, including the authorities."

The accusation stung. Jac hit him with narrowed eyes of her own and leaned in. "I didn't torture him."

Reginald leaned back. "Tortured agreeably may be extreme, but he was far from how nature created him. You *did* leave his body behind."

She threw up her hands. "What was I supposed to do? Carry him with us? How would that have looked? Me walking down the highway with a grown man over my shoulder?"

"The difficulty of the situation is not lost on me. However, I must impress upon you our position in this."

Jac tilted her head and sighed. "What do you want from me, Reginald?"

"Very well, straight to the point."

"Yes, *please*. It's nearly ten, and we have to be out of the room."

"Then, here is our demand." He clasped his hands at his waist. "Leave."

Jac slouched, her lips parted. "That's it? Leave?"

"Leave now and never return to Oklahoma."

"Return? I wasn't planning on it. I didn't even want to come here."

"Planned or not,"—he pointed at her—"never again do I want to see your face in Oklahoma."

"Fine. Never."

Reginald softened. "Very well. Now that we've reached an understanding, we'll escort you out, driving where you drive and stopping where you stop."

"So, you're going to follow us? Track us?"

"Up to the state line, of course." He leaned in. "Jac, you must understand. There hasn't been an incident here in over a decade. These incidents are a fright to clean, especially with humans having phones that take pictures and record. Your face and Billy's are already everywhere. You making it out of Oklahoma without being spotted or picked up by the local authorities will offer a challenge."

"I get it!" Jac clenched her fists. She felt exposed. Vulnerable. Simultaneously, she felt a wave of relief at practically being excused with a slap on the wrist. She had gotten in more trouble with her parents for sneaking up to the roof of their apartment building alone to stare into the starry night sky.

"At least you didn't use your real names when purchasing the bus fare."

Jac pressed a sharp point of her jagged fingernail into the door's leather panel as she stared out of the car window. She spoke softly and matter-of-factly while poking at the leather. "Billy wouldn't have made it to the next stop. I thought I was saving a lot of lives."

"So, Billy had an unplanned craving?"

"He's a kid; of course, he did."

"And you didn't think to bring blood?"

She turned to Reginald, her jaw tensed, fighting against the words she wanted to scream. She breathed, waiting for the desire to berate him to subside. "It's complicated."

Reginald leaned in closer and spoke with what sounded like concern. "Jac, is there something you want to tell me about why you're running? Maybe something your parents told you?"

Unlike Devin, Reginald and emissaries like him were difficult to read. He acted sincere, but she couldn't know for certain and sure as hell couldn't open up to him. "Can I leave?"

Reginald stared at her with pinched eyes for an uncomfortable few seconds. His expression relaxed. He sat straight and smoothed the creases from his pants. The empathy, feigned or not, departed. "Yes, please do."

Jac climbed from the car and stopped at Reginald's voice. "Jac."

She huffed and planted her hand firmly on the door, ready to close it and end the forced conversation. "What now?"

"I'm certain you know the protocol. This marks your first official visit. Don't make me perform a second."

Jac presented an emotionless response while swallowing a lump in her throat. "I understand."

"And, your friend inside."

He knows about Devin, of course. He saw him. "What about him?"

"Does he know about you? About what you are?"

Jac understood Reginald's insinuation. If Devin knew who she truly was, *what* she truly was, Reginald wouldn't let him leave the motel room with breath still in his lungs. He would scrutinize her response for any hint of dishonesty. She leaned into the car, met his stare, and said firmly, "He doesn't know."

He studied her for a moment. "Very good; please keep it that way."

"Of course."

"And Jac."

No words; she glared at him.

"Devin doesn't understand the danger he's in, being in your acquaintance. I don't know the extent of your plans with that young man, but I must warn you—he had better make it home safely."

Heat rose within Jac at Reginald's belief she was on a murderous rampage, killing at a whim. "He's our ride. He's safe with me." She gave Reginald the single finger and slammed the door.

Jac wasn't sure how Reginald knew so much about Devin, but he raised a legitimate concern. She realized the significant complication when she leaned close to Devin in the motel room. She hadn't noticed before because the lingering smell of fresh-baked pizza on and around him had masked the scent. Devin, her ride to San Diego, a human who would sit an arm's length away from her for the next so many hours, was her blood type.

QUESTIONS AND EVEN MORE QUESTIONS

Jac waited with Billy in the car as Devin returned the room key. She had dodged his questions about the visit from Reginald, guiding his interest toward a quick exit before anyone else came along.

Devin suggested hiding behind the seats, as they did the night before. The state of the car's floor had drastically improved. The cans, wrappers, and socks were gone. A coconut air freshener hidden somewhere and whatever cleaner Devin used tempered the pizza odor.

While waiting, Jac rehearsed answering questions from Devin's expected interrogation. The stepfather story had worked so far. There was no reason to deviate. She peeked over at Billy from her spot behind the passenger seat. "You okay, Billy?"

"Yeah, this is kinda fun. Like we're hiding from bad guys." Sadly, he wasn't far from the truth.

Footsteps sounded on the concrete. Devin climbed into the car seconds later. "You two ready?"

"Ready," Jac replied.

"Stay down until we reach the interstate. I'll tell you when."

* * *

They drove for what seemed like too long when Devin gave the all-clear. Jac and Billy emerged from their hiding places like butterflies from chrysalis. Billy stretched his legs, and Jac climbed to the front. Her hip brushed against Devin's shoulder. She apologized as she plopped into her seat and fastened her seatbelt. She pulled at her sleeves and pant legs, getting comfortable for the long drive ahead.

The landscape hadn't changed from when Jac was on the bus—trees, more trees, and a seemingly endless stretch of road in front of them. The farther they traveled from home—from the tall buildings and congestion—the tightness in her chest worsened. It was as if after each mile, a one-pound weight was placed on her ribs, creating a painfully heavy stack. She felt isolated, and it threatened to siphon the life from her like a ghoul. She needed a distraction; though dangerously imperfect, one sat beside her.

Devin fidgeted and stole glances at her, then asked, "Are we going to talk about that guy at the motel?"

Jac played coy. "If you want."

"So, who was it?"

"My stepfather's lawyer; he wanted to make sure I was okay and if I was ready to come home." Jac chewed at her bottom lip. That *sounded rehearsed.*

"Wait. How did he find you?"

"I don't know; I didn't ask."

"You didn't ask? That would be the first thing I'd ask." He looked her up and down, then eyed her backpack. "You're not bugged or something, are you?"

"Bugged?"

"Yeah. Like a tracker on you or your backpacks?"

Jac hadn't considered the possibility of the Philadelphia Coven bugging them. When would they have had the chance? Only she and Billy had access to their backpacks after leaving the apartment. On the money? But where could they have hidden a tracker on the money she wouldn't have seen?

Vampire covens made it an utmost priority to know what was going on in their region. Her dad once said, "Covens have eyes and ears everywhere." She had questioned if the Pennsylvania Coven's eyes aided in her dad's capture and murder.

Reginald showed no sign he had been in contact with the Philadelphia Coven. The Oklahoma Emissary had found her and Billy on his own.

"No. We aren't bugged. I guess they had someone following me, maybe a private detective."

Devin didn't look convinced, but her imagined story was less unsettling than telling him she and Billy were runaway vampires and that fanged killers lived across the world. He drove in silence for a few minutes before he spoke. "Hey, did you hear about what happened on the bus last night?"

Jac tensed. She glanced at Billy, giving him the slightest head shake. That question was not part of her preparation.

She answered, hoping she'd sound believable, "No. We didn't hear about it. Why?"

"I meant to check out the news last night but didn't get to it."

Her thumbnail found its way to her mouth. "We didn't watch TV last night. We pretty much slept." *Please drop it. Please.*

"I heard someone was killed. Crazy, huh?"

"Yeah. Crazy."

"Anyway, it's probably better you didn't. There's enough bad news in the world. There's no reason to go looking for it. It's bad for your soul."

The silence grew thick. Jac didn't mind, wanting nothing more than for the bus discussion to end. She'd forcibly tear the painful memory from her brain if she could.

She broke the silence minutes later. "Oh. Your payment. How should we work that? Pay you now or when we get there?"

Devin shrugged. "You can pay me when we get there. I'm a get-the-job-done-first kind of guy."

"That's ...."

"Trusting," Devin finished.

"Yeah."

"I can ... trust you. Can't I?"

Jac scoffed. "Of course. One hundred percent."

"Good. However, I *will* let you buy me breakfast. There's a diner I like in the next town. Or we can wait until lunch. If ya want."

Jac swiveled in her seat and blurted, "No."

"No to lunch, or no, you don't want to?"

"No, I don't want to." Truthfully, she wanted out of Oklahoma and away from Reginald as soon as possible. Reginald didn't say they couldn't stop on the way out, but she didn't care to risk a follow-up visit from him.

"*I* want to," Billy chimed in.

"It should be safe, if that's the problem. I doubt the Sapulpa Oklahoma Police are on the lookout for runaways from—Where are you from, anyway?"

"Philadelphia."

"No joke?"

Jac cursed internally, watching Devin mull over this additional detail.

"Wow. You've made it pretty far already. How did you get to—"

"Lunch," Jac said, diverting the line of questioning. She had told Devin that taking a bus to San Diego was out of the question, *and* Devin saw the news report covering the bus incident. She couldn't reveal to him they rode a bus ... almost into Tulsa.

"Lunch?" Devin asked.

"Yeah, I want lunch, not breakfast, and some distance between us and Jenks."

"You mean distance between you and that guy at the motel?"

"Him too. All of it."

Devin appeared to be working out something in his mind. "I was wondering. Why did your stepdad's lawyer just let you go?"

Jac's jaw tensed. *Please stop asking questions.* "He's not a cop; he can't arrest me."

"Guess not. Is your dad rich or something?"

"Stepdad."

"Yeah, sorry ... stepdad."

"He is. And he's powerful. It makes it difficult to get away from him."

"What about your dad? I mean, your real dad. Can he help?"

Devin's question allowed some truth, though painful, to intertwine with the fiction. "My real dad," Jac said, looking back at Billy, "Our real dad is dead."

Devin frowned. "Oh, I'm sorry; I shouldn't have asked."

"It's okay. It's been a little while, and I don't want to hide from it. Talking about him makes it more real, a little less painful."

"Well, if you ever want to talk about ... him, just let me know."

In a moment of respite, Jac let go of the heartache and admired Devin's hazel eyes. They were a perfect complement to his tan skin and white teeth. *Damn, he's gorgeous. Wait.* She ran her hand down her mouth, forcefully erasing her smile. She shook her head and closed her eyes. *What the hell am I thinking?* The color of Devin's eyes, and whether they were beautiful, were unimportant to the task at hand. *Devin is the driver,* she reminded herself, *not a friend.*

"So, lunch, if you're okay with waiting another hour, we can eat in Oklahoma City. We'll blend in with the half-million other people."

"Plan," Jac agreed.

"Plan."

"Thank gosh." Billy collapsed onto the back seat. "I could eat like a ton of food."

With the barrage of questions ended, Jac wiped the perspiration from her hands onto her pant legs and quietly exhaled. The moment allowed her to take a slow, deep breath to determine precisely how difficult it would be to sit next to Devin the entire way to San Diego. She flirted around the edges of smelling his blood. The subtle smell of pizza heavily blanketed by coconut air freshener blocked her attempt, thankfully. The horrid food combination was better than dealing with a blast of O-negative every breath for the next thousand miles. Any odor was better than fighting the desire to sink her teeth into the neck of the boy helping them.

"Devin," Billy said.

"What's up, buddy?"

"What's a prostitute?"

BURGERS, FRIES, AND FRIGHT

Devin's connection with music was both endearing and comedic. He had passionately proclaimed that nineties grunge was the best music ever recorded, followed closely by the half-decade of emo rock. His head bobbed with the music from the car stereo when the rhythm found him. That rhythm occasionally warranted using the steering wheel as a drum kit.

Nearly a half-hour passed before anyone spoke. Jac didn't mind. It gave her time to sit and do nothing instead of answering questions. The lack of communication, unfortunately, gave space for her mind to worry. However, the worry ensured her guard would always be up. It had to be. Someone was after her and Billy. Edgar likely had contacts and connections across the country and wouldn't give up easily. Complicating the problem, Jac had no way of knowing the identity of those connections or when they'd cross paths.

Billy stared at the passing landscape for most of the ride, commenting on the lack of tall buildings and the frequent sightings of livestock. Jac met his eyes a few times. He'd hold her hand for a calming moment. This was Billy's way of checking in on her. He sensed her anxiousness, like when a dog sensed its owner's sadness.

Jac scanned the road behind them every few miles for the black Benz. Devin's eyes flickered to the rearview mirror more than usual, as if he thought they were being followed. He wasn't wrong. Jac made out the front of a black car nearly a half-mile away, too far for Devin's human eyes. She imagined Reginald sitting in the back seat with his perfect hair and suit, directing the driver with his perfect diction. The smugness of emissaries irked her. They were the voice of the covens, and the code meant they were untouchable, including from opposing covens. Coven disagreements and battles often happened in the "old days," a term her parents used when reminiscing. However, altercations between covens were now non-existent, with hiding the existence of vampires being the most agreed upon crucial objective.

Jac shifted in her seat and stretched out her legs. "Hey, Devin."

"Yeah."

"How long until we're out of Oklahoma ... after Oklahoma City?"

"Eh, a couple hours, maybe two and a half. Why?"

"No reason, just curious."

"You mean we aren't even out of Oklahoma yet?" Billy groaned. "How big is this place?"

"Well, don't be ready to leave yet." Devin excitedly drummed the steering wheel. "You are about to experience Stan's, the best burger place in Oklahoma City. Heck, maybe the entire country."

Billy sat forward. "Stan's?"

"Yeah, Stan's."

"That doesn't sound like a burger place," Billy said, seemingly unimpressed.

"Okay. If *you* opened a burger place, what would you call it?"

"I wouldn't call it Billy's."

Jac smiled.

Devin laughed. "No, I suppose you wouldn't. Billy's sounds more like a fish and chips place."

"Huh?"

"Never mind, buddy."

"Does Stan's have video games?" Billy asked.

"It's not that kinda place."

Billy sat back, pouting. "Oh."

"How about you?" Devin turned to Jac. "Do you like burgers?"

"Of course, who doesn't?" Honestly, she would love any complete meal at this point. Living the last two days on snacks and soda had lost its appeal.

"Funny." Devin smirked.

"Funny what?"

"I pictured you as a vegetarian."

"You have no idea," Jac muttered, eliciting a giggle from Billy.

"What's so funny?" Devin asked.

Jac shook her head. "Nothing, burgers it is." She dismissed the "vegetarian" comment. *What does a vegetarian look like, anyway?*

* * *

They pulled into a parking lot ten minutes later. It read Stan's Burgers and Fries in large red letters across a white exterior and gray-roofed building that looked one notch above a dive.

Devin either noticed the look on Jac's face or read her mind. "It's not much to look at, but trust me." He parked, and Billy dashed from the car toward the front door.

"Billy!" Jac yelled.

"I got him." Devin climbed from the car and turned to her. "I have a skull cap in my glove box. I doubt anyone here will recognize you, but it couldn't hurt to have a disguise. Oh, and it's clean, in case that matters." He closed the door and ran after Billy.

Devin reached Billy, waiting at the door, and wrapped his arm around his shoulder. Jac raised her pointer finger and mouthed, "One minute." Devin gave a thumbs up, and the boys disappeared into Stan's.

Jac found the green skull cap in the glove box sitting atop a mass of folded paper, receipts, and, surprise, an empty energy drink can. Coins of some sort accumulated in the crevices. She pulled a blue and black coin centered by the number twenty-four and "One Day at a Time" across the top. There must have been a dozen coins, some marked with "ONE MONTH." She wanted to dig in, sift through the accumulation of random stuff, and learn more about Devin—peer into a small window of his life. But it wasn't the time. Reginald had ordered her to leave Oklahoma permanently and intended to honor that agreement as soon as possible.

Steady traffic passed Stan's, and one car was on Jac's radar. The one that intended to escort them out of Oklahoma. A minute passed. Cars left Stan's, and a couple pulled in and parked. She nearly gave up watching when a black car came into view. Flawless exterior, black tinted windows, and the Mercedes emblem—it was Reginald. The Benz slowed, drawing even with Stan's, continued past, and turned off a side street two blocks down.

"A quick lunch, and we're out of here, jerk."

Jac entered Stan's without expectation, but it didn't surprise. It smelled of grease, with hints of grilled beef, bacon, and onions. The walls were a bland shade of brown. Framed black and white photographs of what may have been the city's past hung in spots, along with rectangle metal signs bearing clever sayings like, "Keep it to yourself if you don't like the coffee, there's a reason it's free," and "Unattended children will be taken to wash dishes." The ambiance and country music playing from a radio somewhere matched the patrons' attire.

Devin waved her over to the booth where he and Billy sat.

The feeling of being watched, of being noticed, overwhelmed her. Imagined voices called her the 'girl from the bus' while imagined fingers pointed in her direction. She lowered the skull cap, ducked her head, and hurried to the booth. She scooted in next to Billy.

Devin smirked. "That wasn't suspicious ... at all."

"Is anyone looking at us?" Jac sat low, like a teenager embarrassed at being caught having lunch with her parents.

"Not yet, but people will if you don't start acting like you belong here."

"I *don't* belong here."

"I get that, but trust me, no one is looking at you. You look like a dude wearing that cap."

Jac shot a disgusted look at Devin. "I do not look like a dude."

Billy fell back in his seat, giggling.

"I didn't mean it like that." Devin's face reddened. "You obviously have some girl parts, but, ya know, no makeup, your clothes, and you're kinda scrawny."

Jac scoffed. "Scrawny?"

"Tiny, maybe. Is that the right word?" Devin's eyes squinted. "You're like, what, four-ten?"

"Whatever." Jac rolled her eyes and muttered, "I'm four-eleven."

"Hey, don't be mad about it. No one is looking for two dudes and a kid. Besides, it's not like you're on the news."

On the news? We are *the news.* Jac looked away, tucking strands of hair under the skullcap.

"Wait." Devin leaned forward. "Are you?" he asked in a harsh whisper.

Jac crossed her arms. "Just shut up."

Devin grinned at her, opening his menu. "Billy, are you ready to order?"

Billy sat straight and rubbed his hands together. "I've been ready. I'm, like, a million times ready."

"That much, huh?" Devin chuckled. "Order whatever you want, your brother, I mean, your sister's payin'."

Billy eagerly scanned the menu. "Good, 'cause I'm starving."

Jac repaid the "brother" comment with a kick to Devin's shin.

"Ouch! Son of a—"

"Language," she warned.

Devin rubbed his shin and grimaced. "That really hurt."

"Good, it was supposed to."

As if an apparition, a waitress materialized from nowhere and placed three glasses of water on their table. "Welcome to Stan's. I'm Sally. I'll be serving you today." Sassy and country came to mind in Sally's presence.

Devin smiled. "Hi, Sally."

Pretending to scratch her face, Jac glanced at Sally and meekly said, "Hi."

"Are ya'll ready to order?" Sally asked.

"I'm ready," Billy said.

Sally positioned her pen above her order pad. "All right, little fella."

"Me too," Devin agreed.

"How about you, darlin'?" Sally asked Jac.

Either the skullcap's power of disguise didn't work on Sally, or she called everyone darlin'. "Uh, yeah," Jac said, finding herself awkwardly speaking in a deeper voice. "I'll have the hamburger special with a cola."

"How do you want that burger?"

"Medium rare, please." Jac handed the menu to Sally, gave her a quick smile, and put her hand on her forehead, concealing her face.

"You got it. How 'bout you boys?"

"Same," Devin and Billy said in unison.

"Easy enough." Sally pocketed her order pad. "I'll have your food out in a jiff."

Jac waited for Sally to leave, then sat up straight. "We haven't had an actual meal in days."

"Then you're in the right place," Devin said, mimicking Jac's deep voice.

She pouted at him. "Real funny."

"Why were you talking like that?" Devin suppressed a laugh.

"I don't know." She puffed out her cheeks and covered her face with her hands. "It seemed like the right thing to do."

"Well, it's not. So let's use our regular voices." Then he made that face again, like he'd been given foreign language instructions for self-assembled furniture. "We've been in a rush since you stowed away in my car. I was thinking you could catch me up on a few things."

"What few things?" Jac plucked a piece of ice from her glass of water, plopped it in her mouth, and crunched down.

"First, how did you get to Oklahoma from Philadelphia?"

Jac internally cursed at herself for having shared that bit of knowledge. She said the first thing that came to mind. "A friend."

Billy gawked as if amazed at her on-a-whim storytelling ability.

Devin leaned back from the table. "Wow. A friend? That's a pretty good friend to drive you that far."

"Yeah, pretty good," she agreed. "I guess it can't be that big of a deal. You're driving us to San Diego, and *you're* not even our friend."

Devin cringed. "That's not hurtful, but close. So, your friend, he ...."

"She."

Devin wasn't at all subtle when he said 'he' and paused. He smiled as if her "friend" being a girl held some importance. Like his chances of dating her had improved. The "friend" story was a lie. Other than Billy, Devin was the only person in her life. Besides, he had no idea who she liked. Her imaginary girl friend could have been a girlfriend for all he knew. Regardless, they were not on a date or anywhere near dating.

"She couldn't take you all the way?" Devin asked.

"She couldn't."

"And your plan in Jenks was to hide in some handsome guy's car and talk him into taking you to San Diego?"

"No." Jac smiled wryly. "The plan was to pay someone to take us to San Diego, and luckily, the handsome part wasn't a necessity."

Devin placed a hand on his chest. "Oh, really? That one ... that one hurt, just a bit."

She crossed her arms. "Any other questions?"

"From what you've said, your step-dad is an ass, and your dad is ... no longer with us, but your mom, you didn't say much about her. Where is she in all of this?"

Jac paused. She had told Billy that Mom was alive and in hiding, waiting for the right time to come out. But for Devin, she wanted to give the most straightforward reply, one that didn't require fitting a square answer into a round question. "She's dead."

It hurt to say, but it created continuity for the story she had been feeding Devin. Jac wanted to believe their mother was alive and hiding. She needed that to be true for Billy. However, their mother could be dead, and saying it aloud made it a bit too real for her. More so for Billy, she imagined.

Jac glanced at Billy, flashed a frown, and winked. Billy couldn't read minds, but he knew his sister's expressions. His furrowed brow softened, and his frown straightened.

Devin slapped his forehead. "Oh, dang, I'm sorry ... again."

"It's okay, but no more questions."

Devin nodded. "Yeah, no more questions."

"But I have one for you."

"Okay, sure." Devin sat up and leaned forward.

"Why are you *really* helping us? And don't give me that 'giving back' and 'helping others' crap."

Devin bowed his head as he fiddled with his fork and knife. "It's not crap; I really believe in it." He grew quiet, placing his hands firmly atop the utensils, and looked her in the eyes. "Also ... I needed to get away from life in Jenks for a bit. Work. Home. It'll be a nice break."

The tin bell above the door rang, announcing a customer's entrance. A tall, muscular man entered, looking out of place. He wore a black suit; his black slicked-back hair framed his head; his complexion was perfect, aside from the jagged scar cutting across his chin at an angle. In less than a heartbeat, Jac pegged him as a vampire—Reginald's driver.

She grabbed Billy's hand while Devin said something about something. She squeezed once, and Billy squeezed twice.

"Yeah, I see him," Billy whispered for only her to hear.

Jac surveilled the vampire, listening to every word he said to Sally. "That booth over there." The vampire pointed to the booth behind theirs.

Sally said, "Sure, hun," in her cheerful southern manner. With a menu in hand, Sally led the vampire to his selected booth. She winked at Jac as she passed.

Jac's eyes met the vampire's, who grinned. Surely, he wouldn't try something in here, not in public. Deftly, Jac moved her hand to the tabletop and gripped the knife, barely sharp enough to cut through butter. She figured she could stab it through skin and possibly skull bone if it came to it.

"Jac," Devin said. His voice barely registered with her. He repeated, louder, breaking her trance, "Jac."

Jac turned her attention from the vampire to Devin. She huffed. "Yes. What?"

"Were you listening to me?"

"Yes, I mean, no ... sorry." She closed her eyes and shook her head.

"Stare much?" He motioned to the booth behind them.

She didn't answer, trying to gather her emotions into something functional.

"And, what's up with the knife?"

Her reversed, white-knuckle grip had the knife's rounded end digging into the table. She eased her grip and gently laid the knife flat. "Nothing, I was just thinking."

Truthfully, she *had* been thinking. Evaluating her chances and best opportunities to shove the knife into the vampire's neck if it came to it. There were likely others outside, at least Reginald. Could she overcome them as well?

"I guess you weren't thinking about what I said."

"No. Sorry. What did you say?"

Devin studied his phone. "We're about two hours from Texas, according to my map app. We can drive awhile and stop in Amarillo, or keep going and stop in Albuquerque, New Mexico."

"Amarillo?" Jac asked.

"It's a city in Texas."

She shook her head. "No, let's keep going."

The vampire sat face forward behind Devin. The menu obscured the fanged killer's face, but with certainty, he was there to watch, listen, and report back to Reginald.

Listen away, Jac thought. She wanted him to hear of their plan to leave Oklahoma, to know they were still on their way out.

"To Albuquerque?" Devin asked.

"Yes. But how long will it take to get there?"

Devin punched the face of his phone and frowned. "From here, about eight and a half hours with a few stops."

Jac's eyes narrowed. "Do we need to stop?"

"Uh, *yeah*. To rest, get drinks and snacks, and you know, to pee."

She didn't like the idea of stopping when the goal was to reach San Diego as quickly as possible. Taking longer to reach the destination risked another hunger incident from Billy, or worse, from her. The stops had to be limited. "We can get snacks and drinks here. And can't you hold it until we get there?"

Billy giggled, apparently amused by the talk of pee.

"Well ... maybe, but why would I want to?"

Obviously, asking Devin to drive for nearly half a day without stopping was ridiculous. So, she compromised. "Fine, one stop."

"Good choice." Devin tapped the side of his head. "Being flexible is a sign of intelligence."

"Yeah, well, don't get used to it."

"We'll stop in Amarillo and sleepover in Albuquerque."

Jac sat forward with clenched fists and, a few decibels above attention-getting, asked, "What?" Taking a moment to calm herself, she continued in a quieter voice, "A sleepover?"

"It'll be nine by the time we get there. Sleep will be nice."

Jac internally cursed. They could have taken turns behind the wheel and sleeping if she had learned to drive. "Do you have to?"

Devin pursed his lips, and his head tilted to the side. "Sleep? Yeah. You sleep, don't you?"

Jac sighed. "Fine. We'll stop in Albuquerque." She looked into his eyes to ensure there was no misunderstanding. "But from there, straight to San Diego."

Devin typed on his phone again. "I don't know; it's another twelve hours from there. We might have to——"

"Okey-dokey. I got your burgers and fries." Sally approached, carrying a tray of food with one hand as if she'd been performing the server's skill for a lifetime. One by one, she placed the plates of food on the table.

Jac used the distraction to check on their chaperone. Over Devin's shoulder, her eyes met the vampire's. The iris of his eyes was a deep and lustrous black against bright white. The smirk on his face, both creepy and confident, sent the message of superiority without saying a word. He flashed a peace sign. Jac returned the gesture. She cringed and dropped her hand, looking disappointedly at her fingers as if they had autonomously fraternized with the enemy.

"That's three hamburger specials and three sodas. Is there anything else I can getcha?" Sally asked.

Jac broke her eye-lock with the vampire and agreeably said, "No, thank you," simultaneously with Devin.

"Okay. Holler if y'all need me." Sally sashayed to the booth behind them, calling the vampire "Hun." The vampire, now affectionately known as Hun, ordered a coffee—black.

Billy grinned as he chewed his burger and fries. Jac took a bite and experienced the same fulfilling sensation. The food was greasy and fried but substantial, and the soda was on ice.

"Here's to a couple of days of adventure." Devin raised his red plastic glass of soda for a toast.

Jac and Billy shared a grin, shrugged, and clunked their red plastic glasses against Devin's.

Jac put her lips to the straw for a refreshing drink when the doorbell chimed again. She choked mid-sip, placed her glass on the table, and slid down in the seat as she coughed up the fluid.

A man in uniform stood in the doorway, removing his state trooper hat.

Devin blew the paper from the end of his straw, hitting Billy in the face. "You okay, Jac?" He fought back a laugh.

"Sit with me," said a faint voice.

Who said that? Distracted by the boys, Jac focused on pinpointing the voice's origin to ensure she wasn't just hearing things. The voice came again, clearer this time. "Sit with me, now," said the vampire in the booth behind them.

Billy apparently didn't hear the voice, too distracted from dodging paper projectiles.

Jac coughed. "I'm fine, just choked on my drink."

"I guess you need more practice drinking from straws." Devin laughed.

Jac ignored Devin's sarcasm, focusing instead on the state trooper having a friendly conversation with Sally as if Stan's was one of his regular stops. He probably dropped by every day for lunch and in the morning for complimentary coffee. He likely knew almost everyone who ate at Stan's, the regulars at least. Not regulars, she and Billy would stand out like giraffes on a pig farm.

"Quickly," the vampire whispered.

"Devin," Jac said hushed, striking the front of his shoe with hers.

Devin dodged a fry thrown by Billy. "Yeah, what's up?"

She nodded sideways toward the trooper, then met Devin's wide eyes when he turned back to her. He stiffened as if siphoned of life.

"Wait here." She tapped the table with a firm finger.

"Yeah, sure."

"Tell them to go to the men's room," the vampire whispered.

"I heard him," Billy mouthed to Jac.

With the trooper still distracted by what must have been a gut-busting story from Sally, Jac slid from her seat and deftly slid into the vampire's booth. Billy asked Devin to take him to the restroom.

Jac firmly gripped the tabletop, ready to run if needed. She no longer feared the behemoth sitting across from her. He had a vested interest in the teenage killer vampire not getting apprehended and risking their exposure.

"Be calm," the vampire said through gritted teeth.

"What if the waitress asks why I'm sitting with you?"

"Tell her we're friends, and you saw me when I came in."

"Then I need to know your name, friend."

"Otto."

"Otto?" Jac raised an eyebrow. The name didn't seem to fit. He looked more like a Bear or Goliath.

"Yes, Otto. It's German, a family name."

Jac tugged at the cap on her head, firming it in place. She and Otto covertly listened to the conversation between Sally and the trooper.

"I'm going to wash up," the trooper said. "I'll sit in my regular spot when I get back."

"Okay, hun," Sally replied, as sweet as southern tea. Evidently, she had more than one hun. Otto didn't bat an eye at this knowledge.

Jac rubbed her arms, fighting the urge to dig her nails into her skin. She glanced at the trooper, then back at Otto.

"It will be okay," Otto said, in a tone Jac guessed intended to sound reassuring.

"How is this okay?" Her hands switched from rubbing her arms to fingertip grabs. "My brother's in the bathroom."

"They aren't looking for a boy and his brother; they're looking for a boy and his pain in the ass sister." He glanced at the skull cap. "Good disguise. You look like a boy wearing that. Though, softer."

Jac took only the slightest offense to the comments. "That's not helping."

"We told you to leave, not stop for hamburgers."

"Then, I guess I misunderstood."

"Yes, you did."

"Why did you come in here, anyway? To spy on us?"

"Reginald is in the car outside. He sent me in to keep an eye on you."

"*Spy* on us."

"That too."

A burst of adrenaline hit Jac at recognizing the significance of Otto's presence. "Hold on. This is a second visit." She leaned away. "You're here to take us, to kill us."

"No. I'm not an emissary." He pointed to himself and then to her. "Me sitting with you doesn't count. We're here to follow you, bumper to bumper, to the Oklahoma State line, where you will never return."

"You heard."

"Heard what?"

"Where we're going ... Albuquerque."

Otto shrugged slightly. "Yes. And?"

"I wanted you to hear us so that you knew we intended to leave." She scratched her cheek. "Now I'm not sure it was a good idea."

"Why is that?" Otto asked, still monitoring the trooper.

"If you—If the Oklahoma Coven is working with the Philadelphia Coven, with Edgar, you could tell him where we're going next."

Otto scrutinized her as if debating between what he *wanted* to say and what he *could* say. "Listen. I think you're a real little pain in the ass. But what you've been through ... what's happened to you is wrong on many levels. Trust me, we have no love for Edgar." He clenched his fists, and the vein in his forehead bulged. "If I had a chance to put my hands around his neck

....." He glanced around as if worried someone was watching, released a long breath, and eased back into his seat.

Jac chewed on her bottom lip. She wanted to believe Otto but couldn't trust her judgment. Reading humans was simple. Reading vampires? Not so simple. Concealing emotions was an essential nonphysical vampire trait. The attribute lost effectiveness with turned vampires—those not born into vampirism but turned by the vampire bite infection.

Lack of time worked against Jac, forcing her into a decision. She got an inkling Otto was a turned vampire. The angry vein in his forehead was an emotional giveaway. Also, his scar was more revealing: too deep, too jagged, and too unhealed to belong to a full-blooded vampire. Being a turned vampire, Otto couldn't completely hide deceit, even if he intended. Considering the situation and her options, she decided to trust him.

"Do you want more black coffee, hun?" Sally asked Otto, sneaking up on them in that waitressy way.

Jac jumped in her seat.

"No, thank you. I'll be leaving soon."

Sally gawked at Jac. "You changed booths, darlin'."

Jac fidgeted in her seat as if caught breaking some diner rule that would unwillingly force her to the kitchen to wash dishes. "I noticed my friend Otto sitting behind us. I came over to say hi."

Sally grinned and placed a hand on her hip. "Well, it *is* a small world, ain't it?"

With a syrupy, small-town affectation, Otto guffawed deeply and replied, "Ain't it, though?"

"Well, don't say hi too long; yer food will get cold."

Jac gave a thumbs up. "Okay."

"Ya'll let me know if ya need anything. I'll bring your check."

"I'll take both," Otto offered. As Sally walked away, he whispered, "Get boxes for your food, and I'll check on the boys."

"Sally," Jac called.

Sally turned a few yards away. "Yes, darlin'."

"Could you bring boxes for the food? We have to go."

"You got it. Three to-go boxes are coming up."

"Jac, listen to me. Carefully." Otto placed his hands on the table, readying to stand. "If anyone else had done what you did, they'd be dead by now. Do nothing else to provoke us. I don't want to be obligated to ... punish you. Leave and don't come back."

Jac, unsure how to respond, only offered a slow nod. She might have considered Otto a decent guy if he wasn't a bloodsucking killer vampire.

* * *

A minute ago, Otto left for the men's room, and Jac finished stuffing the to-go boxes. Though Otto offered to pay, Jac stuck a hundred-dollar tip under the ketchup bottle. She imagined a future with Sally burdened by detectives asking her about the suspicious kids who came into the diner for burgers and fries.

Devin and Billy came bustling over to the booth.

"The cop—" Devin said with shaking hands. He paused, looking around for anyone listening, then lowered his voice. "The cop came into the restroom."

"I know." Jac closed the last box lid. "Grab a box. We're leaving."

They each grabbed a food-filled box and hurried for the exit. Sally waved and said goodbye as they filed out of the door. They clambered into the car, situated their food boxes, and strapped in.

Devin zipped out of the parking space and stopped. "Hey, isn't that the same Benz from the motel?"

"Yes, it is." Jac rapidly slapped the dashboard. "Go."

The Benz's window lowered, revealing a stern-faced Reginald sitting in the back seat. As Devin pulled away, Jac shared a look with the Oklahoma Coven Emissary. The look conveyed nothing, which was a good thing. It was time for Jac to leave Oklahoma and never look back.

GETTING TO KNOW YOU

"What the heck am I doing?" Devin white-knuckle gripped the steering wheel, maneuvering around traffic as if racing toward a finish line.

Jac gripped the oh-shit handle above her. "What do you mean?"

"I don't know what I'm doing. I just hid from a cop in the bathroom with your brother. I've never hidden in Stan's bathroom from a cop, or in any bathroom. It's like I'm kidnapping you guys."

"You are not kidnapping us."

Devin eyed her as if her comment was utterly ridiculous. "I know that ... it just seems like it."

"It's nothing like it."

"And that giant guy you sat with? What was that about?"

"He works with my stepdad's attorney."

"I guessed that. I saw the Benz when we left. And why did he help? I figured he'd want the cop to pick up you two."

"He doesn't want the cops involved."

"Unbelievable." Devin gripped the back of his head with his right hand. "I'll be just like my dad. I'm going to jail."

I'm losing him. I can't lose him. Jac touched Devin's arm and spoke calmly. "You are *not* going to jail. Let's get out of Oklahoma and leave the cops behind. Speaking of cops, if you don't slow down, we'll be pulled over by one."

Devin glanced at the speedometer and muttered, "Damn. You're right."

Cops were second on Jac's list of concerns, right behind vampires. The same was true for Devin. He just didn't know it. If the cops caught them, he'd be okay. He was the getaway driver for a murderer, but unwittingly. But if a vampire who wanted to harm them found them...

Jac alternated between looking for the Benz and waiting for Devin to declare that her crazy life was more than he could handle. She again questioned her decision to bring him into this ... mess.

Devin shifted in his seat and rolled his shoulders. "This is so not what I expected."

"Are you backing out?" Jac asked.

"Devin, you can't leave us," Billy said from the back seat.

Devin glanced at her, in the rear-view mirror at Billy, and back to the traffic. He pressed his lips and alternated between nodding and shaking his head. "No, I'm not backing out. We're going to San Diego. Though I probably should have asked for more money."

"Done." Jac jabbed her finger at Devin like an auctioneer to the winning bidder.

Devin raised both eyebrows. "Done?"

"I'll double it, ten thousand dollars."

He craned his head toward her. "What ... you ... you said ten thousand?"

"Is that not enough? I can pay you more."

"No ... no, I don't—"

"Then it's set? You drive us to San Diego for ten thousand dollars?"

"But I didn't—"

"Devin's staying with us!" Billy hopped up and down in his seat.

Like a sloth watching a tennis match, Devin struggled to keep up with the conversation. He appeared to be working out something in his head, then nodded. "Yeah, buddy, we're on our way to San Diego."

"So, you're good?" she asked.

He offered a grin instead of a smile. "I'm good."

Jac studied him. Was he truly okay with continuing the trip or just being agreeable? Or worse, was he being agreeable just from being in her and Billy's presence? Especially Billy's. She couldn't know for sure, nor could she ask him. She settled in her seat and chewed on the inside of her mouth. *Please be okay with this, Devin. Please be okay.*

* * *

Devin maintained a steady speed on the highway while Jac and Billy chowed down on their boxed food. Jac handed Devin his burger and positioned his fries in the center console for an easy grab.

Thirty minutes into the drive, they relaxed and listened to music. Jac slipped off her shoes and rested her socked feet on the front console. Billy had dozed off, still coming down from the blood high that kept him tossing and turning all night, like a kid burning off a day's worth of candy and caffeine. Devin focused on the road before them.

The music wasn't enough of a distraction to keep Jac's mind from wandering toward painful thoughts of her father, mother, and the man from the bus. Her thoughts swirled like a festering whirlwind of negativity, with the splinters of her fragmented life striking and pricking at what little mental health remained. If she could just think of something to ask Devin, to get her out of her freaking mind, but conversation starters were not in her repertoire. She turned toward her window and wiped away the pooling tears.

Billy slept in the back with his mouth open and his hands over his head as if dreaming of confirming a successful field goal. Jac settled her eyes on Devin's profile. His messy, dirty blond hair fell just below his ears, his skin tan and smooth with only the modest beginnings of facial hair. He had a positively ordinary and unremarkable nose. Her gaze lingered over his arms, his hands, and his torso. He was handsome, not that she had the time and proper circumstances to think about him that way. Jac's only focus when it came to Devin was to keep him safe from *her*. Shallow breaths and distance from him were vital in preventing her from ever considering him a meal.

Jac had lived a sheltered life for as long as she could remember. Rarely was she allowed outside alone, and family excursions from her apartment were short-distanced and to familiar locations. Mom homeschooled her and Billy for a "better education." The ugly truth was that Mom and Dad feared she or Billy would harm other children or, in a nightmare scenario, kill them. There were no sleepovers, birthday parties, or playdates except with other vampire children. In Philadelphia, there were only a few.

She never attended Friday night high school football games, dances, or proms. She never had a love interest, making Devin the first boy—human or vampire—she had been around for an extended period. Getting the chance to look at him in a normal, everyday setting—aside from the fact they were running for their lives—felt indescribable.

"Take it all in," Devin said, breaking Jac from her reverie.

"What? No. I wasn't ...." Jac dropped her head and hid her burning cheeks behind her hair.

"Well?"

She turned toward him, dropping her feet to the floor. "Well, what?"

"You were checking me out." He grinned as if told he had a secret admirer.

She stammered. "I—No. I was ... becoming familiar with you. We haven't had much time to—"

"Check each other out."

"Uh, no. I wasn't going to say that." Jac slumped in her chair.

Devin smirked. "Oh, okay."

"Shut up."

"I will. As long as I can return the favor."

She rolled her eyes. "Sorry, but I'm not much to look at."

"Let me be the judge of that."

Jac sat straight and pulled her hair from her face. "Judge?" She scoffed. "I certainly don't want you judging me. I hate to disappoint you, but I'm not one of those beautiful people you see in magazines and on TV." She counted with her fingers. "I dress in young boy's clothes, mostly for functionality. I don't have a hairstyle, and my eyebrows are … just eyebrows. So, whatever bullshit you have to say, you can keep to yourself."

"Whoa, hold on. You are *way* too hard on yourself."

"Not even close. I didn't even get to the bad stuff." She turned away. Sitting around her home nearly every night didn't require fashion, make-up, or a stylized haircut. Looks were not high on her list of conversations, especially with Devin. The discussion was utterly and embarrassingly over.

After a gap of silence, Devin asked, "Why were you crying?"

"You saw that?" Jac clenched her jaw. She couldn't be completely honest with Devin and still stay true to the fiction she had fed him.

"Yeah, sorry for noticing."

She turned the tables.

"I'll tell you, but you first. I have questions for you."

"Okay," Devin said tentatively. "Shoot."

Jac shifted in her chair to face him. "What are *you* running from?"

"What am *I* running from?" he repeated, then chuckled.

"Yeah. That's my question." She poked his arm. "And be honest." Regardless of how unfair it was to ask for honesty, Jac wanted to know Devin and discover what made him tick. She needed a better feel for exactly how far she could trust him.

"Well, lately, I've been running from the police and your stepdad's attorney, who has enormous and scary henchmen."

"You're not being honest." She punched him in the arm.

"Ow! What the heck?" Devin grimaced, rubbing away the pain.

"Be honest."

He gave her a stern look, then returned his focus to the road. After some contemplation, he answered, "Life."

"Life?"

"Yeah, life."

Jac frowned. "I need more than 'life.'"

Devin audibly exhaled. "Wow, where to start? I'll have to give you the abridged version."

She crossed her arms. "I'll accept that … for now."

"My parents …" His lips pinched, and he slightly shook his head. "I hate my parents."

He hated his parents? How could he hate his parents? "I wish I still had parents."

He palmed his forehead. "Oh, I'm sorry. I didn't mean it like—It's just … I don't have parents. Normal ones, anyway." He lightly pounded the steering wheel. "My dad sucks. He's been in jail for half his life and most of mine. He got out about a month before my fourteenth birthday. I guess he didn't care about me enough to stay out of trouble and out of jail because he got arrested one week after getting out."

"What about your mom? You live with her. Right?"

"Oh yeah, she's a prize. You wanna know what she likes more than me?"

Jac met his eyes.

"Alcohol. The brown paper bags my mom comes home with aren't filled with groceries. She fills her bags with bottles of vodka and whiskey. Or whatever knocks her out the fastest. She can't stop drinking long enough to act like a mom."

Though stark in comparison, neither had an enviable parent situation. Imperfect or not, Jac would do anything to have her parents back. Give her a dad she could help keep on track and out of trouble, give her a mom to sober up and show support. At least Devin and his parents had a chance at reconciliation and a future together.

"You want complete honesty? You wanna know a big reason I'm taking you to San Diego?" He firmly gripped the steering wheel. "I need to get away from my life in Jenks. Work on my dreams before they become regrets. Jenks isn't unique, I know. But there's a ton of regret in Jenks. I deliver pizza to it every day. People whose lives didn't turn out the way they expected." His words came quick. "I want to know what it means to live, have a better life. Be a better person. I want to see the world and thought California was a good place to start. And I've been thinking this way for years. Now, all of that is finally within my grasp."

"Why haven't you left already?"

He scratched his head and dropped his hand onto the steering wheel. "First, I just graduated from high school last year. I thought about dropping out, but I didn't want to start off as a quitter. So, I got in the habit of finishing what I start." He glanced at her. "Second, my mom. I guess I felt obligated to take care of her. I've been fighting that feeling more lately. Enough is enough. Ya know?"

Devin shared more than Jac imagined he would, as if he'd been holding it all in, waiting to tell a listening ear. She could relate. At the same time, his getting it all out made her jealous. Billy was the only one with whom she could share her emotional baggage, but he was living through the same thing.

"For two years, I've been saving as much money as possible, and I'm about a year away from leaving Jenks. Well, until you came along."

Jac smirked. "Oh, so you *are* helping us for the money."

Devin placed his hand on his chest. "It wasn't a lie … about wanting to help you. But it's true. What you're paying me is like a bonus and gets me to my goal quicker, a lot quicker." He winked at her. "Plus, you're cute, and I couldn't resist."

Flushed cheeks, again. The only people who ever called her pretty, beautiful, or cute were her mother, father, and Sunny. Although she didn't have time for being cute or anything other than Billy's protector, a warm, tingling sensation of mutual attraction flowed through her.

"You look good with a little color in your cheeks," Devin said.

She put her face in her hands. "Oh God, shut up."

Devin laughed.

"Are you two done?" Billy spoke up from the back seat.

"Yeah, buddy, we're done." Devin grinned smugly, like he had won an award for successfully holding a conversation with her. "Welcome back to the land of the living."

"Thanks." Billy stretched and yawned. "Hey. Turn up the radio. I love this song."

"No way. Me too, buddy."

Devin pushed the radio volume button to twenty.

Jac glanced between the boys, singing along to the song that, apparently, was their favorite.

"I'll be with you whenever, wherever," they shouted the chorus off-key, "I'll stay with you forever and ever."

"You two are too much." Jac covered her smile, leaned back, and slowly turned somber. She wished she could pause for the simple pleasures in life—a mid-day nap, singing a song at the top of her lungs, flirting with a boy, or just being happy. However, this journey was about nothing more than getting Billy to long-term safety.

What about her future? She had no plans. Nothing to look forward to. It was dark, beyond reaching the Castillos. She blinked hard, once. *Focus on getting to San Diego, Jac. Nothing else matters.*

* * *

"Are we close?" Billy asked Devin.

"To where?"

"Texas."

"We are maybe ... twenty minutes away. We'll stop soon and stretch our legs."

"Stopping again?" Jac sat up. "Where?"

"Yeah, for a few minutes in a little town named Shamrock. You can't drive through Shamrock without stopping."

"And why not?"

"Because it's bad luck. Stopping there is good luck, and we could use some good luck. You know, luck of the Shamrock?"

Jac stopped believing in luck after the murder of her father and mother's disappearance. When her life turned to crap. The world was a horrible place, and the universe had its boot firmly on her neck.

The world, the universe, and luck aside, they *had* managed to escape Oklahoma and Reginald's reach. Things seemed to be going well, so she decided to be agreeable. "Yeah, sure, we could use that luck."

Devin drummed the steering wheel. "Alright, Shamrock, it is."

One state down and a few to go. With every passing mile, they were closer to safety and farther away from Reginald, the man she killed, and the Pennsylvania Coven that killed her father, possibly her mother, and wanted her and Billy dead.

Jac surveyed the empty road behind them and hugged herself. They were still a thousand miles from California, and Edgar would not just let them go. She shivered. Someone was out there, somewhere, looking for them.

THE ORANGE ROOM

After failing his coven, Sunny again sat alone in the White Room with the white orchid, waiting for his meeting with Edgar. News of the bus incident had reached the Philadelphia Coven and likely every coven in the United States, Canada, and Mexico. And who knows where else? Jacqueline foolishly risked riding a public bus without a drop of blood to satiate her hunger. Could he blame her? What other options were there? What other means of travel could he have expected her to use to reach San Diego?

Sunny pinched the bridge of his nose, attempting to squeeze away a headache. Having already visited the Yellow Room, orange would be next, maybe red. He flexed the fingers of his right hand and wondered if his time with them was short. He listened for Ava's heeled footsteps. She would disclose the destined room so he could prepare. Trust had been difficult to come by since the reign of Edgar. Fortunately, Sunny had a few remaining friends within the Coven's sprawling operational complex. Ava was one of those friends.

Not all members of the Philadelphia Coven accepted Edgar's takeover upon the demise of their previous leader, his sire, from old age. The younger vampires were especially reluctant. The Coven held a vote, of which Edgar received slightly more than half. Soon after Edgar's takeover, some members left Philadelphia to join other covens.

Edgar had a secret known to only his closest inner circle, which included Sunny. That secret was compromised, resulting in the disappearance and death of a few Philadelphia Coven members. Edgar promised a thorough investigation. However, his involvement in the tragedies rendered investigations pointless.

Sunny sat straight at the sound of Ava approaching. He closed his eyes. Were her steps firm or light? Could he garner any indication of her emotions from the rhythm of her steps?

Ava opened the door, adding gray to the color scheme, a welcome relief to Sunny's eyes. She wore a tight white dress that stopped an inch above her knees, her hair pulled back tight in a bun, and flawless makeup.

Ava smiled, but it faded like love lost. "He's ready for you."

"So, he is." Sunny stood and smoothed the wrinkles from his suit. "Lovely as always, Ava." His eyes followed the line of her body, from her head down to her high heels, her orange high heels. His eyes returned to meet her gaze. She winked. He was safe, at least today.

After a couple dozen unhurried steps down the hall, a pumpkin orange door stood before Sunny. Knowing the room's occupant, it would have been appropriate had the door been carved in the manner of a jack-o'-lantern. A terrifying countenance acting as a warning to all who enter.

Ava, stoic, raised a hand, guiding him toward the door.

"Thank you for accompanying me." He gripped the handle, mentally preparing to enter the room and face who he feared most.

"I don't want to see you here again," she whispered. "I have zero interest in walking you to Red."

Sunny stared at his hand resting on the door handle while considering Ava's words. Yes, he *could* trust her more than any other Coven member. He paused another beat, opened the door, and stepped inside. Ava closed the door behind him.

It wasn't Sunny's first visit to the Orange Room. However, it was his first for something *he* had done or failed to do. He despised the overwhelming, engulfing, and off-putting orange compared to the White Room's clean crispness and the Yellow Room's sunny feel. The horrible color came with realizing he was only a room away from physical harm, the lasting type, even for a vampire.

As Emissary for the Coven's region, he too had called upon others to meet him in the Yellow or Orange Room for a talking-to. Next in line, the Red Room was reserved for punishment. The Black Room was for final judgment, the responsibility of the Coven's leader, the vampire now sitting before him.

"Hello again, Edgar," Sunny said. "I hope you've found the day to your liking."

"The pleasantries of an emissary, with a name to match." Edgar stood and strode toward Sunny, moving more like a spider with spindly limbs than a man. If Sunny didn't know better, he'd swear venom dripped from Edgar's teeth.

"I am here as you ordered."

Edgar grasped Sunny's hand like a comforting priest and stood uncomfortably close. "Please, please take a seat."

Sunny sat while Edgar loomed above him, sneering.

"Sunny, I want to make this brief and perfectly clear. Brief, because I truly hate this room." Edgar scrutinized the room with eyes like dark, cold orbs. He snarled and extended his arms with claw-forming hands, just short of fists. "Yes, the color is awful, but that's not the extent of it. In this room, I don't get to express myself ... physically. This, you know. So, I'll be unequivocal."

Sunny sat in silence, knowing it was best to speak to Edgar only when asked a direct question.

"The Kelley children have been naughty." Edgar's slender fingers flexed and curled like tendrils as he spoke. "No doubt you've heard about the bus incident."

"I have." The thought of Jacqueline killing someone mortified Sunny. Or worse, Billy taking such action. They had never taken human life, never having the need. They were only children. Vampire children, yes, but innocent.

On the evening of Jacqueline's fourteenth birthday, Sunny reminisced with her parents—his friends—James and Lelah. After Jacqueline and Billy had turned in for the night, the three friends discussed, after too many glasses of wine, ways they had killed people—before easily accessible blood. He didn't know how long Jacqueline eavesdropped on stories of death from her room's threshold. Likely long enough to be an end-of-childhood moment.

Edgar stood and paced, the vein of his forehead throbbing. "Those kids for whom you were, and still are responsible, are causing me significant grief." He plucked the potted orchid from the table, looking at it as he spoke. "I, however, am responsible for the death on the bus. Mind you, I feel no sorrow for the human. In fact, it pleased me when I first envisioned the Kelley girl tearing apart the man—the horror, the blood." He licked his lips. "But I am now indebted to the Oklahoma Coven." He scratched the pot with an elongated fingernail, then hurled it with a scream, smashing it into the wall. Dirt, orange clay shards with bright white edges, and delicate orange orchid petals littered the floor.

Sunny flinched.

Edgar quickly shuffled toward Sunny and leaned within inches of his face, wearing a scowl. The tips of his canines peeked from his lips. Sunny recognized the look. It said, 'I want to kill you, but there is protocol.'

Edgar glared at his Emissary a moment, rose, then took in and slowly released a deep breath as he started pacing. "Sunny, I like you ... I always have. You were my Sire's emissary. Besides, who doesn't like you? But I must impress upon you the importance of bringing the Kelley children back here, back home ... back to me."

"I can ask the Oklahoma—"

"No, you cannot!" Edgar's eyes were a fury, his complexion a fiery red.

Sunny risked continuing his line of thought. "I'm in good standing with Emissary Reginald. I'll—"

Edgar growled and struck the wall with an open palm. "Oklahoma is no longer an option!" He closed his eyes and raised his hands to the sides of his head. "Sunny, Sunny, Sunny," he murmured. "I've already asked their emissary to aid in returning the children. Politely, he said no, though a distasteful tone coated his response."

"Do you suppose ..."—Sunny paused, concerned with causing another outburst—"Oklahoma knows what we're doing here?"

Edgar bolted toward Sunny, their noses mere centimeters apart. His fingers, like pinchers, tightly gripped Sunny's thighs just above the knees; his nails threatened to pierce his pant legs.

"You don't suppose they know?" Edgar sneered. "You told me the kids don't know, that their parents hadn't told them." Spittle flew from his mouth onto Sunny's face. "Was that the truth, Sunny? Or did Lelah and James tell those brats, and now they're sharing our secret with every vampire with ears?"

Fighting against the urge to wipe away the spit from his lips and cheeks, Sunny calmed himself and dared a look into Edgar's furious eyes. "I am your Emissary, and, as an Emissary, my words are my truth. The kids do not know."

Edgar's countenance softened, as did his grip on Sunny's thighs. He grinned, then chuckled as he straightened. "Always the consummate diplomat; however, Uncle Sunny, you may be too close to the family to help with my endeavor. I desperately need our young bargaining chips returned to bring their dear mother from hiding."

"I can still help."

Edgar pulled a handkerchief from his pocket, wiped his brow, and tossed it into Sunny's lap. "Maybe you can; you are indeed still my Emissary." He returned to pacing. "But first, we have Texas."

Sunny envisioned a map of the States and what lay between Oklahoma and San Diego. "Texas *is* on the route they'll likely travel."

Edgar waved a finger. "Oh, I'm betting on it. So much so that I've called the Dogs on the Kelley children. Unlike Reginald, they were 'rarin' to help for a significant payment," he said with a southern twang.

Sunny stiffened in his chair. The Dog Brothers: bounty hunters, scoundrels, and all-around bad guys. He knew of the Dog Brothers all too well and silently opposed sending them after Jacqueline and Billy. "What have you asked them to do?"

A toothy smile jettisoned across Edgar's face, stretching thin the skin of his cheeks. "Whatever it takes to bring them back alive. Broken or not."

SHAMROCK

"Feelin' lucky?" Devin flashed his goofy smile Jac hadn't yet warmed to.

Jac blinked. "What are you asking me?"

"We're here."

"Where? Shamrock?"

"Precisely." He drummed the steering wheel. "And I'm feeling luckier by the moment."

"Finally!" Billy unlatched his seatbelt, and his head invaded the space between Devin and Jac. "I'm ready to get out of this coconut pizza box. I mean, I love pizza. But coconut pizza? Yuck."

"And I'll feel a ton better with something to drink and a lady's room," Jac added.

"So, you're a lady, are you?" Devin asked.

Jac rolled her eyes. "Shut up."

"Okay, grumpy. Geez."

"I need to pee," Billy said. "I couldn't at Stan's because of the cop. And Devin was in the stall with me."

"You keep holding it," Devin said. "We're stopping up the road here."

"And then straight through to San Diego," Jac added, angling for a reaction from Devin.

Devin smirked. "Yeah, sure."

Jac raised her eyebrows, leaning forward to ensure Devin could see her disapproving expression.

He raised a palm. "I'm serious; it's a long drive. We need to sleep over at least one more time."

"I'm paying you to drive us to San Diego, not to sleep in rented beds."

"No, you're paying me to *get* you to San Diego, and I'm not a robot. I need sleep, or I'll fall asleep driving, and we'll all die."

"Hey, I don't want to die," Billy said.

Jac punched Devin's arm, eliciting a pained exclamation and causing him to swerve briefly into the other lane. "You are not going to die, Billy." She maintained a disapproving glare at Devin as he rubbed his arm.

"Seriously, where did you learn to punch?"

"One stop,"—she held up a finger—"that's it ... and I have to approve the hotel, or motel, or whatever."

"Sure, you got it, Rocky Balboa." Devin slowed the car and turned into the parking lot of a curious-looking brown-painted, stone and brick, one-story dome-shaped building with an art déco flair.

Two cylindrical towers rose from the building, one short and the other dozens of feet high. In white letters, "Shamrock" ran from top to bottom of the taller tower. At the top sat a large, green, metal four-leaf clover.

"Welcome to Shamrock's Visitor Center. Snacks, drinks, bathrooms, and … stuff."

"What kinda stuff?" Billy asked.

Devin shrugged. "The coolest kind."

Billy looked at him doubtfully.

"I've never seen anything like this." Jac gawked at the building. Somewhere in the last fifty miles of road, they had left Earth through a wormhole, traveled through the depths of space, and reached a Martian colony.

"I guess you haven't. There's nothing else like this in the States."

Billy pressed his face against the car window, straining to look up at the tower. "I think it's cool."

* * *

Inside the visitor's center, Jac pointed to the bathroom sign and asked Devin to watch Billy. "I'll be right back."

Devin saluted. "Got it." He pulled Billy into a side hug. "He's safe with me."

Jac's gaze lingered on Billy as if she were seeing him for the last time. A twinge of anxiety pinched at her insides. During her time with Devin, he showed no signs of being disingenuous in his desire to help them reach San Diego. Her distrust of Devin waned when he opened up about his jailbird dad and alcoholic mother, as if the veil protecting his secrets had fallen. Yes, she had grown closer to trusting Devin, but she didn't trust the world or anyone else in it.

Jac wanted to be comfortable when not having Billy at her side. Realistically, she couldn't watch his every move and every breath. She was his sister, his protector, but they weren't fused at the hip. Devin would suffice for bathroom visits, but without question, he couldn't protect Billy from a vampire if one were lurking, waiting to strike, waiting to take him away. Being a public place, the visitor center offered an excellent opportunity to test Devin. To be absolutely sure, she could trust him.

Jac relieved herself, washed her hands, and examined her reflection in the bathroom mirror. She pushed her hair behind her ears. The white of her eyes had cleared up nicely, and the dark circles underneath her eyes lessened. She didn't look half bad, nearly photo-ready. Staring at her reflection, she shook her hair free from her ears to cover her cheeks, like some shampoo commercial model. She brushed her hair back and repeated. She smiled coyly, biting her bottom lip.

She frowned.

What am I doing? Her mind had strayed from concern for Billy, to Devin's face, smile, and voice, like some idiotic love-sick girl. She closed her eyes, shook her head, and left the bathroom, utterly disappointed in herself.

The store buzzed with an influx of customers. Removed from Oklahoma or not, Jac kept her head low and hid behind her hair, stealing glances and using her peripheral to locate the boys. *Devin, where the hell are you?*

Her anxiety grew like a stomachache every passing second. Her throat tightened as if being choked, and her heart thrummed like a hummingbird's wings. Although her legs were jelly-like, Jac quickened her pace, scanning the aisles. They weren't in the checkout line or at the drink machine. They weren't anywhere. *Wait. The bathroom. Devin took Billy to the bathroom.*

An elderly man wearing belted pants too high around his waist exited the men's room. "Excuse me." Jac tugged at her shirt sleeves. "Is there anyone else in there? I'm looking for my brother."

"No one else, young lady, just me." The old man offered a pleasant smile, hiding in the wrinkles.

Jac's hands crept to her arms, and her nails dug into her skin through her sleeves. Her mind raced to worst-case scenarios. Devin had deceived her. It wasn't a coincidence he had talked to her in the store in Jenks. He had played her for a fool. The Philadelphia Coven had been following her and Billy the entire time. They had eyes and ears everywhere, and, dammit, Devin was one of them.

"Billy," Jac murmured. Her tense body eased like a stretched rubber band removed from its purpose. Her hands released their grip on her arms and dropped to her sides into fists. Devin and Billy stood outside the store in the afternoon sun. Billy shielded his eyes, looking upward.

She stormed out of the store, shoving the glass door, sending it rattling on its hinges. Her voice caught the boys off guard, erasing the glee from their faces. "Do NOT do that again!"

Devin turned his focus from the tower to Jac's verbal explosion. "Whoa. Don't do what again?"

"Don't...." Jac paused, unsure of what to blame Devin for. She was angry and scared, and that's all that mattered. "Nothing, never mind ... I didn't know where you were. I'll never leave him with you again."

"Okay." Devin's shoulders slumped; his smile melted. "Sorry."

"It's my fault." Billy grabbed her and Devin's hands as if acting as a conduit of peace. "I told Devin I wanted to see the tower."

Jac wasn't ready for peace, but the firestorm subsided to a simmer. Her eyes, no longer piercing slits, regained their almond shape. "Just forget about it. Billy, let's go back inside; I need a drink."

Devin released Billy's hand, pulled an orange soda from a paper bag, and presented it to her.

How did he know? She snatched the bottle from his hand and muttered a thank you.

"I have to go *now*," Billy announced, doing a little dance as he grabbed the crotch of his pants.

"Yeah, buddy, I'll take you," Devin offered. He held the paper bag out for Jac. She grabbed it, and her hand with the bag dropped to her side.

Billy ran inside as Devin stopped, leaned in close, and spoke into her ear. "He'll be fine. We'll be out in a couple minutes."

Jac closed her eyes and held her breath. Her jaw clenched as a war waged inside of her. She resisted the desire to grab Devin by the hair, wrench back his head, and sink her teeth into his neck, allowing the metallic-tasting warm blood to pour into her mouth and slide down her throat. She could do it. No one could stop her, not Devin, not Billy.

Devin had become a confounding temptation. She couldn't determine if the problem was the beginning stages of blood hunger or a basic vampiric primal desire for the O-negative blood flowing through his veins and arteries. However, one thing that overpowered her lust for blood, including Devin's, was her hatred for everything vampire. She'd never drink from Devin. She could never hurt him.

Minutes later, Billy bolted from the store, with Devin lagging behind. Jac barely had time to call his name before he darted past her into the parking lot, jumping up and down excitedly and beating on the Pizza Mobile's hood. Devin trotted from the store, shaking his head as Billy taunted him from across the parking lot.

"What was that about?" Jac asked.

"I challenged him to race to the car," Devin said in a mix of defeat and astonishment.

"Yeah, bad idea."

"Tell me about it." He scratched his head. "How about you? Want to race?"

Jac smirked. "No. You already lost once; no reason to make you a double loser."

"Yeah, thanks for your concern for my ego."

She smiled, her teeth on display.

"Wait ... was that a legitimate smile? Not another fake one like you've been giving me?"

Her mouth snapped back to a straight line. "I don't fake smile." She walked away toward the car as Devin followed behind.

"Everyone fakes smiles at some point," Devin said to her back. "I fake smile. Anyway, it was just a compliment. You have nice teeth."

"I'll pretend you didn't say that."

"I win," Billy cheered with his hand still on the car hood, making it abundantly clear he touched first.

"You did, buddy," Devin conceded. "You are *fast*."

"I know."

"No, I mean you're super fast. You should try out for track or the football team at school."

"I'm homeschooled. Remember?"

Billy's education hadn't crossed Jac's mind. Mom and Dad had always been their teachers in English, arithmetic, science, history, and life in general. Who would teach him now? Billy couldn't attend school in San Diego. He'd be as dangerous around kids there as he was in Philadelphia. Maybe the Castillos had a plan. A tutor or something.

"Oh yeah, well … maybe in college, then."

Jac waited at the passenger side for Devin to unlock the doors while the feeling of being watched pricked her senses. She inconspicuously and slowly scanned the area, taking deep breaths. Nothing or anyone appeared out of the ordinary, though everything, everyone, and everywhere outside of Philadelphia was new to her. Heck, anything outside of her apartment had the potential to appear unique, strange, or awe-inducing. Again, the prick at her skin. *Whoever is out there, leave us alone.* "Devin. We need to go."

Devin must have picked up on Jac's freaked-out expression. He nodded, quickly slid into the driver's seat, and hurriedly backed out of the parking spot as Jac buckled up.

Jac continued to scan the area for danger as Devin pulled onto the street. She half expected Reginald's black Benz to pull up, regardless of his authority ending at the Oklahoma State line. It was a ridiculous worry. He wouldn't be around. If someone were watching or following them, it would be someone else, someone new, and possibly someone worse.

"You okay?" Devin asked.

She tucked her hair behind her ears and hugged herself. "Yeah, sorry, paranoid, I guess."

"That makes sense, but relax. We'll be out of Texas in no time."

"Thanks." Though not feeling Devin's reassurance, she played along, not wanting her worry to spread, especially with Billy in a great mood.

"Besides, we have luck on our side now." Devin extended his hand toward her. A shamrock-shaped keychain dangled from his forefinger; the green petals sparkled and shined in the sunlight as it spun.

"What's this?"

"It's a keychain," he said, as if her question was ridiculous.

"Yeah, I get that. Why are you giving it to me?"

"For your upcoming birthday." He smiled conspiratorially at Billy in the rearview mirror. "Men talk in the men's room."

Jac slid the keychain from Devin's finger and placed it in her palm.

"It's not much, I know. I thought you might like a memento from our trip. Maybe later, I can get you something better." He glanced at her as if waiting for a response. "They had a mug with your name on it, sort of. It had Jac but with the 'k.' You haven't said if you drink coffee, so I didn't get the mug. Shamrocks are lucky, so now you have portable luck."

Jac admired the keychain. She had only received gifts from Mom, Dad, that bastard Sunny, and Billy, though Mom always bought gifts for Billy to give her. She would have to remember to throw away or burn every gift Sunny had ever given her, assuming she saw the contents of their apartment again. The keychain was inexpensive but also an unexpected and sweet gesture. Internally, she adored the sentiment; outwardly, she thanked Devin and scorned Billy for divulging her age and upcoming birthday.

Jac squeezed the keychain and wished for whatever luck it could bring. However, her inside voice, the one that offered warning and guidance people had a knack for ignoring, warned her they needed more than luck. Much more.

BAD DREAMS
AND COWBOYS

Every mile closer to San Diego, to safety, was one mile farther from Philadelphia, from danger, from death. The sense of being watched at the Shamrock Visitor Center had abated but remained as the slightest itch. An itch Jac decided was best not scratched. Instead, she let it linger to keep her more aware.

With the drone of wheels on the road, Jac eased into her seat. It wasn't long before the monotony enveloped her. Itch or not, her eyelids lost their fight against gravity, and she dozed off.

The blare of a car horn awakened Jac with a jump. She whipped around in her seat to check on Billy. Her tension washed away. He slept; he was safe.

"Welcome back to the world," said a familiar and unexpected voice.

Jac froze. She recognized the voice above all others. Where Devin had been, with his dirty blond hair and nearly ever-present smile, was the person who shouldn't be, who *couldn't* be. Behind the steering wheel sat the person she missed the most—her father. Smiling. Breathing. Driving. Alive!

"Shit, Dad! What are you doing here?"

"Language," Dad said, mocking seriousness.

Jac inherited her father's curse word fluency: four-letter words, closed compounds, hyphenated, and the silent and most powerful middle finger. Those words found their way from his voice box to her impressionable ears during afternoon baseball and football Sundays. Opposing teams and the refs were frequent targets of his verbal assaults. Political shows elicited his most virulent attacks. "Politics is a reason people hate each other," he would say.

Jac kept the curse words stowed away in her arsenal for when needed and appropriate. Mom disapproved of the colorful language, but Dad taught Jac to never fear a word or asking for what she wanted. If she didn't speak up for herself, she shouldn't expect anyone else to.

"How are you here?"

"You asked me to be here, Jackie Q."

'Jackie Q,' she hadn't heard that in years, her father's play on her name. She didn't care for it all that much, and after age twelve, she forbade him from using the nickname, but today, at this moment, it sounded like verbal gold.

"I *asked* you?"

"Yes. You needed me, and I'm here."

"I don't remember asking you," she said, her voice trailing off. "Wait." She checked the back seat. "Where's Devin?"

"Devin? Who's Devin?"

"He's the guy driving us to San Diego. This is his car. He was here a minute ago."

"Oh, him. He'll be back."

Jac stared at her father's profile as he drove. She had missed him so much. All would be perfect if Mom were in the back seat with Billy. "Oh, Dad. Where's Mom?"

He shook his head and looked grimly at her. "Jacqueline, don't do it."

"Don't do what?"

"Do what you're planning … in San Diego. After you leave Billy with the Castillos."

How could he know about her plan to … end things? How could he possibly know? Maybe he doesn't, and he's talking about something else. "Dad, I don't understand. What plan are you talking about?"

He frowned. "Jacqueline, I know you better than anyone. I've known how you felt for years. I'm sorry, Mom and I haven't been there for you. But Billy needs you more than ever. Don't do it."

Jac's eyes flooded with tears. He knew. From a young age, she told her father she never wanted to hurt anyone. There were occasions when she almost had. The first incident occurred during a routine trip to the grocery store when she was only five. Her mother turned her back for only a moment, and Jacqueline explored. That's the watered-down description of what Jac had done. More accurately, "explore" meant Jac had caught a whiff of O-negative and wanted to find the owner. Mom found her an aisle over, wrestling a kid two or three years older than she.

Mom pulled her off the kid a split second before the bite. Jacqueline knew better, but knowing didn't always trump desire.

She despised living in the world as a predator, as if she were a Savanna lioness and every human with O-negative blood was a gazelle. This danger became a reality after choking the breath from the man on the bus and draining his life from a hole in his neck.

"I have to, Dad. I'm so sad." Jac hugged herself, wishing instead she could collapse into her dad's arms and have him squeeze away the sadness. He'd tell her everything would be alright. He would turn the car around and drive them back to Philadelphia, back to their apartment. It was Mom's night to cook dinner. She'd be finishing a pot of beef stew, a family recipe passed down through the generations. Jac's favorite. The family of four would sit at the dinner table, eating from bowls filled with delicious food and talking about their days, futures, and lives.

"What's got you so sad now that you want to end it all ... that you want to leave your brother alone?"

Didn't he know about the man on the bus, the man she broke, the man she killed? Didn't he realize she could never forgive herself? That she could never live with herself? Sadness blended with disgust, creating a messy watercolor of emotions. Her tears continued to fall. "I'm a monster! I don't want to hurt anyone anymore. I don't want to kill anyone else."

Dad rested his hand on her shoulder and, with a kind of psychic effort, kept the car in the lane while looking at her empathetically. "Jacqueline, you are not a monster. The simple fact you feel this way proves it. I know what happened on the bus. But monsters, actual monsters, have no regard for others. Monsters hurt and kill for pleasure, for sport."

"I killed him. His face ... he stared into my eyes when I pulled him from the seat. He—"

Dad squeezed her shoulder. "You did what was needed, for Billy."

"I know, but it hurts my heart. It hurts everywhere, all over."

"I know it does, Jackie Q, but you're strong. You can handle this." He refocused on the road, smiling as he drove.

Jac lived in the conversation break with their heartbeats and the drum of the tires the only sounds. Dad didn't consider her a monster, but didn't parents always think the best of their kids or support them when they were at their worst? On the crime shows she'd watch, parents of murderers were often in the courtroom sobbing after the judge convicted their child. What would Mom think?

Jac asked again, "Dad. Where's Mom?"

Dad chuckled. "Your mom's at home, silly."

She stared at him, confused. "No, she's not."

"She certainly is. You left her there."

Her face flushed. "Dad, she's not at home. Billy and I just left home. She's not there."

Dad kept his eyes on the road. Staring into the distance as if looking for an answer, he murmured, "I died." He cupped his mouth with his right hand, stifling a small gasp, then returned it with his left, firmly gripping the steering wheel.

Jac studied her father. He said he died as if he had only just realized it. "Yes, I know. You died or ... were killed. The Coven said they didn't know who killed you. Mom didn't believe them; I didn't believe them."

"I died." Dad's expression softened until his mouth hung wide open. His face slowly collapsed into itself as if a tiny black hole had appeared where his nose had been. His grip eased, and his hands fell from the steering wheel to his lap. The car crept across the lines and into the next lane.

"Dad!" Jac yelled. "What are you doing? Grab the steering wheel!" She vigorously shook him when his limp head, or what remained of it, slumped against the driver's side window. The car veered erratically, and tire rubber squealed, fighting for grip. A strange wailing came from where her father's face once offered a smile. He shook violently, broke into large pieces, and dematerialized. Devin instantly reappeared in the driver's seat with his intact, handsome face. He slumped against the window, eyes closed. Blood oozed from two puncture holes in his neck.

Jac clawed at her head. "Oh my God. What did I do? Devin! Wake up! Grab the wheel!" She reached for Billy. Inexplicably, he still lay asleep in the back seat, his belt buckled.

The tires shrieked as the car swerved. Jac grabbed the steering wheel, which she had only done a few times before when her dad would let her sit in his lap in a parking lot. She had fantasized that first time holding the wheel at age six, that she could order Dad to the passenger seat, slip on her seat belt, and take off down the road. Little did she know that even at sixteen, she wouldn't be allowed to drive; her parents forbade her from getting a driver's license. Now, at age seventeen, she gripped the steering wheel of a moving car for the first time, this one traveling at seventy-something miles per hour.

The driver-side tires hit the rumble strips on the wrong side of the highway, making the "Wake up!" sound. Jac jerked the wheel to the right, over-correcting and sending the car toward the opposite side of the highway. The car careened off the road and crashed into the tree line.

"Devin!" Jac woke, exploding from her seat, screaming and flailing.

"Holy crap!" Devin yelled, jerking the car into the adjacent lane, narrowly missing the car behind him and to the left. The driver blared their horn, sending a message of disapproval.

Jac's eyes moved wildly, taking in her surroundings. Dad had vanished, Devin drove, and Billy sat in the back seat, giving her a what-the-heck look. When Jac was seven, Dad explained the vampiric proclivity for vivid dreams and how amazing those dreams could be. He didn't explain that those dreams could be absolute nightmares when you're an adult vampire dealing with adult problems.

"What the heck is going on?" Sweat beaded Devin's forehead.

"Devin." Jac held a hand over her heart, threatening to beat out of her chest.

"Yes, I'm Devin."

"Pull over."

"But—"

With pleading eyes, she repeated, "Pull over. Now."

Devin offered no opposition as he applied the brakes, looking more at Jac than the road. The car reached the shoulder and slowed to a stop.

Jac shoved open her door and bolted from the car as if it were aflame and on the verge of exploding. Billy yelled for her, but she needed space and to be alone. She went full sprint, stopping a dozen yards west of the car. Her hands clawed at her arms as she walked in circles, mumbling to herself. The fabric of her sleeves tore in tiny holes as her jagged fingernails found their way through the thread and into her skin. Tears poured from the eyes of her grief-wrenched face.

Devin ran to her, stopping a few feet away.

"Get back!" Jac yelled, her hands outstretched.

"I am back. I am." Devin reached a tentative hand toward her. "Tell me what's wrong."

He thinks I will hurt him. I don't want to hurt him.

Devin would be rightfully concerned if he knew she was a vampire and he was her blood type, her life-giving food. The grisly hidden reason for his life was to elongate hers, to be her six-foot-tall blood bag. That was the horrid truth she couldn't run away from.

"Get away!" Jac urged.

"Jac, I'm coming." Billy rushed next to Devin and gripped the back of his shirt. Devin extended his hand across Billy's chest, keeping him by his side.

"I can't do that, Jac. You're scaring me... you're scaring Billy."

Billy. He didn't look like her regular Billy; he looked scared, a look he had rarely worn. He had always been emotionally resilient. Vampires had better control over their emotions than humans. It was a strength of theirs, a superpower. Dad often claimed that Jac's vampire emotion-control switch was faulty. "It was never installed," she'd joke. As the years passed, instead of a joke, it became an obvious fact.

"You should be," Jac cried.

"I should be what?" Devin asked.

"You should be scared." She met Devin's eyes. "Get away before I hurt you."

Devin opened his palms at his sides. "Why would you hurt me?"

"Because I'm a monster." Her knees weakened, nearly sending her to the ground.

Billy slipped past Devin and ran toward her. She dropped to a knee and enveloped Billy in a hug.

"Calm down," Billy whispered, gently stroking her hair. "You're okay. It will be okay."

Jac pressed her eyes closed and hugged Billy tighter. He would get her through it. He would bring her back from the edge, and they could continue the trip. For Devin, she would come up with a reason she acted like a lunatic. Some story that didn't include biting him in her dream. A calming feeling saturated her. "I'll be okay. I'll be okay." She pulled back from Billy and gave him a pained smile. "I'll be okay." He was always there for her, even when *she* should have been there for him.

Billy nodded.

Blaring music and tires braking on gravel interrupted the moment. A jacked-up, red pickup truck with oversized tires—a mini-monster truck—rumbled up and stopped behind Devin's car. Two men, a driver and his passenger, sat in the truck. A country song blared from the open windows.

Jac's emotional switch, faulty or missing, couldn't prevent her sadness and anger from being whisked away and replaced with fear. The type of fear a mother bear experiences when someone or something threatens her cubs. That itch she had felt in Shamrock became a burn.

"Stay here," Devin said. "They probably think we've broken down. I'll tell them we're okay."

Jac's slowed heartbeat ramped up again as adrenaline coursed through her. "No! Don't get near them. Get in the car. Now." She hustled Billy over to Devin and handed him off like a chore.

"Just let me talk to them."

She stepped close to Devin, uncomfortably close, and whispered intently, "Take Billy to the car, get in, and if I yell for you to leave, leave and don't stop. Don't stop until you reach San Diego." Jac pulled a small, folded piece of paper from her pocket and pressed it into Devin's hand. "Call the number on this paper, and help will come to you." She watched for compliance in Devin's confused hazel eyes and understanding in Billy's.

"Jac, seriously. I know I've been asking this a lot, but what's going on?"

Billy pulled at Devin's hand. "Let's get in the car."

The truck engine sputtered and stopped. Both doors opened, and leather-booted feet hit the gravel-covered shoulder of the highway. The doors closed, revealing two men wearing long-sleeved button-up shirts, blue jeans, and cowboy hats. The broad and tall passenger must have stood at six-four or six-five. His lowered hat covered the top of his face, and a brown and well-grown beard hung from his jaw.

The driver was leaner and tall by any measure: six-one or six-two. He had a clean-shaven face, a crocodile smile, and walked like a peacock, showing off his plumage. But he didn't impress Jac; he terrified her.

Devin called for her. She waved him off when the smaller of the men, the peacock, spoke with a Southern drawl.

"Well, well, who do we have the pleasure of meetin' on this fine afternoon?"

Where have I heard that voice? Jac couldn't place it. Maybe the peacock reminded her of the cowboy played by Walton Goggins in the Jackie Chan and Owen Wilson movie she watched with her dad years ago. The movie was a comedy, and Walton Goggins played the part of a funny and almost likable bad guy. Jac's life *wasn't* a comedy, and the cowboy standing before her didn't exude likeability.

"We're okay … no car troubles or anything." Jac swallowed hard. "We just pulled over for a minute."

Walton, or the peacock, tipped his white Stetson, his face still full smile. "Car troubles?" He glanced at his large passenger and then back at her. "By the look of your teary eyes, I reckon ya'll got more than car troubles."

Jac felt his eyes examining her, following her hand as she wiped a stray tear from her cheek. "We're okay; we're just now leaving."

A gust of wind blew at the Cowboy's backs, sending gravel, glass, and what no amount of cologne could hide—the stench of a vampire. Jac didn't know these men, these vampires, but she knew they were a threat and guessed Edgar sent them. Devin had to leave. He had to drive as if their lives depended on it. Because they did.

She turned to yell for Devin to drive away when he exited the car. "No! Get back in the car!"

"Well, howdy," the white-hatted cowboy said, pulling his gaze from her to Devin. He stepped closer. "Is this your car …." he paused and extended his hand toward Devin as if waiting for a name.

Jac looked fearfully disappointed at Devin as if she were a defied parent. *Damn it, I told you to stay in the car!*

"I'm Devin, and yeah, it is. Why?"

"Just curious. It's … practical." He took a few sniffs. "That smell … is … is that coconut and … pizza?" He turned to the hulking cowboy and laughed.

"Yeah, it comes with the job."

"Now, I've never tried coconut pizza, but I'll try anything once." He grinned, evidently amusing himself.

"What do you want?"

"My brother and I are huntin' for someone," the cowboy said, his voice trailing off. He chewed on his tongue or something that wasn't really in his mouth.

Jac followed the cowboy's eyes, fixated not on the car but on who was in it. Billy peeked over the back seat, his hands gripping the headrest.

"And we weren't sure we had the right folk until little-man showed himself."

Jac yelled for Devin to run. He turned to her, frozen and wide-eyed, like a pervert in a brothel. The passenger—the giant vampire wearing a black Stetson—grabbed Devin, spun him around, and applied a chokehold. Devin's face reddened, and his arms flailed, alternating between pulling at the bulging arm around his neck to attempting awkward punches toward the face of his assaulter.

"Don't kill him!" Jac rushed toward Devin and slid to a stop when the white-hatted cowboy stepped between them.

"Uh-uh. Don't get no closer, darlin'."

This marked the second time in a day, and in her entire life, she had been called darlin'. Once by Sally, the waitress with southern hospitality, and once by the peacock cowboy with zero hospitality.

"Please don't hurt him." Jac's knees buckled, and she stumbled back. She pressed her fists against the sides of her head. "He has nothing to do with this."

The white-hatted cowboy sauntered closer to her, wearing an I'm-the-asshole-in-charge grin. "Darlin', we ain't gonna kill him. At least not yet. Nah, my brother's just puttin' him in a more cooperative state."

"Who are you? What do you want?"

"There'll be time for introductions later." The white-hatted cowboy surveyed the surroundings and highway, presumably for witnesses to the mid-day assault and abduction taking place. "But we found who we wanted, Miss Jacqueline Kelley. We got *you* and your brother. We've been contracted, ya understand."

Jac didn't ask who contracted them; she already knew. Edgar's grasp was far-reaching when he could hire someone else's hands to do the job.

Devin's arms had gone limp; his fight had ended. The giant of a man in the black hat tossed Devin's limp body over his shoulder as if he were a father carrying his toddler.

"Tie him up in the truck bed and pull the tarp over," the white-hatted cowboy ordered. He tapped the back window of Devin's car, getting Billy's attention. "Come on out, kid. You're ridin' in the truck. I can't have ya back there causin' me grief while I'm drivin'.'"

Jac motioned to Billy. He slid out of the car and stood next to the now-kneeling captor. She watched closely, ready to jump in to protect him.

The cowboy tipped his hat. "Listen here, kid, I can tell by the look on your face you're sore at me, but don't get too big for your britches. I need ya to ride in that big ol' truck with my brother and don't cause no trouble."

Billy nodded once, slowly.

The cowboy patted Billy's head and stood. "Good boy. Now, if ya cause any trouble, I'll know it ... and remember, your sis is ridin' with me." He looked at Jac, continuing his orders. "I can be nice, but if ya try me...."

The cowboy laid his arm across Jac's shoulders, sidling up to her, and waved bye to Billy, walking toward the truck. He stood closer to her than she could stand; the one too many sprays of cologne nearly smelled worse than the vampire he was. His big brother came from behind the truck, presumably finished securing Devin. He plucked Billy from the ground like a doll and placed him in the passenger seat.

"Where are you taking us?" Jac asked, her eyes still glued to Billy.

"The five of us are goin' for a chit-chat."

Jac didn't want to leave the spot. It didn't matter who or what the cowboys were—they wouldn't harm them, not on the side of the road in plain view.

"We can talk here," she offered.

The white-hatted cowboy removed his hat and held it to his chest. An indentation in his clean-cut brown hair encircled his head. He leaned close, too close. Jac nearly recoiled, fighting against punching his stupid face. She wanted to be unwavering, unflinching, and unafraid.

"This kinda chit-chat ain't for public consumption. Besides, we gotta hand ya off tomorrow."

Jac wanted to fight, but she'd be no match for even one of them alone. Besides, Billy's vulnerability, sitting in the truck with the giant vampire, erased the idea of combat.

"Then take me." She locked onto the cowboy's eyes. "Let Devin and my brother go."

"That's a no-can-do, senorita. You two are a package deal, and we aim to get paid. Now, get your narrow butt in the front seat."

Jac reluctantly moved toward the car, stopping next to the passenger door. "Who's driving?"

"My brother's drivin' the truck, and I'll drive ol' practical here."

They slid into their respective seats and closed their doors.

"How long's the drive?" Jac wanted information, any details she could pry from her captor. She didn't know what good the information would do, but it gave her a sense of control.

"Somewhere not too far from here. Somewhere we go to unwind, get crazy, and when the feelin' arises, where we take our prey." He stuck the key in the ignition and raised a finger. "Just a warnin' ... if ya try anything, ya best know that your brother will be dead before this car stops."

Jac glared at him. However, she *was* partial to the idea—she and Billy would be dead, and the pain and turmoil of their lives over. Pushing aside the nihilism that had found a home in her, she settled on the idea of leaving with her abductor. She could never bring harm to Billy.

The cowboy started the car and paused with his hand on the gearshift. "Now, buckle up."

VARIABLES

The white-hatted abductor pulled onto the highway, crossed the grass median, and headed back east.

Jac clenched the doorframe with her right hand. Her chest tightened like a knot in a vise. By the second, a damn gravitational pull yanked her back to Philadelphia and farther away from San Diego. She glowered at the driver, wanting him to see how she felt. The violence she desperately wanted to inflict was not an option.

"Pretty, ain't I?" he asked with a stupid grin.

Jac remained silent, maintaining her focus on him.

"Drink it in, darlin'." He smirked. "But now, don't get too enamored; I ain't part of no boy band. Though, I've been known to cut a rug on occasion, and my karaoke ain't too awful once I have a couple beers in me."

Her stern look turned to disgust before turning away. Absolutely anything was better than looking at the jerk driving her back east. *Seriously, old man?*

"I think it only fair I introduce myself, seein' I know your name, Jacqueline Kelley."

Of course, he knew her name; he had been hired to capture her and Billy. However, something irksome hid in how he said it, as if they'd already met or he thought they had. She had neither seen nor met him before today. Maybe he knew her parents. Had he ever stopped by their apartment? Doubtful. Why would her parents have any connection to this trash?

"My brother and I are famously known as the Dog Brothers. You're welcome to address me as Tanner and him Curtis."

Jac heard but acted disinterested, choosing instead to watch the truck behind them to confirm Billy was safe. It wasn't much to have the names of their abductors, but she added it to her mental information list.

"Since the cat's got your tongue, how about I lay out the ground rules?" He paused for her acknowledgment that never came. "Though this may seem like a pleasant afternoon drive, you and I restrained only by easily removable seat belts. Just know if ya try anything causin' this car to deviate from its forward trajectory, my brother, though a big teddy bear, will pull over, yank your friend Devin from the truck bed, and snap his neck like a chicken. Which, truth be told, ain't easy. Don't let them movies fool ya."

Jac gave him the finger.

Tanner chuckled. "Breakin' fingers, however, is nothin'. Heck, I might say I've become an expert at phalangeal fracturing."

She lowered her finger and stuffed her hand into her lap.

"Now, the most important ground rule is ya do what I say when I say it. That includes answerin' when I ask ya a question. If ya follow this rule, we'll get along like bumble bees and honey."

She pretended to ignore him.

"Now, I'm gonna need some indication of compliance ... nod your little pixie head if that's all the communication you can muster."

Jac wasn't interested in giving him the satisfaction of conversation, but she nodded, with compliance being the wisest course of action ... for now.

"Good girl. Now, at first, I thought Devin was food for the road, but ya showed your cards right away when Curtis grabbed him."

Tanner claimed to have seen what Jac feared admitting to herself—she cared for Devin. And why wouldn't she? Devin helped her and Billy escape Oklahoma and would have been the only reason they made it to San Diego. She analyzed the pros and cons of admitting her blossoming feelings of friendship for Devin. Any answer could result in his untimely death, but she had to pick one. She met Tanner's stare, unwavering. "I don't care about him. He was just my dinner."

Tanner studied her for a moment and smirked. "Hell, then." He pulled a phone from his shirt pocket. "I'll tell my brother to pull over and do it now."

Jac's stomach clenched; her heart fluttered. Still, her mouth remained shut, her face that of a phlegmatic poker player.

Tanner called her bluff. He fidgeted with the phone and placed it against his ear. "Hey, brother, turns out we don't need ol' Dev—"

"No, wait!" Jac desperately grabbed at Tanner's phone.

He slapped her hands away and laughed, showing the phone still on the home screen.

"You didn't even call?" Heat rose from her head. She fought the urge to strike him, choosing instead to cross her arms. "Jerk."

Tanner slid the phone back into his shirt pocket. "What we're doin' here, Jacqueline, is playin' chess. Now, I've been playin' chess a long time, long before you were born. There's no 'gettin' out of this.' In the end, you'll do what we say, answer what we ask, and then my brother and I will receive our deserved payment."

"Assholes," she muttered. Jac thought the moniker fit Tanner and Curtis the moment she saw them. Now, it felt empowering to say it, even if under her breath.

"Oh, I'm more than that, but look who's talkin'."

She scoffed. "What is that supposed to mean?"

"You're like some evil little creature. Killin' people on buses, leadin' on that boy, him not knowin' he's along for the ride up until when ya lose the strength to resist and poke holes in him. Drain him like an old above-ground pool."

"You don't know what you're talking about." Truthfully, Tanner spoke facts. A vampire spending too much time with a human of matching blood type was a pending tragedy. Still, she felt better denying it in words.

"Did ya tell him he's your type, and you're waitin' for the moment to suck the O-negative from him like a neck canteen?"

"He doesn't know what I am. And, just so you know, I wasn't saving him for anything. I would never hurt him."

"Tell me, little killer-pixie, what you'd have done if a cravin' hit ya somewhere in the middle of New Mexico and your favorite snack sat right there in the seat next to ya?"

Jac looked away, hugging herself. "It would never happen."

Tanner nodded mockingly. "*Sure* it wouldn't."

"I wouldn't do it." She spat the words. "I'd rather die."

"I guess we'll never know." He rested his left arm on the door and drove with his right. "Devin is what I'd call a short-timer."

She stared him down. "Screw you."

"Woah, now. Calm down there." He laughed. "I'm only playin'. Havin' a little fun to kill time."

* * *

They drove miles without speaking, with the tires on the road and Tanner singing an awful twangy song, the only sounds. Jac pressed her lips to keep from telling him to shut up. Unsure of what she could get away with, she didn't test his ire, with Billy and Devin only a phone call away from harm.

Tanner twice glanced at the backpack between her feet before he broke from the song. "What's in your satchel?"

"Nothing."

Tanner sighed. "Are we gonna do this?"

Jac shrugged. "It's ... just stuff. My stuff."

He raised an eyebrow. "Stuff?"

"Yeah. Clothes, toothbrush, toothpaste, girl stuff." The bag contained much more, but nothing she cared to share with him.

Tanner appeared unconvinced. "I need to know. Got any weapons in there?"

Jac considered her spare chopstick, the mate of the one in the right-side pocket of her cargo pants. She slid her hand over the pocket, feeling its long, thin shape. "No weapons."

"Let's keep it zipped for now. I'll be checkin' it later, anyway."

"No, you—"

Tanner raised an interrupting finger. "Uh-uh, ground rules."

Jac gave him a blistering look. She didn't want him to find the cash, much less poke around her belongings. Then again, she and Billy headed somewhere none of it would retain any value, monetary or sentimental. If she had given up hope, she would have thrown the backpack out of the window.

A cluster of single-level buildings came into view half a mile ahead. Jac sucked in her lips, sighed, and closed her eyes. She opened them as they passed the Shamrock Welcome Center, but this time in the opposite direction. *Some great luck you were.*

"Ya know, it's considered good luck to—"

"Yes, I know." Jac stared solemnly at the trees and buildings as they passed. "How much farther?"

"You in a hurry? Got somewhere to be?"

She balled her fists at the sarcasm in his voice. "Yes, I do. I want to get done with whatever you have planned. I want to get to wherever we're going and get this bullshit over with."

"Patience there, darlin'. We got hours yet until our time together ends."

Jac tensed to keep from exploding. How had this idiot bested her? While in the car, she couldn't do anything to improve her and Billy's situation. Fighting back in a moving vehicle wasn't wise, and besides, it would mean permanent lights out for Devin.

She barely knew Devin, but she had lost so much already; more than ever, she understood the permanency of death.

Despite her frustration and fear, Jac believed she could get them out of this predicament. She would never, could never, let harm come to Billy. But what about Devin? Could she leave Devin behind if it meant freedom for her and Billy? She cringed at the thought. In her heart and mind, yes, she could leave Devin behind, and she hated herself for it.

Tires on gravel brought her focus back to the here and now. The car kicked up dirt and dust, creating a cloud and camouflaging the truck behind them. A desolate landscape spread out before them. Wide open plots of dry grass stretched in all directions with the occasional outcropping of trees. Dense woods, like a wall, stood in the far distance.

Jac doubted she'd receive a straight answer from Tanner but asked, "Where are we?"

"Almost there."

"Where? There's nothing here."

Tanner lifted his chin, pointing in the distance. "Over yonder."

A single-level building stood under a tree outcropping, a football field away. "That ... house?"

"That's the one."

The brick home stood underneath the trees like a forgotten relic. Green mold had taken root at the base, bordering the dirt and weed-covered ground. Two windows were on the side facing them, and the front had a single door. Worn gray shingles covered all but a few spots of the roof, like the scales on the back of a decaying dragon. Pinewood bark covered the parking area.

To Jac's relief, no other cars were parked out front. Whomever the Dog Brothers were passing them off to didn't seem to be there. "Aren't you giving us to someone?"

"Indeed, we are, pixie girl."

"They aren't here," Jac said, half statement, half question.

"They won't be comin' here. They're flyin' in tomorrow. Private jet and all." Tanner turned to her as if analyzing her expression. He gave her an uncomfortably creepy look. "We're havin' a sleepover."

Jac recoiled. "Oh, no. Whatever you think might happen tonight, I guarantee you it isn't. No way in Hell."

Tanner laughed.

"Laugh all you want, asshole, but if you get ... it ... anywhere close to me, I'll rip it off."

"Hey, hey, hey. Calm down there." He met her stare, appearing sincere, if that was even possible. "Listen. I won't deny I represent negative things to many a people. It comes with me being me. However, there are a few things I'm not. First, I'm not a liar. I may withhold information when called for, but if I tell ya somethin', it's the God's honest truth. Even when I tell ya, I can't tell ya somethin'.

"Second, I don't force myself on anyone, much less you. You, Jacqueline, are a child." He removed a hand from the steering wheel and held it as if making a vow. "I do swear that nothing untoward will happen to you while in the company of yours truly."

Jac read Tanner as well or as poorly as any other vampire. Vow or not, she didn't trust him. Tanner's belief that withholding the truth didn't equate to lying, revealed that deceit was part of who he was. A level of deceit so ingrained in his being that he couldn't disseminate between lies and truths.

Even if Tanner was as truthful as he believed, the thought of spending the night in the dank building with Creepy-Guy-One and Creepy-Guy-Two repulsed her. Still, the sleepover gave her something she desperately needed—time to find a way out of this mess.

Tanner parked Devin's car on the bark driveway and killed the ignition. Curtis parked the truck behind them. Both vehicles rested under a thick, towering, water oak tree, throwing shade over the parking area and house, providing relief from the late-day sun.

"Just a heads up," Tanner warned, "the first item on our agenda is to flesh out the variables of this circumstance."

"What do you mean, variables?"

"Variables are like a hidden copperhead." He formed a snake head with his hand. "If ya don't know what you're doin' and don't watch where you're steppin', you'll get bit."

Jac threw him a look. "I *know* what variables are. I didn't need your stupid analogy. But what do variables have to do with you abducting us?"

In her short time with Tanner, Jac had come to know his reluctance to provide a straight answer, and that reluctance continued. "Just know, when we're inside, we're gonna find those copperheads and stamp 'em out ... kill 'em dead."

Tanner grabbed Jac's backpack at her feet, needing a second tug to pull it from her grasp. "Stay in the car." In a serious tone, he continued, "Now, if ya get out before I say, or if ya try anything, we'll end your friend, Devin. No pretend phone calls, just him going nighty-night real quick like." He stared at her as if gauging her understanding and compliance. Seemingly satisfied, he took the keys and her backpack, slid out of the car, and closed the door.

Tanner walked to the back of the truck with Curtis, undoubtedly to retrieve a hogtied Devin. They had driven for nearly forty-five minutes; he must have been all kinds of confused when coming to.

Tanner stepped out of view, allowing Jac time to search the car for a weapon—anything other than her chopstick. Devin never mentioned having a gun or a knife, but she had to be sure. She had variables of her own to consider. Under the seats hid forgotten wrappers, coins, and hardened french fries that had once escaped Devin's grasp to live on in darkness. The glove box contained papers, Band-Aids, pens, an old dead mobile phone, and the coins—nothing that could help, and she had nowhere left to look.

"Damn it." Jac clenched her fists and struck the dashboard.

Sounds of a scuffle arose from behind the truck, followed by an exchange of harsh words. One voice she recognized as Devin's. Moments later, Tanner came from the back and opened the truck's passenger door. Billy's eyes met hers as Tanner pulled him from the seat and gently lowered him to the ground. He walked hand in hand with Billy toward the car. Devin lagged behind them, staggering, his hands behind his back. His t-shirt collar sagged down his chest, stretched to the limit. Curtis towered over him with one giant hand clamped on his shoulder.

Jac and Billy exchanged a pained look as everyone reached the car's side. They were safe and alive, for now. Tanner gave her the two-finger wave to exit the car as if getting a waiter's attention. She opened the door and stepped from the vehicle. Her stomach turned at the sight of Devin, his head wobbling; his eyes squinted, even in the shade. He wouldn't survive the day. This was her fault, all her fault.

Tanner spoke, alternately looking at each of them. "Now, we're gonna go inside, and each of you is gonna do what we say and have some get-to-know-you conversations. If any of you try anything," Tanner continued, looking only at Jac, "we'll make this a miserable night for each of ya." He grabbed Devin by his hair. "Now, we can all be agreeable and uncover those variables while we wait for our sponsor to arrive, or things can get awfully ugly in there. Which will it be?"

Growing up, Jac played chess for hours upon hours with her dad. He taught her the pieces' movements and various strategies. Because of its versatility, she favored the knight, which he had allowed her to call the horsie. He would beat her mercilessly, never letting her win. He said allowing her to beat him would make her first true win less monumental. After several years of play and practice, she improved enough to challenge him, and a couple of years later, she put him in checkmate. Dad was right—the win *was* monumental.

Tanner claimed to have been playing chess long before she was born. But chess had been part of much of her life. As far as she was concerned, her chess game with Tanner had just begun, and she hadn't yet gone on the attack.

Jac glowered at Tanner, intent on not showing him an ounce of fear, and said, "Variables."

WHO'S IN SAN DIEGO?

"Alright, let's get to steppin'," Tanner ordered.

Jac pulled Billy close as Devin's eyes finally focused on hers. Terror and confusion registered on his sweat-coated face. Two red-lined scratches crossed his cheek and chin as if he had lost a fight with a cat.

Devin rubbed his neck as if feeling for damage. "Jac ... what's going on?"

She opened her mouth to speak but jumped at a loud clap of Tanner's hands.

Tanner nodded toward the door. "Now, get on inside before I drag ya in."

A gush of guilt swallowed her. She never intended for Devin's involvement to reach the extent it had. Her expectation of a carefree drive to San Diego was a childish dream. The dream of a seventeen-year-old who knew little more of the world than her Philadelphia neighborhood and endless hours of television. She would have never imagined this dilapidated building somewhere in Texas being the last location of her and Billy's freedom and Devin's life. Once inside, the brothers wouldn't allow Devin to leave with a heartbeat.

Tanner sent Jac and Billy stumbling toward the front door with a shove.

"Don't touch me." Jac shot an angry look at him.

He pointed toward the door. "I said get on in."

"Jac ... Jac, what's going—" Curtis yanked up the back of Devin's shirt, instantly silencing him and bringing his face to a bright, choking red.

Jac stepped into the building with Billy at Tanner's motion to do so. She pulled Billy along, keeping him close. Devin and Curtis entered second and third, followed by Tanner, who closed the door.

The heat and humidity followed them inside. The air smelled damp and musty. If the building had a working air conditioner, it wasn't on. Dust and dirt covered the tiled floor like a disgusting carpet. Yellowed and torn wallpaper clung to the walls. Graffiti in the form of legible and illegible words, various shapes and figures, and vulgarities covered the bare spots.

Tanner stepped from the rear and flicked a switch on the wall next to Jac. A light above them flickered on, dully illuminating the hallway. "Yeah, it's a fixer-upper. Jac, your room is second on the left. Billy, you're goin' with my brother and Dev boy to the room at the end on the right."

Jac pulled Billy next to her. "He stays with me."

"Hmm." Tanner pondered a moment and stepped close to Devin. He pulled a white handkerchief from his back pocket and gently wiped away the sweat from Devin's face. Devin winced at the handkerchief crossing his scratched cheek and chin. Jac's heart raced, immediately regretting being disagreeable and breaking one of Tanner's ground rules. Regardless, she would not leave Billy alone with Curtis.

"Jacqueline, I can appreciate ya wanting to watch after Billy there. Heck, I've been lookin' out for my baby brother since he was a youngin. But your brother's goin' with Curtis, whether ya like it or not." Tanner grabbed Devin's hair, yanking up his head for Jac to see the fear in his eyes. "Now, this can get ugly faster than grease through a goose, or you can trust what I'm doin' has a purpose. Heck, I don't even need you to trust me; however, I insist you do what I say."

"Don't—" Billy blurted before Jac pulled him behind her and stepped up to Tanner.

"Do not hurt him," Jac said with venom. "I *will* kill you if you do."

Tanner's eyes widened underneath raised eyebrows. He laughed, mouth closed and shallow at first, then it built into a hearty laugh, sending him leaning against the wall. "Did ya hear that, Curtis? She thinks she can kill us. Ain't that the funniest?"

Curtis half smiled as if he were humoring Tanner.

"Oh, don't mind my brother; he doesn't say much on account of him losin' part of his tongue. Come on, Curtis, show 'em ... show 'em."

Curtis looked disapprovingly at Tanner but obliged and stuck out what remained of his tongue. Three-quarters of a normal tongue remained, misshapen with jagged edges.

Tanner stepped close and used his hands to cover Billy's ears. "Yeah, he pissed off a lady of ill repute who gnawed off half of his tongue when he stuck it in her mouth, uninvited, though he denies it." He raised his right hand as if taking an oath. "Swore it was consensual."

Curtis shook his head.

"It's one additional detail cementing the fact that I'm better lookin' than him." Tanner pointed to the room behind Jac. "Now, get your murderous pixie self in there and mull around a bit. I'll be there as soon as we settle your boys in."

Jac matched Billy's look of concern—they didn't want to leave each other, but they didn't have a viable choice. "I'll be right here if you need me. Okay?"

Billy pouted and mustered an "Okay."

Their fingers parted, and Jac walked into a room no more pleasant or inviting than the hallway. A dingy, newspaper-plastered window, half-covered by three narrow pieces of plywood, centered the right wall. In the far right corner lay a filthy queen-sized mattress. A chair on wheels stood at the room's center; its faux leather seat and back were torn in spots, revealing the cushion underneath. Strips of disintegrating wallpaper and remnants of what may have been a piece of furniture scattered the floor. The room felt wrong, uninviting, haunted by some unseen residual anguish. *Nothing good has happened in here.*

A conversation seeped through the walls. Tanner surely knew she could hear. In a building, this small, only whispered conversation could evade a vampire's hearing.

"Just keep an eye on them for now," Tanner said. "Billy won't cause ya no trouble ... and no taking any fingers or ears off Devin unless I say it. We good?"

Jac edged closer to the hallway. She suspected Tanner meant for her to hear the part about taking Devin's fingers. She imagined Curtis nodding, playing along.

"I do have one question for you, Billy. May I ask you somethin'?"

Jac peered at the room at the end of the hallway where Tanner stood, his back turned to her.

"How old are you, Billy, nine, ten?"

"I'm eight, but I'll be nine in a few months."

"The big nine. One away from double digits. Almost a man." Tanner laughed his stupid laugh. "Tell me, Billy, where were you and your sister headed?"

Silence.

"Come on now, you can tell me. I'll keep it a secret. Just between us guys."

Silence.

"Idiot," Jac murmured. Did Tanner seriously think he could talk to Billy like he was a six-year-old and get information out of him? Billy was brave and clever. He knew better than to tell Tanner anything.

"Alright. One thing's for sure: before the night's over, someone's gonna talk. What information I can't get out of *you*, I'll get out of your sister or Devin, or fingers will start comin' off of someone."

"Don't you do it!" Devin yelled. "Don't you touch her, you son of a—"

Then came the sound of something slamming into a wall or the ground, and Devin fell silent.

Tears welled in Jac's eyes at the cries of protest. It had to stop. The brothers had to be stopped. She'd rush into the room, chopstick in her dangerous hand, and let fate take over. *No. Don't be stupid. I can figure this out.* She gritted her teeth and gripped the door frame to help prevent her from charging down the hallway and making that mistake.

"I guess we ain't gettin' answers from Devin at the moment. Put him over there ... and no contact with our sponsor just yet."

Boots shuffled on the ground, and a door closed. Still high on adrenalin, Jac stumbled from the door and fell back onto the chair, sending it rolling a few feet. She hugged her knees, buried her head into her arms, and squeezed her legs tight. He would not touch her; he wouldn't do a thing to her. A hand slid down to her side pocket, and her fingers traced the edges of the chopstick.

Tanner practically pranced into the room as if he'd reached the end of the rainbow, and she was the pot o' gold. He bowled her backpack, sending it sliding across the dirty floor. "I have to say, your little brother, he's got that look in his eyes, ya know, that look that tells ya he's done talkin' because he knows better. The look that tells me I gotta get my questions answered by his big sis."

Jac's expression hardened. "You will *not* touch me."

Tanner held out his hands. "Hold on now. There's time for civil discussion before we have to resort to anything dastardly."

"What did you do to Devin?"

"Oh, that boy's fine. He got a lump on his noggin, is all. I'm just keepin' everybody compliant."

"Promise me you won't hurt him."

"I can't very well do that, ya know, with the noggin' thing already happenin'." Tanner settled into his stance, gripping his leather belt. A sturdy-looking knife handle protruded from a sheath attached to the belt.

"You know what I mean."

Tanner moved closer and squatted in front of her. "Jacqueline, you know I can't promise that. You know the rules when it comes to people and vampires gettin' friendly. He can't walk outa here knowin' what he knows."

"I never told him. He doesn't know. You never said anything; Billy hasn't ... your brother, he hasn't."

Tanner looked at her with sincere curiosity. "You honestly weren't savin' him for dinner? What kinda vampire are you?"

"The worst kind. Like you. But I would *never* hurt Devin. I would never drink from him."

"At least not until the cravin' starts. How long has it been? Two, three weeks since your last feeding?" He tilted his head and squinted. "What if I brought Dev boy in here right now and put a cut in his neck? What then?"

"Not even then. I would kill myself first." She pointed a fierce finger at Tanner. "I'd kill *you* first."

Tanner peered into her eyes as if he were searching for her soul, to figure out how her clock ticked. He rubbed his chin, stood, walked to the window, and stared out of a small spot of glass not covered by newspaper and plywood. "Tell me, where were ya headed?"

Surely, he knew their destination. Why ask? Why play this game? She played back. "Away."

"*Yes.* I know that, but what was your destination?"

"It's not a secret." She placed her feet on the floor and leaned forward in the seat. "Didn't your sponsor tell you?"

Tanner wagged a knowing finger at her. "I figured he knew and was keepin' it a secret. West is all he told us."

Jac considered answering. Telling him they were on their way to San Diego, to Asilo Colina, to deliver her brother to the Castillo's where he could stay, live, and be safe. Maybe he didn't need to know her exact destination. She would open up to him but play it out slowly, possibly saving her and Devin from losing fingers or ears. Surely, he wouldn't hurt Billy. "California. We were halfway there when you showed up."

Tanner turned to face her. "Sunny California. Where? Los Angeles? Hollywood? Did ya wanna see the movie stars, or did your little heart desire to be one?"

She didn't answer, leaning back in the chair.

Tanner stepped closer and spun the chair, bringing Jac eye-level with his gaudy belt buckle in the image of a pit bull. His crotch in her face was more than enough to avert her gaze to the sheathed knife connected to the wide brown belt at his hip. The blade was six or seven inches, she guessed. Long enough to hurt, to kill.

"I need to know the city. It might seem trivial, but it is indeed a salient nugget of information."

Tanner stood over her in a dominant position. He'd be mistaken, believing she'd cave and simply answer because of his perceived superiority. She wavered between lying and telling the truth. A fabricated story would falter eventually and risk the immediate safety of her, Billy, and Devin. So, she caved, but on her own terms. "We were going to San Diego, to safety," she said quickly, studying him as if his reaction might open a crack in the window of his reasoning.

A knowing grin formed on Tanner's face.

"Why are you smiling? What's in San Diego that's so important?" She knew San Diego's importance for her and Billy but was curious to know what it meant for Tanner.

He sauntered around the room, gawking at her as if she had asked something stupid, like 'What's in a peanut shell?'. "Now, there are many *wonderful* reasons to visit San Diego: the weather, the beach,"—he grinned a creepy stomach-turning grin—"the ladies. I don't think it's a 'what's in San Diego' that's important, but a who."

He continued pacing, then paused as if mulling over a thought. "Safety, ya said." He paused again. "Who were ya goin' to see in San Diego?"

Jac sensed he already knew the answer. Still, she tried her luck at a lie. "No one. Billy and I were going to start a new life."

He wasn't buying it by the look on his face. "It ain't cheap to live in California. How would ya make a livin' until your *big break*? Wait tables?" He gyrated his hips in a motion she never again wanted to see. "Savin' stacks of dirty dollar bills stuffed into your naughty undergarments by the hands of dirty old men?"

Though not versed in strip club employment, on cop and lawyer TV shows, Jac had seen quick visuals of guys with money ogling girls twirling around poles. Not once did she consider future employment as a stripper, not that she had the curves for the job, anyway. "No, dumbass. I have money."

Tanner raised an eyebrow. "You have money? Where? Ain't you too young to have your own bank account?"

Her eyes betrayed her with a glance toward her backpack lying on the floor. Like a hawk, Tanner saw.

He walked over and plucked the backpack from the ground. "I had been meanin' to go through this to see what baddies or, now I learn, what goodies ya have in it." He pulled the shamrock keychain hooked to the slider and unzipped the main compartment.

Jac stood from the chair, edging closer to him, holding out her hand. "You don't have to go through it; the money's in there."

"Oh, I believe you, but I'm goin' through this backpack, *regardless*. How much cash do ya have in here?"

"Thirty ... thousand."

Tanner froze, eyes wide. "Cash?"

"Yeah, what else?"

"Point taken, and I believe ya, but ya can't expect my peepers to not want to see its green glory." He pulled her clothes from the backpack and tossed them to the floor.

The invasion of privacy poked at her patience. She moved a step closer. "Will you stop?"

Cargo pants and shirts lay strewn across the floor at his feet. Revulsion struck her as he stopped to ogle a pair of her underwear—plain white cotton. He let them slip from his fingertips. "A tad boring, if ya ask me."

"Yeah, well, they aren't for you."

He gave a quick chuckle and reached again into the backpack, pulling out the candle her father gave her. Her hands alternated between forming fists and claws as she moved closer to him. "Don't drop that," she urged, extending her hand toward him. "Please ... please give it to me."

Tanner rubbed his finger against the candle, giving it a once-over. With a shrug, he tossed it to her.

"Damn it all, unzip the inside pocket; the money's in there."

Tanner zipped open the inside pocket and whistled. He grabbed a strap of cash and thumbed it. "Now, will you look at that?"

The cash impressed Tanner, giving Jac an idea.

"You can have it. Just let us leave. Maybe let us keep some for gas and food?"

Tanner returned the cash, zipped closed the backpack, and tossed it to the floor. "Now, I won't pretend thirty thousand isn't a lot of moolah. But my brother and I, we ain't cheap. We are the professionals of professionals." He placed his left hand inches above his right, illustrating levels. "Our sponsor, the one responsible for your predicament, offered us over two hundred and fifty grand for your return. And heck, that was without Dev. We might get another ten thousand for him."

Jac hugged herself as tears formed in her eyes. She had never had much money. Thirty thousand was a lot to her. Two hundred fifty-thousand seemed impossible. The options available to save her and the boys were thinner than ever. "Won't you take it and let us go? Billy is just a kid, and Devin ...."

Tanner stepped close to her, his fingertips flitting about the knife handle. She flinched as he wiped the tears from her cheeks. "Just tell me, who were ya goin' to see in San Diego?"

She recoiled from his hand and mulled over answering his question, wholly and honestly answering his question this time. What did it matter if he knew? It couldn't hurt; maybe it could help. She sighed. "The Castillos. We're going to stay with the Castillos."

Tanner smiled and patted Jac's cheek. "I thought so."

"Why? Do you know them?"

"Know them? Jac, you just said my second favorite last name. I need ya to hang tight while I work on some business. Good God, I love variables." Tanner strutted from the room as if he had won a giant stuffed animal at a county fair. He stepped into the hallway and closed the door.

A warm feeling of possibility rushed through her. Could the Castillos be the answer? Were the Brothers and the Castillos friends? She collapsed onto the chair.

A SECRET
WRITTEN IN BLOOD

A half-hour had passed since Tanner left Jac alone in the room—her cell. Tanner's voice came from down the hall for the first few minutes. He was too far away when he spoke again for her to hear clearly.

Jac sat for a few minutes, paced for a few, and killed time reading the words scrawled and sprayed across the walls. There were crude jokes and phone numbers attached to messages offering lurid services. Attempts at amateur graffiti covered most of the walls, well below the quality sprayed across train cars that would pass her apartment. She'd spend hours watching trains from her bedroom window and would imagine who else would also see and appreciate the art as she had.

The words on the walls ranged from being entirely illegible to near-perfect print. Two words different from the rest caught her eye. They weren't there to represent someone's artistry; they weren't braggadocious nor a crude joke or reference. The two words seemed instructional: "LOOK CORNER."

Jac traced her fingers over the letters, not written with ink, but something else. She leaned close, put her nose to the wall, and breathed deeply. The scent was faint but unmistakable. "LOOK CORNER" had been written in blood—A-positive, she guessed. She stepped back from the wall, and the words tumbled in her mind as she worked out if they held any importance. Why not take them in their basic meaning?

Jac moved to the corner of the room, next to the closet covered by a collapsible door. The top and bottom corners appeared unimpressive, with remnants of spider webs and the edges of graffiti. She inspected the corner by the door. It matched the other—spider webs and small strips of old wallpaper hanging on.

She turned to where the disgusting mattress lay cornered and flush against two walls. The mattress had stains, tears in spots, and frayed edges. Some stains appeared to be blood, but she wouldn't put her nose close enough to find out. She gained an appreciation and longed for motel mattresses.

With the soles of her Chucks protecting her feet, she could safely traverse the mattress of horrors. Stepping on with both feet, she checked her balance, walked to the corner, and studied where the wall met the ceiling. Nothing stood out. The mattress partially covered the bottom corner of the wall, as did various unidentifiable stains faded from the passing of time. She had to move the queen-sized atrocity to see this "LOOK CORNER" search to its end.

Standing on the dirty floor, Jac leaned down and reached for the mattress edge. She grimaced. Her trembling hands moved toward and away from the mattress as if they were sentient and had to be convinced to touch the disgust. Maybe "LOOK CORNER" meant nothing, and she had wasted her time. She didn't really need to move the mattress. "LOOK CORNER" was merely the prelude to a joke someone didn't finish … in blood.

Failing to talk herself out of performing the task, Jac gritted her teeth, grabbed the cleanest part of the fabric she could find, and pulled. Years of use weighted the mattress, but it slid easily away from the wall in her firm grip. She made barely a noise, but she stopped to listen for approaching footsteps. A faint mumbling seeped through the walls. *Hold on, Billy. I'll figure some way out of this.*

Refocused on the task, she wiped the imagined disgust from her hands onto her pant legs, stepped around the mattress, and squatted for a closer look at the corner. Nothing more than a curled piece of old wallpaper clung to the wall.

She gave a cursory look at the corner to her left; not even spider webs hung. She sighed. *What did you want found in the corner?* Her fingers fiddled with the wallpaper strip as she considered how foolish she had been. What did she expect to discover, anyway? She had wasted time that could have been used to devise a plan to escape.

With a slight push from her finger, the wallpaper strip lost its battle to stay connected to the wall and fell to the ground. Where the wallpaper strip had been were small letters just above the warped baseboard, written in the same style and with the same blood ink. It read "CLOSET CEILING."

A wave of nervous excitement struck; she swiveled toward the closet. What was the message's importance? Was a weapon hidden in the ceiling? Something that *could* help her and Billy? A place to hide or a way to escape?

Jac maneuvered around the mattress and walked to the closet. A tug at the collapsible door revealed it was off track. "This will not be quiet," she murmured. With the doorknob firmly in her right hand and the left edge in her left, she pulled. A *creak* accompanied the first pull. She stopped and listened, only hearing her heart thump against her ribs.

Measuring the space between the closet edge and the door with her shoulder, she attempted to slip inside—not quite. She wiped her brow and re-gripped, gently pulling the door and moving it a few inches, resulting in a louder cracking noise. She paused, breath held, ears and eyes alert. There were no audible words or rushed footsteps.

Her shoulder easily slipped in on the second attempt, followed by the rest of her slender frame. Darkness enveloped her, save the light from the room shining through the open space and splayed against the closet's back wall. Her eyes quickly adjusted to the dark, bringing the rest of the narrow closet into view. The freaking empty closet. The message was meaningless; nothing here would help, nothing offering a way out.

Wait, it read "closet ceiling."

Darkness loomed above the clothing rod and shelf. She shimmied to the right. Her back scraped against the closet door, when her foot met something firm, a footstool she hadn't seen.

Nice. This will help.

She pulled the footstool away from the wall with the toe of her shoe and stepped on, giving her nearly two extra feet in height, now eye-level with the shelf. Dust covered the barren shelf from end to end, but again, the message read "closet ceiling."

Jac ran her fingertips across the rough popcorn ceiling, sending tiny particles like snow onto her face and head. She gave a push—no give. Her fingers moved along the ceiling inches at a time; she pushed again—no give. She ran her hand in every direction, pushing every few inches until, finally, a cut-out ceiling piece gave.

Her heart skipped; her labored breath was the only sound as she listened for any sign of Tanner's return. Confident he hadn't heard and wasn't returning to snatch her from the closet, she pushed up and away, revealing a black square of darkness where the ceiling piece had been. Mere attic dusk met the tips of her fingers, barely breaching the approximately two feet by two feet opening.

Jac stepped from the stool, positioned it directly under the hole, stepped back atop it, and rose to the tips of her toes. The opening's edge met her wrist as her fingers desperately felt for anything. *There has to be something up here. Why else would someone have taken the time to write the message, in blood, of all things?*

At the last edge, her fingers met something substantial. The object slid further away at each attempted grasp until only her fingertips brushed against whatever it was.

The shelf, of course.

Jac rubbed and blinked away a burning sweat that dripped into her eyes. She shook out her hands. "Okay. I can do this."

She grabbed the shelf with her left hand, pulled herself up with a jump, and clawed at whatever was there. The brief fight against gravity and a fortunately timed grab pulled the object to the edge of the hole. She landed atop the stool with enough of a thump to warrant a pause and listen—no incoming footsteps sounded.

On the next reach, she pulled the object from its hiding place. She couldn't precisely identify what she held in the dark. Its surface was smooth and cold, like metal, and shaped like a shoebox.

She shimmied to the closet door opening and slipped back into the room. Now in view, she held a green metal box, maybe a square foot in width and four inches in depth. A thin metal handle was attached to the box top for carrying, and a latch secured the lid. Time had aged the box; its paint peeling from or missing from sections; rust lived at the corners and the edges.

Anticipation swelled from her abdomen and gushed to the end of each limb as she flipped the latch. The hinged lid creaked as her right hand moved it up and away; that same right hand rushed to cover her gaping mouth below her shocked eyes.

"What in *Hell*?"

The box wasn't concealing a gun or any weapon to help her fight the Dog Brothers, nor did it hold anything that would enhance their chance for freedom. It contained dozens of photos. Photos that clearly were meant to remain secret. She flipped through the images that resembled mug shots of women, children—girls and boys—her age, and many much younger. First names, last initials, dates, and blood types were written in black ink on the white strip beneath each photo.

The photos had a disturbing mood: hurt, pain, and fear. Some images buckled her legs and caused her to choke back her lunch. "What happened to you? What did they do to you?" Jac muttered. Women, their faces bruised and cut, had terror in their eyes. Many sat on a dirty mattress, the same mattress in the room where she stood. Audible voices and footsteps broke her from disturbing thoughts.

"Oh, crap." Jac shut and latched the lid. "Where do I put you?" She scanned the room with only a mattress and chair for hiding places. Returning it to the ceiling would take too long.

My backpack.

Tanner had removed and carelessly strewn most of her clothes about the floor, leaving ample room to slide the box into the backpack. She pulled the backpack flap over the box edges for complete concealment and gently placed it on the floor precisely as Tanner had left it.

As the footsteps neared, Jac scanned the room for anything out of place. The chair was acceptable wherever. She pushed the mattress back against the wall. And the closet door—*The closet door!*

Before she could move to close the closet door, the room door opened, and Tanner strutted in, wearing a Texas-sized grin. "It's your lucky day."

But it wasn't Jac's lucky day. Her concern with the open closet turned to the camera in Tanner's hands.

FAILED VISION

The click, the flash, the buzz as the film ejected, and the delayed gratification from waiting for the image to slowly emerge from some seemingly mysterious unknown realm. Jac had never used an instant camera, their relevance being before her time. She had often seen them used on TV, usually in old '80s movies. The cameras on TV, misshapen black boxes, resembled the one Tanner held. It sickened her to think the same camera had taken the photos hiding in her backpack.

"I'll tell ya. Our sponsor wasn't happy with me askin' for an update to our financial agreement, but after hearin' of the Castillos havin' an interest in you and tellin' him about your boy Devin, well, he suddenly became agreeable." Tanner stepped closer to her. "Truth be told, we would have honored the initial agreement. We always do. But at my bein' suggestive, he threw in more money. Now, gettin' back to it bein' your lucky day, he asked for Devin as well."

Jac sneered. "How is that lucky?"

"Well, darlin', it means we won't be killin' Devin. You've got more time to see the light in his pretty eyes and long for the blood pumping through his veins."

"So, you talked to the Castillos? Did they—"

"The Castillo name was mainly a bargaining tool."

"But you said you told your sponsor that the Castillos were interested in us."

He pursed his lips. "It was more or less an insinuation."

"Screw insinuation. Call the Castillos. Maybe … maybe they would offer more for us."

Jac had no reason to believe the Castillos would pay for their release. She knew nothing of them aside from occasional mentions of the last name during her parents' discussions and then on the note her mother left her. But the Castillos must know that she and Billy were on their way to their home. They should have some interest in their safe arrival.

"Like I said, we honor our initial agreement. There's nothing the Castillos could offer to change where you're headed."

Jac lost interest in talking to Tanner, but she feared what would happen if the conversation stopped, what would come if he learned she had found his secret. Her eyes darted from the open closet and back to him. *Talk to him. Distract him.* "When do we leave?"

"Smile," Tanner said. The camera flashed.

She raised a hand and looked away as spots and stars filled her vision, then slowly faded. She turned and glared at Tanner as he pulled the fully ejected photo from the camera and gave it a few shakes. He examined it and returned to shaking it.

"Ya know, they say shakin' 'em doesn't help, but ... it just seems like the right thing to do."

She stepped back, and her hands found their place, clawing her arms.

"Now, that's a pretty picture." He held up the photo for her to see. There she was, memorialized and destined to be another image in his box of horrors.

"When are we leaving?" she asked again, her voice cracking.

Tanner's hands fell to his sides as he walked toward her, one hand autonomously shaking the photo, the other holding the camera. "Oh, we got time, lots of it. Tonight is like a celebration. With the amount of money Edgar offered, my brother and I are goin' on a long-due vacation somewhere *scandalous*."

Jac moved back from him, step by step, stopping when her heels met the mattress. She wanted to keep him talking and distracted. He said he wouldn't touch her, that he saw her as just a kid, and wouldn't force himself on anyone. But those photos, those disgusting photos. What had he done to those women? Was she next?

"Let me see Billy and Devin before we leave. I want to be sure they're okay."

"You'll see them soon enough. And don't worry your heart none. Billy is safe and sound. Devin, though, he's a little banged up."

Her hands clenched. "What did you do to him?"

FLASH

She turned away, again blinded. The camera buzzed, and Tanner chuckled.

"I don't 'spect this one will be as pretty as the first, but damn girl, that look you give when you're furious."

"I'll pay for Devin; let me be your sponsor for him."

Tanner scrutinized her as if she were a child going on about having some imagined superpower. "You?"

"Yes, me."

"A sponsor?"

"You saw the cash ... thirty thousand dollars. You take it, and Devin goes free." Jac winced at mentioning the cash.

Tanner turned to look at the backpack. "Now, if you think that money in your—" He paused. His gaze moved from the backpack to the closet. The damn open closet.

A heaviness poured through Jac like wet cement, testing the stability of her legs. He would know she had been in the closet, breaking an unspoken ground rule; he would see that she had found his secret. Nothing that well-hidden was for anyone else's eyes. He shuffled to the closet and gripped the sliding door.

"Jacqueline," he said accusatorially. "What were you up to while I was gone?"

The room's door stood open, a clear path to escape. But to where? And she couldn't leave Billy behind. No. She had to stay, to make a stand right here and now. She fiddled with her pants pocket, pulled the chopstick free, and slid it up her shirt sleeve.

Tanner tossed the photos of her to the ground. With a grunt, he pulled the closet door from its rails, dropped it like a carcass, and peered at the closet ceiling. "You sneaky pixie brat." He turned and stomped toward her, wearing an incensed expression she hadn't before seen.

Jac pressed the chopstick against her neck and held her empty hand in the stop position. "Don't come any closer."

Tanner's eyes darted from the chopstick at her neck to her intent-filled eyes and complied with her order. "Where are they? Where are my photos?"

"I'll tell you, but you have to accept me as your sponsor for Devin, and you can't hurt me,"—she pressed the chopstick firmly against her jugular—"or I'll do it."

"Girl, I'm royally pissed off with you right now, but damn if you ain't a spitfire."

"Deal?" She extended a shaky hand into the space between them.

Tanner only glanced at her hand. Instead of a deal-making shake, he stood square and kept his hands at his sides. The fingers of his empty hand hovered above the sheathed knife. "Now, I told ya I wouldn't touch ya, and I intended that to mean I wouldn't hurt ya neither, but ya best answer. Where are my photos?"

Jac pulled back her unmet hand and let the question linger between them for a few heartbeats. First, she had her own questions. "What happened to them?"

"That's what I'm askin' you, darlin'."

"No, not your sick photos: the kids, the girls, and the ..."— she fought back tears—"the women."

Tanner shrugged. "Do ya mean while in the company of yours truly, or after?"

Jac glowered at him with hard eyes. Her nostrils flared. "After, you sick jerk."

"That's not a need-to-know for you." He took a couple of steps forward, stopping again when she pressed the chopstick more firmly against her neck.

"If you don't answer my questions, I *will* shove this into my neck, and you'll lose your contract ... and I had damn sure better believe your answers."

Tanner's jaw clenched; the camera groaned from his tightening grip. "I sold them, all of them."

"To who?"

He sighed. "Whoever paid us to get them, sometimes at auction, to the highest bidder."

Jac pressed the chopstick with increased pressure, breaking the skin. A warm drop of blood ran down her neck. "To who?" she repeated, her voice tremulous.

Tanner held a palm toward her and spoke slowly, "Covens, all across the States, sometimes individual buyers."

"What for?"

"For the money, of course."

"No. Are you stupid? Why did they want them, the kids, the women?"

"For whatever need they had: manual labor, companionship, blood." Tanner shrugged. He glanced at the chopstick.

She pulled the blood-tipped chopstick from her neck and pointed it at him with a shaky hand. "That's disgusting ... that's cruel!" Tears streamed down her cheeks.

Tanner took a casual step forward. "People are a commodity. For vamps, the young ones are top dollar."

Jac countered his step forward, maintaining the distance between them. She brushed against the half-boarded window—farther from the mattress and closer to the door.

"Lately, ya know who's been our best buyer?"

She shook her head.

"The same sponsor who paid us for you and your brother. That turned-vamp jackass who took over in Philadelphia." He took a step. "Edgar."

Edgar, of course. She returned the chopstick to her neck in response to Tanner's step. "Stop. Do *not* come any closer."

"Jac, in my line of business, if someone's been acquired for a price—"

"Abducted."

Tanner sighed and slowly shook his head. "If someone's been *acquired,* I tend to know about it. And Edgar, he's been callin' on me and Curtis quite a bit the last few months. I reckon he may be up to somethin', somethin' the other covens might not like if they got word, but I know it's in my best interest to pay it no mind. I won't say anything on account of...." Tanner lowered his gaze and rubbed his chin. He looked back at her, waving a knowing finger. "Hold up now."

Jac stood rigid with her back against the window and the chopstick pressed against her neck. Tanner had said their contact with Edgar increased lately. Was Edgar's business with the Dog Brothers related to her dad's murder? Did he uncover Edgar's plans? Is that why her mom disappeared and left her and Billy alone? Did she know too?

"That's why he paid big money for a teenage vamp from Philadelphia and her little brother. Ya know what I reckon?

Edgar's up to somethin' naughty, and he thinks you know, but you don't. You don't know nothin' about nothin'."

"I know I'm going to kill him."

Tanner grinned. "Jac, under different circumstances, I bet you would. I'd put money on it." He raised a finger, brought his left hand to his nose, and turned away as if to sneeze. He whipped back around, unleashing the camera from his obscured right hand, sending it hurtling toward her. The camera grazed Jac's head and smashed into a space between the boards covering the window, sending shards and fragments of glass onto the floor at her feet.

Tanner lunged, slamming his weight into her and sending her onto the boards and what remained of the glass window. Grabbing her shoulders, he slammed her upon the mattress, breaking her grip on the chopstick and sending it skittering across the floor.

Jac screamed as Tanner pressed the full weight of his body on top of her. "Get off me!"

He grabbed and pinned her arms, only for Jac to break free each time. "I didn't ... want ... to fight with you."

Jac pressed against his chest with one free hand, creating space between his body and her compressed lungs. She gasped. Billy and Devin yelled for her. They would hear the struggle; they would hear her screams. *No, Billy. Don't listen ... don't listen.*

Tanner's hand wrapped around her neck, pushing himself into a straddle across her waist. She fought for breath as his full weight fell upon her abdomen. With what little nails Jac had, she drew blood, frantically clawing at the arm attached to the hand choking her. With wild imprecision, she struck at his chest and face. Her eyes widened as Tanner cocked his arm, and all went dark when his fist struck the side of her head.

Jac awoke to a ringing in her ears and a dull pain. Shapes and shadows undulated around her like demons. A blurred and dark form stood next to her, speaking muffled words. She shook her head, clearing the image. To her right, an object fell upon boots.

Rope. He's … going to tie me up.

She croaked a groggy "no" and crawled away. A hand firmly gripped the back of her pants, pulling her toward the mattress center. She shelved a scream, not wanting Billy to hear. She would save him from anything, including having to listen to her pain and anguish. But the moment to act had come. The opportunity to fight and escape would be lost if Tanner immobilized her with the rope. She could no longer worry about protecting Billy from hearing a fight and possibly her end.

Lying on her back, once again, Tanner straddled her waist. He held a thin white rope and wore a fanged 'I told you so' smile. "If ya stop fightin', this will hurt a lot less."

Jac looked at him through blurry eyes; her fingers flexed, and she reached for the chopstick she had forgotten was no longer there. "What are you going to do to me?"

Tanner frowned and dropped his chin. "Jac, I'm sure I'm not your favorite person, and you may find it hard to believe, but I told ya … I don't lie. I am not performin' whatever inappropriate act you think I am. You're leavin' here as complete as when you entered. But with a few new scratches and bruises."

Jac closed her eyes, relented, and sighed heavily. "Fine. Okay. I give up."

"Yeah?" Tanner chuckled. "I hafta say I'm surprised. You're makin' an excellent choice."

She met his stare. "I won't fight you anymore."

With a relieved grin, Tanner removed his Stetson, ran his arm across his sweaty forehead, and replaced the hat. He slid from atop her and grabbed the waist of her pants. "I'm sorry it came to this, tying ya down. Now, I'm not all concerned with ya hurtin' me, but we can't have ya takin' yourself out of this game and costin' my brother and—"

A kick from Jac to the side of Tanner's head cut short his speech. With a second kick to the underside of his chin, Tanner flew off the mattress and onto the tile with a thud. The rope fell from his hands like a dead snake, and his Stetson slid across the floor.

Jac scrambled to her hands and knees and scurried across the mattress. Her scream marked her short-lived escape as Tanner reached her the moment her hands touched the glass-covered floor.

Tanner grabbed the waist of her pants, yanking her back to the middle of the mattress. "Now, I'm gonna make this hurt."

Jac gripped the mattress edge with all the strength she could manage, lifting it from the floor with each of Tanner's pulls. Then it caught her eye. The glass from the window—small and large shards—was within her reach. In between pulls, she reached for the glass, for a piece that would cut, for a piece that could save her.

Her pant button popped off, and the zipper gave way, exposing her backside and sending Tanner off balance. She released the mattress; her hands desperately fumbled amongst the shards, cutting and slicing her skin as she gripped the pieces, feeling for something substantial.

"Get back here!" Tanner grabbed her waist, pulled her back to the middle of the mattress, and flipped her over, ending her moment of freedom. His furious eyes burned down at her, and his bloody fangs had fully descended as if he were a hungry vampire preparing to feed.

"Screw you!" Jac's left fist shot up toward him, falling short of the target as he caught it with his left hand, inches from his face.

"Now it's come to throwin' fists?" He growled, raring back with his free hand.

Jac's right hand shot toward Tanner's face. A spray of blood rained over her. Tanner only managed a look of surprise as the glass shard pierced his left eye, stopping when the shard's wide end met his eye socket. His shocked, delayed scream shook the walls.

Dog One fell from her and onto the mattress, his legs kicking wildly, pushing him back as he screamed. He stopped when his back contacted the wall. Gently, he touched the shard, feeling for the extent of the damage.

A momentous rush of adrenalin coursed through Jac. She slid backward across the mattress—her right hand leaving behind bloody prints—while keeping a careful eye on Tanner. Her barely pant-covered bottom slid off the mattress and smacked the floor.

"You bitch, you stupid bitch," Tanner said, sobbing. "I'm gonna kill ya now, right now. Screw the bounty."

"Curtis," she muttered.

Jac sprang to her feet, wavering from the effects of the concussive blow. She pulled up and zipped her button-less pants. A blood-letting clean cut ran an inch across her palm and below the first knuckle of her four fingers from the shard. A brief acknowledgment of the pain was all that time allowed. Scanning the room for the chopstick, she remembered the knife attached to Tanner's belt.

She rushed to the agonized Tanner and swiftly kicked his gut with unplanned brutality, collapsing him like a deck chair. As he gasped for breath, she went straight for the sheath, unbuttoned it, and pulled the long, polished, serrated knife free with her undamaged hand. Tanner didn't notice she had removed the knife from its home.

Footsteps came loud and fast.

"My brother ... he's gonna ruin your world. We're gonna kill Billy and your boyfriend and make you watch," Tanner agonized. He wore a mask of blood, the shard sticking out of his eye socket like a knife in a ripened apple.

"That will not happen."

Jac rushed to the door and pressed her back against the wall. Her heart raced like that of a victorious sprinter. She gripped the knife, cuts or no cuts, in her bloody right hand.

The door flew off its hinges with a loud bang and slid to the mattress. Jac firmed her grip on the blood-soaked knife handle. Tanner said something she only half-heard outside of focusing on dealing with Curtis. What he said next came loud and clear: "Kill her!"

Jac stood firm, her hand clamped around the knife handle. With his eyes bloodied over, Tanner couldn't see her; he couldn't warn his brother. Curtis rushed toward Tanner, only to stop a few steps into the room when he released a gasp, followed by a gurgled wheeze. He regarded the knife hilt protruding from his chest, his shirt around it turning a bright red.

She stood frozen, fully expecting a blow from one of Curtis's massive arms, but they hung at his sides like wavering pendulums. He met her stare, stunned, his jaw slack. Something lived in his eyes, a sadness, almost an empathy for her.

"Brother?" Tanner said, close to a cry.

Jac's resolve kicked back in at hearing Tanner's voice. She slid the knife out of Curtis's chest, squeezed her eyes shut, and screamed as she pierced his chest a half-dozen times in rapid repetition. The feeling returned of skin separating at cut lines on her hand and fingers, along with a fresh flow of blood. Curtis held her shoulder as he fell to his knees, his grip dropping away as he landed face down with a resounding thud. He made a final gurgling sound and went quiet.

"Brother!" Tanner yelled again. "Curty!"

Jac had stabbed no one in her life, but in a matter of days, she stabbed the man on the bus, Tanner's eye—under hazy duress—and now Curtis. She dropped the blood-covered knife and clutched her stomach as a wave of nausea overcame her. "Oh, my God. Oh, my God. I never want to do that again." Pulling her eyes from Curtis's apparent corpse, she focused on finding her chopstick and gathering her things.

With her backpack re-stuffed, she dumped the photos of the women and children from the metal box into the remaining backpack space. She slid the chopstick back into her pant pocket and surveyed Tanner and Curtis; the once formidable, ageless vampires were dead or dying.

"Jac," Tanner called when she turned to leave.

Tentatively, she turned to face him one last time.

"Did you kill my brother?"

She didn't answer.

"Did you kill my brother?" he repeated, his voice shaky.

Jac stared at him for what felt like too long. Feelings of empathy lingered in the recesses of her mind. But how could she feel sorry for Tanner after what he did to her and would have done to Billy and Devin? And the women and children. He was the worst kind of monster.

She snatched the knife from the floor, squeezed the handle, and took a deep breath as she considered ending Tanner. It would be easy to slide the knife into his heart—more than enough to kill him, a vampire.

She wouldn't.

She didn't decide to spare him out of pity. No. She wanted him to live the rest of his stupid life alone and with only one eye.

"I stabbed him. A lot. He's dead."

Tanner wailed.

"I'll leave your phone, wherever it is, so you can call for help. If you can find it."

"I can't see, Jac. Please, I can't see."

"Then you better clean off your good eye."

"You little pixie—"

"Listen to me, Tanner. If you ever come after my brother, me, or Devin, I will take your other eye." Jac walked away and paused at the doorway. "Checkmate. Asshole."

Jac sprinted down the hallway to the room where she expected to find the boys. She tested the lock. "Billy, step back from the door. I'm coming in." Her foot ferociously met the door. Its hinges held as it swung inward and slammed into the inner wall. Devin lay sprawled on the floor, blood dripping from his scalp. Already wearing his backpack, Billy sat beside Devin as if he had expected her. Billy, red-eyed, half smiled. His eyes darted between her face and the bloody knife in her hand. His mouth straightened. He ran to her and hugged her waist. "What happened to your face? Are you okay?"

Jac dropped her backpack and ran her fingertips across her cheek. The tips of her fingers brought with them a layer of blood. Tanner's blood. "I'm fine, mostly," she lied. She just suffered through the most traumatic event of her messed up life but had to stay strong for Billy. "Let's get you outta here. How's Devin?"

"Curtis choked him again, and he hasn't woken up all the way."

"Drag him." Jac grabbed her backpack and led the way. Billy held Devin by his left wrist and pulled him along the dirty floor like a toddler with his oversized stuffed animal.

Jac stopped at the room where she had left the Dog Brothers. Curtis lay in a growing pool of blood; beyond him, the fractured door and the mattress. Only a blood stain remained where Tanner had sat. "Oh, the Hell." Whatever adrenaline remained kicked in. "We have to hurry." With her head on a swivel and ears focused, she led them down the hall and out to the pine bark driveway in the late afternoon sun.

"Get Devin in the car. I'll be there in a minute."

"Got it." With apparent ease, Billy continued to pull Devin, his legs trailing behind him.

Jac ran to the brothers' truck with her backpack slung over her shoulder and the knife in hand. She transferred the knife to her left hand, the one not noticeably emanating pain and dripping blood. Unsure of how to hold the knife for stabbing a tire, she tested grips, held it like a hand-shake, and thrust the knife into the sidewall. With a pop and hiss, the blade easily plunged into the front driver-side tire as if stabbing gelatin. The truck creaked as it tilted.

With the front passenger tire and the rear passenger tire also bleeding air, she reached the rear driver-side when Billy shouted from the car. "Jac, let's go!"

Maybe three tires were enough, but Jac wanted to be sure. One more tire and she will have done all she could to disable the truck. She signaled 'one more' to Billy. Her hand shot forward, but the tire moved farther away, and her back slammed onto the ground. Pain shot across her scalp, and the knife fell from her grip. Frantically, she reached for the knife, which moved out of her grasp as she slid across the ground. Squinting through the sun's glare, a hand had her by the hair, pulling her toward the building. Tanner had hobbled his way out of the house. He had freed the shard from his eye socket, leaving behind a bloody, gaping wound where an eye used to be.

"You ain't goin' nowhere, not anymore," Tanner said, his voice gruff.

"Let go of me!" Jac grappled with Tanner's hands. Her legs kicked, her feet planted into the bark, searching for purchase.

Jac's back scraped against the concrete walkway to the front door when a chunk of her hair pulled free, and Tanner's grip failed. She stumbled to her hands and knees, only to feel Tanner's hold upon her again, raising her off the ground. His arm snaked under her chin, applying immediate and immense pressure to her neck. Jac yanked with all her strength against Tanner's vice grip. In seconds, her consciousness faded. In the blur of the last moment, before it turned black, someone ran toward her.

* * *

It could have been a minute or an hour for all Jac knew when her vision returned. *Where am I?* Stifling heat engulfed her. A circular object in front of her morphed into a steering wheel. Her head flopped from side to side. Someone said something, in almost a cry.

"Jac, wake up! We have to go!" Billy screamed and shook her.

She was in a car, Devin's car. Billy sat in the passenger seat to her right, and Devin lay in the back, barely moving.

Tanner! Where's Tanner? She looked through the dust-covered windshield. Tanner, barely recognizable from the blood on his face, sat slumped against the building. He pulled at his knife sticking from the side of his knee like a fleshy sheath. His face morphed into something out of a demonic exorcism with each pull.

"We have to go. Now." Jac had a cursory understanding of a car's mechanics; it would have to do. She reached for the ignition. "The Hell." Her hands trembled. "Where's the key?"

"I don't know," Billy cried.

"Look ... look in the glove box. Look under the seats."

Tanner had removed the knife from his knee and attempted to stand.

"Wait a second." Billy gripped his hair. "Curtis has the key in his pocket."

"Oh, my God." Not an ounce of Jac wanted to return to where Curtis lay dead at her hands. Not to mention, Tanner, though disabled, waited in a slump by the front door. But they needed the key to leave; only she could get it. "Billy. Wait here. I'll get the key."

A hand fell upon her shoulder. "No, a spare," Devin said, his voice weak, "under the wheel well, front left ... in a small box."

Jac shot out of the car and fell to her knees at the tire. She tentatively reached into the wheel well, not knowing precisely the feel of a key-box versus any other object related to the car. Her hands moved quickly and purposefully, but she failed to locate the key box.

"Jac!" Billy stood in his seat and pointed toward the building. Tanner had managed to stand and hobbled toward her, taking a step on his good leg and, with a skip, putting only a minimal amount of pressure on the bad. He gripped the knife, now a mix of bloods, in his right hand.

Immediately, Jac regretted sparing Tanner; she cursed herself for wanting him to suffer. If it came down to it, could she fight him off again? Now that he had the knife? She didn't want to find out. "Devin, I can't find it!"

"Feel underneath at about three o'clock."

Jac stuck her hand into the wheel well where the short hand would be at three. "Where are you, damn it? Come on!" Her fingers searched greedily, gripped, and pulled the magnetized box free. The tiny box's lid opened with a push, and she pulled out the key like a found treasure. "I got it!" She slipped into the driver's seat and slammed closed the door. The key stabbed at the ignition in her shaky hand. "Come on! Come on! Please. Get the—" The key slid in and turned, bringing the car to life.

Billy grabbed her arm when she gripped the gearshift. "You don't know how to drive."

She glanced at Devin sitting in a slump and swaying with his hand upon his head. "No choice."

Jac slammed the car into gear and pressed the gas pedal to the floor. In horror, the car hurtled forward, striking Tanner where he stood, sending him flying to the ground and rolling boots over head. He came to a stop in a broken clump. Billy screamed and pressed his hands against the dashboard as Jac slammed the brakes. The car slid over pine bark and settled to a stop.

Billy looked at her with wide eyes, his chest heaving. "Holy cow, Jac."

"Put on your seat belts," Jac ordered as her foot released the brake and gently pressed the gas pedal, easing the car forward.

Billy fell into his seat and secured the seatbelt around his waist after several failed attempts to marry the tongue and the buckle.

Jac turned the wheel to the right, facing the car toward the road, and pressed the gas pedal more firmly. In the rearview, the truck stood immobilized with three flat tires, and Tanner lay crumpled on the ground, a broken version of himself. With Tanner down and Curtis likely dead, no one could come after them. They were safe, for now.

WHOSE BLOOD IS THAT?

The tires fought for traction as the car swerved along the dirt and gravel road. A cloud of trailing dust obscured the view of imaginary pursuers.

No one is following us; there's no way. The mantra did little to calm Jac's nerves. Her sweaty-palmed hands—one with a mix of sweat and sticky blood—shook as she drove, struggling to keep the car on the country road.

Ahead, the main road—blacktop—came into view. The prospect of driving on a paved road did little to calm Jac; it meant driving around other people. *I can't do this. I have to stop.* She slammed the brakes, engulfing the car in a dust cloud and sending Devin from the back seat to the floor with a thud.

"Oh, crap. Devin, are you okay?" Jac asked.

"Yeah," Devin replied, with a weakness still in his voice.

Billy gave her an "okay" and a thumbs up.

With the dust settled, Jac parked the car, lowered the window, and breathed fresh air.

Devin righted himself and leaned back. "You okay?"

"Yes ... no. No, I don't know." Jac examined herself, cataloging the damage. Blood coated her hands, shirt, pants, and, with a confirming look in the rear-view mirror, her face. She met Devin's eyes. He looked *there*, but not quite all there.

"You're bleeding," Devin said—half statement, half question.

"No, at least I don't think so." She focused on the horror of blood covering her, barely giving a second thought to her sliced hand and fingers. Was she bleeding from somewhere else? A cut or gash she wasn't yet aware of?

"Then, whose blood is that?"

Billy gave her a knowing look. He must have heard what happened in the house. Death, again, surrounded Billy.

"It's their blood ... the brothers'." Jac pulled down the sunshade, leaving bloody prints behind, getting a closer look at her cheek that took Tanner's punch. She was growing accustomed to not looking her best, but her reflection revealed something worse than any pimple break-out, or dark circled morning-eyes. Tanner's blood—not yet dry—streaked across her face like Viking war paint, from left hairline to right ear. Her left cheek had begun to swell and color. Jac was the final-girl in a horror movie who, only moments before, escaped the masked, ax-carrying madman's clutches.

I look horrible. I'm disgusting. "Billy, stay in the car." Jac slammed closed the visor, turned off the car, and climbed out before Billy could argue.

She staggered away, cradled her face in her hands, and focused on her breath—the only thing she could control. *Breathe, just breathe. Billy is okay. Devin is okay. I am okay. Just. Breathe.*

A hand grabbed Jac's shoulder and turned her around. Her hands dropped from her face, revealing the full extent of the damage. Devin's horrified reaction told her all she needed to know. He raised his hand to touch her cheek but pulled back as if he thought it would do more harm than good.

"So, is it?" Devin asked.

"Is it what?" She had forgotten the question. Her head was on, mostly straight, but her brain was scrambled eggs a minute too long in the pan.

"Is that your blood?"

"No, it's not. Well, most of it isn't. I cut my hand." The cuts on her hand and fingers no longer bled, with hemostasis complete. Vampires healed quicker than humans, but not instantaneously. If she were careful not to reopen the cuts, they wouldn't be visible to the human eye in a week.

"My God. What happened in there?" Devin's eyes scanned her, stopping for a second look at her pants. "Your pants, your button's gone." His face morphed into a combination of confusion and horror like he'd been given horrible news.

Jac's pants had slightly slipped down her waist, revealing the top of her underwear. She pulled them up, gave the zipper a firm yank, and gripped the pants where the button had been, and only a single dangling black thread remained.

"Yeah, a lot happened. Tanner, he … yanked them, and the button popped off." Images flashed through her mind of what happened in the room and on the mattress. The shard of glass piercing Tanner's eye, slicing perfect lines in her hand and fingers. The look on Curtis's face with the knife blade deep in his chest. She trembled.

"Did he—" Devin's hands moved between covering his mouth and forming fists, as if forgetting where they belonged. "He didn't … please tell me he didn't—"

Jac saved him from saying the words and her from hearing them. "No, he didn't. He tried to tie me down, and we fought. I couldn't let him tie me. I had to get us out of there."

Devin released a long breath, ran a hand through his hair, and did a double-take at a streak of blood across his palm. He patted at spots on his head, searching for the area of damage.

Jac tensed. A metal aroma hitched her breath. She covered her mouth and stepped back, squinting away the sunlight from her dilating eyes. If she hadn't already known, Devin's blood type was obvious, with it displayed in front of her in horribly glorious red streaks. She slid her tongue across her top teeth and back, hoping for a smooth line. *Please, please, please, no.*

"Are you okay?" Devin asked.

Jac's heart thumped like a drumline. She shook her head and hands, attempting to exorcize the desire for Devin's blood. Her tongue, back and forth, back and forth. Smooth. Back and forth—smooth, bump, smooth, bump. *Oh crap. Oh crap.* She turned at footsteps—Billy had disobeyed her order to stay in the car. She opened her mouth to scold him but decided against it. She desperately needed him … *now.*

Billy slid his hand into hers. She blinked. Tongue back and forth. Smooth, bump, smooth, bump. *Oh my God, Devin. I don't want to hurt you.* She took slow, deep breaths. *Calm down. Calm the hell down.*

"It's okay," Billy whispered. "You'll be okay."

Jac dropped to a knee.

"Are you alright, Jac?" Devin moved closer.

Billy gave him a thumbs up. "Just a second. She's just ... upset."

"Billy," Jac said in a quivering whisper, "I don't want to hurt him."

"You won't." He placed his hand on her shoulder. "Just focus on your breaths. Count them with me."

Jac nodded. "Okay." A shaky breath filled her lungs and forcefully blew past her lips. "One." Another breath. "Two." Another. "Three." Jac's tension eased, and her thumping heart slowed. "Four." The brightness dimmed. Again, with her tongue—smooth. She squeezed Billy's hand. "Thank you." In control of the savage vampire inside her, she focused on Billy. "Are you okay?"

"I'm okay, I guess," Billy replied. "Are you?"

"I'm better. Thanks." She pushed the hair from Billy's eyes and scanned his body. "Your hand. Is it cut?"

Billy scrutinized his bloody hand, turning it over and back again. "No, it's Tanner's. When I stabbed him in the knee."

She recalled the image of someone running toward her as she passed out from Tanner's choke. Her sweet, brave brother had come to her rescue. "That was you? You did that?"

He grinned. "I stabbed his leg, and he cried like a baby."

Jac resisted a hug, not wanting to cover Billy in the Dog Brothers' blood, and instead opted to rest her forehead—the cleanest part of her face—against his. "You saved me, Billy; you saved us."

"And Curtis never touched me, but he beat up Devin."

"Yeah, I heard it happening." She looked up at Devin. A tinge of guilt gnawed at her, bringing her to her feet. She had neglected to ask what had happened and how he felt. "Devin, are you okay?"

Devin touched his head, where the blood began. "Yeah, well, I'm a little banged up … and I have a major headache." He looked at Jac with pained curiosity. "Who the heck were those guys? What did they want?"

"I've never seen them before. Tanner told me he was paid to take Billy and me back to Philadelphia." Jac wanted to tell Devin everything; he deserved to know at this point, but it wasn't safe for either of them if he knew the whole truth. He had nearly died knowing nothing.

Devin shrugged. "That's it?"

She averted her eyes. "That's … all I know."

He shook his head, pumping his palms at his sides as if trying to calm himself. "I said I would take you to San Diego, but I didn't agree to being chased, beaten up, and nearly killed." He motioned to the Pizza Mobile. "There's blood in my car … most of it isn't mine."

"I know and—"

"This was supposed to be a drive to San Diego," Devin continued, his voice rising.

Devin was right, and guilt continued to rise within Jac. Asking Devin for a ride was a horrible idea, but it was their only option. How utterly stupid she was getting him involved. It was naïve to assume he would be safe. Being honest with herself, he was in danger from the beginning, from her alone, being her blood match.

"I know." She paused. "You don't have to take us any farther. I'll still pay you what we agreed, and you can drop us off in Shamrock. I'll get us there another way."

Devin looked at her as if she'd asked him to stand on his own shoulders. "Dammit, Jac. I can't just drop you off somewhere. As screwed up as this has been, I'm not a jerk." He placed his hands on his head and turned in a circle. "Where are we, anyway? We need help; we need to call the police."

"No!" Jac replied quickly, emphatically.

"Why not?"

"They can't help with this." She paced, her hands moving manically at her sides. "I can't trust anyone other than you."

"We were kidnapped ... held hostage," Devin said, enunciating the words, "and you and Billy are covered in blood. I'm guessing those guys are horribly messed up or dead."

Jac stepped close to Devin, leaned in, and met his eyes, no longer concerned with her appearance or his alluring blood-drenched hair inches from her lips. "You either go to the police or take us to San Diego. You can't do both."

Devin returned her gaze and opened his mouth as if to speak, but words failed to form.

"Deal?"

"There are two people back there; as bad as they are, they might be alive and need help. Let me call the police, and they'll—" He paused and dropped his head as if realizing the complication of making the call.

"What happened to Tanner and Curtis, even though it's their fault,"—she pointed to her chest—"I'm responsible. The police will have your number if you call them, and when they find you, they'll find me." She maneuvered to look into his eyes. "We have to leave. We have to keep going. If we're caught, or someone finds out we were here and what happened, it's on me." She pressed her lips. "And we don't owe them anything with what they did to us."

Devin closed his eyes and tapped his palm against his forehead. A moment passed, and he nodded less than enthusiastically. "I don't like any of this ... but you're right. At least, I think you are. I've never been in a situation like this." He rubbed his head. "I'm not thinking straight."

Jac gave an empathetic, barely there smile.

"Are we good?" Billy asked.

Jac watched for Devin's response.

He looked down at Billy, holding his hand. "I think so."

"Then, are we ready to go?" Jac rubbed her hands together.

Devin nodded. "I'll drive."

"You sure?"

"Yeah, I'm good."

* * *

After driving back east to the first major exit, they stopped to clean up and change clothes in a gas station outside-access restroom. They stuffed their blood-stained clothes into a bag and stashed them in the trunk.

Devin bought a liquid cut sealer and applied it to Jac's cleaned and disinfected hand and fingers. He marveled at how quickly the cuts had already sealed. Jac returned the favor by sealing a quarter-inch cut on the top of Devin's head and cleaning the superficial scratches on his cheek and chin. They grabbed food to go and got back on the road.

The sun hung low in the sky as they drove. Without explanation, Devin pulled onto a short gravel road a few miles later that led to a church. They parked out front on the tire-flattened grass and weed-covered ground. The small church had a white wooden exterior with blue-trimmed stained-glass windows. A small white cross hung above the door, and one stood atop the steeple, casting a long shadow across them.

Jac studied the church, and then Devin. "Um. Why are we stopping here?"

"I don't know." Devin scratched his cheek. "I guess it's just a safe place to park while we eat. You know, being a church and all."

Billy sat forward in his seat. "What's so safe about a church?"

"I uh …"—he turned to Billy—"I can't say I have a good answer. Other than it's a church."

"Maybe because of God and stuff?"

Devin chuckled. "Exactly. God and stuff."

"More like it isn't Sunday, and no one's here," Jac added.

"Actually, now that you mention it, empty churches are kind of creepy."

Jac opened the car door, stepped out, and turned to Devin. "No people. Perfect."

The trio sat on the Pizza Mobile's hood, ate microwaved burritos, and drank Slurpees. Not much was said as they chewed, slurped, and ruminated. Jac and Devin groaned at pains that became evident during the calm.

Billy reached the bottom of his Slurpee with a final suck from his straw and broke the silence. "Some day, huh?"

Jac and Devin nodded absentmindedly, absorbed in thought and bathed in exhaustion.

"Those guys were scary," Billy continued.

Chewing, they languidly nodded again.

"Things can only get better from here," Billy added.

At this, Jac and Devin gave Billy a look, asking that he not provoke the universe. Their luck was already in question.

Jac returned her focus to the church as she ate, curious about its interior. How the hell did she end up just outside its doors, to begin with? What a horribly wrong turn her life had taken that brought her here. She had brought Devin with her on this wrong turn, murdered a man, killed a vampire ... maybe two. And now, she sat atop the hood of a car she had dubbed the Pizza Mobile outside of a church somewhere in Texas. But why here, of all places?

Billy giggled, dodging pieces of tortilla thrown by Devin while returning fire with tortilla pieces of his own.

"Hey, kids. That's enough."

They fought back laughs.

"Yes, Mom," Devin fired back.

"Funny." Jac wrapped the rest of her burrito and slid from the hood. "I'm, uh, going to check out the church."

Devin dodged a rather cheesy piece of tortilla and shot Billy a quick, stern look. "What for?"

"Just something I want to do."

"Hold up, and we'll go with you."

Jac raised a hand. "No. Stay here with Billy and finish eating."

Devin eyed her a moment before agreeing. "Okay. I'll watch Billy."

A piece of tortilla struck Devin's cheek.

"Yes," Billy cheered. "You better watch out."

"Nice one."

"And, Billy, please put more food in your mouth than on Devin's face," Jac urged.

* * *

Jac slowly approached the church, rethinking her curiosity. She didn't belong anywhere near this church or any church. Not only because it wasn't Sunday but because of the horrible things she had done. The closer she got, an unwanted feeling crept across her skin as if she risked being struck down by God. The sky was absent of dark clouds, but certainly, the Almighty could send down a single lightning charge upon her, storm or not.

Jac hesitated on the first step to the door. "What am I doing here?" The stair beneath her foot wouldn't offer a response, no matter how long she looked at it. Without providing an answer to her own question, she conquered the final two steps with determination. She grabbed the metal doorknob and paused. It cooled her warm and sweaty hand. *It will be locked, anyway.* After a purposeful, tension-easing breath, she turned the knob, and the door creaked open. She winced, looking around for anyone else who may have heard her practically breaking into the church.

Aside from her breathing, the church was library quiet. It somehow seemed smaller from the inside. An aisle to the pulpit separated two rows of ten dark wood pews. Bibles and hymnbooks sat in cubbies at the back of each pew. Sunlight pouring through stained glass windows painted the pews in a rainbow of colors. Dust particles hung in the air. Not one to frequent anywhere, especially churches, something seemed to be missing, but she couldn't put her finger on it.

Thinking better of barging in uninvited, she softly called out, "Hello." No one answered, not even God. For both, she was thankful.

Jac gave an it's-all-good-wave to the boys and stepped inside, leaving the door open behind her, just in case, and paused. She waited for something to happen but wasn't sure what exactly. The whole crosses-hurting-vampires thing was complete bull, but standing inside an *actual* church? Could she be evil enough for God to appear and strike her down? Burn her into a pile of ash? So, she waited. Still, nothing happened.

Jac strolled down the aisle toward the pulpit, letting her fingertips gently touch the pew tops as she passed. The air was stale and musty, with a hint of lemon cleaner. A closed door to another room stood on the right side of the back wall. Then it hit her. *Now I know what's missing.* The back wall was barren—an unadorned gray slab. *Where is Jesus on the cross?* How strange for the sanctuary of a church to not have a cross.

A bible lay on the pulpit, opened to the book of Luke. Jac traced her finger across the page and read the holy words when the door opened behind her.

"Holy shit!" She swiveled, arms wide, nearly toppling the pulpit. "I mean, damn. I mean …."

"Afternoon." An imposing figure of a man stepped from the doorway. He wore jeans and a blue, long-sleeved button-up shirt that fit him like a glove. Not because the clothes were too small, but because he was so large. He had muscles upon muscles, making Jac question if the church doubled as a gym for bodybuilders.

Jac steadied the pulpit. "Sorry, I was just ... the door,"—she pointed toward the entrance—"it was open, so I came inside. Of course, you know that because you see me standing here and...."

The man raised his hands in a calming gesture. "It's quite alright. This church is always open."

"Really?" Jac tilted her head. "Aren't you worried about people just coming in whenever and—"

"Stealing a bible?"

Jac thought it over. "Yeah, that wouldn't make much sense. I suppose if they really wanted one."

"I'm Ezekiel, but you're welcome to call me pastor, if you prefer." Ezekiel stepped closer and extended his hand. He had a head of clean-cut salt and pepper hair and a closely shaven, imposing jaw. His eyes were a deep blue, and his teeth were as white as freshly fallen snow.

Jac reached for Ezekiel's hand and then thought better of it. She returned her hand to her side and stepped back. "Sorry. Trust issues lately."

"That's fair." He pointed at his cheek and eyed hers. "Does that bruise have anything to do with your trust issues?"

Jac instinctively placed her hand over her cheek and looked away. "Yeah. I suppose it does."

"Anything to do with the boy you left outside?"

"Devin? No." She shook her head. "No way. Devin ... he's kind."

"That's good to know. We don't have a service tonight, but you're welcome to join us tomorrow."

"No. I mean, thank you, but I was just stopping in for a minute."

The pastor rested his massive hand on the pulpit. "What brought you into my humble house of worship?"

She looked down and patted the pew next to her. "You know … I'm not sure why."

Ezekiel pulled the bible from the pulpit, shut it, and held it at his waist. "People come to my church for many reasons. Fellowship. To feel closer to God. To hear an uplifting and faith-strengthening sermon." He eyed her curiously. "To seek forgiveness."

Forgiveness. Is that what brought her to enter the church? Seeking forgiveness? God knows she needed it. A damn truckload of it. Maybe she was curious about how wrong she was for the world and if the world would be better off without her. Who better to ask than a man of God who knew the difference between good and evil? "Yeah, well, forgiveness can't be why I'm here. I'm not worthy of forgiveness."

"Forgiveness is available to everyone, including you."

"Even those who do bad things?"

"All God's children are worthy." He gave her a strange, conspiratorial look. "Even those under the burden of sin."

Jac tugged at her sleeves and laughed. "What if I'm not one of God's children? What if I'm … something else?"

"We are all God's children. You step upon this earth with God's feet and breathe the air with God's lungs." He pointed to her, then to himself. "We see each other through God's eyes."

"Yeah, but I'm not good, like you."

Ezekiel extended his arms at his sides. "Do you think offering sermons makes me more worthy than anyone else to receive God's love?"

Jac's eyebrows pinched. "Isn't that why you do it ... why you became a pastor?"

"What, to give me an inside line to God's favor?"

She shrugged. "Yeah. I mean, it seems like a pretty good reason."

Ezekiel laughed and clasped his hands around the bible. "In God's eyes, I am no more special than you. The only difference between you and me is that I know God is everywhere and within everyone, and you doubt it."

"He can't be within me," Jac muttered.

He craned his neck toward her. "What was that?"

"Um. Nothing. Sorry." She clasped her hands. "Can I ask you, does God forgive everyone for any wrong they do?"

"The question isn't whether God has forgiven you," Ezekial countered. "God forgives all. The question is, have you forgiven yourself?"

Jac lowered her head and peeked at him from behind her hair. "I don't know if I can."

Ezekiel gave her that knowing look again. Like he knew everything and was humoring her with conversation. Reading him was not as difficult as reading a vampire, but it wasn't easy either.

Jac stared into his eyes for a long moment, then blinked. "Do you ... know who I am?"

He stared at her with his piercing blue eyes. "I do."

Her heart raced. Ezekial knew about the bus and what she had done. She glanced toward the door and took a backward step, preparing to run. "Are you going to call the police?"

"No."

"Why not?"

"I don't have a phone."

"You don't have a phone?"

"Phones have an energy of their own. I want nothing to block my connection with God and spirit."

Jac took another backward step. "Are you going to stop me from leaving?"

"Could I?"

She scoffed. "Have you seen yourself? You're huge."

"Could I, Jac?" He pushed his sleeves up his arm, revealing two bulging, veiny forearms. "Could I stop you even if I tried?"

Delayed understanding exploded in Jac's brain like a pin-less grenade. "Oh." She swallowed and lowered her voice. "How do you know about *that*? About what I am."

"I know about all of God's children. Call it my ... specialty."

"Wait a minute." She raised her hands in front of her. "No human on Earth knows what I am, and I just *happened* to stop here and meet you?"

"Maybe Devin's stopping here was a convenience, a coincidence." He shrugged. "Maybe it was synchronicity. Or, maybe I prayed on it ... manifested it."

Jac lingered in the silence, waiting for Ezekial to admit joking about manifesting her presence. She smirked when he didn't falter from the assertion. "I don't believe in any of that."

He chuckled. "There was a time I didn't believe in vampires."

She considered this for a moment. "Fair enough."

"Jac, are you almost ready?" Devin called from the car.

She thumbed toward the door. "I guess I should get going."

"Oh, yes. Don't let me keep you."

"This has been ... yeah." Jac took a step toward the door and paused. "He's safe with me, by the way. Devin. We've been through some rough shi—I mean, stuff." She pointed at her bruised face. "But, yeah, he's safe with me."

"I'm glad to hear that." Ezekiel touched his temple. "Now that I think of it. I'd like to meet Devin and your brother. Then offer a prayer for the rest of your journey."

"You want to pray for us after knowing what I've done and what I am?"

"I don't know of anyone who needs prayer more than you?"

She cleared her throat. "Okay. But Devin doesn't know about me. I hate to ask you to lie, being a pastor and all, but could you not mention it?"

He placed his hand upon his bible. "I promise. God as my witness."

* * *

Devin set his burrito on the car hood and dropped to the ground. He dusted off his hands as he walked toward her and reached for Ezekial's hand for a shake. "Pastor."

"Nice to meet you, Devin. You can call me Ezekiel." His hand engulfed Devin's; they shook and released. "Jac tells me you were passing through and decided to stop at my humble home of worship."

Devin looked at Jac as if to ask if Ezekiel was on the up and up. She gave a slight nod.

"We needed a place to break for lunch. And it's been a heck of a trip so far. Your church seemed like a safe place to be."

"Indeed, it is. And you are welcome here."

"Hello," Billy said, eyeing Ezekiel curiously.

"Hello, young man."

"You don't look like a pastor. You look more like a superhero."

Ezekiel laughed. "Don't tell anyone, but the truth is, I may have a cape or two in my closet."

Devin flexed his bicep and pointed to Ezekiel's massive arms. "Which came first, God or the muscles."

"God was and has always been there. He waited for me with infinite patience until I realized there was a power greater than physical strength."

"You found your purpose."

Ezekiel raised the bible in his right hand. "I indeed found my purpose."

"Anyway." Jac stood next to Devin. "We should be going. Let's have that prayer."

* * *

The white church grew smaller behind them as Devin pulled onto the road. Ezekiel appeared normal-sized in the distance.

Devin glanced in the rearview mirror. "You were in there for a while. What did you and Ezekiel talk about?"

"I was curious. I don't know if there is a God and...."

Devin chuckled. "You thought God might hang out in a small-town church in the middle of nowhere?"

Jac gave Devin a look of disdain. "*No*, I didn't think God would be in the church. You jerk. My family never went to church; we never even stepped inside one. I guess I just wanted to know, if God is real, how much trouble I'm in. You know? How much does God hate me?"

"Did you find out?"

She sighed. "Not really."

Devin glanced at her a few times as if waiting for her to continue. "What happened today was not your fault."

"I know." She chewed on a particularly uneven fingernail. "There's just a lot on my mind."

"Want to talk about it?"

"Is it okay if we don't?"

Devin studied her for a moment. "Yeah. Sure."

In the drive's silence, Jac ruminated on an offer Ezekiel made after Devin climbed into the car. "I'll pray for you," he said. "You're welcome here if you ever need a safe place to stay."

The offer was odd, coming from a pastor, even one like him. Why would he want someone like her, something like her, around? Could he have thought she was worth saving? Was it some elaborate long-game to trap her and kill her? She offered her thanks anyway.

She kept her conversation with Ezekiel to herself. Billy likely heard most of it anyway, and Devin couldn't know.

* * *

They headed west again and had been on the interstate for half an hour. Jac revisited the conversation about forgiveness with Ezekiel. She decided she hadn't forgiven herself and didn't know when and if she would. Regardless of God's pardon, she didn't deserve forgiveness for what she had done. No vampire did.

A revelation hit Jac as she stared out the passenger window at nothing. Devin had said something when they were driving toward San Diego; he said they were "back on track." Back on track to the known destination on the most obvious path. The way anyone would travel to find them. The way anyone could wait for them. It was the route they needed to leave.

"Wait a minute." Jac placed her hands on the dash. "Which way are we going?"

"What do you mean, which way?" Devin replied. "We're going west."

She tucked her hair behind her ears. "No, I mean, we're on the same road, the same interstate we were before?"

"Yeah, it's a direct route to San Diego."

"Get off it," she commanded.

"Why?"

She turned in her seat toward him, her hands animated. "Get off it. Go a different way. They know where we're going, and they know we'll go this way."

"So, then what? Go somewhere else?"

"Someway, go someway else."

"All right, we'll ... head south. Then, we can travel through the middle of Texas. Cut across southern New Mexico. It makes little sense to go that way, so it should work."

Jac placed a hand on Devin's shoulder. "Thank you."

"It'll take longer."

"Fine." She leaned back into her seat. "Perfectly fine."

"Longer?" Billy groaned. "It's already taken like forever. I'm going to need a ton more snacks."

"We'll get you some. I promise."

Devin shifted in his seat and reached into his right pocket. He pulled out the piece of paper Jac had given him just before the Dog Brothers took them.

"Oh, yeah. Thanks." Jac plucked the paper from his fingers.

A moment passed when Devin asked, "Who are the Castillos?"

Jac's mind raced, trying to remember everything she had told Devin. She never mentioned the Castillos by name but said she was visiting family friends in San Diego. What difference did it make whether he knew the Castillos were those friends? "They are the family friends I told you about."

"Oh. That's why you asked me to call them right before...."

She smirked. "Right before you didn't listen to me when I yelled for you to drive away."

"Yeah. I guess I don't take direction very well."

"I think that's called being stubborn."

Devin twitched a smile. "If not wanting to abandon you is stubborn, then I am the king of stubborn."

"Well then, king. The next time you don't listen to me,"—she ran her hand across her throat—"off with your head."

Devin glanced at her twice. His forehead rippled. "You're scary sometimes. You know that?"

Jac grinned and settled into her seat, her anxiety easing with her plan to change routes and Devin's resiliency. Even after going through Hell, he agreed to continue to San Diego. She gazed a moment at the guy who wouldn't leave her. Thankfully, Devin still found his smile. That wonderful boyish, we-got-this smile.

She ran her tongue across her teeth—smooth from molar to molar. She believed again. They would make it to the Castillos, all in one piece.

"Hey, look." Devin pointed ahead.

Jac's eyes followed Devin's finger toward a roadside sign that read "Shamrock City Limit, Population, 2030". She sighed, and he offered an empathetic smile. It had been nearly a full day, and they were barely farther than when they started.

MARCO ... UH OH

The roadside sign read, 'Welcome to Abilene City.' They'd been driving for over three hours. The sun set on a day unlike any day they had experienced, giving way to the moon. They were exhausted, worn, and a little broken—emotionally and physically.

The trio said little along the way other than confirmations of wellness, minor landscape observations, and checking in with Billy's need to pee. All mixed in with radio station changes and consumption of snacks and drinks.

Devin turned west at an intersection. "We'll stay here tonight, in Abilene."

Jac surveyed the surroundings. "Is there anything special about this place? Like Shamrock?"

"I've found it's not where you are that's special; it's the people you're with."

She raised an eyebrow. "Where did you come up with that? A song?"

"No." He chuckled. "Well ... maybe. But that doesn't make it any less true."

She rolled her eyes.

"I'm serious. You haven't lived with an alcoholic for eighteen years."

"Yeah. I guess I haven't. However, I haven't been alive for eighteen years. Old man."

Devin smirked. "You'll be eighteen soon enough, and join us, old folk."

"You're like ancient," Billy interjected.

They laughed.

Jac hadn't yet been anywhere on this trip as sprawling as Philadelphia. She never liked the city's congestion with the constant movement of cars, trains, and people. And the noise, it never stopped. She couldn't have imagined missing the city's suffocating feel, but now, a few days into the journey, she had grown an appreciation for city life. Anxiety visited her at moments during the drive. Especially when the view was nothing but road, trees, and the sky. It felt like abandoning society and charging head-on into a world of isolation. Not having anyone or any place to return multiplied the stress. If it weren't for Billy and Devin, those twinges of anxiety might have swallowed her.

Abilene was larger than Shamrock and seemed a good-sized fit. As they drove the main town strip, Jac's attention turned to the passing restaurants and retail shops.

"Stop!" Jac sat forward and slapped the dashboard. "Pull in there."

Devin slowed and followed Jac's finger, pointing to a mega-store—its bright lights a beacon for commerce. "What for?"

"That store is *huge*," Billy marveled.

Jac kept her wanting eyes on the store. In previously worn clothes, she felt unclean and didn't want to be near anyone else, much less herself. "I need clothes. All of mine are dirty or ... bloody."

Devin shared his agreement. He pulled into the parking lot and settled into a spot. "Are we all going in?"

She shook her head. "No, just you."

"I am?" Devin asked, taken aback. "Buying you clothes?"

"I need an extra shirt and pants," Billy said from the back.

Jac placed a reassuring hand on Devin's shoulder. "It will be easy. I promise."

Devin smirked. "Yeah, I can imagine."

"For me, go to the boy's section and get an extra-large long-sleeved shirt and a size fourteen pants ... cargo pants. And a medium shirt and size eight pants for Billy. Oh, and boy's large white socks."

"And ... that's all?"

"That's all. Is there something else I should get?"

Devin made an uncomfortable look, clearly struggling for the words. His hands motioned up and down his torso. "No, under ... things?"

Jac squinted at him. "Are you asking if we need underwear?"

He held up a you-guessed-it finger.

"Billy's okay, and I can go a couple days without any." The words spilled from her mouth before her mind caught up. She cringed, wishing she had somewhere to hide.

"Um," Devin said, covering his mouth.

She pushed at his shoulder while averting her gaze. *"Please* stop thinking about whatever you are thinking and go."

His hands fidgeted and formed two thumbs up. "Yeah, okay ... yeah, I'm gone."

* * *

Devin was in and out of the store within thirty minutes. He climbed into the car and handed a plastic shopping bag to Jac while keeping another bag and placing it on his lap.

Jac peeked into the bag and gave Devin an approving nod. "Thanks. What's in *your* bag?"

"Something for me." Devin grinned suspiciously and tucked the bag between the door and his thigh.

She narrowed her eyes at him but let it go.

A couple of blocks from the store, Devin pulled into the parking lot of a Motel 6, as announced by a towering, illuminated sign. "Here's our home for the night."

"We're moving up in the world," Jac said. "This motel has two levels."

"And a pool." Billy nearly climbed into the front seat and pointed to the sign. "Awesome."

"That's not happening," Jac said.

"Oh, come on. I haven't been swimming in *forever.*"

"You went last summer, which isn't forever."

"Close enough." Billy crossed his arms and sat back in his seat.

"I'll take you to the pool," Devin said. He pulled the car into a space out of direct sight of the motel front desk.

"Yes!" Billy raised his hands at landing the victory.

Jac frowned at Devin. She worried Billy had been through too much and needed rest. The reality was they all had a hellish day by any standard.

"Why are you looking at me like that? It will give you time to clean up. And relax, you know."

"Oh, you're doing it for *me*?"

Devin opened his mouth, paused, then continued, "Yes, I'm doing it for you. You might not believe it, but I like doing things for you ... when I can." He released his seatbelt. "I'll be back."

Jac grabbed Devin's arm when he opened the door. She gave him a long look before finding the words. "Thanks for everything. Only one room this time." Heat radiated from her cheeks when she said it, wondering if it came out as alluring instead of strictly instructional.

The grin on Devin's face answered her query. "One room? *Really?*"

She rolled her eyes and groaned. Devin's life experiences had dragged him into adulthood much sooner than a kid should have been. However, with the adult Devin came the teenage Devin—always ready with a joke and endless innuendo. She answered the teenage boy, "Yes, with two beds. And stop with the grin before I punch you ... hard."

Devin recoiled and raised a hand in defense. "Okay, no more violence today. I'm bruised enough."

Jac felt the urge to qualify the request, to remove any chance of misunderstanding from the adult *and* the teenage Devin. "I think we should stick close together. That way, we can watch out for each other. Ya know?"

"Got it: one room, two beds." He surveyed the surroundings. "We're probably off the radar, but let's keep playing it safe. You two stay here."

Jac agreed and watched Devin walk into the lobby. Truthfully, she wanted one room to be close to Devin, nothing more. She wanted to watch over him, to protect him if needed. If the weight of caring for Billy and making it to the Castillos wasn't enough, now the burden of keeping Devin safe from anyone who would harm him, including herself, fell on her shoulders. The all too familiar feeling of blood lust grew within her. Still only slight, a minor itch underneath a long-sleeved shirt. Experience told her Devin would be safe in the room with her tonight. There'd come a time when he wouldn't be safe from her while in the same city, and that time might only be a day or two away. They needed to reach San Diego soon so she would no longer need him, and he could return to his normal, everyday life in Jenks, far from her fangs.

"Are you going swimming with us?" Billy asked, breaking her from thought.

"Swimming?"

"Yes. Are you swimming with us?"

"No, I'm not going swimming. I don't have a swimsuit."

Billy tugged on his shirt. "You can swim in shorts like me and a T-shirt."

Aside from the cringe of prancing around the pool with a wet, clingy T-shirt, Jac didn't want to expose her arms to Devin. Her scarred arms from years of digging her nails into her skin. She wore long-sleeved shirts to add some protection from herself and to hide her arms from the judgmental world. However, neither excuse for not wanting to swim was necessary—she didn't have shorts and a T-shirt. And she didn't like the idea of getting her damaged hand wet, especially by motel pool water.

Jac examined her hand; deep red lines crossed her fingers and palm. The cuts appeared mostly sealed but were still cuts. She lifted her hand to show Billy. "I don't want my hand to get wet. Besides, I don't have any shorts."

"Well, will you watch me?"

"That, I will do."

They shared a smile as Billy did a sitting happy dance.

A few minutes passed when Devin returned with the room key.

"All good?" Jac asked.

"Perfect. I got a room on the second floor overlooking the pool. It has two full-sized beds."

"See, Billy, I can watch you just outside our room."

"You're not swimming with us?" Devin asked.

"She doesn't have a swimsuit," Billy said.

"Just wear shorts and a T-shirt."

"I already told her that," Billy clarified.

Devin shot Jac a confused look. "You can wear shorts and a T-shirt."

She pointed to her hand. "I don't want to get my cut wet."

"The liquid sealer is waterproof. You'll be good."

She huffed. "No, you two swim."

"Can't you swim?" Devin asked.

Her jaw dropped. "I *know* how to swim, but I don't want to in a T-shirt."

"If it makes you more comfortable, I'll wear one too."

"Yeah, come on," Billy urged.

Jac threw her arms in the air. "Billy, look away for a moment."

"Why?"

"Just do it."

Billy responded with a simple "fine" and turned to look out the window.

With the excuse of her hand being dismissed and not wanting to disclose her self-inflicted damage, she played a last card. She slapped Devin's arm and pointed at her chest, "I am not swimming in a wet T-shirt."

Devin's eyes lingered on her chest beyond her comfort level and garnered an additional slap to the arm. "Okay," he said, choking. "Okay, yeah, I think we lost this debate, Billy. It's only you and me swimming tonight." His eyes moved to hers and her chest, and he playfully smiled. "You have those?"

Jac sighed and placed a fist on her forehead. "Let's go to the room, please."

Devin seemed to regain focus, no longer alluding to what was under her shirt. "Here, take the key. I'll park somewhere away from the room, just in case."

She agreed but asked, "You don't think we're safe?"

"I do, but why take the chance?"

"Okay. Makes sense."

"Take your bags; it's room two-ten." He pointed toward the right. "I think if you take the stairs right there, it'll be close."

Jac exited the car with Billy and watched Devin back away. Behind the car's headlights, he waved them off. Her breath hitched. *He's leaving us. He's not coming back.* Devin had enough of the danger. He used the guise of hiding the car to leave them at this Abilene motel, which was as good, or bad, as being in the middle of nowhere.

She grabbed Billy's hand and reluctantly headed for the stairs. Ten steps later, the car and Devin were gone. Her chest tightened. *He's gone for good.* She couldn't blame him. The trip up to this point was a disaster. A vampire coven chased them out of Oklahoma, and they nearly died at the hands of a couple of vampire cowboys who abducted them. She'd be disappointed if Devin didn't return, but honestly, he should point his car east, head back to Jenks, and never look back.

"The pool!" Billy sprinted past the stairs toward the hole in the ground filled with chlorinated water.

"Billy, wait," Jac called, receiving no response. She caught him at the pool gate and persuaded him to wait in the room for Devin. Assuming he hadn't left for home.

A flick of a light switch illuminated their room. The floors were hardwood or manufactured wood. The walls were white, except for the orange one behind the beds that matched the comforters.

As he liked to do, Billy leaped onto a bed and jumped. "I love staying in motels."

"Careful." Jac closed her eyes and smiled at a memory. *Mom would have said that.* Mom would have stopped Billy from jumping, but his excitement outweighed Jac's worry that he'd hurt himself.

"When ... is ... Devin ... getting ... here?" Billy asked, timing each word with a jump.

"Soon, real soon." She wanted to sound believable for Billy and for herself. *What's keeping him from leaving? The money? The money isn't worth his life. He's probably driving back to Jenks, back to his safe, dull, and miserable life.*

"Please go swimming with us?" Billy asked, wearing his best beggar's face.

"I'm not going swimming."

"It will be more fun with you." Billy flopped to his stomach.

She met his eyes to ensure he heard her. "Billy, don't ask again."

He frowned. "Okay."

Jac sat on the edge of the bed, not being used as a trampoline. Every passing second reaffirmed her belief that Devin was gone. Still, she wanted to believe. She needed to believe. *He'll walk in the door any minute now.*

Full disclosure: she needed Devin not only for the ride and general societal knowledge but for something else, something she didn't understand at first or care to admit. *No. Stop thinking about that. Devin's the driver, that's all—just a ride, nothing else.*

The room door opened, and Jac audibly exhaled.

"Devin," Jac and Billy announced simultaneously. She sprang excitedly to her feet, wearing a full smile.

"Sorry it took so long. I parked in a secluded spot, just in case." Devin ran a hand through his hair and mirrored her smile.

Jac pressed her lips to a straight line and turned away. *Way to play it cool. Jumping up like I'm some stupid girl happy to see a boy.*

Billy sprang from the bed, his excitement brimming over. "Pool time?"

"You bet, buddy. Let me change into my trunks."

Devin took his bag into the bathroom and came out a few minutes later, shirtless and wearing blue swim trunks. Billy skirted past him and into the bathroom for his turn to change.

Jac stared.

Devin stood shirtless in front of her. He was tan and lean, an alluring mental image burned into her memory. He had a defined chest, well-rounded shoulders, and clearly delineated abdominal muscles. His smirk clued her in that she had been ogling him. She might as well have had her tongue wagging.

"Want a picture?" Devin pouted his lips and made a silly pose like a clothing model.

A warm rush flooded Jac's cheeks. She shielded her eyes as if Devin were the sun. "Oh, God, no. Disgusting." *Disgusting? Did I really just say he's disgusting?*

"Ouch." Devin placed his hands over his heart. "Change your mind about swimming?" He plucked the shopping bag from the bed, pulled out shorts and a T-shirt, and tossed them to her.

Jac caught the clothes, checked the sizes, and sighed. "Really? This is what was in the bag you hid from me in the car? You bought me shorts and a T-shirt?"

Devin tried to stuff his hands in the swim trunk's nonexistent pockets and hugged himself. "To be honest, I looked at the swimsuits for girls ... because that's what you are. But I wasn't sure what size your ... what size—"

"Fine, I'll go." She didn't want to swim but wanted to save Devin from saying anything else stupid. "But you have to promise one thing."

"What, no splashing?"

"I'm being serious. Obviously, no splashing, but something else."

Devin ran his hand down his face, erasing the smile. "Okay. Serious. I promise." He crossed his heart. "Hope to die, and all of that."

"No questions, or you'll wish you were dead."

"No questions? What do you mean, no questions?"

"That's just it; you can't ask me anything."

"Okay, sure ... no questions."

Billy came from the bathroom, shirtless and wearing shorts.

"All right, skins." Devin gave Billy a high five. "Your turn, Jac."

"Serious? She's going?" Billy asked hopefully.

"Yeah, but no splashing her, *and* we can't ask any questions, so...."

Jac grabbed her backpack and paused at the bathroom door. With a finger pointed at Devin, she reminded him, "No questions." She slipped into the baggy shorts and the anime T-shirt Devin had purchased. "Nice choice," she muttered, rolling her eyes.

She studied her reflection in the bathroom mirror. Her arms were a topography of damage. A visual record of the torment she had always strived to conceal would be on display. Some old scars, and many new and healing, covered sections of her arms.

The habit of clawing at her arms began with her first bloodlust. It wasn't long before the clawing became impetuous during bloodlust and as a reaction to any stressful or nerve-induced situation. The fact she was about to reveal her arms to Devin was one of those situations. She resisted the urge to claw away.

He'll notice and think I'm disgusting. My stupid scars. After a couple of deep breaths, she opened the door and announced she was ready. Immediately, her hands moved to her arms, nervously sliding up and down as if she could hide every scar.

Devin's eyes move from her feet to her face, wandering over her body as if he were a yet undiscovered Peeping Tom. His eyes narrowed at her arms, then met her eyes. She frowned and looked away.

"So, uh, ready?" Devin asked, breaking the awkward silence.

"Ready." Billy rushed toward the door.

Jac hugged herself and averted her eyes. "Just remember our agreement."

* * *

The crescent moon hung in the starry Texas sky like the Cheshire Cat's smiling face, sans eyes. They swam for nearly an hour, Jac staying mainly on the pool stairs, attempting to stay as dry as possible. Despite a pathetic volley of pleading from the boys, she refused to be Marco or Polo.

The boys splashed each other, compared cannonballs, and had a breath-holding contest. Devin's proud celebration at holding his breath for one minute and twenty-five seconds turned to astonishment when Billy stayed underwater for three minutes and thirty seconds.

For the moment, Jac stopped dwelling on the day's tragic events and quit worrying about the future. She smiled at seeing Billy happy, playing like the little boy he was. Her appreciation for Devin grew exponentially. She saw kindness in him and an unmatched resilience.

Other feelings for Devin surfaced, feelings she never had for anyone—not that she ever had the opportunity throughout her sheltered life. New, exciting feelings drew her to him, urging her to be with him. More than a lust for blood, the draw was natural, human. Something irresistible. The feelings were an all too confusing emotional puzzle box, and she was all thumbs.

She hung her head. *What's wrong with me?*

* * *

The trio walked back to the room with wet feet and dripping clothes. Devin slid in the keycard, opened the door, and Billy ran into the room, announcing his claim to the bathroom. He had broken kid-law by refusing to pee in the pool.

A blast of cold air rushed from the room. "It's an icebox in there." Devin shivered and wrapped his towel around his shoulders.

Jac stepped a foot inside when Devin grabbed her hand. She turned to him, their eyes locked. "Billy, take a shower to wash the chemicals off."

"Ah, come on."

Keeping eye contact with her, Devin reinforced Jac's demand, "Your sister's right. Shower off, and then it's our turn." He winced. "I mean, her turn ... your sister's turn." Devin's slip of the tongue flushed his cheeks.

Jac covered her mouth and bit her lower lip. She turned to Billy. "We'll be just outside."

"*Fine.*" Billy's shoulders slumped as he trudged into the bathroom and closed the door.

Devin grabbed Jac's hand and eased her away from the room. Her fingers lingered on the handle until the door quietly closed. They leaned against the rail overlooking the pool; the night sounds were their only company.

"It's getting chilly out here." Jac pulled her hand away from his and rubbed her arms.

"Because you're wet." Devin placed his towel around her shoulders, helping her grab the ends to pull it tight around her. "You need to take that shirt off." He closed his eyes and sucked in his lips, turning a brighter shade of red.

Jac let him stew in the embarrassment.

"What I mean is—"

"Relax, I know what you meant. What I don't know is why we're out here."

"I wanted to talk ... alone." Devin hugged himself and looked around. Even when nervous, he exuded an innocent charm that warmed Jac's core.

"About what?"

His eyes focused on the exposed parts of her arms. "What happened to your—"

"No questions. Remember?" Jac pulled the towel tighter around her.

"Yeah, sorry. I assumed that rule ended when we left the pool."

"Uh, no. That rule lasts until I say." She flashed a playful smile. "So, as far as you know, that means forever."

"I'll have you to your destination soon, so I don't really have forever."

"Sucks for you."

"Come on. You have to let me ask you *some* questions."

"Like what?"

A bead of water slid down Devin's neck. Jac chewed on her bottom lip, following the drop's path between his pecs and the center of his abs. She hummed.

"I'm up here."

"Oh, my God." Jac closed her eyes and put a hand to her forehead. "I just did that."

Devin laughed.

She turned away, bathed in embarrassment.

"It's okay. You can turn back around."

"Okay. But here's the deal. We don't talk about ... that."

"Deal."

Jac regained her composure and tentatively turned back to face Devin. "Hi."

"Hi."

"So, is there a question?"

"Yeah. What's going on in that head of yours?"

Jac blew out her cheeks. "Oh boy. You're sure you really want to know?"

"One hundred percent."

"Hmm. So, yeah. Have you ever put together a Lego set?"

"Yeah. A lot, actually." He looked away, lost in memory. "My mom would get a Lego set for me for Christmas. I would put it together, take it apart, and put it back together. I didn't get many toys, so I got as much use out of them as possible." Devin shrugged. "So, what's the analogy? You're trying to piece your thoughts together?"

"Sort of. My mind is like a finished Lego set you drop, and it breaks into pieces." She frowned and looked away. "Except I'm not sure if I can put it back together."

Devin brought his hand to her face. "Maybe I can help."

She stood motionless, unsure how to react, uncertain she wanted to. A warm rush swelled inside her. She flinched when his fingers brushed against her bruised cheek.

"Does it hurt?" he asked.

"Only when I think about it ... or touch it."

He quickly pulled his hand away and returned it to the back of his neck. "Oh, sorry."

"That's okay." Releasing the grip on her towel, Jac grabbed his left hand and slowly brought it to her face, placing it on her right cheek. She left her hand atop his. "This one is okay," she said, her voice softly trailing off.

Her breathing shallowed as his thumb gently stroked her cheek. A fire welled within her, locked in the gaze of his hazel eyes. They edged closer as if pulled by gravity. Devin leaned down, narrowing the space between them, his lips a breath away from hers. Her heart raced. She couldn't resist, and why should she? She had never experienced affection from a guy. Only recently, she became aware these feelings were missing from her life. She wanted it, needed it. This moment with Devin meant everything.

The door to the room opened, instantly shutting off the gravitational pull between them.

"Your turn!" Billy announced.

As if Billy were Moses, Jac and Devin parted, their faces as red as the sea in the Biblical tale.

Devin stuttered, "Hey, buddy. That—That was a quick shower."

Jac felt like she was stepping away from the edge of a ten-thousand-foot cliff, no longer taking the plunge. She wrapped the towel around her. "You can go next."

"You sure?" Devin's hands awkwardly moved from his neck to his hips, then back to his neck as if looking for a home to hide from the embarrassment.

"Yeah. I'll take too long."

"Okay. I'll be quick."

* * *

Jac sat atop a dry towel on the bed.

Billy crawled under the covers and cozied up to her. "I smell bleach. The sheets are clean."

With her mind elsewhere, she acknowledged this bit of information with a grin. Still anxious, still aroused, her heart continued to race. In one way, Devin brought out feelings and sensations in her she had never experienced, feelings she didn't know were inside her. Unfortunately, he also brought forth an all too familiar feeling. One she had hoped to avoid on the trip. One overshadowed by the almost kiss. This feeling outweighed all others and terrified her more now than ever. She slid her tongue across her top row of teeth—twice, to be sure. Smooth, bump, smooth, bump, smooth. As she feared, her fangs had slightly descended. And worse ... she was getting hungry.

I NEVER WANTED
THIS TO HAPPEN

Jac lay next to Billy. He was out. It had been a grueling day, and swimming wiped out his reserves. She turned toward the table between the beds, struck a match, and with a crackle and pop, her candle burned with a steady flame. She clicked off the lamp and laid her shower-damp head atop a pillow.

The ceiling was awash with wavering shadows from the licks of the flame. The room was quiet, allowing her mind to wander. It wasn't long before it settled on Devin and the kiss. Well, the almost kiss. She didn't know then that she was in the early stages of bloodlust. She had been careless getting *that* close to him. He had risked too much already and deserved to be safe around her. She braved a look toward Devin, already looking at her from his bed.

"Hi," Devin whispered.

"Hiya, creep. Why are you staring at me?" Jac whispered back.

"Wow, thanks. Creep, huh?"

"Yeah, a little."

Devin nodded at the side table between them. "What's with the candle?"

Jac gazed solemnly at the candle and back to Devin, his face aglow in its light. "My dad gave it to me." She smiled at the memory. "He said I should light the candle whenever he wasn't around, and he would be here, in spirit. Kind of corny, huh?"

"No, not at all. That's really cool. How long have you had it?"

"Since I was around Billy's age. But I don't keep it lit for too long. I'm worried it won't last, especially now that he's gone." Tears welled in her eyes. "I don't know what I'll do when it finally burns out."

"Sorry. I didn't mean to make you sad. We don't have to talk about it anymore."

"No, it's okay. I was already thinking about him. It tends to happen when I light the candle."

They lay quietly, staring at each other until Jac's bravery broke. She blushed and pulled the blanket over her face.

"Hey." Devin propped up on his elbow. "No hiding."

"Stop staring at me," she said from behind the blanket.

"Stop being so cute," he countered.

She groaned. "Now I'm never showing my face again."

"Then the world would be an uglier place."

She pulled down the blanket, revealing her smirk. "You're dumb."

"I've been called worse."

"Why don't I find that hard to believe?"

They shared a laugh.

Jac lay on her back and stared at the ceiling. Devin, unfortunately, continued to be a wonderful distraction. She imagined a life where she could act upon her feelings for him. Their story would be nothing special. She'd be an ordinary girl, and he'd be her guy. It wasn't fair that ordinary was too much to ask. Despite the power of imagination and her feelings, she couldn't have a life with Devin.

Devin pulled another pillow under his head and plopped back down. "Jac. I was thinking. When you get to San Diego, things will get better. I'm sure it will be complicated with your stepdad and all, but it will get better."

"Thanks. But how can you say that?"

"Because I can."

"You can't just say it will get better and it magically happens."

"Why not?"

Jac propped up on her elbow, looking quizzically at him. "Because it doesn't work that way."

"I choose to believe it does. It's the same reason I believe we'll make it to San Diego. Think about everything we've already gone through."

She stared into the nothingness of the room's darkness, imagining reaching Asilo Colina and feeling relief. And the possibility of a reunion with her mother? Billy would be thrilled. They'd come together as a three-person family and figure out how to live out the rest of their lives. But Devin was foolish for believing in the fantasy, and she for imagining it. Life didn't just happen to work out for her. "I wish," she muttered and blew out the candle. "Goodnight."

"Night."

Devin *was* right about it being a miracle they'd made it this far. Still, she didn't buy into his positivity nonsense. She wanted to continue talking with Devin, but their closeness was getting a bit too cozy for her current comfort. Her fangs had descended, not at full bloodlust or pre-bite length, but enough to keep her distance from him, physically and emotionally.

* * *

Jac woke in the darkness, lying still and listening to the ambient sounds: Billy's soft breathing, the rumble of the air conditioner blowing cold air into the room, the distant sound of passing traffic, and, faintly, a heartbeat, a pulse.

Narrowing her focus and filtering out all other sounds, she focused on the heartbeat, a distinct, unadulterated beat. Concentrating first on herself, she ruled out the rhythmic thump being that of her own heart.

She reached over and gently placed her hand atop Billy's covered chest, timing the beat with the sound. It wasn't Billy's. She turned over to her side. Devin's darkened shape lay beneath the covers in the other bed. She focused only on him, watching intently as his chest rose and fell with every breath. Blocking out all other sounds, it became clear—the heartbeat was Devin's.

A rush of adrenaline brought Jac to her feet, and a step from Devin's bed at a surprising and frightening speed. Her heart pounded at the sight of him, the sound of him, the smell. Her breath quickened as blood rushed into her gums, descending her canines between her throbbing lips to their fullest biting length.

With clenched hands, she took the last step toward his bed, her thighs resting against the mattress's edge. She leaned over him just slightly. *What am I doing? Please, no. I don't want to do this.* Her conscience fought between returning to her bed and moving closer to Devin. Her humanity begged her to go back to sleep but shouted against sealed ears.

An intoxicating O-negative aroma surrounded Devin. Her gaze followed his profile down to the pulsating vein in his neck and lingered there as if it called to her, invited her.

Her fingertips caressed Devin's neck, tracing the line of his jugular vein. Closing her eyes, she brought her fingers to her lips and licked. Her tongue traced her teeth, stopping to flick and swirl around her fangs in perfect form for a penetrating bite. Desire burned within her. Hunger consumed her and locked her conscience away.

Jac crept to the other side of the bed, lifted the covers, and slid behind Devin, pressing her body against his. She sniffed his neck, slid her hand underneath his shirt, and rubbed his chest, stopping only when he made a sound and turned to his back. Gently and slowly, she pushed herself upon him, straddling his waist.

Devin opened his eyes. "Jac?"

"Shhh." She leaned forward, kissed his forehead, then pulled back just inches from his face. His pulse thumped an enticing rhythm; in his veins flowed an intoxicating drug to be consumed.

"What are you doing?" he whispered. "Billy's right over there."

She laid a finger on his lips. "No talking."

Devin slid his hands under her shirt and firmly gripped her waist. She tensed as she dragged her rigid fingers down his chest, gouging at his skin. He pulled her close, their bodies coming together with mutually radiating heat.

Jac placed her hands on Devin's shoulders and slid them along his arms to his wrists. In a blur, she pinned his arms above his head. He playfully struggled to free them. "Don't fight it," she ordered.

He smiled. "You have control."

Jac leaned forward, gently brushing her lips upon his cheek, creeping to his neck. He turned his head, granting her full access. She passionately growled as she kissed and sucked the tender skin of his neck. "Devin," she whispered softly, intimately.

"Yes." He pressed his hips against hers.

"Do something for me."

"Anything. I'll do anything for you, anything you want," he said between passionate breaths. "Just ask."

"Devin." She pecked at his neck and slid her lips across his skin, up to his ear.

"Yes. What is it? What do you want me to do?"

Her lips brushed against his ear, and she whispered, "Die."

All passion left Devin, and his body fell limp. "What?"

Maintaining a firm grip on his wrists, Jac rose to leer at him, exposing her bloodlust eyes and protruding fangs.

"Jac!" Devin's eyes bulged as he fought against her grip. "What's wrong? Your eyes. What the—My God, your teeth?"

She smiled broadly, revealing her complete set of gleaming white teeth, two like tiny daggers.

"Jac!" Devin struggled against her grip, his legs and torso joining the resistance to no avail. "What's going on?"

She moved close to his face, and with unimaginable speed, her mouth enveloped the side of his neck, and her jaw clamped tight. Warm, salty blood poured into her mouth as she took long, satiating drinks.

Devin's body writhed as he pleaded for her to stop, desperate for her to understand she was killing him. His hands twisted and turned, searching for freedom from her grip.

Blood trickled from the space between her lips and the skin of his neck as she took prolonged and ravenous drinks. A minute passed when Devin's struggles weakened, and he fell silent. His passion had left him, and so did his life.

Releasing his wrists, Jac pushed herself up. Blood dripped from her mouth to her chin and streaked down the front of her shirt. She watched with detachment as Devin's head twitched, and the light left his eyes.

Devin's mouth moved.

Jac moved the hair from his vacant eyes and cooed, "What do you want to tell me, my sweet meal?"

She placed her ear upon his quivering lips. His voice came as a pained whisper, "You're ..."

"What, Devin?" She kissed his cheek. "What am I?"

"... a monster."

His words struck her as hard as any blow. Whatever compassion she had turned off, allowing her to drain Devin of his blood, flooded back in. She sat up and watched in horrified comprehension as Devin breathed his final breath.

"No, no, no," Jac cried, clawing at her hair. "I'm not a monster. I'm not a monster!" She shook him and pounded his chest.

"Take it back! Take it back! I'm not a monster!" She swiveled at a hand falling upon her shoulder and looked into Billy's eyes.

"Jac?"

Her bloody chin quivered. "Billy, I'm sorry. I didn't mean to do it. I'm so sorry." Her head collapsed into her hands.

"Jac?" Billy repeated.

She met Billy's stare. "What have I done?"

Billy narrowed his eyes at her. "You *are* a monster."

Her face cracked, overcome with a river of anguish and shame. Tears poured from her eyes at the sight of Devin's lifeless body. "No, no, no ... NO!"

Jac shot up from the bed, screaming. The lamp on the table clicked on, filling the room with light.

Devin placed his chilly hand on her fevered arm. "Jac! What's wrong?"

Her breaths came rapidly. An unbridled heat boiled within her.

Billy sat next to her on the bed and gripped her hand. "Are you okay?"

Jac pressed her lips and squinted at Devin. Though disoriented, she turned away, knowing her eyes and teeth were things of nightmares. She ran her fingers through her sweat-laden hair and focused on slowing her breaths. *It was just a dream. Another damn dream.* She stifled a sob. "I'm fine ... I'm okay. It was just a bad dream."

"It must have been a heck of a dream," Devin said. "Want to keep the light on?"

"No, it's okay. You can turn it off." She frowned at Billy. "I'm sorry. Go back to sleep."

"Do you want to stay up?" Devin asked. "Talk about it?"

"Just turn off the light, *please*, and stay away from me," she said curtly.

Jac didn't want to be short with Devin but needed distance. She didn't care to discuss the dream, much less expose her bloodshot eyes and weaponized mouth to him. Most importantly, she couldn't have the urges for him—for his blood—play out in real life.

"Okay. Okay. Sorry. Let me know if you change your mind."

Devin clicked off the light, and Jac collapsed onto the bed. Though only a dream, guilt filled her from toe to crown. She had done what she believed she could never do—drink from Devin. Nightmare or not, she killed him. Her bloodshot eyes met Billy's when she turned to her side.

"I know," he whispered for only her to hear.

Jac squeezed her eyes shut to hide from the guilt and ran her tongue across her fangs as they slowly receded to their pre-dream length—not flush with her other teeth, but not jutting from her mouth. She opened her eyes. "I'm scared," she whispered back.

Billy pushed her hair from her face. "I'll help you."

Despite all that had happened, Jac couldn't fool herself into imagining the second half of the drive to San Diego would be any easier. Now, she was hungry. Now, *she* was the danger.

FRAGILE BOX

J ac woke to Billy's laughter. She silently turned to her side and watched as he and Devin interacted. Wildly animated and smiling, Devin told a painfully corny joke that had Billy in a giggle fit.

The guilt she felt for killing Devin lingered. The dream was all too real, and with the hunger growing, the possibility of his death at her hands crept closer to becoming reality. Devin, the boy who carried her life-extending blood, would sit beside her for hours. She ran her tongue across her teeth and winced. Toothless smiles were the rule today ... if she found a reason to smile.

Her father had taught her a method for self-control, for when blood wasn't immediately available—like now. He would purposely deprive her of blood for hours, at first, and eventually up to a couple of days beyond initial hunger. Blood fasting, as he called it, was a handy asset when living in a world with untouchable humans. He instructed her to close her eyes and search her body for any sign of the hunger. When she found the hunger, she'd put it in an imaginary box and hide it away. Her longest time without blood was two and a half days after the first hunger pains. Today was day one. But this situation differed significantly. She wasn't resisting a refrigerated bag of blood—mere sustenance—she was resisting a living, breathing, six-foot bag of warm, delicious O-negative. Devin was the blood bag within her reach for at least two more days. He'd be moving in and out of her space, tempting her not only with bloodlust but with the desire for touch, an embrace, and his lips upon hers.

Pushing thoughts of Devin aside, Jac focused on locating the hunger. She found it in only a minute of meditation. Or did she? It wasn't a perfect science and might not even be real. Still, she placed the faintest of desire inside a box—one she always imagined was wooden with intricate carvings possessing the power to ward against evil. She locked the box and threw it into the black, imaginary nothingness. *Thank you, Daddy.*

"Good morning." Billy hopped onto his knees on her bed. "You should hear Devin's jokes."

"Good morning," Jac said through a hand-covered yawn. "I can't wait."

"Oh, there will be plenty of time for jokes during the drive," Devin said.

"Great," she said with a smirk and blatant sarcasm.

"You should probably get up. Check-out is in half an hour. I let you sleep a little longer, with that dream keeping you up."

The dream—she hoped Devin wouldn't mention it. Not only did she want to forget, but she didn't want him to question the dream's content.

When the questions didn't come, Jac offered thanks and left it there, appreciative of the extra sleep.

* * *

Devin handled the motel check-out, and they were back on the road with San Diego still a thousand miles away. After referencing Devin's phone map, they picked Las Cruces, New Mexico as their destination. They would decide what to do from there.

Jac didn't want to stop but instead drive straight through. The box with her hunger was lost in the nothing, but the craving for blood couldn't be contained forever. It grew by the minute and eventually would break free, splintering the tiny, intricately carved box. They had planned for at least one more overnight stay, and she had already decided to sleep in separate rooms. Hell, if she could convince Devin, she would have him sleep in a different motel or city.

During the first half hour of the drive, she pondered when an answer to the blood problem arrived. *The Castillos!* "Yes," Jac said aloud, drawing an odd look from Devin.

"Yes? Yes, what?" Devin asked.

"Oh ... nothing. I was just thinking about something."

Devin narrowed his eyes and returned his focus to the road, dropping the conversation to Jac's relief.

New Mexico might be within the Castillo's influence. They could have information on blood supply or arrange a delivery. Though only a plan, it gave her a modicum of relief. Now she needed time alone to call.

"When are we stopping again?"

"I thought we'd drive a couple hours. We're good on gas. Why?"

"Just wondering. I haven't been on a lot of long car trips."

"You haven't been on any long car trips," Billy corrected her.

Jac sighed and continued, "It's just ... I like to get out and stretch my legs. Move around a bit."

"Really?" Devin raised an eyebrow. "The girl who wants to get to San Diego yesterday wants to stop more?"

"Yeah. I guess I'm a paradox."

"What's a paradox?" Billy asked.

Jac opened her mouth to answer, but Devin beat her to it. "It's like when you contradict yourself."

"I don't get it."

"It's *like* when someone wants to be funny but purposely tells lame jokes," Jac said, throwing a look at Devin.

"What? That's not it at all. I see how you're gonna be," Devin said, feigning hurt.

She laughed behind her hand.

"And for that, an hour of jokes shall commence."

"No. Please. I take it back." She placed her hands in prayer position, pretending to grovel.

"I think I get it," Billy said.

Devin drummed the steering wheel and glanced at Jac as if making sure she was ready. "Joke number one: What did the driver say to his passenger?"

Jac eyed him with suspicion. "Wait. Is this joke supposed to be about me?"

He shrugged. "It could be about you."

She sighed. "Okay. What *did* the driver say to his passenger?"

"Be nice, or you might drive me away."

She stared straight-faced at Devin.

Billy laughed. "I got that one."

Devin's smile and Billy's contagious laugh got Jac laughing at the joke's ridiculousness. "That is the dumbest joke I have ever heard. It doesn't even make sense."

"Maybe not, but it did its job; you're laughing, and I have dozens more."

She shook her head. "No, please, no."

Devin flashed the peace sign. "Fine. Truce for now."

"Truce forever."

* * *

Jac studied Devin as he drove. Her emotions were a conflux, creating a mess in her mind. The previous night, she nearly let him kiss her. She would have if it weren't for Billy's timely or untimely interruption—she hadn't yet decided which. Regardless of her detest for the vampiric desire, there'd come a time when she'd want to snap his neck and drink every drop of blood from his body. Thankfully, at the moment, she'd prefer a kiss.

"What is it?" Devin checked his reflection in the rearview mirror and ran his hand through his hair.

Her face flushed; she had been staring at him. "Nothing." She looked away.

Devin chuckled. "Why were you staring at me?"

"I was just...." She glimpsed Devin from the corner of her eye. He caught the glimpse and laughed. She covered her mouth and joined him.

"It's okay; I like looking at you, too."

"You guys are being weird again," Billy said.

They laughed more.

"You got that right, buddy, but we *are* talking about your sister."

Jac punched Devin's arm. He winced.

* * *

Hours passed, and the laughter and talk died. The synergistic hum of the road and the monotonous scenery eased Jac into losing herself in thought. She replayed memories of when her dad taught her about boxing the hunger. She wanted to be sure she followed all the instructions. Also, she enjoyed thinking about Dad being alive. An earlier memory of being with her father bubbled up to the surface. She was five or maybe six.

"Jac. Jacqueline," Dad said, shaking her shoulder. "I need you to listen to me."

Jac lifted her head from the pillow and swept her sweaty hair from her eyes to better look at his gentle face.

"There's my girl."

She forced a grin, with only the right corner of her mouth winning the battle against the gravitational power of pain.

"Did you box it?" he asked.

She frowned and curled into a ball, wrapping her arms around her shins. "I can't. It's too big."

"But it's not, Jacqueline. It's only just started. But the hunger will grow too big and quickly if you don't box it." He sat next to her on the bed and rubbed her arm. "If you want to give yourself more time, you need to box it from the beginning."

"I tried, Daddy, but I'm just a kid."

He patted her arm. "I know you are, sweetheart."

"Are you mad at me?"

"No, I'm not mad at you."

"Are you disappointed in me?"

"I am not disappointed in you. You're learning, and that's what's important."

Jac sniffled and wiped her nose. "Will I ever get it?"

"You certainly will. It takes time."

"What if it takes forever?"

He laughed. "It won't take forever. One day,"—he snapped his fingers—"just like that, you'll have better control over your hunger and forget you ever struggled with it, to begin with."

It was a quiet minute before Jac spoke. "Daddy?"

"Yes?"

"I don't want to kill anybody."

He gently eased her onto her back and looked into her teary eyes. "Why are you thinking about killing someone?"

"Because ... it's what we do."

"But that's not what we do, Jakie Q. Your mom and I will always make sure you have blood without you ever needing to kill someone."

"But what if you and Mommy are gone, and you're not here to help me?"

He swept the remaining sweaty hair strands from her face and kissed her forehead. "Don't worry about things like that. We're here with you now, and we never plan on leaving you."

A sharp, stabbing pain swept through her, from the top of her head to the tips of her toes. She stiffened, releasing a scream reserved for the worst of pains as she clawed at her arms. "Daddy! Help me!"

"Fight it, Jacqueline. Put it in a box."

A heat emanated from her shaking, sweat-drenched body. "I can't, Daddy! I can't! Please give me some blood! I promise I'll do better next time."

"Are you sure?"

"PLEASE!"

Then there was pain. Not in her memory. Here. Now. A wave of quick pinpoint strikes of searing pain, as if a thousand burning needles stabbed her. The stupid box had already broken. Her lack of focus had doomed it. Before Jac fully recognized her surroundings, Devin yelled a curse. Her hands had formed violent grasps: one on the faux leather siding of her door and the other on his forearm.

"You are hurting me," Devin said, enunciating each word.

Jac released Devin's forearm and backed as far from him as possible. The aroma of Devin's blood swelled her gums and burned a path from her nostrils to her lungs. She had to escape the car. Now.

"Devin," she said desperately.

"What's wrong?"

Billy's hand rested on her shoulder. "Jac, it will be okay."

Jac shut her eyes and rocked back and forth. A need grew inside her like a forest-fed fire. She had to find the hunger and shove it back into the box.

"Jac?" Devin cried.

She ignored him, quickly looking for the hunger, her mind a comet desperately searching through the space that was her body.

"Jac?" Devin repeated.

"WHAT?!" She faced Devin, her hands trembling at the sides of her head.

Devin regarded her, his face registering only disturbed surprise, and he turned back to look at the road.

Guilt weighed on Jac. She had yelled at Devin, the only person, other than her parents and Billy, whom she cared about and trusted. But none of that mattered. Only the hunger mattered, running free within her like a damn juggernaut speeding her closer to sinking her teeth into his neck.

Without apologizing, she took a deep breath, settled into her chair, and refocused.

"It will be okay," Billy whispered so only she could hear. Jac tilted her head, creating a calming sandwich with her head, Billy's hand, and her shoulder.

"What the heck was that?" Devin asked.

Jac owed Devin an answer. Some explanation for why she nearly ripped his arm from his body. A reason for—"Jac sometimes has panic attacks," Billy said.

Billy's lie wasn't far from the truth. Blood lust shared some symptoms of a panic attack, but times ten. The excuse would suffice for now. It had to.

"That's one heck of a panic attack."

"Yeah. It happens when she gets … scared and stuff."

"Jac," Devin said. "Are you going to be okay?"

"She'll be okay," Billy answered.

"We'll be stopping soon. You can get out of the car. Breathe some fresh air."

Jac didn't answer and instead refocused on her meditation. She had to slow the monster awakening inside of her. Box ready, she searched for the hunger starting at the tips of her toes, fearing she was already too late.

GAS AND A PHONE CALL

Devin pulled the car up to the next gas station and convenience store combination. Jac had stayed in silent meditation for nearly an hour after being assaulted with pain from bloodlust. She found the hunger a short time later. It had grown to an intensity she could no longer lock away. Manage it, yes, but her intricate wooden box was useless.

Devin stopped the car beside a gas pump. "I'll go in and pay. Can I get you anything?"

"So many things." Billy removed his seatbelt and leaned in between them. "I need a lot."

"A water ... and your phone. I need to make a call." Jac glanced at Devin behind her sunglasses to the extent she could stand.

"Sure. Who are you calling?"

She tilted back her head and sighed. "The Castillos. Not that it's any of your business." She instantly regretted the verbal assault but didn't apologize. She couldn't bear to look at Devin and witness the confusion and pain he likely felt from her words.

"Oh. Your family's friends. Okay. Here." The light in Devin's voice had dimmed. He gently placed the phone on the console between them. His hand lingered on it a moment before release. "Do you want to go inside with me, Billy?"

"No, I'm—"

"Just go with him." Jac snapped, then softened. "Please."

"I guess I'm going," Billy relented.

"Yeah, before she bites one of our heads off," Devin said playfully.

She got it. Devin tried to lighten the heaviness caused by her attitude. He wouldn't return if he knew how close he was to the truth.

Devin and Billy closed their doors. Jac pulled the paper with the Castillo's phone number from her pocket and urgently punched in the digits. She turned the car key to the first click, then lowered her window, ushering in gas-tainted air to replace the scent of O-negative. It rang three times before an answer.

"Hello. You've reached Asilo Colina. I'm Ximena," politely answered a girl.

"Um … hi."

"Hi."

"Is this the Castillo house?"

"Oh, it's much more than a house, but yes."

"This is Jac—Jacqueline Kelley."

The girl gasped and dropped all affectation. "Oh, damn, girl. For real? You straight?"

"Am I … what?"

"Okay? Are you okay?"

"Yes ... no, I mean no. I need help."

"Chica, you got people buggin' around here. You cuttin' up the Dog Brothers and all. Honestly, I'm a little tired of hearing your name."

Jac's brow furrowed. "What? I don't understand. Can you help me?"

"Fine." Ximena sighed, slowly. "Whatcha need, girlie?"

"Blood. Is there somewhere in New Mexico I can get blood? Or maybe someone who can deliver it to me?"

Silence.

"Hello?" The conversation wasn't progressing as quickly as Jac had hoped. The boys weren't on their way back, but they wouldn't be long.

"Are you trying not to eat that boy with you?"

The accusation was spot on, hurt to hear, and Jac didn't want to think about it. She put her fist to her forehead and asked again, "Can you help me?"

"I gotcha covered," Ximena said, sounding uninterested. "The Castillos run Southern Cali and New Mex. Where you gonna be?"

"Some place called Las Cruces."

"Oohh."

"Oh, what?"

"Nothing. Our supply station is in Albuquerque. It's a few hours north of Las Cruces."

Jac scanned the storefront again for the boys. They were still inside. "Is that a problem?"

"No, it's all good. When do you need it?"

"When we get there."

"Ya. And when is that?"

Jac tapped her forehead with her fist and closed her eyes. "Sorry, I'm not thinking straight."

"You jonesin' girl?"

"No ... wait ... maybe. What does that mean?"

"Are you in a bloodlust?" Ximena said slowly and succinctly.

"Yes!" Jac said louder than she intended. A man pumping gas in an adjacent car eyed her, then turned away when she noticed. She lowered her voice and slid down into the seat. "I'm on day two and don't want to go another night. I don't want to hurt anyone."

"So then, how long to Las Cruces?" Ximena asked again.

Devin had mentioned the drive time to Las Cruces. Jac estimated the time they had been driving and made her best guess. "Two to three hours."

"Well, girl, you need to prepare to wait five to six hours."

Jac's head slumped. The nails of her right hand dug into the skin of her left arm.

"You there?"

"I'm here," Jac said softly, verging on defeat.

"Should I place the order?"

"Yes, please."

"Do you have cash to cover it?"

"Yes. Wait. How much?" Jac's parents had always bought blood for the family; she never had to for herself. For all she knew, it could cost five dollars or five million.

"O-neg ain't cheap."

How does she know my blood type? There wasn't time to ask. The conversation had to end before Devin returned. "Just tell me."

"One pint of O-neg and the delivery fee ... probably five thousand."

Jac worried she would kill Devin at any moment, making her more of a monster than she already was. Five thousand? Five thousand was a freaking bargain.

"I can pay for it."

"Okay, chica. Call me when you know where you're staying, and I'll have it delivered."

"Thanks." Jac worried she heard something in Ximena's voice, that she wasn't thrilled to be helping her. The Castillos were waiting for her; surely, they would have told Ximena to help when she called. Wouldn't they?

"No prob. And Jac,"—Ximena paused—"don't go killing that boy before the blood gets to you. We don't wanna have to clean up your mess."

Jac scowled at the phone as if Ximena could see her and ended the call. Her hands collapsed into her lap, and she relaxed into the seat. *I can do five to six hours. I can do it.*

The driver-side car door opened, and a hand holding bottled water reached out to her, followed by a gust of wind carrying the scent of O-negative. She trembled as a lustful feeling flowed through her like a sugar addict stepping into a bakery. Holding her breath, she forced a fangless grin, plucked the bottle, and pulled it close to her core. At the end of the outstretched arm was Devin's smiling face. The face that seemed to say, 'I'll never quit on you.'

Devin lingered as if he were awaiting a response, an apology, or a thank you, but Jac remained silent, and his smile vanished. He closed the door and walked to the pump to refuel the car.

Billy crawled into the back seat with hands full of drink and candy. "You okay, Jac?"

Her sweet Billy was always there for her, seemingly emanating an empathetic aura that covered and healed her. Jac wanted to be okay, but the blood delivery was up to six hours away, and her resolve weakened by the minute. Ximena had warned her not to kill "that boy." She secretly watched Devin pumping gas in the side-view mirror and quietly gave herself the same command, "*Please* don't kill that boy."

WHO IS THIS GIRL?

"Separate rooms." The words flew from Jac's mouth like a fist to a table.

They had reached the motel, and Devin had one foot out of the car. He paused, looking despondent, before climbing out and closing the door.

Jac heard and felt the agitation as the words left her mouth. Devin likely thought she had a personality disorder or was the absolute worst. Depending on the time of day, either or both could be true. Under the hunger, the pain, and the exhaustion, she felt terrible for how she'd been treating Devin. However, distancing herself from him mentally and, especially physically, was imperative. It was the only way for everyone to survive the trip.

"Jac," Billy said from the back. "Why did you call the Castillos?"

"For blood. I ordered a delivery of blood." She turned toward Billy after a brief battle with her ego, letting go of hiding her weakness from the only person who could relate.

Billy brightened. "Oh, that's great." His expression flipped to concern. "When are they bringing it?"

"Tonight. I have to call from our room."

"That's why you wanted our own room? So you won't kill Devin?"

Jac groaned. "How many times do I have to tell you?"

"I know. Just making sure."

Jac checked to confirm that Devin wasn't yet returning to the car. Something bothered her about Billy asking if she'd kill Devin, like he was preparing for the eventual act. Like he was readying himself to forgive her or give her permission.

"Billy."

"Yeah."

"If I needed … to kill Devin to survive, would you let me?"

"But you said—"

"I know what I said, but if I had to?"

"I don't want you to. I like Devin, a lot."

"But … if I had to. If the choice was between me and Devin."

"Well, I guess if you had to … then yeah."

Jac turned in her seat and focused intently on Billy. He appeared troubled by his answer. She unfairly asked a lot from him, but it was the difficult position they were in. "Don't, Billy. Do not let me."

"But—"

Devin appeared in her peripheral.

"No more. He's back."

Devin opened the door and slid into the seat. He handed a keycard to Jac. "I'll park the car around back and out of sight from the street."

* * *

Jac wasted no time calling Ximena—who acted equally indifferent to her as the first time—and gave her the motel's address and room number. She said the driver was already on the way, a couple of hours from Las Cruces. Curiously, Ximena asked for her clothing and shoe size and replied, "Oh, that figures," in a tone crossing the border into disgust, and hung up.

The sun was setting on the day, elevating the sense of urgency. Jac collapsed onto the bed and stared out of the window. Everything hurt: her bones, her skin, her teeth—everything. Still, there was relief in not having Devin sitting beside her, acting as a living, breathing temptation.

Despite knowing better than to focus on the imagined outcomes, her mind ran through worst-case scenarios. *What if the driver doesn't show up? What if he gets lost or can't find the motel? What am I thinking? Everyone has a phone with GPS. Except for me. What if the blood bag breaks, and he doesn't have a second one?*

She imagined herself roaming the streets of Las Cruces like some junky, searching in the shadows and alleys for someone with veins filled with O-negative—someone other than Devin.

Her feelings for Devin had grown over the last couple of days. The emotions were ... unfamiliar. New. And she wasn't sure what to do about them and if they were even real. She loved Devin's kindness and how he made her feel safe—when not confronted by other vampires—in this new and unknown world. He always had a smile for her, even when she needed to be mean. She wanted to be near him, hold him, and kiss him. Or … it could be the blood talking.

Billy curled up beside her, laid his head in her lap, and grinned at her.

"Hi." She smiled back and played with his hair.

"Do you want to lay your head in my lap, like you let me when I'm feeling bad?" Billy offered.

"Thanks, but that's okay."

"No, come on." Billy sat next to her. He dangled his legs off the bed, the tips of his toes touching the floor, and patted his lap. "It works. I promise."

Jac believed wholeheartedly it would work. Her dad spent hours comforting her during hunger attacks. She didn't believe it to be a miracle cure, but much like the boxing technique, it delayed the inevitable. Relenting, she stretched out on the bed and laid her head on Billy's lap. The tension in her cheeks and eyebrows eased as Billy stroked her long black bangs from her face. He instructed her to relax and repeated, again and again, it would be okay. Though still there, the pain slightly dulled, and the tension melted away.

KNOCK KNOCK.

The tension returned like a taut rubber band released upon a wrist. Jac sprang from the bed, put on her sunglasses, and rushed to the door. She nearly ripped a hole in the wall, forgetting to release the latch before opening the door. She didn't mask her disappointment. Devin's handsome face at her threshold would be welcome any other time. At this moment, he was an annoyance.

"What?" Jac gripped the door with one hand and the frame with the other.

Devin frowned. His resiliency to her verbal assaults clearly wavered. This time, he appeared genuinely hurt. No, more like hurt compounding on hurt. "Yeah, so ... I'm next door."

"Fine," Jac shot back, sounding instead like 'Okay. Bye.'

Devin's mouth opened, but the words never formed. Whatever he wanted to say, or scream, he didn't. He stepped back, looked down, then over her shoulder. "Night, Billy."

"Goodnight," Billy replied.

"I guess I'll see you in the morning." Devin turned away, then paused. He lowered his gaze. "You know, if you need to talk about ... whatever, I'll listen." He glanced at her.

Jac let Devin's offer hang uncomfortably between them. God, she wished he could help. If he were just some other freaking blood type, she'd still lust for blood, but not his. He'd be safe from her. Through gritted teeth, she muttered, "Yeah," slammed the door, and slumped her head against it. She threw her sunglasses across the room and squeezed shut her eyes, sending tears to the floor. Whenever she treated Devin horribly, it felt like she was killing whatever kindness remained inside her.

"Why do you have to be so mean to him?" Billy asked.

"So that I don't *eat* him," she snapped. Her voice was ragged. Exhaustion had taken over, and she had lost patience with everything and everyone, including Billy, and he deserved better.

She took a moment to regain her composure before facing her little brother. "I'm sorry, Billy, but that whole time, it took all my strength to fight the monster inside me that wanted to drag him into the room and drink his blood."

"It's okay. Come back and lie down."

Jac lumbered to the bed, settled her head on Billy's lap, and breathed through the pain as he stroked her hair. He whispered reassuring words, drawing her into a meditation of sorts, separating her mind from her breaking body.

Slowly, the light filtering through the window changed from sunlight to fluorescents and moonlight. She had checked and rechecked the clock on the table: first, a half-hour passed, then one hour, then two.

Where the hell is he? Ximena said two hours, and it's been almost three. He's lost. I knew it.

"What's wrong?" Billy asked.

"They're late. It's been almost three hours." She shook and rambled. "Ximena gave him the wrong address. She must have. On purpose. Ximena did it on purpose. She hates me. I'm going to call her."

Jac sat up, grabbed the phone's handset, and punched in the Castillo's number. It rang without an answer. She slammed the handset back in place. Violently, she shook her head, groaned, and tried the number again. Still, no one answered. "Damn it!"

Jac hurriedly paced around the room while grabbing and clawing at her arms. Her eyes closed at the subtle release of tension when her stubby, jagged nails broke the skin. Pausing, she opened her eyes and flinched. The reflection of her broken face in the mirror atop the drawer stared back at her. It resembled the face she wore on the bus, her face moments before killing the man. It resembled her fledgling vampire face as her father helped her fight the hunger. But this face was unrecognizable and terrifying. She wore the face of a vampire on the verge of killing to survive.

"This can't be me," Jac muttered. Terrified, she ran into the bathroom, flicked on the light, and stared at her reflection. The signs were there: thin ashen skin pulled tight over cheekbones, two dilated eyes with whites turned the color of sacrifice, and sharp white fangs protruding from her mouth. The face of a killer. The face of a monster.

"Billy," Jac said, her voice raising.

Billy ran into the bathroom. "What's wrong?"

She turned to him, and the gravity of the situation registered on his face. It was too late—for meditation, stroking her hair, and gentle words. She needed blood. Now. "Don't let me do it." Her voice was hoarse, pained. "Don't let me."

Billy held her left hand as she clawed at her arm with her right. Tiny spots of blood had formed on her sleeve. "Stay here. I'll find someone for you. Someone with O-negative."

Her jaw clenched, and she stopped clawing at her arm to pull him close. "You will *not*. I will *never* let you hurt anyone."

Tears welled in Billy's desperate eyes. "Let me help you. I'll get him ... I'll get Devin. We can explain it to him. Maybe he will understand and let you drink from him. Just enough. Just enough to make you okay."

Jac eyed her brother and covered her mouth with a trembling hand. *Just enough. Of course. Devin was her friend. He would understand. No. No. My bite would infect him; he would change. He would become a*—"No, Billy. I can't bite him. I can't turn him into one of us?"

"Maybe ...." Billy scanned the room as if an idea would jump out at him. "I don't want you to hurt Devin, but I don't want you to hurt either." He dropped his head. "I'll get him."

Jac's eyes widened. Billy was the watcher of the door, the barrier between her and Devin, and he just offered her a pass. "You will *not*. Damn it, Billy, I told you not to let me."

"But—"

"No. No!" She pushed past him, rushing from the bathroom. Her speech was choppy, frantic. "I'll leave. You—You tell Devin. Tell him. Tell him to take you to San Diego. I'll get there on my own. If I make it."

Billy ran after her, tugging at her arm. "You can't leave me! You're all I have!"

"I can't do it ... I don't want to," she pleaded.

Billy dropped his voice to a firm whisper. "Let me get him; please let me get him."

Jac violently shook her head, stopped, and settled into a dead stare in a reprieve from the pain. *Why is this happening? Why me? It doesn't matter. I have to get Billy to the Castillos. He's my only family. I have to be here for him. I'm the adult. I have to—*"No, Billy. Not you. I'll—I'll do it."

"You'll do it?"

The relentless hunger inside her reasserted control. Jac gritted her teeth and gripped her hair as her body contorted. Painful groans escaped her mouth like haunted spirits from unearthed tombs. Billy held her hand through the agonizing convulsion until the torment subsided, and she hunched over, heaving breaths. She looked around the room as if to confirm she was truly living through the nightmare and bent herself back into as much of an upright position as manageable.

Jac spoke in bursts. "Yes. But not here. Not in here. His room. Stay here." The clock read minutes after midnight as she walked to the adjoining room door. She bent at the waist and dry-heaved twice, then righted herself. "Get our stuff together. After this, we'll have to leave."

In a moment of clarity, questions arose from the darkness of her mind. *What will the Castillos do to me for killing Devin in their territory? Ximena warned me not to. They'll find out. They'll know I did it … and have to clean up after me. Will they forgive me? Kill me?*

"Jac." Billy held her hand. "I love you."

She gave her little brother an exhausted grin. Their time was up. Her body could shut down any moment, leaving him alone with Devin. Billy would have one hell of an explanation to come up with, but that wouldn't happen. She had chosen Billy over Devin and was okay with it.

Jac released Billy's hand and grabbed the door handle. Blood like a torrent rushed through her veins; her heart visibly beat from her chest. She shut her eyes, embraced the hunger, and allowed the monster inside her to take over. Empathy and humanity, which were a faint cry, escaped her when she turned the handle. Whatever caring feelings she had for this boy were meaningless. A room away had what she needed to survive, and she would have it.

She opened the door to her room, and to her surprise, Devin had kept his door open. It would be easier than she expected—Devin lay asleep on the bed, unaware and helpless. The light from the TV illuminated his face and cast evil shadows as if associated with her. No one would stop her. She would drink her fill, and Devin would be no more.

BREAKING POINT

Jac crept into Devin's room, gliding across the floor toward him like a phantom. The only light and sound came from an action sequence of some cop show. The sounds of a car chase and gunshots masked her movement. In seconds, she stood next to his sleeping body.

She craned her head forward and loomed over Devin like a reaper, eager to claim a soul. His jugular pulsated in rhythm with his heartbeat. The sweet-smelling substance was only a foot away, and Devin—the guy with beautiful hazel eyes who offered to help and hadn't given up on her—was nowhere. Devin existed as a means to an end, and that end was to satiate her hunger. Her protruding fangs ached and throbbed with her every heartbeat, and only the pressure from unbroken skin would ease the pain.

Stay still, boy. I promise it will all be over soon. It will hurt, I'm afraid. But not for long. The experience would be new, having never fulfilled her need directly from the source. A surge of endorphins like she had never experienced rushed through her like water breaking through a dam. Like a starved animal, she panted, anticipating a meal. She was powerful, invincible. She was a god.

Jac's mouth opened like a python preparing for prey, inching closer to Devin's exposed neck. His jugular thrummed, guiding her like a beacon. Nothing else existed in the world, just her and—She flinched. Quick footsteps sounded on the stairs leading up to the second floor, breaking Jac's murderous trance like a hypnic jerk, a breath away from Devin's neck. She straightened and shook her head. *The blood delivery.*

Devin still lay asleep, and she was still desperately hungry. All she needed lay next to her. She only had to bite Devin's neck and drink, and the aches assaulting her entire body would dissolve. The blood would be fresh and warm like she had never experienced. How could she pass it up for the refrigerated blood bag being delivered?

She placed her hand on his neck and stifled a groan. *I want to drink from you, boy; I need to. It would be so good.*

The steps sounded outside of the room. She leered at Devin, at the vein throbbing in his neck. It would have been easy, like a lioness taking a lamb. But she had just enough awareness to recognize the other option, the one planned to keep her from killing him. That option stood outside her door, which received a knock.

Fearful Devin would awaken and see her ghoulish face hovering over him, Jac stepped lightly but quickly, leaving the room. She gently shut her door, leaving his open as he had it.

A second knock sounded when Jac opened the door to the smell of cigarette smoke, liquor, and an amalgamation of perfumes. A male vampire of diminutive stature stood before her. He had dark and neatly slicked-back hair and sunglasses-covered eyes. He held a mini cooler, the kind you would buy from a superstore, in his right hand. *Classy*, Jac thought.

"Where the hell have you been?" Jac demanded, louder than she would have liked. She never thought she'd ask that question. Her mother occasionally asked her father the same after coming home late at night.

"Good evening," the vampire said, bowing. "Bonaventure at your service. You may call me Bonnie." Bonnie straightened and lowered his sunglasses. "Holy Hell. You look like whatever scares the crap out of death. You really *do* need this. If I knew, I would have skipped the club and come straight from Burque."

Jac shook, making nervous movements as if she were getting into a song only she could hear. Didn't he know how badly she needed the blood? Didn't Ximena tell him? "Give it to me. Now," she growled.

"Normally, I would ask for cash up front, but the Castillos sent me, so—"

"*Now*, I said." She reached for the cooler with shaky, addict-hands.

"Okay, okay," Bonnie said, pulling the cooler away. Nervously, he scanned the surroundings, then motioned Jac to step back. She complied, and Bonnie stepped into the room, closing the door behind him. He and Billy exchanged hellos.

"Hurry," Jac cried in a voice more animal than human.

"Ask no more." He pulled back the cooler top, releasing a waft of cold air, and pulled out a pint bag of blood. He barely got to say O-negative when she snatched the bag from his hand.

Jac popped open the PVC bag. She shoved the opening into her mouth, tilted her head back, and squeezed the bag, ravenously sucking it dry. Blood droplets trickled from the corners of her mouth, like an infant drinking from a bottle. She pulled the bag away from her lips, coughing and gagging.

Bonnie held a wineglass in his hand. "I thought you might want this. It's an added touch the Castillos—"

"One more. I need one more," she said breathlessly, pushing away Bonnie's hand.

"They are five thousand—"

"Give. Me. Another," she ordered, sticking her still horrifying, bloody, dagger-toothed face close to his.

Bonnie held his palm toward her. "Okay, okay. Merda." He handed her a second bag and stepped back as if he had just fed a pound of beef to a lion. "You know, you're lucky I came prepared. Everyone always asks why I take two bags on my deliveries." He tapped his temple. "You know what I tell them? I tell them it's because I'm a businessman. Eh?"

Jac gulped down the second bag as quickly as she did the first and sleeve-wiped away the blood dripping from her mouth.

"Are you okay, Jac?" Billy asked.

Billy. She had forgotten about Billy. "I'm ... good," she said, catching her breath. "It's going ... to be okay." The hunger relented, and the pleasure chemicals pouring into her system replaced the pain. In a moment of clarity, she focused on Bonnie. Her eyes narrowed. "Why did you close the door?"

Bonnie glanced at the door, then back at her. "Isn't it obvious? You being all vampire National Geographic. Privacy was definitely in order."

Bonnie had a valid point; still, the closed door bothered her. Tanner was the last person to close her in a room.

"Do *not* try anything." Jac assumed a defensive stance.

"Try anything?" It took a moment before Bonnie understood. "Oh, no. I don't take advantage of ladies. I'm a lover of ladies." He gave an awkward look toward Billy. "In the most respectful and mutually agreeable way. Like between mommies and daddies, for example. Besides, I heard what you did to the Dog Brothers." He mouthed an exaggerated 'wow' and held up a unity fist. "One of them a pin cushion and dead as death, and the other ready to play an extra in a pirate movie." He placed a hand over his left eye.

Jac reflected for a moment. Curtis *was* dead. She believed she had killed him, but hearing it from someone else made it real.

After a stretch of silence, Bonnie spoke with a salesman's smile, "That'll be ten thousand, and I accept tips." He winked.

Jac pulled two straps of bills from her backpack and a single one-hundred-dollar bill from a third strap. She shoved the straps at the vampire's chest and placed the extra bill on top.

Bonnie clumsily grabbed for the cash with his free hand.

"Here's another tip, Bonaventure," Jac said. "Never keep a hungry girl waiting."

He shrugged and laughed uncomfortably as he moved his sunglasses back into place. "So I've been told." He plopped the money into the cooler, closed it, and opened the door to leave. Pausing, he turned around. "The Dog Brothers, they truly are

... were assholes. Tanner more than his brother. I applaud what you did. But you should know that many influential vampires are friendly with them. And Tanner is still breathing. When you're in San Diego—you and your brother—don't leave."

Bonnie's last statement challenged the powerful, feel-good endorphins coursing through her bloodstream. She hadn't had time to consider how the covens and whomever else benefited from the Dog Brothers' human trafficking would react to her killing Curtis and severely disabling Tanner. Having the Philadelphia Coven after her was enough on its own. At least she knew they were. Who else would come for her? For all she knew, someone stood outside the door, waiting for her and Billy.

Bonnie held up a finger. "Oh. It's Chuck Norris, by the way."

Jac blinked. "What?"

"Death. Death is scared of Chuck Norris." He chuckled in that awkward, questioning way when wondering if someone had got a joke. "A moment ago, I said—"

Jac closed the door and flipped the latch.

Her once raging blood-high waned from worry. She was eager to leave Las Cruces and beyond ready to reach the safety of Asilo Colina.

SOMETHING'S WRONG

Jac paced the room, wringing her hands. Her heart crashed against her ribs like a pinball against a bumper. The fresh blood intake coursed through her, elevating her senses and emotions.

"We should go. We should go," she repeated like a crazed mantra.

"We can't go right now," Billy said. "You'd freak Devin out."

She paused and stared into the mirror. Crazed, bloodshot eyes with quarter-sized pupils leered back at her. "I can wear sunglasses." She paced again, and her hands resumed their wrestling match. "I've done it before, in the store. Devin didn't think I was crazy ... well, maybe he did. It's dark. Maybe he won't notice."

"It's not cause your eyes. You shouldn't have had the second bag of blood. You're acting super crazy." Billy slipped his hands between hers and laced fingers, bringing Jac to a stop. "We should get in bed. You'll be normal in the morning."

Normal ... in the morning. Jac slowly nodded. She gave Billy a half-there look. "Normal."

"Yes. Come on."

Billy pulled her toward the bed. She slid atop the covers and blanket, soaking them with her sweat. *I will be normal in the morning. I want to be normal.*

Jac lay in bed with her mind stuck in high gear. How stupid she was to not consider how killing and maiming the Dog Brothers would put a giant target on her back. But how could she have known or considered it? She was too busy driving here and there, fighting off the urge to kill Devin for blood and seeing Billy safely to San Diego. Regardless, what was she supposed to do? Let Tanner tie her up, then turn her, Billy, and Devin over to Edgar? "It's not my fault," she muttered. "I did what I had to."

Thoughts of Tanner brought her wandering mind to darker places. She had glimpsed a photo from Tanner's Hell-house when getting money from her backpack for the blood delivery. Eventually, she'd have to decide what to do with the photographic proof of the Dog Brothers' inhumanity. She *could* keep the photos to herself and figure it out on her own. Maybe she should anonymously turn the photos over to the authorities. Or she could show them to the Castillos and ask for their help. The second and third options required reliance on someone else when she could only depend on Billy and herself.

Jac turned to her side. Who was she kidding? She wasn't long for this world. The abducted women and children would have to be someone else's burden. Maybe she had already played her part in the story by disabling and killing the Dog Brothers.

She huffed, turning to her other side. Billy, her sweet little brother, lay asleep beside her. "Where almost there, big guy," she murmured. "We're almost safe." They were a day's drive away from San Diego. She will have brought Billy to Asilo Colina as Mom instructed, as she hoped. Yes, Devin was essential in getting them there, but *she* had convinced him to drive them. She didn't need anyone else. *Screw it. I'll figure it out on my own. I can't trust this with anyone else.*

Jac turned to her back. The room's adjoining door loomed in the darkness. It acted as a reminder of being seconds away from making the biggest mistake of her young life. While cursing the late blood delivery, she offered gratitude for Bonnie showing up just in time.

Devin slept only a room away, finally safe from her. She considered sneaking into his room to snuggle up to him. She'd apologize to add balance to their little universe, not caring if he slept through her words.

Apologize? She cringed. She'd prefer to forget how awfully she had treated Devin during the last twenty-four hours. However, an apology was the least she could do. In the morning, she would give one blanket apology—done and done.

Jac pulled the cover to her chest and settled her arms at her sides. She closed her eyes and started a meditation. Thankfully, this time, she wasn't searching for hunger to hide away, but instead a pathway to sleep. She focused on her toes, feeling their presence, relaxing them, and moved to her feet. Sleep won out when she reached her waist, and all turned dark.

Hours later, Jac opened her eyes to a dark room; the clock read 6:30. Ready to start the day, she showered and dressed in the clothes Devin had bought. While brushing her teeth, she gave her face a once over. Looking for anything vampirey, she scrutinized her eyes: perfectly white with pupils of a normal dilation. Her cheeks were full and flush; her teeth were white, in line, and blood-free. The punch bruise from Tanner had faded to a light brown.

The clock read 7:15. Billy still slept but made waking movements and noises.

Jac's worries had dissipated, leaving room for a wave of motivation. She hopped in place as if jumping rope. "It's time to wake up Devin." She checked her hair in the mirror and then hurried to the adjoining door. With a deep breath and exhalation, she grabbed the door handle and pushed. "Oh!" she exclaimed, taking a step back.

Devin, already awake, stood at the entrance. "Jinx."

She studied him. Was he angry, sad, or frustrated? He was entitled to feel all three.

Devin flashed a grin short of his usual smile. "Morning. I ... don't know what I did to make you—"

Jac rushed to him before he could finish what she was too ashamed to hear. She pulled his face close and lightly kissed his lips, sending a tingling sensation across every inch of her body. Fearing his reaction, she buried her head into his chest.

"Uh ... okay." Devin slowly wrapped his arms around her in a gentle hug.

"I'm sorry. I've been so mean to you. I'm so sorry."

"Mean is a good word for it, though I called you something worse in my thoughts and maybe under my breath a few times."

Loving his embrace, she hugged him tighter. He wasn't as mad at her as she feared, certainly not as angry as he should be. Perhaps she had time to salvage their friendship, or whatever it was they had.

"So, what was the kiss for?"

Jac considered the myriad of cheesy retorts and lazy answers she could give but went with the truth. She pulled back a little to meet his gaze. "Ever since the motel."

The space between Devin's eyebrows narrowed. "The motel? What does that mean?"

"I didn't think you'd come back after leaving us at the Jenks Motel. To be honest, I was scared you'd call the police. When I saw your face through the door,"—she cut her eyes, then gained the strength to meet his stare—"I was so relieved, but I wasn't sure how to show you how much I appreciated you. I wasn't sure I wanted to kiss you, until now."

Devin smiled. "Well, guys work a bit differently. I wanted to kiss you the moment I saw you at the store. No question. You had this tomboy, I don't care how I look, hotness about you."

"Wow, thanks, I think." She punched him gently in the chest. "Just so you know, you were an arrogant jerk."

"Yeah, sorry about that." He rubbed the back of his neck. "I thought it might work on you."

She punched him again. "And why would that work on me?"

"I don't know. You were a little rough around the edges."

"*I* was rough? What about you? Your clothes were stained, and you reeked of pizza."

Devin scratched his chin. "I probably should have considered that before walking up on you."

"Besides, I don't have a type." She placed a flat palm on his chest. "I've never had a boyfriend."

His eyebrows rose. "You? Really?"

"Don't laugh, but that was my first kiss." She scrunched her face and looked down. "It was good, I think?"

He lifted her chin, bringing her eyes to his. "I can't say I've never kissed a girl, but I can promise, knowing it was your first, makes it the best kiss I've ever had." He closed his eyes and leaned toward her when Billy spoke.

"Are you two done being weird again? We need to get out of here and get some food. I'm starving."

Jac stepped back from Devin with a shove, sending him stumbling backward onto his bed. She made a sound nearly resembling a word and fidgeted with her hair. If someone's face could melt from embarrassment, hers would have. "Yeah, we're almost ready." She mouthed 'sorry' to Devin, and Billy walked away with morning hair and a suspicious look.

* * *

Packed, in the car, and ready to leave, Jac hoped she had seen her last motel. Motel rooms were acceptable for a night, but the bed, bath, and air inside were used. She thought of home: lying in her bed on sheets that smelled of the lavender detergent her mom used, her dad cooking in the kitchen, and vanilla candles burning in her bedroom. Looking at the motel a final time, she gave it a mental middle finger.

* * *

"I'll be back. Don't leave me," Devin joked.

Jac beamed at him as payment for the quip. She'd never leave him, not that she could. The two-minute drive when fleeing the Dog Brothers equaled the extent of her driving experience. An observer would likely have considered the dirt road ramble less driving and more not-crashing.

Devin opened the car door and stopped to gaze at her as if they were saying goodbye. In the reflection of his hazel eyes was an intoxicating place, a place to reside and call home. Still, her face flushed from a bout of shyness.

"*What?*" Jac placed her hands over her reddening cheeks.

"I ... I just...."

"Yeah. Me too." Jac bit her bottom lip. She understood without him saying another word. Devin came as close as he would to saying, "I like you." She wanted to fully embrace how it felt to like Devin but had sense enough to temper the excitement. Soon, they would go their separate ways. He would go home, and she would stay in San Diego. Complicated thoughts already crowded her head without adding on how they would meet again. She was happy in the moment, which was enough.

Devin slid from his seat, closed the door, and strolled into the motel lobby.

* * *

Eight minutes had passed from the moment Devin left the car. About six minutes longer than Jac expected the key drop-off to take.

"What's taking him so long?" Billy asked.

"Don't know," Jac said. "Maybe there are other people in line."

"Go check on him."

"You know we can't let anyone see us. He'll be out soon." She tapped a knuckle on her lips. "He probably went to the bathroom."

Jac wasn't an expert in motel checkouts, but the other checkouts were quick. She *was* an expert in bathroom trips, but even that excuse was questionable. A logical reason existed for Devin taking so long. *Be patient,* she told herself.

Billy broke the silence. "Jac. I have a question."

"Okay. Ask away."

"Do you like Devin?"

She turned in her seat toward him. "Of course I do, silly."

"No, I mean, like him, like him."

Jac stared out of the window. When it came to liking Devin, she didn't trust her feelings. She might have been experiencing the exhilarating feeling of a first crush. But the horrible lie hiding underneath it all gave her pause. The Jac Devin had come to know was not the real Jac. The Jac Devin had come to like was a charade. Their feelings for each other were built upon a lie. Despite the complications, she had a simple answer: Unquestionably, she liked Devin.

Liking Devin wasn't enough to solve the complications. When they reached San Diego, the trip from Hell would be over. Billy would be safe with the Castillos, Devin would head back home to his drunkard mother, and she would find a quiet place to hide and slip away from the world. At least, that had been her set-in-stone plan. However, that once-hardened stone had a vertical crack through and through. Things changed since leaving Philadelphia. Now, she had a steadfast goal of helping the women and children in Tanner's photographs. Did Devin fit into her life? At all?

"Well?" Billy said, breaking her from thought.

"Huh? What?"

"Do you like him? Geez."

"I ... it's hard to—"

"There's Devin." Billy pointed toward the motel lobby.

"Finally." Jac sighed. She smiled and waved at Devin as he walked toward the car.

Devin frowned and lowered his head instead of returning the gesture.

"That's strange," Jac muttered.

Minutes ago, Devin couldn't take his eyes off her. Now, inexplicably, he looked away at the first chance. He walked hesitantly, sluggishly, as if he was questioning returning to the car. His face was ashen. It seemed like he would vomit or already had. The fifteen minutes he had been gone now felt like an eternity; a lot can happen in an eternity.

"Billy," Jac said, keeping her eyes on Devin.

"Yeah."

"Something's wrong."

I HAVE TO TELL YOU SOMETHING

Jac regarded Devin as he climbed into the car. Stiffly, he closed the door and turned the ignition.

"You two ready?" Devin asked, his voice empty of life.

Moments ago, Jac was the center of his world. Now she felt like a stranger, as if for the first time he truly was the driver and she was the passenger.

"You okay?" Jac clutched her arms to her chest.

He glanced at her. "Yeah, I'm good. We ready?"

"Yeah, sure, we're ready," she said, unintentionally matching his uninterested tone. *He's lying. Something* is *wrong.*

Devin had changed sometime after entering the hotel and returning to the car. He acted distant. Billy sat in the back with his hands clasped at his chest. He cut his eyes to Devin and then back to her.

"It's about ten hours to San Diego. We'll stop for a break in about five."

He found out about us. Somehow, he found out. Jac swallowed hard. "Devin—"

"I don't feel like talking right now, if that's okay." He looked at her, then turned away and lowered his head. "I just want to focus on the drive. I'll be out of your life in ten hours."

Jac couldn't disagree with him, but she didn't care to be hit in the face with it. Yes, the moment they left Oklahoma, the trip was planned as one-way for her and Billy, and Devin would return to Jenks alone. She's a vampire, and he's her life-giving blood type; they could never be together, but it stung anyway.

No one spoke during the drive. Music played, but Jac only noticed an occasional lyric. Billy quietly sang along to some songs. Devin sat as close to his door as he could, and peripherally, she caught him stealing glances at her.

Jac sat in contemplation, working out her confusion. The silence, and Devin acting distant, revved her anxiety. She wanted to protest, scream, and demand he tell her what was wrong. Maybe he was pushing her away because he believed it would make it easier to say goodbye. But easier for who? Knowing Devin for the short time she had, if he were trying to make the goodbye easier, he acted this way to make it easier on *her*. But she couldn't discard the theory that he found out about what happened on the bus.

"Devin," Billy said.

Devin scratched his forehead. "Yeah."

"Are you going to miss us when you leave?"

Devin's left hand squeezed the steering wheel. He lightly pounded his forehead with his right.

"When you go back to Oklahoma," Billy continued as if he needed to clarify.

Jac looked back at Billy and then at Devin, hoping Billy's question would get him to open up.

"I can't do this." Devin slammed the brakes without warning, slowing the car from seventy to nearly zero in seconds. He pulled to the road's shoulder, parked, and turned off the ignition.

Gripping the handle above her seat, Jac checked on Billy and turned to Devin. "What the Hell!"

"Geez," Billy exclaimed, righting himself.

Devin pounded on the steering wheel, then looked at her. His eyes welled with tears, and his face burned a bright red. His expression lived somewhere between a scowl and a frown. "Tell me about Sarah."

The comment didn't click at first. Then it did, and it clicked hard. *He knows. My God, he knows.* Sarah, the name on her fake identification Sunny had provided. Sarah, the name under which she purchased the bus tickets. The heat from embarrassment and guilt raged through her. If she were ever to spontaneously combust, this would be the time. She deflected. "Sarah? Who's Sarah?"

"Really? Is that how this is going to go?" Devin said coldly.

Jac shrugged.

Billy pulled his legs up to his chest and buried his head behind his knees.

Devin's eyes deadlocked with hers. "Are you going to kill me, too?"

"Devin, I would never hurt you. What are you talking about?" Her throat tightened as if the truth were suffocating her.

"You and Aaron, you're going to kill me ... when we get to San Diego ... when you are done with me."

"Devin,"—Jac slowly shook her head—"*no.*"

Devin pulled a folded piece of paper from his pant pocket and tossed it in her lap. "I had the motel clerk print this out for me. Open it. Take a look."

She opened the twice-folded paper with shaky hands, revealing grayscale portraits of two people—a young boy named Aaron and a girl named Sarah. The image of the boy resembled Billy, and the image of Sarah looked exactly like her. Exactly.

Horrified into silence, Jac struggled for breath. The world spun around her in bright, blurred colors and into black nothingness. Faintly, Billy called for her as his hand grabbed her shoulder. Devin yelled at Billy to stay back or to stay away.

"Billy," Jac muttered.

Billy rubbed her shoulders. "Breathe, just breathe."

Her sight returned, and the world was a wave pool. She pressed her hands against the dashboard, attempting to force the world to stop moving.

Devin scoffed. "Is this part of the act? The Sarah and Aaron show?"

"What did—What did you hear?" she asked.

"Do you honestly want me to tell you? You should be the one telling *me.*"

Unsure of what Devin knew, Jac didn't want to divulge more than needed. She wanted to hear it from him. "You. You tell."

Devin grabbed his door handle as he spoke. "It was you two; you killed a man on the bus in Oklahoma. It's all over the news. The police, the FBI, everyone's looking for you." He pointed a finger at her. "Those images are dead on."

Jac ducked her head and hid behind her hair. "Devin, do you trust me?"

He laughed nervously. "Trust you? I don't know who you are. You told me your names were Jac and Billy. I believed the BS story about your stepfather. And those people after us, like you're in the mob or something." His eyes widened as if he had solved some great mystery. "That's it. You're some mobster's daughter, and you killed the guy on the bus as a hit job or something."

Jac shook her head, then surveyed the barren landscape. A car drove by every few seconds. They weren't alone, but they were alone enough. She needed time to figure this out.

"And you, Billy, or is it Aaron? Whatever your name is, you were like a little brother—"

"Shut up!" She wheeled around toward Devin.

"Or what? Are you going to—"

"I said, shut up!" She glared at him.

Devin opened his car door and moved to leave, but Jac grabbed his right arm and pulled him back. He yelled and kicked his feet, attempting to tear himself away.

"I need to tell you something," she urged.

Devin, looking terrified, fought against her grip, grabbing and clawing. "Let ... go of me!"

"I'll let you go, but you have to close the door and sit with me. I also need you to understand that if you run away, I'll run you down and drag you back into this car!"

Devin's eyes showed understanding after failing to free himself from her grip. He slumped into the seat, the fight from him gone.

"Are you done?" she asked, as if Devin were a kid just finishing throwing a tantrum.

Devin nodded once, huffing.

Jac released his arm and watched him closely as he shut his door. He straightened his shirt and winced as he rubbed his reddening arm.

"How are you so strong?" he asked.

"Like I said, I need to tell you something."

"I know where you can start."

She humored him. "Where?"

"What are your real names?"

"Jacqueline and William Kelley. Sarah and Aaron are fake names we used to help keep us safe."

Devin shook his head. "Safe, that's funny. Then answer this."

Here it comes.

"Did you kill the man on the bus?"

"Devin." She leaned toward him. He pulled back against his door. "If I tell you, will you promise to hear me out?"

His eyes bulged. "Oh God, that's a yes."

"Please, hear me out. Then, if you still want, you can leave us here and drive back home."

He locked onto her eyes. "The truth? You'll tell me the truth?"

"The absolute truth."

Billy sat forward with a look of concern. "Jac. What are you doing?"

"Billy, please shut up and let me do this."

"But—"

She raised a palm at him. "Billy, please!"

Billy sat back in the seat and, again, pulled his legs to his chest. "You really shouldn't."

"Devin." She reached for his shoulder, but he pushed her hand away.

"Just talk. Don't touch me."

Jac rubbed her sweaty hands down her pants and tapped her knuckles together. She would do it; she would tell Devin the truth. Not only the truth about what happened on the bus, but all truths. Billy was right; she shouldn't. But the time for lies was over.

"I did it ... I killed the man on the bus." She said the words without breaking down.

"Wha—" The admission stole the breath and words from Devin. He reached for the door handle.

Jac grabbed the back of his shirt and held him in place. "You promised."

"That was before I knew for sure you killed him." He pulled at her arm and pulled away, stretching out his shirt collar.

"I killed him to save Billy."

The fight in Devin halted. "What? How could killing him save Billy?"

"Jac, no," Billy pleaded.

She raised a firm, hushing finger at Billy. "Devin, you cannot tell anyone what I'm about to tell you."

"Or what?"

"Or your life will be in danger."

"Are you serious?" He tittered. "Then don't tell me."

She released his shirt, leaving it crumpled at the back of his neck.

"Devin—" Jac paused to listen to the inner voice urging her against disclosing their secret. The voice cautioned against making an enormous mistake and putting them all in greater danger, especially Devin. But it was not the time to heed that tiresome voice. It was time for honesty, to pull off the Band-Aid in one quick pull.

As if he were a child, Devin covered his ears.

"Devin ... I'm a vampire." The words left her mouth with a rush of relief, guilt, and adrenaline.

Devin's hands dropped, and he slowly turned his head toward her, his mouth slack.

Jac smiled widely, revealing her extended canines.

His eyes bulged. "What in Hell?"

ASK ME ANYTHING

Devin's butt hit the road first. He clambered to his feet, wiped the gravel from his palms, and looked around wildly, as if searching for somewhere to run on the long stretch of highway.

"Devin, get in the car," Jac called from her seat.

"No freaking way. You get out."

And just like that, they replayed the first night they met outside Devin's trailer.

"*Please* get back in. I won't hurt you."

Billy opened his door and pulled himself up between the door and the frame. "Yeah, we won't hurt you."

"I'm not getting in the car." Devin pointed at her. "You get out."

"Devin—" Jac began.

"A vampire? A damn vampire? Are you kidding me? Please tell me those are fake teeth you got at a Halloween store."

Talking him down wasn't working. Jac had to prove she wouldn't hurt him. "Billy, get back in the car, and don't talk back." She climbed from the car and walked toward the front end, close to Devin. He circled toward the back, keeping the distance between them like a kid playing a game of tag.

"I can do this all day," Devin said.

"I could catch you if I wanted to. Easily. If I wanted to kill you, I could have and would have by now." She slowed her pace but continued to circle the car.

Devin kept track of her while glancing at Billy. His eyes darted toward each passing car as if he considered flagging them down but decided against it each time. "Were you waiting for when you don't need me anymore? I thought you liked me. I thought we were friends."

"I *am* your friend. If I didn't like you, then why did I kiss you?"

He laughed. "Hell if I know. To make it all more real? You probably used some vampire mind powers on me. Glamor, or whatever it's called."

"We don't have mind powers or glamor." Jac smirked and shook her head. She'd heard the term on her most beloved and entirely unrealistic vampire television show.

"That's not exactly true." Billy pressed his hands and face against the window, watching her and Devin as if they were zoo animals.

A jolt of understanding appeared on Devin's face. "Oh, my God. Billy, too?"

Jac's eyes cut to Billy, then back to Devin. "Yes."

Devin placed his hands in a prayer formation to his face and bowed his head. "I can't believe I've been driving across the country with vampires. I can't believe vampires are even—How are you even real?"

She scowled at him. "You can think the worst of me, and I won't disagree, but Billy has never hurt anyone. When we get to San Diego, the Castillos will make sure he never has to."

"Oh yeah? Then what about you? What were *your* plans in San Diego?"

Jac paused. A passing car, too close to the shoulder, kicked up dirt and sand, sending her hair flying. She considered admitting what she had told no one. Billy shouldn't hear, but she wanted to earn Devin's trust; honesty was vital. "I wasn't going to do anything."

"You weren't going to do anything?" Devin asked. "I don't understand."

She looked at Billy, already watching her intently through the fingerprint-smudged window.

"I planned to leave, go somewhere far from everyone, and just ... fade away."

"No, Jac." Billy opened his door. She motioned for him to stop.

Devin stared at her as if he were working out the meaning of her words. "Wait." He raised a hand toward her. "Go away, fade away. What does that mean?"

Jac dropped her chin to her chest, unable to face Billy. "I can't—I couldn't live like this anymore, being what I am. I've suffered through it for so long. I'm done. Or, I *was* done. But along the way, during this trip, something changed."

"What do you mean, something changed? What changed?"

She removed her hair from her eyes and waved away the airborne dirt kicked up by a car blowing by at seventy. "Can we finish this in the car?"

Devin shook his head. "That's not happening. Tell me what changed."

"I don't know." Jac shrugged. "Something to live for."

"Like what?"

She moved toward the front of the car, distancing herself from the traffic. Devin took countersteps toward the passenger door while keeping an eye on Billy.

Jac knew the answer to his question, and with sincerity being tantamount, she told him. "The women and children in the photos. I think I can help them. I want to help them. And ... you."

"Me? You want to help me? I don't need your help."

Her words weren't clear, and now, embarrassingly, she'd have to spell it out. "No, not help you. I just ... like you. You get me out of my head, and my head is a horrible place to be."

Devin scoffed. "There will never be a you-and-me if that's what you're thinking."

"Yeah, I'm starting to get that."

Devin's words stung. But he was right—there would never be a them. She was stupid, ever thinking otherwise. More so, she was tired of arguing, tired of this trip, tired of who she was.

Jac gasped. A flash of blue light reflected off of the car window. In the distance, a state trooper vehicle approached them from behind, slowing and easing onto the roadside.

Devin focused intently on the approaching car. He seemed to consider his options, shifting his weight from one foot to the other.

Jac's eyes urgently flashed between Devin and the trooper pulling close. A heaviness grew in her chest, challenging her breaths. Devin would expose them, ending their journey together in an explosion of violence. She didn't want to fight the trooper, but she'd let her monster loose before she'd let him handcuff her and stuff her into the back seat. Someone would lose. Someone would die.

Maybe it wouldn't come to a fight. There was time to convince Devin he was safe with her.

"Devin, please." Jac clawed at her arms. "Let's get back in the car. Finish the trip with us."

Devin's eyes remained on the vehicle as it continued to slow.

"You can trust me. I won't hurt you, but if it comes to me defending myself and Billy from this cop, I will choose us."

The patrol car came to a stop about ten yards away.

"Devin," Jac said desperately.

He narrowed his eyes at her.

"Please," she mouthed.

"Billy, climb in the trunk," Devin said, keeping his eyes on her. "Pull the handle on the seat, crawl in, and pull it closed."

Billy pulled the seat latch, disappeared into the trunk, and his little arm reached out and pulled the seat-back closed. Now, only she and Devin knew of his existence.

Jac hoped she had gotten through to Devin, but she wasn't convinced he wasn't tricking her into dropping her guard.

"Let me do the talking," Devin said.

"Wait. Are you sure?"

He didn't reply.

Jac readied herself for a fight if Devin was lying or if whatever he planned to tell the trooper didn't work.

The trooper slid from the seat of his patrol car, closed the door behind him, and sauntered toward them. He had a square jaw, eyes hidden behind dark sunglasses, and wore his hat pulled low on his forehead. A patch on his blue, crisp shirt read Johnson. A holstered gun hung on his hip.

"Hi, Trooper," Devin called out over the passing traffic.

"How you folks doin'?" Trooper Johnson asked.

"We're good. Just pulled over for a minute," Devin explained, his voice calm.

Trooper Johnson pointed at the Pizza Mobile. "Got car troubles?" He stood beside Devin near the car's trunk.

Devin laughed awkwardly. "No, to be honest, I pulled over to pee. I should have gone at the last stop, but I thought I could make it."

I think he's actually trying to help. Jac wanted to feel safe, believing Devin was still on their side, but Trooper Johnson asking questions had her stomach in knots and her fingers feeling for her chopstick.

"You know you can't do that, son. It's illegal."

"Then it's good you got here before I had a chance to. Good timing, I guess."

Johnson scanned the area like he was searching for a pee spot. "Do yourself a favor; find an empty bottle in your car and use it as a portable urinal." He chuckled. "But be in your car before you do, or I'll have to arrest you for indecent exposure."

Devin gave a thumbs up. "Empty bottle ... got it."

Jac couldn't help but imagine the comedy of Devin sitting in the car and peeing in a bottle. Thankfully, he didn't actually have to go.

"Guess we'll be on our way." Devin waved casually at the trooper. "Thanks for stopping to check on us."

Johnson walked past Devin and peered into the car. "I noticed your Oklahoma plates. You're a long way from home. Where ya headed?"

Devin met Jac's eyes. "California."

She nodded in approval of his vague answer.

Johnson peered into the back seat, raising the sunglasses from his eyes. "Oh yeah? What part?"

"Disney. She's never been."

Johnson straightened and looked at Jac, allowing his sunglasses to fall into place. His expression was a mix of disgust and astonishment. "Never been to Disney?"

Jac shook her head. "No, first time." She always wanted to visit Disney. A couple years ago, she got hooked on watching people live stream while walking through amusement parks. She realized living through the experience of others was the closest she'd get. Despite being free from the confinements of her apartment, she was no closer to visiting the castle and animated characters. Keeping herself and Billy alive and finding their mom was her life.

Johnson gripped his belt and eased into his stance. "Well, that'll be fun."

"Yeah, I've heard," she said. Her hands now only gently scratched at her arms.

"Anyone else traveling with you?" Johnson asked, looking at her straight on.

Jac swallowed hard. *He seems suspicious of us. He saw something in the car, and now he's looking for Billy.* Maybe Johnson believed their story, or maybe he didn't. Perhaps he recognized her from the sketch of Sarah from a bulletin released to every police department in the country. Adrenaline coursed through her. "No, just the two of us," she said matter-of-factly.

Devin thumbed west. "Yeah, we're going to head out if that's okay. I have a bottle to find."

Johnson studied Devin for several heartbeats and turned to Jac. "You have a drink cup in the back seat."

Jac shrugged. "Yeah, so?"

"So, if the two of you are sitting up front? Who was in the back?"

Jac tensed. She reached into her side pocket, grabbed her chopstick, and stepped toward the officer.

Devin spoke up quickly, throwing her a stern look. "We take turns lying down in the back. It's easier to sleep that way."

"So, no one else is off taking a piss?"

Devin laughed uncomfortably. "Oh, no. I see where you were going with that."

"You do, huh?"

"Yeah, it's only the two of us. You can watch us pull away if you don't believe me."

Jac walked to Devin.

Johnson grinned, pushed the top of his sunglasses against the brim of his hat, and stared at Devin for an uncomfortable few seconds.

Jac sidled next to Devin and grabbed his sweaty hand, giving it a slight squeeze.

"Just the two of you?" Johnson asked.

Jac raised her eyebrows. "Just us."

Johnson tipped his hat. "You two drive safe, then."

"Will do." Devin extended his hand. "Thanks again for stopping to check on us."

The trooper shook hands with Devin and walked toward his patrol car. He waved as he slid into his seat and closed the door.

Jac breathed, exhaling slowly. She turned to Devin, already looking at her as if questioning the benefit of what he'd done. The look suggested he could dash to Johnson and give them up. An intense, uncertain moment passed before Devin motioned toward the car. They both climbed into their sides and closed their doors.

"Can I come out yet?" Billy asked. "It's hot as heck back here."

"Not yet," Devin said. "I'll tell you when."

"Why didn't you tell the trooper about us?" Jac asked.

Devin gave her a cross look. "I did it more for him than you."

It took a moment for understanding to kick in, then she cringed. Devin wasn't wrong. She *was* prepared to disable the trooper if it came to it, but she'd have killed the man only if it meant keeping Billy safe.

"No. I didn't want to ... I didn't want to kill him."

"Put on your seatbelt," Devin said distantly.

TAP TAP TAP

Jac would have flown through the car's roof if not strapped in. Trooper Johnson stood at Devin's window, pointing a finger down for him to lower it. Devin looked at her wide-eyed before calming his face and turning back to face him.

"Billy, stay quiet," Jac said in a whisper only he could hear.

Johnson wore an expressionless face, and the sunglasses made him difficult to read. He had figured them out. There was something they said, something they didn't, or they had acted suspiciously.

Jac slid her hand to her seatbelt latch and positioned her finger to press the release.

Devin lowered his window. "Hey. What's up?"

"I got this for you." Johnson held out an empty plastic sixteen-ounce soda bottle. "I was gonna put it in the recycle when I got back to the station, but...."

"Yeah ... thanks." Devin reluctantly took the bottle, holding it with his fingertips as if the trooper had already used it for the unintended purpose.

"Careful, though. I've filled two bottles in one sitting, so control the flow." He lowered his head and tipped his hat at Jac. "Sorry about the guy talk, ma'am."

Jac raised her eyebrows, grinned, and gave a quick wave before turning away.

Trooper Johnson pivoted and returned to his patrol car.

Devin handed the bottle to her. Lip curled, she tossed it to the back seat, where it rattled around and then came to a rest. They vigorously rubbed their hands against their pant legs as if friction would kill the imagined germs.

"Now?" Billy asked.

"Not yet," Devin said. "A few more minutes." He pulled the car back onto the freeway and sped off.

Trooper Johnson pulled onto the highway behind them about fifty yards. He followed them for a few miles before slowing and cutting through the median with flashing lights, off to ticket a less egregious lawbreaker.

Devin gave Billy the okay to leave his hiding place. The seat dropped, and Billy sluggishly crawled through the hole. Sweat soaked his hair, face, and shirt. "It's so hot back there," he said, panting.

"Put your seatbelt on, if it makes a difference."

Jac glared at Devin. "What do you mean by that?"

Devin grinned wryly. "You're serious? It's not like you two can get hurt."

"Of course, we can get hurt. What makes you think we can't?"

"You're vampires. You're, like, indestructible."

"Do you remember the cut on my hand,"—she pointed to her face— "and bruised cheek from getting hit by Tanner?"

Devin considered it, and then some realization came to him. "Holy crap! They were vampires, too; that's how they hurt you. The big one, Curtis, was strong, but beyond any strength I've felt before."

"You're right," Jac said flatly.

He slapped the steering wheel. "I knew it."

"They are, or were, vampires, but we can be hurt like anyone else."

Devin laughed. "You being a vampire explains *so* much. I couldn't figure out how you were so strong. The handshake. The punch." A spark of curiosity lit up Devin's face. "So, if you can be hurt, does that mean you're not, you know, immortal?"

"Not exactly," Billy said.

"How are you not exactly immortal?"

"We live longer, but not forever," Jac clarified. "Three hundred, maybe four hundred years. It depends."

"Depends on what?"

Jac sighed. *Here comes the blood talk.* "Vampires have to do the same stuff humans … regular people have to do. Eat healthy, exercise, don't drink or smoke too much—"

"Don't get hit by a car," Billy said, laughing at his cleverness.

"That can't be it. There's something you're not telling me."

"Blood." The word left her mouth with a layer of disgust and guilt. "We have to drink blood. It rejuvenates us." There was more to it, but she erred on the side of simplicity.

"That. Is. Disgusting." Devin grimaced. "Blood does not taste good. Have you tasted it? I mean, of course, you have. Haven't you?"

"Yes. And it is disgusting. Well, it doesn't taste bad … to us. I just hate the idea."

"What happens if you don't drink it?"

"At first, the craving hits. It's called blood lust. If we don't drink soon after that, our bodies hurt, horribly. It's so unbearable that we lose control. The timing is different for each vampire, but if we don't drink, our organs start shutting down."

"And then?"

Jac frowned. "After our organs shut down, we go into a kind of coma and eventually die."

Devin studied her for a moment, then refocused on the road. "What else? Can you fly? Turn into smoke?"

She grinned. "No. That's silly."

"How am I supposed to know? My entire vampire knowledge is based on TV shows, movies, and books."

"Then you can forget almost everything you know. We're biological, not magical."

"Based on what you've told me, other than the long-life part, being a vampire sucks." He glanced at her a couple times as if gauging her reaction. "What else makes you special?"

Jac felt an easing from Devin, like he was no longer worried about becoming her dinner. However, she doubted opening up to him could repair their relationship entirely. Still, his willingness to talk to her and his desire to learn more about vampires was encouraging.

"A lot of stuff makes us special," Billy said proudly.

"My dad would always say we're as fast as a cheetah and strong as a gorilla." Jac flexed her biceps.

Devin's expression soured. "Your dad. Was that a lie, too?"

Jac mirrored his expression. "No, that's mostly true. Our dad is dead, murdered. Our mom isn't actually dead. She's missing."

"Missing?"

"Yeah. We hope to find out where she is when we reach San Diego."

Devin looked into the distance, nodding as if he were manually replacing all of her lies with truths.

"But I don't have a stepdad."

"Wait, if you don't have a stepdad—which is good because the one you dreamed up was an a-hole—then who's after you?"

"We left Philadelphia to escape from the coven there."

"The coven?"

"Yeah, it's a community of vampires with a ruling class. My family is ... *was* part of the coven. My dad was a driver for Edgar, our coven leader. Edgar is probably up to something illegal to vampire and human law. I think my dad found out, so they killed him."

"And they're after you because they think you know, too?"

She lowered her head. "Yeah."

"And you thought getting me involved was a good idea?"

Jac frowned and reached for Devin's shoulder, but her hand froze in the space between. She pulled it back, fearing he would reject her touch. "No, I didn't. I didn't expect this to happen. I thought you'd drive us to San Diego, drop us off, and go back to your life."

It grew quiet, and Jac maintained the quiet to give Devin time to think. A minute passed when he broke the silence. "Have you been controlling my mind?" he asked slowly as if he feared the answer or was embarrassed to ask.

"No. We're biological. Remember?"

"But when I asked about mind powers, Billy said—"

Jac sighed, placing her hands on each side of her head, then dropped them onto her lap. "We do not have mind powers. We're more like super empaths. We can feel and sense the emotions of others, like an empath. If committed to it, we can improve moods."

"That's *kinda* like mind powers," Devin said.

Her head bobbed from side to side. "Kind of, but it's not as impressive as you're imagining. Vampires are highly attuned to the feelings of others. It's not just hearing an emotion in someone's voice or their facial expressions and posture. It's more than that. Like everything that makes someone who they are emits an aura. We can't see it, but we can sense it on a deep level." Jac nodded her head at Devin, wanting to promulgate his comprehension. "We can use that knowledge to manage and manipulate conversations and … relationships." She paused a few beats to study his reaction. "Just being around us can change someone's mood. And we can be very persuasive."

"Mind powers," Devin repeated. "Those are freaking mind powers."

"Yeah, I never thought about it that way, but I guess they are, sorta."

"You've been controlling me," he said accusingly.

"But not like that. Not how you're thinking. We can't tell someone what to do, and they'll do it. We can only improve someone's mood. What someone does is still their decision."

"When you kissed me, were you playing with my emotions?"

Jac's face flushed; she looked at Devin with sincerity. "No. I meant that."

Billy groaned. "Are you two going to talk about kissing?"

"Hush, Billy," Jac said, maintaining her focus on Devin.

"How am I supposed to believe you? You could be empathing me or whatever, right now."

Jac laughed. "I am not empathing you."

Devin frowned. "Right."

She reached out and, this time, placed her hand on Devin's shoulder. He flinched but allowed it to stay. "When I decided to tell you that Billy and I are vampires, I promised myself you would have my full honesty. You already know our biggest secret; there's nothing left for me to hide."

"So, I ask, and you will answer any question, honestly?"

Jac considered being completely honest, thought better of it, and then agreed.

"Anything?"

"Yes," she said exasperatedly. "If it's appropriate around Billy."

"I'm a big kid," Billy said. "I can handle it."

"Billy. Hush." She held her hand toward Devin to shake. "Deal?"

Devin glanced at her hand but passed on the shake. "Deal."

He doesn't want to touch me. Jac's cheeks flushed at her outstretched and unmet hand. She returned her hand to her lap and carried on like a big girl. "Ask away."

Devin settled in his seat as if getting comfortable for a long journey. "The kiss? Was it real?"

"Oh no, not kissing questions," Billy said with a heavy sigh.

"Billy, sit back and hush, I said." If Jac's tone wasn't effective, the look she gave him was. Recomposed, she answered, "Yes, the kiss came from a real place."

"And I *was* your first?"

"Yes."

"Then, that means you like or liked me?"

"Like," she said, nodding, "very much."

"Like," Devin said softly, then mouthed, "very much."

"Do *you* still ... like me?" Jac asked slowly, preparing herself for the answer that most assuredly would hurt. Her question only garnered a glance from Devin.

A moment passed, and he gripped the steering wheel tighter. "Do you want to drink my blood?"

Embarrassment smacked Jac as if he'd asked to read her diary, front to back. She took a deep breath. "That's difficult to answer."

Devin changed lanes to pass a car. He nodded at her. "The truth, you promised."

"Fine." She chewed on her bottom lip. "I am a vampire, and you *are* my blood type. Yes, the vampire part of me wants so badly to drink your blood." Saying the words was as difficult as she expected. She folded her arms and retreated, fearing his response.

"Wow. That elaboration made this much more real." He removed one shaky hand from the steering wheel and ran it through his hair. "I'm your blood type. What does that mean?"

Jac clawed at her forearms. Answering Devin's question would expose him to the part of her she hated the most and the impetus for her desire to leave this world behind. She wanted to scream at him to stop asking about his blood and her desire to drink it. She yearned for the mundane questions: What is your favorite color, music, or movie? Not what is your favorite blood type? She closed her eyes, followed her breath in and out, and straightened her fingers. "O-negative. We can only drink from someone with the same blood type or cross-type. It's the same rule humans have for blood transfusions."

"O-neg, huh? I donate every few months—the extra cash helps—and they are always pleased to see me. Universal, but only one way." He shook his head and laughed. "That sucks for you."

"Yeah, it does, I guess."

"Okay, one more question, and I'll give you a break. I know *I* need one."

She eyed Devin sheepishly. He had already asked the worst question; they would get easier from here.

"At any time during this trip, did you ever think of killing me or almost kill me ... for my blood?"

Jac went numb. Her mind twisted into a bramble of thoughts. The previous blood question was *not* the worst. She reflected on the night in the Las Cruces hotel, where she was mere moments away from biting Devin's neck and draining the life from him. The blood delivery arrived in time to save them both. His question was a dagger to her gut, and her answer would likely be one to his. She answered timidly, like a child admitting fault to her parent, "Yes."

"Holy crap." Devin took his hands from the wheel, sending the car adrift before grabbing the wheel and righting it. "Which one? Think of or almost?"

She clenched her hands against her chest. "First, you have to know, I would never hurt you."

"That doesn't answer my question."

"I'll answer, but I want you to know that I won't ever hurt you. Never."

He glanced at her and waited for the answer.

Jac felt small, as if she were shrinking in her seat. Her answer could move her further away from reconciliation, from any relationship with Devin. But she promised the truth. It was time to share with Devin what he was never meant to know. "Both."

WILL YOU STAY WITH US?

Fifteen minutes had passed since Devin's last question. Jac gave him space to work out whatever he was thinking. During that time, his lips moved as if holding a conversation with himself. She picked up on a few words he said under his breath: Can't believe; worth it; and home. It wasn't difficult for her to fill in the blanks.

Then, it seemed his curiosity got the best of him. He rattled off a few less intrusive and lighthearted questions. Questions as rudimentary as her favorite cereal—she promised him her favorite wasn't the chocolate one with the vampire cartoon character—to if she could shape change into a bat. The bat inquiry led her to question his intelligence, though she realized he was being a smartass.

A warming came from Devin but from somewhere frigid, far from the happy place they comfortably inhabited before he discovered she was a bloodthirsty murderer. She had broken his trust, maybe his heart, and deserved the animosity he had toward her.

The questions came sporadically and eventually stopped. Billy lay asleep on his stomach, spread out the length of the back seat, his arm dangling from the side. Jac fished through her backpack for the photographs she stole from Tanner. She placed a handful on her lap and pulled out a notebook and pen she had picked up from an earlier stop.

"Are those the photos you found?" Devin asked, glancing at her lap.

She frowned. "Yeah."

"What are you doing with them?"

"I'm studying them until I memorize their names and faces."

"Those guys, the brothers, they abducted people? Took kids?"

"They were human traffickers, kidnappers, complete trash. You name it."

"Vampires," Devin said coolly.

Jac nodded. "That too. That's the worst."

"Wait. Out of all of those, being a vampire is the worst?"

She tightly gripped the pen. "Yes, because of all the bad things they are, being a vampire makes them killers."

"Like you."

She winced. "Yeah. Exactly like me."

Several heartbeats thumped before Devin spoke again. "Why write down their names if you're going to memorize them? I mean, there are a lot, so it's a good idea ... just asking."

"There needs to be a record of their names if something happens to the photos ... or me. A notebook can easily be passed on to someone else. And, when I save them, one by one, I'll mark through their names until there are no more names to cross off."

Devin blew out a breath. "I'd never say I have girls figured out—any guy who says he has is lying. But you, other than the obvious complexities, are too freaking much. You are difficult on top of impossible."

Jac blinked and smiled at a memory. "My mom always said I'm the easiest vampire to read because I'm always so emotional, but also the most tiresome to be around *because* I'm always so emotional. Thankfully for her, she had Billy. He was always content and happy ... until recently."

"It sounds a lot like you want to live now."

She lowered her pen. "I hate myself, I really do. More than ever, to be honest. And other than the Castillos and Billy, I wish every vampire was dead. I'm not sure how to reconcile that. You know? Get it straight in my head?"

"If you hate them so much, then why save them?"

"Who?"

Devin jabbed his chin toward the photographs. "The women and children, the vampires in the pics."

Jac examined two photos, one in each hand, then stared at the pile in her lap. "They aren't vampires, well, most of them aren't. Most of them are human."

"Really?" Devin grabbed the top photograph and took a quick look. "How can you tell?"

"We can tell our kind by sight. It's a little more difficult in a photo. It's hard to explain."

"Empath thing?"

"Yeah, sort of, but not entirely. It's easier in person because movement and speech can give them away. Mostly, it's the smell. With a photo, it's the look in the eyes."

Devin handed the photograph back to her. "First name, last initial, date, and blood type. How far back—What's the oldest date?"

Jac flipped through the small pile in her lap. "Not sure overall. In this pile, it's May 2005."

"Man, how long have they been taking people?"

"I don't know. It could be decades."

"And how do you plan to save them?"

"That, I haven't figured out."

"I mean,"—Devin slightly shook his head—"how would you even know where to start to find them?"

Jac wrote in big letters at the top of a page in her notebook, "I DON'T KNOW," held the notebook close to Devin's face, and tapped her finger on the words.

He raised a hand. "Okay. Okay. Sorry. I'm just curious."

She picked up the photograph dated May 2005 for a closer look. Scrawled in black ink on the white bottom border, it read *Amanda T. O-neg*. She appeared to be Billy's age. The photograph was blurry, and the lighting was poor. Still, it appeared that Amanda T. was in Tanner's room, despite the walls having less graffiti, more wallpaper, and a different mattress. "She isn't a vampire; I can tell by her expression. It's her eyes; I can see the human in them: terror, helplessness,"—Jac wiped away a tear—"the fading hope someone would save her."

"How are those feelings any different from yours when they had you?"

"A lot different. I didn't feel helpless. I knew no one would save me." She studied Amanda T's face and stared into her frightened eyes. "Yeah, I was scared as hell for all of us. But I was getting out of there. Nothing else mattered." She looked at Devin. "These girls, these humans, were already broken. They had given up. It's all in their eyes."

Devin frowned. He opened his mouth, but the words didn't form.

"What is it?" she asked.

"I'm … sorry I couldn't help you with the Brothers."

She placed her hand on his shoulder without a flinch from him. "If it were a human situation, I'm sure you would have been my hero."

He smirked. "Your hero?"

"Yeah, you would have knocked them out with furious punches,"—she mimicked a boxer—"then swept me up and carried me to safety."

"You make it sound like an old western movie. Thanks, I think."

"You're welcome. But don't worry, I don't want a vampire-Devin to save me. I like you exactly as you are—human."

The words "like you" came out before her mind caught up with her mouth. She shied away, looking down at her notebook and peeking at Devin from her peripheral. He glanced at her several times but never spoke, never returned the words she desperately wanted to hear. For him to say, 'I forgive you for what you are and what you did. Can we be friends again, or whatever we were?'

Reconciliation and forgiveness were too much to hope for.

"When will we reach San Diego?" Jac asked, saving her, and likely Devin, from the awkward silence.

Devin checked his phone. "I think around ... seven. That's about three hours."

The corners of her mouth twitched. "We're finally almost there." She nodded for no reason while finding the words to say. "You'll be free of us soon. I guess you'll be relieved." She fished for an answer, one she wasn't sure she wanted to hear. With Devin recently learning her truth, she wanted clarity on what grounds their relationship stood.

"Yeah, just don't forget to pay your fare."

It wasn't the hoped-for response. There was a time she would have punched him in the arm for being snarky. But that's not who they were, at least not now. Her heart hurt at the thought of Devin dropping her and Billy off in San Diego, getting paid, and then unceremoniously driving away.

Being honest with herself, she wanted more time with Devin. Time to make things right, to fix their relationship. He was only hours away from leaving and forever thinking the worst of her. But there could be hope with the sun dipping on the back half of the day. They would have driven for eleven hours; there was no way he'd start home tonight. Maybe she had one more night.

"Devin," Jac said.

"Yeah."

"It's gonna be late when we get there."

He scanned the sky for the Sun through the window. "Not *too* late."

She hesitated, then asked, "Are you driving back home tonight?"

"I haven't decided yet."

Devin's answer hovered above her like a helium balloon, ready to grab. The possibility she had hoped for. "Will you stay with me ... with us for one more night?" She couldn't bear to look at him. For the first time, she didn't want to read his expression but let the words alone cut her in half or make her whole.

A half minute passed without an answer. Jac gained the resolve to look at Devin. He was already looking at her, but with only the slightest semblance of how he did before discovering her secret—when she was special to him. He said nothing and refocused on the road.

Jac kept her eyes on him, awaiting an answer. He met her stare in the cold, empty space between words, clearly forced a smile, and gave a single nod.

SUNSETS AND GOODBYES

Jac had believed, had hoped, that the motel in Las Cruces was her last, but here she was in San Diego, again placing her backpack on a rental bed. She concluded that with her newfound motivation to locate the people in the photos, she'd live as a motel resident for the foreseeable future—which, for vampires, was a long time.

Overcome by an urge to find each woman and child Tanner and Curtis abducted, she had viewed, memorized, and documented the names of nearly half of the photographed victims. First on the list: Amanda T.

She couldn't know if Amanda T. or any of them were still alive or how she'd find them. However, she had a good idea of where and with whom to start. How she would save them if she found them was a completely different question and a ten-story hurdle. For now, all of that would have to wait.

She opened the adjoining door of her room, revealing the closed door to Devin's room, and gently turned the locked handle. The rejection and mistrust hurt more than she expected. Maybe he forgot to unlock it, or perhaps he smartened up. She considered knocking but didn't, unsure of what to say. *He probably wants time alone.*

Billy grabbed her from behind and tightly hugged her waist. She held onto his arms. "Hey, Billy boy."

"Hi, Jackie girl."

They gently swayed.

"We made it; we're finally in San Diego." Loosening Billy's grip, Jac turned to face him. "And soon, we'll be at Asilo Colina with the Castillos. Safe."

"What does the name of that place mean, anyway?"

"I don't know, but it sounds amazing."

He frowned.

She ran a hand through his hair, removing a few strands from his eyes. "What's wrong?"

"You're not staying ... you're leaving me."

"Oh, Billy." She walked Billy over to the bed and sat him next to her. "I will never leave you forever. I just have stuff I need to do, and I can't do it if I stay at Asilo Colina. But I will come back, I promise."

"Every day?"

She pouted and pulled him in for a hug. "No, silly, not every day."

"Every week?"

"Closer, but no promises."

Billy fell silent and looked as if he had a question he wasn't sure how to ask. "Jac?"

"Yes."

"You don't want to leave me forever anymore? Do you?"

Not long ago, she would have been terrified to answer that question for Billy. But now? Searching for the answer in the dark places of her mind, she didn't find that hideous, defeating belief that the world would be a better, safer, more peaceful place if she were dead. Relieved, she answered, "No, I don't."

With damp eyes, he looked at her. "You'll be my sister forever?"

"Forever, *that* I can promise."

A noise came from outside the door. Jac's heart raced, searching the room for something to use as a weapon, somewhere to hide Billy, when a knock came.

KNOCK knock-knock KNOCK

Jac breathed. "That's Devin." She opened the door, revealing Devin's gorgeous face against the remaining blue sky, juxtaposed with orange clouds and red and yellow streaks from the sun setting behind him. A moment seared into her memory.

Devin stepped aside, giving her an unobstructed view from their fourth-floor room. "I thought you might want to see a West Coast sunset."

Jac, eyes wide and jaw dropped, stepped from the room with Billy close in tow.

"Wow, that's so cool." Billy rushed to the railing for a closer look.

Jac felt Devin's eyes upon her as she marveled at the sunset.

"First real sunset?" Devin asked.

She gave him a smile, then turned her gaze back to the sky. "Where I live in Philly, I can see a decent sunset from the roof of our building,"—she slowly shook her head—"but nothing close to this. Nothing like this."

"We can watch from the beach. But we have to hurry; it'll be gone in about thirty minutes."

"That would be amazing." Jac rushed into the room and returned with her key card. "Let's go."

They took the stairs to the floor level, passed through the lobby, and the poolside deck lined with loungers and umbrella-covered tables with surrounding chairs. Billy, for once, was disinterested in the pool, knowing a much grander body of water awaited him.

They walked down wooden stairs worn from the elements, past flanking palm trees, and onto the beach sand.

Devin bent over and loosened his shoelaces. "Take off your shoes and socks and leave them here."

Jac tipped her head to the side. "Why?"

"Trust me."

She and Billy slipped off their shoes and socks and placed them in a pile.

Jac dug her toes into the cool, soft white sand, sending a wave of satisfaction through her. She beamed at Devin.

Devin chuckled. "Are you okay?"

"This feels weird." She twisted her feet, burying them in the sand. "I love it."

"First time on a beach, I'm guessing."

She raised her palms. "Yeah, I'm from Philadelphia, remember?"

"Well, I'm from Oklahoma, so."

"I'm a vampire from Philly who was rarely let out of her apartment."

"Oh, yeah ... that clears it up."

Billy had already taken a seat, grabbing fistfuls of sand and letting it slip between his fingers.

"Hey, Billy. Want to check out the water?"

"Oh yeah! Yeah!" Billy hopped up and sprinted toward the shoreline.

"Careful!" Jac yelled. "Don't get in the water!"

"Wait," Devin said, looking concerned. "Can saltwater hurt vampires?"

"No. Why would salt water hurt us?"

"Oh, yeah. Never mind. I confused saltwater with holy water."

She smirked. "Holy water can't hurt us either."

He winked at her. "So, you aren't a *real* vampire, then?"

A gentle arm punch sent Devin stumbling across the soft sand. "Ouch!"

She steadied him, and they shared a laugh. Their eyes met, sending a warm rush through her.

Devin tilted his head toward the shoreline. "We better get him."

Jac agreed, and they sprinted to catch up to Billy at the water's edge. They stopped a few feet from the rolling tide, where Billy splashed around ankle-deep. The sunset waned but remained as mesmerizing as when viewed from the hotel room.

"It's like I'm walking into a watercolor painting," Jac said, ambling. She closed her eyes and took a deep breath as a cool breeze blew against her skin. "That smell. I can actually smell the salt in the air."

"We humans smell it, too, by the way."

Jac side-eyed him.

"I love the beach," Billy cheered.

"*He's* happy," Devin said.

Nervously, Jac slipped her hand into Devin's and squeezed. She tentatively met his eyes, waiting for him to pull away. He stayed, holding her hand with a matching firm grip.

Unexpectedly, Devin pulled her close, sending her momentarily off-balance. They giggled, and she snuggled up against him, holding his bicep with her free hand. Her heart fluttered like a kaleidoscope at meeting his stare. "Thank you."

"For what?"

"Everything. You have meant everything to us. We wouldn't have made it here without you."

Devin blushed underneath the red and orange sky and turned away. "Yeah, maybe."

She grabbed his other hand and turned him to face her. "Not maybe. It's a fact."

He stoically stared into the distance past her shoulder.

"Do you regret it?" she asked.

He met her stare with his hazel eyes. "Regret what?"

"Helping us monsters?"

Devin swallowed. "I...." He lowered and shook his head. "It's just...."

"You do. You still do." Jac pulled her hands away, and he quickly grabbed them back.

"Listen. I won't pretend to know what you are or why you do what you do. I can't be sure you aren't using your empath thing on me right now."

Her eyes teared at his continued doubt.

"What I know, for sure, before any of this happened, is that I saw a cute girl in my neighborhood store who I wanted to know. And when I found you and Billy in my car,"—he smiled nostalgically—"it was the most strangely amazing moment of my life."

Jac took a moment to revel in holding Devin's hands, his skin against hers, wishing it would last forever. She gazed at him as the remaining sunset's glow shone in his eyes and asked the question she feared, but the one she needed answered. "And now? How do you feel about me—that girl in the store?"

"It's … complicated."

She furrowed her brow and nodded. "It is."

"I really thought, before I found out about you, that we had a chance at being something. It felt like we fit, like two puzzle pieces."

"Yeah, but from different puzzles. Your puzzle is a snowy landscape, and my puzzle is a dark alley with rats and scary things in the shadows."

Devin chuckled. "Maybe I can learn to like dark alleys."

A stiff breeze hit Jac from behind, sprinkling her with sea spray and whipping her hair across her face. She shrieked. Devin laughed, and she giggled, pulling the curtain of hair from her face.

Devin grabbed her free hand and pulled her into an embrace. "You're still as cute as the moment we met."

The moment and the world were nearly perfect: the waning sunset's soft glow, the cool breeze, the gentle waves crashing, and the ever-closer lips of the guy Jac longed to kiss. A rush of warmth flowed through her. Lost in Devin's eyes, lost in the passion, her lips moved closer to his.

Cold struck Jac's legs. "Billy!"

Billy stomped the water swirling around their feet, soaking Jac up to her waist.

She held her hands at her sides. "Are you kidding me?"

"Let's get him," Devin said.

"You better run!" Jac warned her little brother as she chased him down the shoreline. "Try to keep up," she yelled to Devin.

She quickly reached Billy, grabbed him around the waist, and twirled in a circle until they were both dizzy and flopped onto the squishy beach sand. Devin caught up, laughing at them.

* * *

After the sun hid behind the horizon, they returned to their adjoining rooms and cleaned up, ready for their last night together.

Jac walked from the bathroom, brushing her hair straight. She wore the shorts Devin bought her and a clean, too-long T-shirt she borrowed from him that fell to her knees.

"I love the beach. Can we come back?" Billy asked from the bed, snuggled in the covers.

"You live here now. I'm sure you'll come here so much you'll grow tired of it."

"Never." Billy stretched and released a long yawn.

"It's amazing here, huh?"

"A-maze-ing."

Jac giggled.

KNOCK knock-knock KNOCK

"That's Devin," Billy said as if he were introducing a late-night show host.

Jac trotted to the adjoining doors and opened hers to find Devin standing before her, fresh from the shower. She took in a deep breath. "You smell like soap."

Devin threw her a strange look. "Yeah. That's the result of taking a shower, I guess."

She gripped the door frame, leaned in toward him, cocked her head, and cleared her throat, fishing for a compliment.

"Oh ... and you too. You smell like soap."

She pouted, not getting the desired compliment. "You're stupid."

Devin laughed, gently pushing her away. She scoffed and held a hand to her chest.

"So," he said.

"So," she returned the volley, her hands sliding to her arms, still embarrassed for him to see her old and new scars. She knew what she wanted to say (what she needed to say), but the words eluded her.

Devin slid his hands over her arms and underneath her hands. "What's wrong?"

"I don't know. I guess when we started this trip, and even before it, my life was taken away from me. I planned to take away what was left of me in San Diego. Along the way, that changed." Jac dropped her hands, taking his into hers on the way down. "There were moments that changed everything ...

that reminded me I have a story to tell, a life to live. I learned, again, that life is precious and is worth fighting for."

He freed a hand and pushed a stray strand of hair from her cheek to behind her ear. "What moments?"

"There were a few. Like when the Brothers had us. I found the courage and the will to fight them. I found the desire to live, and not just for Billy, but for the women and children they took. It's the good moments, too." Her eyes widened. "The world is so much bigger and more amazing than I imagined. The sunset was gorgeous. And the feel of the sand between my toes. This trip, this experience, reminded me of the beauty in the world. And...."

"And?"

She turned away; her cheeks and neck flushed. "And when you—When we kissed. You made me feel special ... wanted. That I'm not only this monster."

Devin stuck out his chest and proudly lifted his chin. "Ah, the power of my kiss."

"Don't let it go to your head." She grinned and placed her hand on his chest.

"This power is free whenever you want it." He puckered his lips.

She rolled her eyes. "I'm sure it is."

"Seriously. Whenever. Just let me know." He squeezed her hands. "And, if my opinion is worth anything, you're not a monster."

Jac frowned and gave a single nod. She leaned back into her room. Billy's eyes were closed, his mouth open, sucking in air.

In the hand of his extended arm, the TV remote. The audience, laughing at the TV show host, fell upon his sleeping ears.

"We're leaving in the morning," she said, still looking at Billy. "Early."

"Yeah, I figured," Devin said solemnly.

She smiled warmly at memories of their cross-country trip. "He'll miss you." She turned back to Devin. "Thank you for being so nice to him."

"He's like the little brother I never had,"—he bobbed his head side to side—"who can pretty much beat me at everything."

"Well, you know, vampires."

"Tell him I said whenever, wherever, forever, and ever."

Jac touched her chin, unsure of the reference, then remembered. "Oh. The song."

"Yeah."

"I'll miss you two singing it."

"*That's* a lie." Devin chuckled.

"I said I'll miss you singing it, not that you sing well."

He pursed his lips. "That's fair."

"I'll leave our door unlocked and your cash on the bed."

"That makes me feel a bit like a male escort."

She poked his chest. "I would have *way* overpaid if that was the service you provided."

Devin feigned hurt while she laughed.

"So, I got you something." He stuffed a hand into his pocket.

Her eyes scrunched. "Really? Why did you get me something?"

"Because it's almost your birthday." Devin pulled a white, woven cord bracelet from his pocket, held her by the wrist, and fastened it. "It's not much."

Jac held her wrist at eye level and admired the bracelet as if it were the most incredible gift she'd ever received. Indeed, the bracelet wasn't the most expensive or extravagant gift, but it was special. More than that, it was a piece of Devin she could keep with her.

The room was silent save for the murmured voices from the TV. A somber mood filled the space between them. That voice in Jac's head begged her to close the door between them for good. It would be easier that way.

"So, you have my number; if you ever need me ... just call."

Jac wiped away tears. "I will," she said, her voice cracking.

Devin hugged her, squeezing her as he kissed the top of her head.

She wanted badly to lean back, pull his head down, and kiss him with all the passion coursing through her. To do everything she could to make the moment last, to freeze time and stay right there, forever. Her sensibility and the voice in her head won out. A kiss would only make saying goodbye all that more difficult. She pulled away, looked at him through teary eyes, and placed her hand on his cheek.

"Good night," Devin said softly.

Jac lingered in the gaze of his hazel eyes a final time. "Goodbye."

ASILO COLINA

He introduced himself as Shaughnessy Heart, Emissary to the Castillos. He had arrived at the hotel precisely at seven A.M. as he promised Jac on their previous night's call. Unceremoniously, Shaughnessy ushered Jac into the back of a black limo with Mateus—the Castillo's personal bodyguard. He graciously accommodated Billy's request to ride in the front with the driver.

Jac looked up at the hotel room and fought the urge to bolt from the car, sprint the four flights of stairs, and hug Devin goodbye. But Shaughnessy couldn't know of Devin's presence. Devin knew too much. For his sake, she wished he was already on his way back to Jenks.

Shaughnessy gave the driver the okay to leave without him. Jac considered it odd that Shaughnessy, the Castillo's mouthpiece, wouldn't ride with her.

"Shaunessy isn't coming with us?"

Mateus shook his head.

Mateus differed from the prototype bodyguard Jac had seen in Philadelphia. He wasn't large by any standard, but what he lacked in size appeared offset by lean muscularity. He was young, maybe twenty in human years, had dark tan skin, and wore a close, thick beard. His ears were deformed and lumpy, like those of an MMA fighter. Tattoos peeked out at the sleeve ends of his white button-up shirt. Not the garrulous type, he only spoke to offer Jac a drink and snack, which she politely declined.

The quiet drive let Jac's mind wander as she stared blankly at the city's buildings and people mulling around in summer clothes. She thought of Devin and how she hated leaving him without a proper goodbye. Her finger ran over the woven bracelet, taking her back to their last moment together.

Should I have kissed him? Each of her decisions could be second-guessed. She cringed at remembering what she *had* said and what she *had* done. When would she see Devin again? Would she see him again? Was he just a forgettable crush? Or would she find out she couldn't live without him?

"First time in San Diego?" Mateus asked, his deep accented voice breaking the silence and Jac's reverie.

Jac's brain pulled her focus from the void to Mateus, awaiting an answer. "Yeah ... yes. Almost everywhere I go is my first time. So...."

"You like it?"

"It's very different from Philadelphia."

"But do you like it?"

"It's ... too early to tell. But it's pretty. Everything looks different and smells different. The flowers and trees are colorful, tropical."

Mateus flashed a brilliant smile, shaming all the other shades of white.

"Are you from San Diego?" she asked.

He shook his head. "No. Brazil."

"Oh, wow. How long have you been in San Diego?"

"Near ten years."

Jac's intuition told her Mateus wasn't a natural-born vampire. From her time in Philadelphia, she knew that bodyguards, more often than not, were turned vampires. Covens preferred turned vampires because of their unparalleled loyalty to the one who created them. Like they were bound in some way. Bound by blood.

"I've been vampire for nine years," Mateus disclosed, seeming to pick up on Jac working out the timeframe in her mind.

"And you protect the Castillos?"

"Yes, and anyone they have me." He nodded once toward her. "Like you."

"Oh. Thank you," she said, marveling at the idea of someone protecting her. Though, she wished she didn't need protection and could completely lower her guard and relax.

"No one can touch you. Promise." Mateus drew a cross on his chest with his finger.

Jac grinned and turned her focus back to the world outside of the limo. The farther they drove, the more impressive the homes' splendor and size grew. She imagined how many of her apartments could fit in any of them. "This is crazy," she said to herself. "Why would anyone need a home that big?"

"Yes. Crazy." Mateus agreed.

The driver's seat window buzzed as it lowered, revealing the back of the driver's head and Billy beaming. "Isn't this cool? We're in a limo like we're famous."

Despite her lack of mutual enthusiasm, Jac put on a happy face for Billy. "This is very cool. I can't wait to get to Asilo Co-lina." Then it hit her—they had been driving for much longer than she expected. "Are we still in San Diego?" she asked Mateus.

"La Jolla. A little north of San Diego."

With coaching from Mateus, Jac practiced pronouncing La Jolla. He gave a thumbs-up for her last attempt. She continued silently repeating it to ingrain it in her memory.

"We're close now," Mateus said.

Minutes later, they approached a guarded entrance. A small hut stood beside a black metal gate, slowly swinging open, clearing their path forward. The limo driver and the guard exchanged a wave as the limo passed, and the gate closed behind them.

The neighborhood had homes of many styles, all enormous, with immaculate yards of green grass, colorful trees, stone gardens, and driveways of brick or stone. The elevation increased as the road twisted and turned. By Jac's standards, they were driving up a mountain.

Jac turned to Mateus. "The Castillos, they're at the top?"

Mateus nodded and raised his eyebrows. "Yes. It's quite something."

A few turns later and a few hundred feet in elevation, they slowly approached another gate. A guard wearing a suit and tie instead of a formal uniform emerged from a small building, slightly larger than the guard's hut at the neighborhood entrance. He walked up to the limo driver's door. They exchanged a few words, and the guard knocked on Mateus's window and pointed down. Mateus lowered the window, and they exchanged hellos. The guard squinted at Jac and nodded at Mateus before waving them forward. Mateus closed his window, shrugged, and quipped about security.

They passed through the open gate, transitioning from blacktop to cobblestone road. The road doglegged to the left and ended in a cul-de-sac. Saying Asilo Colina was an enchanted land far from the city where she had lived for her entire life was an understatement. An enormous, white, two-story house—a literal mansion—with dozens of windows stood to their right. Another home, different but as impressive, on their left. The house at the end was a slightly more modest Spanish-style home with a brown stucco exterior, burgundy-colored tile roof, and a driveway large enough for ten cars. Tall blooming hedges lined the boundaries, neatly delineating the property line and no doubt providing privacy.

Jac looked wide-eyed at Mateus. "They own all of this?"

Mateus smiled at her expectantly. "All."

They rolled onto the expansive Spanish-style mansion's driveway and parked. Mateus asked her to wait in the limo with Billy. He exited the limo, jogged down a walkway toward the home, and disappeared from view. Jac didn't want to wait; she was ready to bolt from the limo, grab Billy, and explore this new and exciting world. But she aired on the side of politeness and waited as instructed.

At the site of Mateus's return, Jac grabbed her backpack and gave the back seat a once-over to ensure she had everything. Mateus opened the car door, and she slid from her seat. Billy stepped out, too, expressing his wonderment.

An overwhelming feeling of relief engulfed Jac as her feet hit the driveway, like she had been playing a days-long game of deadly tag and won. She got Billy to Asilo Colina. He was safe, and all would be right in his world. Intertwined was gratitude for her own safety. If someone had asked her forty-eight hours ago if she cared for her well-being, she would have dismissed the idea. Now, she had more to live for. She wanted to dance, scream, and cry, but she held her emotions, took a deep breath, and released it as she smiled at the sky.

"Welcome to Asilo Colina," Mateus said. "Follow me."

Mateus took the lead, and Jac followed close behind, her eyes engulfing the scenery. Behind her, Billy did the same, interjecting a skip every few steps. They walked along the driveway leading to a slightly declined walkway bordered by the same flowering hedge, easily two feet above her head. She gently touched the pink blooms with her outstretched hands as she passed.

Twenty to thirty feet later, the path opened to a backyard of green grass and gardens of various shrubs and flowers. A metal railing offered a protective view of the pool area on the lower ground level at the farthest point from the house.

Jac stopped. Her eyes widened. A glorious panoramic view stretched out before her of an unadulterated skyline. To her left was a bird's-eye view of the coastline and ocean a mile away, with rolling, silent waves. Ahead and to the right was an elevated view of La Jolla's homes and businesses.

"Wow! A pool!" Billy leaned against the rail. He craned his head for a better view. "No *way*. They have a diving board and a slide."

"Wow, indeed." The pool was an afterthought. Jac's mind was elsewhere, quieted away and receiving a full dose of visual awe. She flinched at Mateus standing next to her. "Oh crap, you scared me."

"I'm sorry."

"It's okay. I was just thinking. This place, it's so ...."

"é lindo," Mateus answered.

Jac didn't need a translation for what she heard in Mateus's voice. "Beautiful, amazing. All of it."

Mateus politely gave her a moment, then said, "We should go inside."

She tugged Billy's shirt. "Come on. Let's go. We'll check out the pool later."

"Oh, okay," Billy groaned, not hiding his disappointment.

They reached the door to the house, and Mateus paused. He turned toward her, hands clasped, as if mulling over something. "The Castillos ... they are something to get used to."

Jac tilted her head. "Something?"

"They are ... a curious couple," Mateus said, seemingly looking for a fitting descriptor.

"Curious. Got it." She decided to be agreeable, though still unsure what Mateus meant.

A waft of cold air greeted them as Mateus opened the door, followed by simultaneous "Ahs" from Jac and Billy, expressing the welcome relief from the California summer heat.

Mateus closed the door and asked them to follow. His dress shoes clicked and clacked against the scarlet-colored tiled floor.

The house appeared to haven't seen an upgrade in years, maybe decades. An old building or library smell accompanied the outdated look. The ceiling reached double the height of Jac's apartment, making her feel smaller than she already was.

The high-ceilinged foyer led to a low-ceilinged, narrow hallway lined with framed photos. Dozens, maybe hundreds of them: color photos, black and white images of various people in various places. Places that seemed unreal or from a different time. Ageless twins were present in most of the photos. She assumed they were the Castillos—Sebastian and Carlos.

Leaving the hallway, they entered an enormous room centered with a sectional leather couch fronted by a large, knee-high wooden table. Atop the table sat numerous drink coasters, magazines, and a well-kept plant. Large potted plants, six feet high or more, sat in two corners. A bar with underlit shelves holding copious amounts of bottled liquor stood to the room's left.

"Please, sit." Mateus motioned toward the leather couch. "I'll tell them you are here."

Jac sat on the couch, facing the direction Mateus had left, and pulled Billy down next to her. She reminded him to behave appropriately as a guest in someone else's home while agreeing he had had little practice at being a guest.

"Let me do the talking," Jac said.

"But what if they ask me a question?" Billy asked.

"Then answer it. No ... wait. Look at me first. I'll nod if it's okay for you to answer."

"That's kinda dumb."

"When you're the older sister in charge, then you can make the rules."

Billy gave her a look. "Fine."

The room smelled smoky and aged, like the foyer at the home's entrance. Only the couch seemed newish. Food and travel magazines lay on the table next to the local newspaper, La Jolla Times. In bold letters, the front-page headline read *Shark Attack at La Jolla Cove*. The story was a friend's account of the events leading up to and during the shark attack. The shark clamped down on his friend and pulled him underwater. Neither he nor the shark resurfaced, and neither was found.

Minutes passed, and Jac considered playing "I Spy" when the clicks and clacks of Mateus's shoes against the tile announced his return. He entered the room and extended his arm, guiding a vampire's entrance, who appeared forty-something in human years. The vampire moved gracefully toward Jac as if gliding and beamed a smile upon meeting her stare. He had tan skin and black hair with hints of gray pulled into a ponytail. He wore a loose-fitting, large-collared blue suit from another time, with a bright white dress shirt buttoned halfway, exposing the vampire's formed and hairy chest. Drawing closer, he clasped his hands, holding them over his open mouth. Jac stood and motioned for Billy to.

The vampire stopped a couple of steps from them. "I wasn't sure this moment would come to pass. My oh my." He spoke with a slight accent, his voice as smooth as he moved. He extended a hand, ringed from pinky to thumb, toward them in some kind of odd pointing gesture. "Jacqueline Kelley and

Master William Kelley. I am Carlos Castillo." He stretched his arms wide. "Welcome to Asilo Colina and my side of our home."

Billy held his chin high and grinned, clearly thrilled at being called Master. Jac considered asking what Carlos meant by "my side" but felt uncomfortable asking questions so soon.

"Sit, please." Carlos motioned toward the couch. "If I may apologize for my brother's absence. Sebastian is occupied with another matter."

The siblings sat as Carlos glided toward the couch across from them and gently lowered himself onto it.

"I suppose, in polite conversation, this is where I'd ask if you had an enjoyable trip."

Jac grinned uncomfortably.

Carlos tapped his temple. "Is there an answer in there?"

"Oh. That was a question. No, the trip sucked, actually."

"It pains me to hear that."

"Well, it pained me to experience it."

Carlos seemed to study her as if she were under a microscope. The conversation stalled long enough for it to become awkward. She broke the silence. "I love your home."

Carlos waved off the compliment with a smile and an obliged thank you.

"And the pool is cool," Billy said.

Jac narrowed her eyes. "Billy. What did I say?"

"Master William, I'm sure you'll become quite acquainted with our swimming pool," Carlos said.

Billy's face lit up. "Awesome."

"And your yard is amazing. The flowers—on the hedges—they are beautiful."

Carlos's eyes brightened. "Ah, yes, the oleander—a beautiful bloom with a heavenly aroma." His eyes trailed away, then refocused on her. "They are a lot like you, Miss Kelley."

"Um, thank you, I guess."

Carlos clasped his hands and leaned forward in his seat. "Please, let me explain. The oleander bloom, indeed, is beautiful, like you. Still, there's more to the oleander than beauty, something hidden within."

Unsure of the direction of Carlos's comparison, Jac remained silent.

"Understand, almost every part of the oleander is poisonous; if ingested, it can kill."

Now she understood. *Beautiful but deadly. Clever. For sure, they know that I've killed. Let's get this conversation out of the way.* "I feel bad about the man I killed on the bus. I had to—"

Carlos waved off her explanation. "The man, yes, you were hungry, and you fed. I'm certain you did it to limit the loss of life."

Jac stopped herself from correcting his assumption and explaining it wasn't she who needed to feed. Billy almost beat her to the admission before she grabbed his leg, which he knew meant "shut up." The thigh grab didn't go unnoticed by Carlos, but he didn't ask.

"But you didn't stop after the bus. You continued to bloom and poison."

The Dog Brothers. They know about them, too. Was the Castillo's relationship with the Dog Brothers personal or professional? What if they were upset with her for hurting and killing them?

She had to speak up and ensure Carlos understood she didn't have a choice.

She sat forward, took a deep breath, and spoke defensively. "The Brothers got what they deserved. They—"

"Yes, yes, yes. I know," Carlos said, nodding in agreement.

Jac's brow furrowed. "No, maybe you don't know. One of them, Tanner, he hurt me. He tried to tie—" She paused. Billy watched her every word. He was content, and a Dog Brothers conversation would only ruin that. She swallowed some of her frustration. "I'll just say ... they weren't kind to us."

Carlos smiled at Billy, then looked back at her. "Sadly, though Tanner may seem harmless on the surface, his true nature is one of depravity."

Wait. When did they know? "When did you know the Brothers had us?"

Carlos sat back, crossed his left leg over his right, and hid a guilty grin behind the knuckles of his left hand.

"Tanner didn't say he called you." Jac felt hot; her fingers slowly curled until her hands were fists. "When did you know?"

"You are a curious little thing."

She craned her neck forward. "*When?*"

"Is this how you typically conduct yourself as a guest?"

"You're my second host since leaving home. It's proving difficult to find one I can trust."

Carlos sat forward, narrowing the distance between them. "Miss Kelley. If you're insinuating that we didn't make an offer for your safe delivery to us, then you are mistaken. We spoke with Tanner. He called to apologize for turning you over to Edgar Guerlich. He explained that breaking a deal was bad for their business. We offered him the chance to name his price, but he declined. He's a principled man if not a good one. Thankfully, you made it out alive in the end." He relaxed back on the couch with open palms. "All. Is. Well."

"Yeah, well, no thanks to you." *Damn, Tanner. He did call them.*

Billy placed his hand upon her knee, easing her tension as if siphoning it from her.

"Six stabs, was it? To the chest and abdomen? As you know, vampires are exceptional at healing, but six stabs?" Carlos clicked his tongue, turning to Mateus, who stood at attention. "Well, that's too many."

"I had to do it. Curtis would have killed me ... after what I did to Tanner."

"Yes, it's quite the topic of discussion. Not everyone is pleased."

Jac couldn't help it; part of her felt terrible about Curtis. He was an asshole human trafficker, but he never touched her or hurt her like Tanner did. It could've been because he never got the chance. And the peculiar way he looked at her the first time the blade entered him. Something she couldn't quite put her finger on.

"And Tanner," Carlos said with a hint of wonder. "I heard he resembled a rag doll when found. Crumpled in a corner, half-blind, cussing and professing to what he had planned for you."

"So, he is alive?" she asked.

"Tanner survived you, but with ocular complications."

Jac found satisfaction in knowing Tanner had suffered and would continue to do so. She had to know if her destruction of the Dog Brothers affected her standing with the Castillos.

More importantly, did it affect Billy's standing with them? "Are you and Sebastian upset with me … for what I did? Did I ruin some business you had with them?"

"Oh, no." Carlos waved off the question. "We were merely familiar with them. Never have we required their services."

Never required their services? The claim didn't sit well with Jac. The Castillos had some knowledge of the Dog Brothers, and Tanner contacted the twins. Carlos was hiding something, but she wasn't sure if that mattered. *Mom, I haven't asked him about Mom!* "My mom, do you know where she is?"

"Oh, yeah." Billy sat on the edge of his seat and placed his hands on the table. "Do you know?"

Carlos eyed them curiously, took a deep breath, and exhaled. He opened his mouth to speak when a booming voice came from the same entrance he had earlier.

"Where are my guests? Where are my Jacqueline and William?"

Carlos rolled his eyes. "That's my brother, Sebastian."

WHAT IS HE DOING HERE?

Sebastian Castillo walked into the room like a caffeinated motivational speaker. He was a twin to Carlos, but Jac wouldn't have guessed. Unlike Carlos, who dressed as if trapped in another decade, Sebastian appeared right out of the current fashion magazines. He wore tight-fitting black jeans and a fitted, half-buttoned white dress shirt that fell inches past his waist and stretched to the limit from his muscular arms, shoulders, and smooth chest. He had cropped black hair as short as his neatly trimmed beard and a smile as big and white as a wedding dinner plate. Like a peacock, he strutted toward Jac and Billy with outstretched arms.

"Welcome home, Billy, my big guy." Sebastian lifted Billy into a hug and twisted back and forth before lowering him to the floor.

Billy looked at Sebastian and then at Jac with a beaming smile.

Sebastian turned to her and placed a hand over his mouth. "Oh my. Look at you."

An attack of self-consciousness hit Jac, sending her hands to straighten her hair and clothes. As far as self-maintenance and self-care were concerned, she was far off track. Her clothes were on their second wearing.

"Preciosa." Sebastian continued. "You're the most precious little thing?"

Oh my God. I must look like a tragedy. She pulled her knees together and lowered her head.

"Little Miss Kelley,"—Sebastian placed a finger under her chin and lifted—"it's so lovely to finally meet you."

Sebastian's perfection stunned her. She didn't see him the same way as a boy her age; still, his beauty was undeniable. His face showed some lines that came with aging, but he had glowing, blemish-free, bronzed skin. She would have guessed Sebastian was a younger brother if she hadn't known he and Carlos were twins.

Seconds passed before he broke eye contact and turned to Carlos. "I pray my stodgy brother hasn't bored you to death."

Carlos crossed his right leg over his left. "We've been discussing Jacqueline's travels and her qualities comparable to the oleander bloom."

Sebastian tilted his head, then nodded. "Yes, yes, I see. Beautiful, but—"

"Yes," Jac interrupted. "Beautiful, but deadly. I got it."

"And Jacqueline explained Tanner acted ungentlemanly toward her." Carlos looked to her for non-verbal approval of his word choice.

"Hijo de puta," Sebastian muttered. "Tanner is a resourceful but disgusting creature. And his brother, a mute brute, or, at least, he was." He maintained eye contact with Jac as he sat beside his brother.

Jac felt intense scrutiny from Sebastian. She believed he was more upset with her than he let on. But there was something else. An odd feeling in the room. They were hiding something; she would bet on it.

"Yes, let's keep this one away from knives," Carlos added, cutting through the layer of uncomfortable atmosphere.

Sebastian chuckled and then broke into a laugh. Mateus and Billy joined him. Carlos simply grinned, and to be agreeable, Jac flashed a couple of quick smiles.

"So, tell me, Miss Kelley." Sebastian relaxed into the couch. "What is your impression of Asilo Colina?"

"I've never seen anything like it in person." Jac genuinely smiled. "The view overlooking the town and the ocean is amazing." She looked around her. "The house is enormous and so ... interesting."

Sebastian scoffed. "Oh, please. What you're sitting in is a relic. My dull brother hasn't renovated in decades. There are ghosts of Studio 54 walking these halls."

Jac wasn't familiar with the reference but got the general idea that Carlos lived trapped somewhere in the past.

Carlos crossed his arms. "You're insufferable. Enough of that already."

"I'll give you a tour of my side of the house," Sebastian offered, "and I promise you won't ever want to leave."

Jac wasn't too sure about that. She was accustomed to staying in one location, understandably being forced to live most of her days with her family in their cramped Philadelphia apartment. However, traveling across the country and the memorable experiences brought out something in her. For now, she was okay with staying at Asilo Colina, where she could rest and recuperate. Still, part of her—a mammoth part—yearned to leave and experience all the world had to offer. She wanted to plan whatever it would take to find the women and children Tanner abducted, maybe reunite with Devin, and, most importantly, find her mom. She nearly asked again about Mom when Sebastian spoke up.

"But, before the tour, I'm afraid there's something uncomfortable to address." Sebastian motioned to Mateus, who motioned to someone unseen in the other room.

Jac hadn't felt for days the security Asilo Colina instantly brought when she stepped out of the limo. Her anxiety had been easing, and her guard cautiously stepped into the background. Then Sunny walked into the room.

She sprung to her feet with a jolt of adrenaline. "What is *he* doing here?" Glaring at Sunny, she waited for a damn good answer to dissuade her from rushing at him and ripping off his face.

"Hello, Jacqueline," Sunny said.

Her stomach turned. "Don't call me that." She pointed a furious finger at him. "Don't call me anything." She moved toward Sunny but stopped when Sebastian stepped in between, and Billy grabbed her hand.

Sebastian raised calming hands. "Jac, he is an emissary, and we granted him an audience."

"He's here to take me back. He and Edgar hired the Dog Brothers." Jac moved from side to side, attempting to gain a clear path to Sunny. "Ask him. He knows where my mom is, and he—" She held back a tinge of anguish, not wanting Sunny to see her break. "He knows what happened to my dad."

"Yes. Yes. Much of that may be true, but Sunny is not taking you to Philadelphia. I made that perfectly clear."

Jac's neck corded. "Get him out of here." Her words were an inferno. She wanted Sunny in her grasp to do worse to him than she did to Tanner and Curtis, but Mateus stood next in line to stop her if she got past Sebastian.

"Sunny was just leaving," Sebastian said, his face an exhibit of worry. "Mateus, show our guest out."

With Mateus close behind, eyeing Jac, Sunny walked around the couch toward the hallway to the foyer. Jac glowered at him the entire way.

Sunny paused and turned toward her. "Jacqueline, I never meant for you or anyone else to get hurt. I am sorry."

Searching for something to throw at Sunny, she grabbed the potted plant from the table. Sebastian grabbed her arm at windup.

"You certainly are an emotional little girl." With his jaw tensed, Sebastian pried the pot from her clenched hand, sending clumps of dirt onto the table.

Jac yanked her arm free and funneled her rage toward Sunny. "Leave!"

Sunny solemnly frowned and walked away.

The safety Jac had felt since arriving at Asilo Colina completely evaporated. "I can't believe you let him in here ... *while* we are here."

"Yes, clearly a poor decision," Carlos said.

"One that will not be repeated." Sebastian wiped a bead of sweat from his brow.

"Why was he here?" Jac shifted her weight from foot to foot, her hands clenched fists at her side. "What did he want?"

Carlos exchanged a look with Sebastian.

"You are the reason he was here, but only to await your safe arrival," Sebastian said.

Unconvinced, she leaned toward Sebastian and pointed at him. "You can *never* let him back in this house or anywhere near Billy. Not for any audience or reason."

"Miss Jacqueline, if I may remind you that you are a guest in—"

"Never!" Jac said emphatically, cutting off Carlos.

Billy hugged her waist. After a dozen rapid heartbeats in the near silence, her breathing slowed, and the tension melted away. However, her hands still shook, looking for an outlet, looking for someone to strike.

Sebastian raised a silencing finger toward Carlos and Mateus, maintaining his focus on Jac. "Yes. Never."

DINNER

After being given time to calm down and allay the urge to remove Sunny's perfect head from his suited shoulders, Jac joined Billy on Sebastian's house tour. Mateus followed close behind, apparently not trusting the diminutive oleander girl alone with his master. Carlos chose not to accompany them.

Jac shook her head at the idea of calling this place a house. By definition, the residence was a house, being a structure for habitation. However, based on its enormity and the surrounding properties she had yet to explore, it more accurately fit the definition of a compound.

Sebastian's side of the "house" starkly contrasted with Carlos's. Everything was new and modern: dark brown hardwood floors, white quartz and granite countertops in the kitchen and bathrooms, elaborate lighting fixtures, and furniture that looked like it had recently come from a showroom floor. And his side smelled new, clean, free from the aroma of smoke and parties, past and present.

Sebastian offered to show her and Billy to their rooms, which, he explained, Ximena had prepared.

Jac had forgotten about Ximena. She wanted to thank Ximena for the blood delivery while asking what her problem was. Although difficult to believe, it seemed she purposely delayed the blood delivery, nearly causing Devin to become a victim of Jac's blood lust. "Is Ximena here today?"

"She's otherwise occupied,"—Sebastian stopped before a closed door—"but she'll grace us with her company later."

Jac appreciated and preferred Ximena's absence. Her anger toward Sunny and the harm she wanted to bring him could have spilled over to Ximena.

"Our rooms are on your side of the house?" Billy asked Sebastian with a tinge of hope in his voice.

"Yes, they are, Master William," Sebastian said, sounding relieved. "Carlos prefers his privacy. He's like an old man." He gripped the door handle. "Welcome to your bedroom, Miss Kelley."

Sebastian pushed open the door, extending his arm with flair as if presenting a game show prize. The reveal, which he called a bedroom, was three times the size of her apartment bedroom.

"Whoa." Billy peeked around Jac. "This room is huge."

Jac entered the dreamlike room. An enormous bed occupied a third of the room, covered with a purple and pink flowered comforter and decorative pillows. Above the bed hung an elaborate chandelier large enough to swing from. Against the walls stood an enormous dresser, a makeup station with a lighted mirror, and a desk with a laptop. A TV, the size of a small movie screen, hung above the dresser directly across from the bed. A closed door was next to the bathroom entrance.

"Closet?" She motioned toward the door.

Sebastian nodded. "Go. Check it out." He grinned, clearly enjoying the give as much as she enjoyed the receive.

She pushed open the closet door, and her jaw dropped.

"Ximena went on a shopping spree for you."

"This is insane." Jac paused and looked back at Billy. "No jumping on the bed."

"Oh, man. But it's so big."

"Not happening." She stepped into the closet and slowly spun, taking it all in. Clothes on brown felt hangers lined the closet walls from ceiling to floor. A dozen shoes filled cubby holes to her right, from sneakers to high heels. There were belts, handbags, and all styles of hats. An amazing wardrobe that was not her style.

"I suppose you have some trying on to do. If there's anything that doesn't fit or you don't like, give it to Ximena, and she'll return it."

The amazement of it all collided with uncertainty as reality hit Jac.

"What's wrong?" Sebastian asked. "You don't like it?"

"No ... I mean, yes. It's all great: the room, the clothes. But I'm not staying."

Sebastian's smile faded.

"I can't stay."

"But now you don't have to leave," Billy pleaded. "Everything you need is here."

Jac pulled Billy in for a hug. "We'll talk about this later."

"But I don't want you to go."

Sebastian's eyes showed understanding. "I assumed that might be the case. And I can relate. You're an adult, and you've tasted freedom. You want to see the world."

Jac's plans involved more than seeing the world, but she wasn't ready to divulge her motives to Sebastian about finding the abducted women and children.

"Regardless," Sebastian continued, "consider Asilo Colina your home to return to whenever you need."

She placed her hands over her heart. "Thank you. I couldn't have asked for more."

Billy moped in the side effects of her pronouncement, but Jac knew how to raise his spirits. "I bet your bedroom is twice as amazing as mine."

Billy snapped to attention; he smiled eagerly at Sebastian. "Can we go to my room now?"

"Yes, of course, Master William."

Billy took off running without direction.

"Take a right down the hall. Your room is on the left!" Sebastian gave Jac a look, then hustled to catch Billy.

Jac gave the room, the amazing room prepared for her, another look and followed.

Mateus lurked outside her door, looking at her inquisitively.

"Hey, stalker."

"Where will you go?" Mateus asked.

She tilted her head to the side. "What do you mean?"

"When you leave. Where will you go?"

Jac wasn't ready to answer the question. Not only because she didn't care to divulge her secret but because she genuinely wasn't sure. She had yet to devise a workable plan. "I haven't decided yet. Why?"

"Concern."

"Concern?"

"Yes, you're a lady of the house, even when you are gone. I am the protector of the house." He settled his feet as if preparing to hold out for an answer. "I have concern for you."

Being called "a lady of the house" didn't sit well with her, but she liked the security it garnered from Mateus. If it weren't for Sunny's unexpected appearance, she couldn't imagine a safer place to be. "I appreciate the concern, but I don't know where I'm going. I only know where I've been, and I can't go back there."

Mateus raised an eyebrow and crossed his arms.

"Honest. I'm not sure. I'll let you know when I am. Okay?"

Mateus pursed his lips. "Okay."

Jac wouldn't promise to tell Mateus anything. It didn't take a vampire sensibility to know he wasn't asking about her plans out of concern for her safety. Instead, he asked on behalf of his masters. She was certain they wanted to learn as much about her as possible.

* * *

Billy frenetically rushed around his room, which was just as fantastic as Jac's. It had a giant bed and closet—not as large as hers—filled with clothes and shoes. It also had a big-screen TV and video game consoles. With an entire room to investigate, testing the bed's jumpability seemed an afterthought.

Sebastian winked at Jac. "We gave you the larger room."

"I heard that," Billy said from the closet, "and I don't care."

Sebastian and Mateus left them alone to explore their rooms and the rest of the house, with a strict and curious order to avoid the basement "for now."

Later in the day, Jac gave in to Billy's pleas to check out the pool. She just needed a swimsuit, and searching her dresser drawers, she came across a few. Most were immodest two-piece strips of fabric. Thank God, she found a black one-piece with full coverage in the front and the back. She twisted and turned in front of a full-size mirror hanging on the closet door, check-ing the fit. The suit offered reasonable coverage, but her hands moved to cover parts of her skin that no one had seen since bath time as a toddler.

With no single long-sleeved cotton shirt in the drawers or closet, she slipped on the one she had been wearing, adding the arm coverage she needed. Certainly, the chlorinated pool wouldn't mind the smell.

* * *

Jac swam with Billy underneath the warm late afternoon sun for nearly an hour. They splashed around, dove, jumped in, and rode a twisty slide that dumped them in the deep end. Peeking just above the waterline, at the horizon and sky, they imagined floating on a giant rock, and everyone else was far below, looking up at them in astonishment.

They felt free to enjoy life without fear for the first time in weeks. The underlying problems still haunted Jac, but this moment with Billy was perfection. He was smiling and happy, and nothing could ruin it.

"We're having dinner soon," said a voice, breaking Jac's daydream.

Jac shielded her eyes from the sun. She didn't recognize the face, but the voice was familiar. "Ximena?"

"Yes." Ximena raised a sculpted eyebrow. She was absolutely gorgeous, an image of perfection. She had long hair with curls to die for and flawless golden brown skin. "We're having dinner soon. You should clean up and get dressed." Her eyes fell upon Jac's shirt; her lip curled. "Though it appears you already are."

Jac glanced at her soaked shirt clinging to her chest and arms. "Thanks for all the clothes. They're great. And the swimsuit … I didn't have one."

"Maybe you didn't need one, chica."

"Oh, yeah … I like my arms covered. It's just something I do."

Ximena rolled her eyes. "Anyway, see you inside. And, soon." She sashayed away.

Jac's self-consciousness returned, as did the uncomfortable feeling she didn't belong.

Billy waded up next to her. "We need to ask them about Mom. Carlos didn't answer when you asked."

"Yeah. It's like they keep getting distracted, or they distract us. We'll ask them during dinner."

"Do you think they know where she is?"

"I hope so."

* * *

Jac, her hair dripping from the shower, stood wearing only a towel in the closet filled with expensive clothes. She wasn't ready to call them "her clothes" and doubted she ever would.

She couldn't help feeling she was only borrowing them. Sure, the sizes were mostly correct, but she would have never picked the way-too-short shorts, sundresses, tank tops, and frilly shirts with sheer sleeves. Thankfully, Ximena stocked the closet with more jeans than she had at home. However, there were no cargo pants or a single long-sleeved cotton shirt. Her choice of dinner attire became clear. She grabbed the baggiest pair of jeans, a jean jacket from a hanger, and moved to the dresser outside the closet.

Praying for fresh underwear, she opened the top drawer. Her prayers were answered, mostly. She picked up a frilly pair as if they were someone else's, using the tips of her fingers.

"Who does she think I am? I'm not wearing these."

During their brief phone conversation, Ximena failed to ask for Jac's bra size and evidently didn't want to guess wrong. There was a wide range of cups, all too large. She added bras to her list of needs, along with the long-sleeved shirts and cargo pants.

The next drawer held precisely what she wanted: full-coverage cotton underwear. A note in perfect cursive sat atop one stack: "I got you these boring things, in case it's your time or if you're a prude."

"You bitch." Jac crumpled the paper and tossed it across the room indiscriminately. "It's never my time," she muttered.

She found a white tank top in another drawer and took the clothes to her colossal bathroom, which Sebastian called an ensuite.

Dressed in the loosest fitting clothes with as much coverage as possible, given the selection, Jac finished getting ready. She brushed her hair straight while ignoring the myriad of makeup products Ximena loaded the counter with. Jac hadn't worn lipstick since playing dress-up as a kid. Applying eyeliner and all the other stuff was foreign to her, and she didn't care to learn. With teeth brushed, she practiced her most polite smile and headed toward where she remembered seeing the dining room.

In the hallway outside her room, Billy strutted toward her with a playful grin. "Look. New clothes."

Jac tucked her hair behind her ears. "You look *so* cool."

"Thanks." He looked her up and down. "Why the jacket? It's not cold."

"Um, yeah,"—she tugged at the sleeves—"there aren't any long-sleeved shirts like mine."

"Oh, sorry."

She didn't need to explain; Billy knew why she wore long-sleeved shirts. He knew of the scars. She shoved her hands in her pants pockets and alternately stuck out her feet. "But the jeans and sneakers are perfect."

"Oh, cool. But not as awesome as mine. Watch." Billy pranced in a circle, the heels of his shoes illuminating every step.

She placed her hands on her hips. "Yeah, you got me beat."

"Race you to the dinner table." He took off running, the lights from his shoes splashing the dimly lit hallway with bursts of color like the Fourth of July.

"Wait up! I might need you to show me the way!"

"I'm not falling for that!"

And with that, Billy sprinted away.

"I'll take you," came a voice.

Jac yelped and swiveled. "Shit, Mateus! Don't do that."

Mateus raised his palms toward her. "Sorry."

"I'm serious. Don't sneak up on me like that."

"I wasn't sneaking."

"Well, you weren't making a lot of noise either." She placed a hand on her chest and took a deep breath.

"Again, sorry," Mateus conceded.

"You *could* show me to the dining room. Or would you prefer to follow me, lingering in the shadows?"

He laughed. "I'll show you."

Jac stepped aside, motioning for Mateus to pass, and he did so, looking down at her with a wry grin. She walked beside him, chewing at her cheek with a question on her mind. Seconds later, she braved up. "Mateus, can I ask you something?"

"Yes. I can't promise an answer."

"Secrets. I get it. We all have them."

He shrugged. "Or, maybe I don't know the answer."

Jac slowly nodded once. "That's fair."

"Then ask."

"Why does Ximena hate me?"

Mateus chuckled.

"Really? You think her hating me is funny?"

"No, sorry." He covered his mouth as if smoothing out his smile. "Ximena doesn't hate you."

"If she doesn't hate me, she sure doesn't pretend to like me."

"It's like this. Until you arrived, Ximena was the only lady in the house. And she was not always a vampire. So, she can be ... emotional."

Jac stopped. "Are you kidding me? I had no idea she was turned. She's so perfect. So beautiful."

Mateus stopped and turned to her. "Yes, she is beautiful, but also intelligent, driven, and completely committed to the Castillos."

"Well, Ximena can relax. I'm only committed to Billy."

"I see that. She will, too. Just give her time." He nodded forward, and they continued toward the dining room.

"How long has Ximena been here ... at Asilo Colina?"

"She was turned in nineteen ninety-three. She was here before me. After Sebastian and Carlos, she is like the third boss."

"Who turned her, Sebastian or Carlos?"

Mateus zipped his lips. "We all got them."

"Secrets," Jac muttered.

* * *

Jac had walked past the dining room during Sebastian's tour when the lights were off. Now, brightened by the chandelier hanging from the ceiling, beads of light danced around the room against the golden-painted walls, the fine china settings, and crystal glassware.

Sebastian and Billy occupied two of the ten gray fabric chairs around the table. A cream-colored rug covered the space underneath the table atop a dark-brown hardwood floor. Long flowing drapes framed the tall windows to the left, letting in the remaining light from the setting sun. A door on the far side of the room led to a galley kitchen.

Sebastian stood at the head of the table. "Welcome to dinner, Miss Kelley."

Every irksome time the twins addressed her as Miss Kelley, she reminded herself she would have to ask that they use "Jac."

For now, she masked her displeasure and allowed the appellation. Billy, however, was perfectly fine with his title of Master William.

Sebastian asked them to sit—her to his left and Billy to his right. He thanked Mateus, raised a hand, and Mateus gave one stiff nod and left.

"Wait a second." Jac placed her palms on the table, her eyebrows raised. "That's how you get Mateus to leave you alone? Just lift your hand?"

Sebastian shrugged. "Yes, I suppose that's how it works."

"I can't wait to try."

Billy played with the silverware, tapping it against the crystal glassware and drumming the table.

"Billy, no more," Jac scolded. "Remember, not our house."

"Yes, it is," Billy said, as if she were ignorant of the title bestowed upon him.

"Well, yes, but not like that."

"Billy, you are correct, but also is your sister." Sebastian calmly took the silverware from Billy and set them on the table. "Proper etiquette would have you sitting politely with your hands on your lap."

Billy grinned and complied.

Place settings sat on the table in front of empty chairs. "Who's eating with us?" Jac asked.

"Oh, the common house rabble: Carlos and Ximena."

"Not Mateus?"

Sebastian smirked. "Certainly not. He's on an assignment. Truth is, he spends most of the day working."

"How much of the day is he supposed to watch me?" Jac had an inclination the twins had ordered Mateus to monitor her. He hovered more often than she liked and had the habit of sneaking up on her. She couldn't blame them; she was new to the house, and they hardly knew her. Still, the constant attention was creepy. How else were they monitoring her? Were there hidden cameras throughout the house? In her room? They wouldn't dare have cameras in her bedroom. Just thinking about it elevated her heart rate. She'd literally tear the place down if they filmed her in such a personal space.

The corners of Sebastian's mouth twitched. He didn't answer.

"Whaddup, people?" Ximena strode into the room, tapping on her phone.

"Speaking of poor etiquette." Sebastian rolled his eyes.

"What-evah Bastian. I can act more like Carlos if you'd like."

Sebastian raised his hands in surrender. "Please, no. I'd move to another home before suffering through two of you."

Ximena wore a skin-tight, strapless blue dress, revealing envy-inducing shapes and curves. She styled her hair in long, loose curls. Her makeup accentuated the perfectness that was her face. She set her phone on the table, draped her gorgeous locks over her lotion, glistened shoulders, and surveyed the room until her eyes settled on Jac. Her face scrunched. "Chica. What's up with the jacket?"

"It's a piece of clothing," Jac said deadpan.

Ximena's acerbic personality clashed with hers, so being besties would not happen. She appreciated Ximena shopping for the clothes and arranging the blood delivery. Obviously, Ximena did it on Sebastian's orders, not out of kindness.

"Guess you're wearing the big cotton panties too?" Ximena motioned from her backside to her front.

Sebastian closed his eyes and rubbed his forehead.

Jac turned a shade of red. She scowled at Ximena and stood, prepared to fire back.

Ximena leaned forward. "Oh, now *that's* hot. Love the jeans and that top." She placed a hand over her gasp. "Oh girl, now that jacket makes perfect sense. Is it that cold in here?" She hovered her hands over her chest. "Do they not wear bras in Philadelphia?"

Horrified, Jac closed her jacket, fastened two buttons, and sat.

"I don't think Jac wears bras much," Billy said, sending Ximena into a giggling fit.

"Billy!" Jac slapped the table, rattling the place settings.

"What?" Billy raised his palms. "I heard you and Mom talking about it one night."

"That was years ago." Jac huffed. "Just stay out of this."

"Good evening, everyone." Carlos entered, unknowingly saving Jac from the discussion of what she was and was not wearing under her clothes.

"Okay, kids, Dad is at the table," Sebastian said. "It's time to stop having fun."

Carlos took the comment in stride, evidently accustomed to chiding from his brother. He wore a loose-fitting silk shirt bearing images of cocktails and ladies in various forms of relief. His skin-tight white pants revealed more than Jac cared to see. She shut her eyes, waiting for him to sit.

"Yes, Father is here," Carlos said. "Our meal will soon be served."

Carlos sat opposite Sebastian at the end of the rectangle table; Ximena sat beside Billy opposite Jac. Billy showed off his shoes to Ximena, who marveled at the flashing colors and gave him a high five, earning *some* positive points with Jac. Still, the score was not in Ximena's favor.

"Jacqueline and Master William. Our meal has been prepared by the finest chef in La Jolla, who gratefully is the chef of Asilo Colina," Carlos said as if cultivating everyone's anticipation.

"His food is the bomb," Ximena said.

"Ximena, please." Carlos gave her a grieved look.

"Loosen up, bruh." Ximena tapped on her phone and held it an arm's length away. She puckered her glistening lips, the phone clicked. She smiled appreciatively, rapidly punched the screen, and set the phone down.

Jac stared blankly at Ximena, receiving a sneer in response. The sneer reminded Jac of her conversation about Mom with Billy at the pool. "Carlos."

"Yes."

"Earlier, I asked about my mom, where she is, but you didn't answer."

"You're right. We were interrupted by a sideshow." Carlos threw a look at his brother. "Would you prefer to answer?"

"Oh, no, Carlos. I defer to you on this one," Sebastian countered.

"Yeah. Where is my mom?" Billy added.

"William, I don't know where your mother is. She—"

"What do you mean you don't know?" Jac interrupted, eyeing Carlos as if he had proclaimed the Earth was flat.

"However," Carlos continued, raising a finger, "I know she is quite alive and well."

A wave of relief washed over Jac; she slumped forward as the tension in her shoulders eased. She shared a smile with Billy. Their mother was alive. She had wanted to believe it, especially for Billy, who had been losing hope. This news changed everything.

"I can go to her. Where is she?" Jac asked, ready to leave Asilo Colina and hit the road.

Carlos opened his mouth to speak when Sebastian cut in. "Her location is a secret." He turned from Carlos to Jac. "She doesn't want anyone to know her location, not us ... not even you."

"But why?" Billy asked.

"Because, Billy, it's the only way she can stay safe while keeping *you* safe."

"From Edgar," Jac added.

Carlos nodded once. "Now that you're here, I suspect you will see her sooner than later."

Mom's plan of hiding didn't make perfect sense to Jac, but she had to believe Mom knew what she was doing. "If we can't see her, can we call her?"

"We don't have her number; she uses a disposable phone, but she does text us," Carlos said. "We expect a text from her any day now."

The possibility of speaking with her mother thrilled Jac. Even if only by text. She reached across the table and clasped Billy's hand.

"Mom's alive." Billy smiled at her, then giggled.

"And here it is, the main course." Sebastian clasped his hands, then motioned to an older gentleman wheeling a cart carrying plates of food into the room. "Ah, one of my favorites: filet mignon, creamed spinach, and fondant potatoes. Juan, it smells"—he scrunched his face and grunted—"amazing."

Juan, who Jac now understood as the chef, bowed his head and expressed gratitude. He placed a full plate in front of everyone and filled their glasses with water, leaving the goblets empty.

The makeshift family held polite conversations throughout the meal and ate bread pudding for dessert. Billy proclaimed it the best dessert he'd ever had, to which Jac agreed.

There were occasional verbal barbs between Carlos and Sebastian that they took in stride. Jac imagined them as an old married couple beyond offense from each other's jabs.

Jac actively ignored Ximena. They exchanged glances, Ximena's slathered in disdain. Jac imagined conversation starters to direct at her, but none were polite or appropriate, neither for the setting nor the company.

Juan, the chef, apparently also performed busboy duties, returning to remove the mostly empty plates and silverware from the table, leaving the water glasses and empty goblets.

The waiter was a curiosity—a subservient vampire, cautious in how he interacted with the Castillos. It felt different from the standard coven hierarchy. Jac considered asking about Juan's status but felt out of place. Maybe she didn't understand the relationship between a vampire and their servant. Her family never had a personal chef or anyone to do their chores. Everyone in her family chipped in if something needed cleaning, cooking, or folding.

"Well, Jacqueline," Sebastian said, patting his stomach and easing back into his chair, "how have you enjoyed your first day with us?"

"I, um,"—she pressed her lips while thinking how to answer—"it's incredible here. And everything you've done for us and got us." She glanced at a smug-faced Ximena. "Other than home, I can't imagine a better place."

He extended his hands. "Consider Asilo Colina your home for as long as you need."

"I've been meaning to ask. What does that mean, Asilo Colina?"

"Roughly translated, Asilo Colina is a refuge. A refuge on the hill."

Jac's forehead creased. "A refuge? A refuge for who?"

Sebastian opened his palms. "For those who need it."

"For vampires who need it," Jac countered.

"Not necessarily."

"It seems like today,"—Ximena lifted her chin at Jac—"we lowered the standards significantly on who is granted refuge."

Jac sneered at her.

"Our dear Ximena, for example, was human when we first met. She was young, beautiful, full of life's energy." Sebastian extended his hand toward Ximena. "And still is."

Ximena held her hands to her heart, faking modesty.

"I don't get it? How did Ximena get from human to vampire? I'm obviously missing something."

"Recklessness," Carlos interjected.

Sebastian gave his brother a look. "Let's just say, keeping the story brief, Ximena needed a place to stay, and we needed an assistant."

"I practically run the place," Ximena added.

"Hold on." Jac leaned forward. "You chose this?"

"Let's see. Long life, youthful beauty for a couple centuries,"—she extended a finger for each reason—"I'm stronger and faster than any human. I'm the complete package."

"It's a good thing you have five more fingers," Jac said.

"And why is that?"

"For when you learn kindness and humility."

Ximena scowled at her. "Now that I think of it, I have one more finger to show you."

The clink of crystal brought everyone's attention to Carlos. He stood holding an empty goblet in one hand and a butter knife in the other. "Family, old and new, thank you for sharing this fine meal tonight."

They exchanged smiles—Jac's forced—and nods around the table as Juan rolled a cart carrying four silver carafes into the room.

Carlos raised his hands at his sides. "And for that, I propose a toast."

Jac's eyes narrowed on Juan. He poured the first carafe's contents into Sebastian's goblet. *The hell.* She blinked hard as Juan filled Billy's and Ximena's goblets with a liquid the color, consistency, and smell of blood. She pushed back from the table when the aroma struck her. Juan made it to her goblet and poured. Jaw clenched, she watched the O-negative swirl and settle.

Sebastian stood, raising his goblet of blood. "May this wonderful meal be the first of many with our new residents. Our new family."

Billy picked up his goblet and rotated it, examining it curiously as the viscous fluid swirled, coating the inside.

Jac shook her head at Billy and mouthed, "Put it down."

The alluring blood seemed to have distracted him, but he blinked, mouthed, "Sorry," and returned his goblet to the table. "What is this?"

Everyone's glass stopped inches short of their lips.

"Um, it's blood," Ximena said in her snide way. "What's wrong? Do you prefer your blood fresh from the bus?"

Sebastian raised a reassuring hand. "Don't worry, Jacqueline. I made certain each of our goblets would contain our individual blood types. We don't want anyone getting sick."

Jac glowered at Ximena with an expression conveying a desire to hurt. "Yeah, I get that." She turned to Sebastian. "But why are we drinking it from these fancy glasses? I don't know about everyone else, but I don't need mine. I'm not hungry for blood."

"Jacqueline," Carlos said, easing into the conversation like a slow-moving stream, "we drink in celebration, not in need."

Jac looked down, clinching her fist before her face. "Okay ... okay ... first, call me Jac, not Jacqueline or Miss Kelley. And second, this is bullshit."

Sebastian lowered his goblet. "Jacqueline, I mean, Jac, your language around Billy."

"Oh, it's okay," Billy said. "Jac says the 'S,' the 'A,' and sometimes the 'F' word around me."

"Billy, not now," Jac said sternly.

"Jac. What's your concern? Everyone's glass has their blood type. We are vampires; this is how we live."

Jac stood, planting her fists on the table. "Drinking blood is a horrible necessity, not a fucking celebration!"

"See, the 'F' word," Billy said proudly.

Sebastian raised his hands in a motion to ask for calm. "We own the blood business in the Southwest. This is donated blood. We take none from anyone by force."

"What?" Jac cocked and shook her head. "I don't care. We should never celebrate what we are. If I had it my way, we'd all be dead."

"That didn't keep your self-righteous ass from killing that guy on the bus," Ximena said.

Sebastian met Ximena's comment with a stern look.

A burning anger filled Jac to boiling. She grabbed her goblet and splashed the blood in a Rorschach pattern across Ximena's dress and chest.

Ximena screamed. She shoved her seat back, stood, and surveyed the damage to her clothes. With her white fangs on display, she struck the table with a bloody fist and growled. "You stupid bitch!"

Sebastian and Carlos offered urgent, calming words, attempting to quell the tension.

Billy watched helplessly.

Jac didn't budge an inch, nor did Ximena at noticing the knife in Jac's hand.

The gleam of silver in Jac's clenched fist caught Sebastian's attention. "Ximena," he said calmly, "I need you to leave, and Jac, I need you to give the knife to me."

Neither girl moved. Their eyes daggers pointed at each other.

"Ximena, ahora mismo!" Sebastian yelled.

Jac flinched. It marked the first time she heard Sebastian yell, which she found pretty unsettling while effective.

Ximena peeled her furious eyes from Jac and looked at Sebastian, her chin trembling. "Fine." She glared at Jac as she stomped from the room, leaving a trail of blood droplets.

"I'll take that." Sebastian scooped up the knife that fell from Jac's now open but clawed hand.

Carlos, seemingly apathetic, sat with a content grin, his goblet empty save the red residue.

"Jac, please sit," Sebastian asked, borderline ordered.

Jac reluctantly dropped onto her seat. Aimlessly, she searched for where to place her shaking hands.

Sebastian lowered into his seat, a full goblet in front of him. He clasped his hands on the table. "Now, I know from your mother that you've lived a sheltered life. I understand. It's part of being a young vampire in your circumstances."

Descending from the precipice of rage, Jac lowered her head and eased back into her seat. "My life was fine."

"To be clear, just because our way of life differs from yours does not make it wrong. Nor does it make us uncivilized monsters worthy of death."

She leered at Sebastian. "We are monsters from birth or by turn. That's what we are. We're a scourge, a disease. We should be exterminated ... all of us, all vampires."

"I'm afraid that based on what we've heard from our guest," Carlos said solemnly, "she should be dis-invited."

"No, she shouldn't," Billy blurted.

Sebastian raised his hands, silencing the room. "Jac, I need to know. Will our lifestyle continue to be a problem for you?"

"Yes, it will," she said without hesitation.

Sebastian sighed, drumming his fingers on the table. "Then, surprisingly, I agree with my brother. Billy may stay. However, you must leave."

"No!" Billy stood and stomped, his shoes adding a brief splash of color to the room's dark mood.

"Billy, it's okay. We already discussed this. I'm just leaving sooner than we expected."

"Then, I'm going too."

"No, you aren't. I just got you here. I can still visit."

Sebastian nodded his agreement. "Yes, your sister will always be welcome to visit."

"I don't want you to go." Billy pouted and crossed his arms.

Jac sighed. "When do I have to leave?"

"Tomorrow. I'll have your belongings delivered to a local condo we own. You can stay there as long as you like and visit Billy if you give notice."

She shook her head. "I can't ask you to do—"

"No," Sebastian interrupted, "it's not a burden nor a cost. We owe it to your mother. Say no more of it."

The mention of owing anything to her mother struck Jac as odd. What did her mom do for them that made them feel obligated to raise and protect Billy and give her a place to live? "Why do you owe my mother?"

Sebastian glanced at Carlos and pushed his full goblet of blood to the side. "That discussion is for another time. Tonight,

Carlos and I need to discuss something much more urgent with you."

"Well, if you won't answer me, then I think I've had enough talking for one night." Jac placed her hands on the table, preparing to stand. "Can I go to my room?"

Sebastian gave Carlos a slight nod, then focused on her. "We had planned to wait until tomorrow for this difficult discussion, but with how the night has unfolded, now seems more appropriate."

She leaned forward. "What is it?"

"Jac." Sebastian placed a hand upon hers. "We have Devin."

DEVIN

A door closed, waking Devin. He yanked the covers from his legs, sat in bed, wiped his eyes, and stretched out a long yawn. It hit him after a minute of gathering his senses. "Jac." He sprung to his feet, rushed to the hotel rooms' adjoining doors, and stopped to knock. "Jac, Billy ... you in there?"

No answer.

The door slowly opened with a turn of the handle and a gentle push. He peeked inside to find an empty room.

The door ... that was them leaving. Shoeless, he sprinted from the room to the end of the walkway overlooking the parking lot. Neither Jac nor Billy was in sight. A black limo with tinted windows pulled out of the lot.

"That has to be them." Devin waved at the limo as it drove away, feeling a bit foolish, not knowing if Jac could see him or if she was in it. Then it was gone.

"I guess last night *was* goodbye," he murmured. His neck and chest tightened, and his legs turned into rubber. Leaning against the wall behind him, he slid down into a sit. Jac was gone; Billy too, and he was alone in San Diego with a long ride home in front of him. Soon, he would return to his everyday life of delivering pizzas and stopping to chat with Rusty. Worst of all, he had his drunk mom to deal with.

Jac circled back into his thoughts. "I can't breathe," he muttered. "I can't breathe." He threaded sweaty hands through his hair, held his head, focused on one breath at a time, and waited for the anxiety to lessen.

"Mommy. Someone's outside." A kid looked down at him, jabbing his tiny finger against the room's window. Fearing being labeled a creepy guy hanging outside hotel room doors got Devin to his feet, and he jogged back to Jac's now empty hotel room.

The room was a lonely quiet. For three days, Devin spoke with either Jac or Billy or listened to them talk to each other. Or fell asleep to their voices' murmuration from the other side of a motel room wall. He missed Jac's sigh and disapproving look when he acted "dumb." He missed Billy's laugh, finding humor and happiness in the most innocent of things. Mostly, he longed for Jac: her dark hair and how it framed her face, and her dark brown eyes that were often sad, frequently angry, sometimes widened in surprise, and occasionally narrowed by laughter and a smile. And, once or twice, softened by tenderness.

A short stack of cash sat neatly arranged on the bed atop a once-folded piece of paper. Devin grabbed the stack and flipped through the hundred-dollar bills. "Ten thousand dollars. Wow," he said, unsmiling. Nearly half his annual income, the small pile of green was the most money he had seen and touched at one time. He grabbed the white piece of paper, unfolded it, and read:

Devin,

What a crazy trip! Right!? I'm sorry we put you through so much and put you in danger. I could never pay you the amount you deserve for getting us here. Thank you for showing me there's beauty in the world and that there are kind people like you. And thank you again for the bracelet. I love it. After Billy and I get settled here, and I'm on the road, maybe I can stop by Jenks for a slice of pizza and company. Though, I'll have to sneak in, as I am rightfully banned from entering Oklahoma. Please take care of yourself and your mom.

PS. Don't grow old too fast.

XOXO Jac (I don't know what XOXO means, but I saw it on a TV show once.)

He folded the note, placed it on the bed, and wiped tears from his cheeks.

* * *

Packed and ready for the drive, Devin gave the two rooms a last look. He left a generous tip for the cleaning staff, acknowledged the memories he was leaving behind with a nod, and let the hotel room door close.

"Oh. Sorry." Devin nearly ran into three men wearing dark suits standing just outside the room. Each was taller than he. Two were built like football linemen.

"Relax, my friend," the first man said with a bright smile. He was smaller and shorter than the others, with sculpted eyebrows and perfect hair.

"Excuse me." Devin adjusted his backpack and took a side-step to move past them.

They moved to block him.

"If I may offer introductions," the smaller man said. "I'm Shaughnessy Heart, and these are my colleagues."

Devin looked up into the behemoths' sunglass-covered faces. If his suspicion was correct, they were vampires. *Play it cool and get out of here.* "Colleagues, as in bodyguards or muscle?"

Shaughnessy smirked and pointed his finger at Devin. "Very perceptive, my friend."

"So, can you let a friend pass? I have a long ride home."

Shaughnessy held up his pointer finger. "Oklahoma ... right? Well, about that, I'm afraid your trip is now canceled."

Devin cleared his throat. "Yeah, I figured, but I thought I would try anyway. So, what's the plan? You grab me, I yell and fight back, and someone calls the police?"

Shaughnessy turned to his henchmen and turned back, pouting. "Oh no, Devin. In that scenario,"—he jabbed his thumb behind him—"I have my muscle snap your neck before so much of a sound escapes your mouth. And should anyone else leave their rooms upon hearing the commotion, they, too, will be silenced."

Devin read the seriousness on Shaughnessy's face and feared that the two giants could easily snap his neck. With the little kid a few rooms down, Shaughnessy's threat made the decision substantially easier. Devin's amygdala revved in high gear, but he could neither fight nor take flight. It seems he wasn't leaving San Diego ... just yet.

"Scenario two," Shaughnessy continued, "is we all walk to our awaiting car, go for a ride, and talk."

Devin nodded toward the bodyguards. "Let me guess. Either way, one of them snaps my neck."

"Honestly, with scenario one, that is an absolute certainty." Shaughnessy pulled at his jacket sleeves. "Option two is out of my hands."

Devin's crest fell, and his head dropped as he cursed under his breath. Shaughnessy didn't need to be any more explicit—his trip home to Jenks ended before it began. He was likely dead in either situation, but option two meant living, for now, and no one else would get hurt.

"Which one will it be?" Shaughnessy spread his arms wide.

Devin raised his head and flashed a peace sign.

"That's an outstanding choice. We'll carry your bag for you." Shaughnessy motioned for one of the giants to take Devin's backpack. The other pulled Devin by his arm, shoved him in front of them, and ordered him to walk slowly.

Devin searched for thoughts to protect his sanity from the gravity of the situation, grasping at every good vision and every good memory of his sad life. He pictured Jac's face, her cute face. He recalled the note she had written for him and her final request. *So much for growing old.*

I'LL DO IT

"You don't have Devin." Jac stared into Sebastian's eyes, searching for evidence of truth or deception. She pulled her hand from his grasp.

Billy's nose wrinkled. "Yeah, he went home."

Carlos walked across the room and stood next to his brother.

"Jac, our secret is paramount," Sebastian said. "There isn't a human inside or outside of the gates of Asilo Colina who knows of our existence. Now, because of you, we have one within the very walls of our home."

Jac trembled, beginning to believe they had Devin, but denying it felt safer. She needed to feel safe. "Devin's not here; he can't be."

Sebastian leaned in and whispered. "He is *here*."

"He can't be here." Her trembling hand removed a strand of hair from her face, then curled into a fist. She struck the table. "He shouldn't be here!"

"We can't have a single human know our secret," Carlos said calmly, leaving the statement in the air like a threatening, ghostly spirit.

Jac rocked in her chair, feeling the warm rush of blood course through her veins, bringing her to stand. Her canines descended, protruded from her mouth, and pressed against her lower lip. "No. No. This is not happening."

Billy—her rock and emotionally stronger of the two—wore an expression that matched her own. Billy couldn't stay; he couldn't hear what she'd say to Sebastian or see what she feared might happen.

"Billy, get out of here," Jac ordered.

"I don't want—"

"I said, get out of here!" She looked at Carlos. "Get him out of here!"

Sebastian motioned to Carlos, who ushered a protesting Billy from the room.

"I'll send Mateus," Carlos said before leaving.

Jac wallowed in the purgatory between anger and anguish. Her clawed hands found their familiar resting place upon her jacket-covered arms. "Why are you doing this?"

"Now, this is when you tell me he doesn't know what you are or that we exist, but he does … he knows."

In a daze, Jac stared at nothing in particular, listening to the rapid thumps of her heart. "He doesn't know."

Sebastian pulled a small piece of paper from his shirt pocket and slid it across the table toward her. She didn't need to examine the paper to know its significance. It was the note she gave Devin when things were at their worst, when she feared they wouldn't finish the trip. The note that she carelessly left in Devin's car. The note with the Castillo's phone number and the name Asilo Colina.

She imagined Devin's face, the face of the boy who had an unwavering commitment to getting them to San Diego despite it all. The face of the boy who smiled during hard times and pulled her from her mind's dark places, allowing her to feel the desire for life and living. The face of the boy whom she had now condemned to death.

"Just let him leave with me." She placed her trembling hands on the table. "I promise Devin won't say anything. He won't."

Sebastian regarded her as if she were a silly child, ignorant of the vampire world and its rules. "You know Devin isn't leaving here, and he can't stay."

Gasping breaths, Mateus rushed into the room, his eyes immediately falling upon Jac.

Sebastian raised a hand to halt any action Mateus intended to take. He smoothed the tablecloth before him and tapped his fingers on the table. "I didn't want to do this tonight," he said, avoiding Jac's stare, "but your actions have forced us. We'll make it painless; he'll peacefully drift off and won't wake up."

Jac straightened, her hands curled into fists. Mateus moved toward her, only to be stopped by Sebastian's hand upon his chest.

"You will not touch him." Jac grew manic, speaking through tears. "You won't. He's my friend. He's my friend!" Her legs buckled, and she planted a hand on the table to steady herself.

Sebastian reached for her.

She pushed away his hand. "Don't touch me."

"Jac, this will happen. There is no other way."

She flung off her jacket and dropped to the floor in a sit. Her fingers tore at the exposed flesh of her arms, drawing blood, offering a macabre relief. Her world had once again shattered. Asilo Colina—a refuge for Billy and somewhat halfway house for her—had become a tomb for Devin, the first and only boy she had grown to have feelings for. *They won't touch him. They won't come near him.* A determined calm came upon her at realizing what she had to do. Stone-faced, she looked up at Sebastian. "I'll do it."

It took Sebastian a moment before the crease between his eyes smoothed. "Jac, no, you shouldn't—"

"I said I'll do it. No one else gets near him. I'll kill Devin."

Sebastian appeared to mull over her request. His expression changed as if an idea had bloomed. "I'll grant you one other option."

As if their minds had melded, Jac vehemently shook her head. "No."

"But you didn't hear—"

"I said no." She stood, releasing her claws from her blood-speckled arms. "That will never happen." Her eyes narrowed. "I'd kill myself before turning him into one of us."

"Jac, please consider it ... for you. If you change Devin, you still must leave, but he can leave with you. You can keep Devin."

"I will not make him a monster!" Anger swelled in her feet and shot to the crown of her head. She grabbed Sebastian's blood-filled goblet from the table and hurled it across the room. Its travel ended in a bloody explosion against the wall, scattering red-coated crystal shards across the floor.

Sebastian groaned as he stood. "We are not monsters. We are what we are."

"What do you call something that wants to kill my friend?" She stepped up to him, inches away. Mateus placed a hand firmly on her shoulder.

"Easy, Miss Kelley," Mateus warned.

Sebastian met her stare, then turned away as if the pointing finger of shame reflected in her eyes.

"But what do you care?" She added.

Sebastian's face tightened, the veins in his neck and forehead bulged, and then he erupted. "There is much worse in the world than vampires! Horrors you could not imagine, many perpetuated by the providers of our sustenance, from which you feel *so* horribly taking." He pointed a finger at her face. "You're a naïve little girl. Parading across the country with an attainable heart when you had no business sharing it with anyone."

Sebastian's facade had cracked, revealing he wasn't the exquisitely charming and gentle vampire he portrayed; he was as bad as them all. Though she couldn't disagree with his assertion that she was a 'naïve little girl,' much of the world was unknown to her, including caring for someone aside from her family. However, she knew evil, and the Castillos were no different.

"That's not fair," she muttered. Her arms and hands hung limp. "I went through Hell to get here."

"Indeed." Sebastian leaned down and pulled a newspaper from the floor. He slapped it on the table in front of her. "I wanted to show you this as part of our little celebration."

Jac glanced at the newspaper. "Show me what?"

"Open it." He repeatedly jabbed his finger at the paper. "*Read* it."

Jac slowly reached for the newspaper, keeping her eyes on Sebastian. She pulled the newspaper toward her and unfolded it.

"Go on," Sebastian said.

She scanned the paper, unsure of what for. It didn't take long to find what Sebastian wanted her to read. *Man Murdered on Bus to Tulsa Identified.* "Why am I reading this? We know what happened."

Sebastian sat in his chair, crossed his legs, and ran his hand over his mouth. "It's in the details. Read."

What did he expect her to learn from the article? The day, time, and horrifying outcome were already known to her. One detail she didn't know was the man's ... name. *Harold Rainey,* she read, *thirty-four, was found murdered on a bus traveling to Tulsa, Oklahoma. His assailants may have inadvertently saved the life of Harold's estranged wife, who was staying at a friend's house in an attempt to escape the abusive relationship. Authorities found a handgun and ammunition in Mr. Rainey's luggage that police feared Rainey may have intended to use against his wife had he made it to Tulsa.*

Jac met Sebastian's gaze. "So, he was an asshole."

He leaned forward. "More than that, *he* was a monster, a veritable monster, and you a hero."

"No. What he did was between him and his wife. What I did to him was between him and me. This just means we both deserve to die."

Sebastian stared at her for a moment and clicked his tongue. "We are a lot alike, you and I: stubborn, hard-headed, and unreasonable. We care too much, and we hate too much." He stood and placed a hand on Mateus's shoulder. In a hurried tone, he ordered him to retrieve two bottles of water from Carlos and to meet them at the stairs to the basement.

Her jaw dropped. "*That's* why you told us to avoid the basement."

Sebastian smoothed his shirt and motioned toward the hallway. "Shall we?"

"Oh my God." Jac lowered her head and closed her eyes. *Stupid! I was so stupid. Devin would be halfway home by now if I didn't talk him into staying with me.* She tensed. The entire day had been a lie. While she swam with Billy, enjoyed her new room, and ate a fancy dinner, Devin was trapped in the basement. *He was here the whole time.*

Sebastian touched her shoulder, breaking her from torturous thoughts. "Remember, if you want to turn him, you must have the strength to pull away, to stop drinking from him."

Jac stared at her host with cold eyes. "Don't worry, I'll forget."

* * *

Jac walked next to Sebastian in silence as they made their way through the house, which had taken on an ominous vibe. No longer was Asilo Colina the wonderful sanctuary she had first imagined. It was now a jail or a tomb, a place to escape from while still alive.

Sebastian's mouth moved as if he had something to say, but the words never formed. Jac preferred it that way. Chances were, anything he'd say would only elevate her anger.

They reached Mateus and Carlos, standing at the top of a flight of stairs Jac guessed led to the basement. Carlos extended his arms toward her with a bottled water in each hand. "Now, don't confuse these. The one half-full is yours."

Her mind a blur, Jac autonomously grabbed the half-full bottle from his hand, unsure of its importance, and allowed her hand to fall to her side.

He snapped an attention-getting finger at her.

She gritted her teeth.

"Pay close attention," Carlos continued. "This full one is for Devin; it's heavily spiked. It's already open, so remember to let him see you remove the lid before giving it to him to allay suspicion."

"Right. We wouldn't want Devin to know his friend is about to kill him." She cut a look at them.

Mateus looked away from her for the first time since they'd met. Proving he at least had a conscience and might care.

"He only needs to drink a little," Carlos continued. "It has the faintest taste. Even if he noticed, it would be too late. He'll lose consciousness in seconds, and then you can do what you need to ... to finish it. Fortunately, you are the same blood type."

Jac wouldn't plead for Devin's release, unharmed and unchanged. Neither brother would listen or care. She swiped the full bottle from Carlos's hand and plodded down the stairs. The vampires' stares at her back were almost tangible, leering at her like they were her gods and, in this house, they were. She turned to footfalls striking the steps when she reached the bottom. Mateus trotted down the stairs.

"I'm going by myself."

Mateus reached the bottom and stood next to her. "No, I'm going with you."

Jac slammed her fist against the wall. "I'm going alone."

"Dammit, Jac. You don't know what room he's in."

"Tell me."

Mateus sighed. "Let me 'least go to the hallway. I'll show you the door, and then you go alone."

"Fine." She appreciated Mateus's predicament. He couldn't return to the brothers at her refusal. He followed their orders, not hers. But she wouldn't let him in Devin's room with her. The hallway beyond the door was an agreeable compromise.

Mateus pulled down the long metal handle and pushed the door inward with some effort. The thick steel door opened slowly with a sound as if hermetically sealed. Beyond the door stretched a long white hallway illuminated by recessed fluorescent lights in the ceiling. On either side of the hall were doors to windowless rooms.

Jac entered the hallway, followed by Mateus, pushing shut the door. She glowered at the twins until the door closed. "Can you help us get out of here?" Jac asked Mateus in an urgent whisper. "Is there another way out?"

Mateus's eyebrows furrowed. "Miss Kelley, no."

"You have to help me." She prodded his chest. "You said you would protect me."

"Miss Kelley, I would protect you with my life, but my first obligation is to the Castillos. Sebastian turned me. I belong to him."

She understood, and though she couldn't blame him, it angered her all the same. "You're just like them."

"Yes, I am, and so are you."

"I'm not," Jac said solemnly, defeated.

"It doesn't matter anyway, Miss Kelley. There are two doors out of here; the other is thick like this one and locked. Carlos has the key. You can't get out."

Hopelessness set in. The last person who could have helped her refused. It was no surprise—Mateus was a turned vampire with allegiance to Sebastian. Turning against a sire was nearly impossible. Mateus would not help her.

The water bottles represented life and death clutched in her sweaty hands. How could she trick Devin into drinking from the drugged bottle, making it easier for her to kill him? How could she live with herself after? How could she live with herself regardless? Sebastian's words echoed in her mind, "You must have the strength to pull away, to stop drinking from him." It didn't matter. Dead or turned, Devin's life was over.

"Miss Kelley," Mateus said, pulling Jac from her thoughts.

She looked up at him; his expression had softened.

"He's in the third room on the right. Push the button on the wall to open the door. There is also an intercom button if you want to speak with him first. I'll wait here. Promise."

Jac's mind blanked. She might have nodded but couldn't remember. Her first step toward the third door on the right took momentous effort. Each step after was like walking through waist-high water with only momentum carrying her forward.

She thought of Devin. How annoying he acted in the convenience store where they first met. The gratitude she felt when he offered to make the drive to San Diego. The way he looked at her when he didn't know she was also watching him. His carefree love for life. His smile. Their brief kiss—her first.

Their painful goodbye. Now she stood at the door to his cell, moments from ending his life.

Jac lurched, clutching at her stomach, and with a convulsion, the evening's dinner shot from her mouth and splattered across the floor. She spat away bile and pieces of partially digested food and ran her hand across her mouth.

Mateus touched her shoulder. "Miss Kelley. Are you—"

She pushed him away. "Stay away from me." She spat again. "Do not touch me."

He raised his hands in defense and stepped back.

As Mateus had explained, there was a button labeled *OPEN* and one *INTERCOM*. She would confirm Devin was in the room and that she wasn't being subjected to some ridiculously drawn-out trick. Some kind of sorority hazing. She'd kill them if they were tricking her. Honestly, she'd kill them either way.

She took a deep breath and pushed the intercom button. The speaker emitted a click and a crackle, then silence.

"Is someone there?" came Devin's voice.

Jac flinched away from the button and sank to the floor. She dropped the water bottles and covered her mouth with her hands. Sobbing tears, like rain, poured from her eyes onto the tiled floor. The twins *had* captured Devin, imprisoned as promised, and soon she'd take him from this world.

She wanted to fight; God, she wanted to fight. Maybe she could get past Mateus, disable him ... somehow, and then catch the twins off guard. She could find Billy, come back for Devin, and then ... and then .... The plan was unrealistic, no plan at all, actually. There was only one option that would keep Billy safe in the confines of Asilo Colina. She had to consider Billy's well-being above her own and Devin's.

"Dammit." Jac stood, bringing the water bottles with her. The plastic crackled under her grip. She couldn't enter the room an emotional wreck. She had to harden, quell her emotions, and prepare for what needed to be done. Silence enveloped her. Her body stilled, and her mind cleared.

A minute later, she straightened, sniffled, wiped away her tears, took a deep breath, and exhaled long and slowly. She dropped the water bottles, neither wanting nor needing them. She wouldn't trick Devin into making this easy for her. This needed to be difficult; it needed to be personal. Besides, like Sebastian and every godforsaken vampire had tried to tell her, taking blood from humans, even if it killed them, was in her nature.

With her eyes wide and dry, Jac pressed her finger against the red, open button on the wall. She pushed the door upon hearing a click, revealing Devin in shorts and a T-shirt, just like the last time she saw him.

Devin stumbled back and slowly smiled. "Oh. Hi, Jac." He ran a hand through his hair. "You scared me."

"Hello." Jac stepped inside, stone-faced, emotionless. She looked Devin up and down and settled on his eyes. She felt nothing for the boy standing before her. The way it had to be.

The door closed.

I NEED TO SEE HIM

One week had passed since the day the door closed behind Jac, leaving her locked in a room with Devin. When she gained coherency a couple of days later, Mateus gave her the event details. The twins didn't immediately come into the room after she finished with Devin. Mateus explained they wanted to give her time to calm down from the anger and come down from the high of Devin's blood coursing through her. She sat beside Devin's motionless body for nearly an hour, crying through the endorphins that overwhelmed her senses.

Jac had been violent. She lashed out at anyone who entered the room and tried to pull her away. She plunged off the emotional cliff after striking Billy, who had rushed into the room to comfort her. Billy flew across the room into a sturdy metal table, breaking his humorous clean in two and dislocating his shoulder. The Castillo's doctor had explained that if he weren't a vampire, the break was bad enough to warrant amputation of his arm. Having already been emotionally wrecked from what she did to Devin, the pain and hurt on Billy's face shattered what remained of her sanity. From that moment, the Castillos didn't trust her around herself or anyone else. She hadn't seen Billy since.

For hours upon days, Jac was inconsolable, suicidal. Sebastian assigned Mateus to watch her day and night, with instructions to keep her away from sharp objects and anything that could be fashioned into a noose, including long pants and shirts. They even went to the extreme measure of serving her food on a paper plate for fear she would break a ceramic plate and use a shard as a makeshift knife.

The brothers later assigned Mateus another task unknown to her and replaced him with other faceless bodyguards. They told her their names, though she cared not to know, much less remember.

The passing days gave her ample time to grieve and time to think. Early on, she had considered ways to kill herself or be killed: refusing to breathe and choking herself didn't work. She should have known better, but she wasn't thinking straight. She had considered fighting Mateus or one of the other bodyguards who entered her locked room, forcing them to kill her. Thinking it through, she determined they would easily overpower her and instead leave her harmlessly screaming and flailing.

It wasn't until the fifth day she decided she no longer wanted to die. The sadness had mostly subsided, but the guilt remained like a suffocating wet blanket, worse than any pain or heartbreak. She accepted the guilt and owned it. The guilt reminded her of her hatred for vampires and her conviction to fight against what they stood for. She would need that hatred for her commitment to finding every woman and child taken from their homes and families by the Dog Brothers.

Earlier in the day, Mateus returned from whatever job he had been on. He brought a cupcake with a single candle—the extent of her birthday celebration. He stayed with her for fear she would burn down the house instead of blowing out the candle and making an undisclosed wish. She received a gift from Ximena of all people—a long-sleeved shirt and cargo pants. Inside the gift box, a card that appeared to have come from the no-special-occasion section read, "For when you leave." Signed, "Ximena."

Jac hadn't even thought of Ximena since the goblet of blood event. The birthday card message clearly indicated that the present was a going-away gift. Ximena wanted her out of the house, and Jac was more than ready to leave. Still relegated to wearing shorts and tank tops, Mateus apologetically took her gift.

It wasn't her birthday candle wish, but later that day, Jac convinced Mateus and the Castillos she was no longer suicidal and asked for her backpack and sheets for the bed. They expressed uncertainty, so she bartered by agreeing to the 24-hour surveillance for a few more days. Later, she decided, she'd insist on seeing Billy. They'd never been apart for seven hours, much less seven days.

After using the floral sheets, pillowcases, and comforter, making her mattress more of a bed, she plopped down upon it and unzipped her backpack. Her nose scrunched. The clothes desperately needed a wash. She pulled them from the backpack and threw them across the room and into her open closet. Despite the smell, she considered them an improvement to the wardrobe that had been removed.

Next, she removed the photographs bound with hair ties and the notebook with the victim's names. She studied the sad eyes of a child named Harley, four or five years old at the time of the photo. *I'll find you, Harley.*

She placed the photographs and notebook to the side and pulled the candle her father gave her. Caressing it with both hands, she closed her eyes, thought of Dad, and smiled. Next came the remaining straps of money, a plastic bag filled with bathroom supplies, and some underwear and socks that also found their way into the closet with an accurate throw. A beef stick pulled from the backpack's bottom recesses assaulted her with memories of Devin. He had warned her that the spicy beef stick—she bought to prove him wrong—was too hot for her to handle. Her chest tightened as she clutched it. As if it were a glowing rock from another planet with power-draining capabilities. She dropped the beef stick and lightly pounded her knuckles on her temples, then stared at the birthday bracelet Devin had given her. She pushed it around her wrist once, then forced the memories aside with a deep breath and an audible exhale.

Jac tore the beef stick from its wrapper. After giving it a whiff, she took a bite and chewed in the manner of a taste tester. The heat was mild at first, then grew into a mini-inferno. She waved her hand over her gaping mouth and scanned the room for a non-existent glass of water. She sprinted into the bathroom and spit the chewed meat into the toilet, sending it away with a flush. A few gulps of water from the sink faucet eased the pain, allowing her to reflect and smile. "Devin was right."

Jac jumped back onto the bed, scooped up her backpack, gave another look inside, and shook it. Something moved. She reached in again, running her hand around the bottom when it brushed against something flat. She pulled two photographs from the backpack she had missed. The first photo was of a woman named Vikki T., wearing the same scared expression as the others. "I'm sorry this happened to you. I'll add you to my list."

In the second photo, a child with a nest of black hair and sorrowful eyes stared back at her. Familiar eyes. "The hell?" She recognized the hair, eyes, and shape of the face. And ... the name.

Jac gasped, dropping the photo. A violent chill rippled through her. She scanned the room, scrutinizing everything, looking for truth, for reality. The world around her must have been an unsettling illusion. She clutched at her chest, fighting for breath. "This isn't real. This can't be happening." The child in the photo fearfully stared at her, a desperate cry for help from years long since passed.

"Okay." She sucked in a breath and blew it forcefully from her lungs. "Calm down. Calm down." She snatched the photograph, jumped from the bed, and bolted to her room's now unlocked door. Mateus, on guard, looked up from a book and narrowed his eyes.

"How can I help you, Miss Kelley?"

After a few rapid intakes of breath, she managed, "I need to see him. Now."

Mateus's brow furrowed as he spied the photo in her hand. "What's this about?"

Jac discreetly slid the photo into her pocket, away from Mateus's hawkish eyes. "It's been a week. I need to see him, and it can't wait."

"Jac, it's still not a good idea for you to be around any—"

"You take me to him now." She prodded her finger into Mateus's chest but stopped after he gave a disapproving look. After a calming, closed-eyes breath, she asked again, "Please. Just for a few minutes. You can stand right behind me."

Mateus wore a familiar, discouraged look on his face. He needed to say no but had a soft spot for her.

"Please," she said softly, with pleading eyes.

"Fine."

She put a fist to her forehead. "Thank you."

"But you listen to what I ask and say. And if he doesn't want you around, we leave."

"I promise."

Jac followed Mateus out of the Castillo's home and over to the American Colonial-style mansion next door, nearly a fifty-yard walk. Their steps led them along a red brick walkway to towering twin front doors. Mateus pushed the button to the fanciest doorbell Jac had ever heard, and they waited. Seconds later, footsteps sounded from inside the home. The clicking of turned locks preceded the door's opening, releasing a gust of cold air. A tall, head-shaved bodyguard answered the door. He regarded her mistrustingly, knowing she shouldn't be standing before him.

"Tyler," Mateus said.

"No. Nope," Tyler responded with a headshake and hand wave. "She can't come in."

Mateus gave Jac a 'you better not be screwing me over' look before replying. "Tyler, jus' get him. We'll stay out here."

Tyler scrutinized her and looked back at Mateus. "How are we supposed to trust her? Besides, he doesn't want to see her. Not yet."

"I'm fine; I promise," Jac said, calming the turmoil inside her enough to sound in control. "Tyler, you watched me a couple days ago. You know I'm better."

Mateus approached Tyler and responded, pulling rank, "I'm not asking this time. I'm ordering. Get him."

Tyler frowned. "It's on you." He closed the door to a crack behind him.

Minutes passed before footsteps returned, two sets this time. The door swung open, revealing Tyler. He reluctantly stepped to the side.

Jac stilled, her muscles stiffened. There he was, just as she remembered, but also undeniably different. He appeared rested, healed, healthy, and absolutely indifferent to her. He was also the worst she had ever seen him. Devin ... was a vampire.

"Hi, Devin," Jac said softly, fearing her voice would send him running away.

Devin fixed his eyes on her but said nothing.

"You look,"—she swallowed—"good. I, uh, I—"

"What do you want?" Devin snapped at her.

Jac flinched. She lost the words she wanted to say.

He leaned in. "What do you want, Jac?"

"I want ... I need to show you something." Jac averted her eyes as she fiddled with the photo in her pocket. She looked back at Mateus. "Can we have a minute?"

"Not happening," Tyler said firmly, stepping closer.

Jac stared into Devin's eyes, and he into hers. "Just a couple minutes ... please."

Devin stood motionless, stone-faced, for a moment, then broke. "It's okay. I'm ready." He patted Tyler's muscular shoulder.

Jac looked up at Mateus. "I'm good. Promise."

Mateus pressed his lips, and then his expression softened. "I'll be a few yards away," he said like a father watching his daughter play on the jungle gym for the first time.

Devin watched as Tyler walked away, saying he, too, would be close. He turned back to Jac, wearing the same stone-faced look. "Here we are, alone ... kind of. Now, what do you want? To finish me off this time?"

The comment hurt momentarily. Jac didn't have time for hurt. "No. God no. I never wanted any of this." She glanced back at Mateus and Tyler, then lowered her voice. "I wasn't given much of a choice."

"What was that you told me, after I found out you're a vampire?" He raised his eyebrows and craned his neck forward. "You said—" He pointed at her. "You said you would never hurt me."

Jac looked down, unable to meet Devin's eyes. She remembered saying those exact words. "I know," she muttered.

"What was that?" He touched his ear. "Oh, never mind. I can hear much better now. Figuring out how to dial back that ability? Not easy. It's nearly impossible to sleep when you hear everything. And that's not the worst of it. Did you know that a turned vampire, which I am thanks to you, feels some strange loyalty to the one who turns them?"

"I know."

"Do you know how screwed up it is to hate you and want to be around you at the same time?" Devin gritted his teeth. "Several times, I imagined killing you right after daydreaming of protecting and kissing you. Right now, I want to hold you in my arms and, at the same time, wrap my hands around your neck and squeeze until your eyes pop out."

"We good over there?" Mateus edged toward them.

Jac nodded, hugging herself. "We're okay."

Devin placed a hand over his eyes and rubbed his temples with his thumb and middle finger.

"Devin, I can't make up for or apologize enough for what I have done to you. I wish I could start over and never climb into the back of your car. But, when it came down to it, I couldn't do it. I couldn't kill you. If I chose wrong, I'm sorry."

Devin frowned, then lowered his head. "I don't think I'm ready for this yet. You should—"

"Wait." She placed a hand on his chest. "I'll go, but I need to show you something. It's why I came over."

He eyed her hand upon him, then met her gaze. "Fine. What do you need to show me?"

The corners of Jac's mouth twitched as she removed her hand from him. Devin's eyes followed her hand as she pulled the photo from her pocket, righted it, and held it in front of his face. At first, he didn't seem to understand what she was showing him, cutting his eyes between her and the photo. The confusion on his face slowly showed a creeping recognition.

He, too, recognized the kid. The shape of the face, the eyes, and the name. The kid in the photo was standing in front of him. He whispered, "Jacqueline P., June, two thousand-five, type O-negative."

EPILOGUE

Sunny waited as Edgar exited a brightly lighted room. Edgar eased the door shut and faced him and Ava. A woman's pained screams seeped through the walls.

The Coven leader stepped close to Ava, leaned in toward her, and smiled to his eyes. "Ava, what brings you and Sunny here?"

Seemingly unfazed by Edgar's breathy closeness, Ava stood firm. "Sunny has returned. He has news."

Edgar's eyes lingered over her briefly, then focused on Sunny. He held a finger inches from Sunny's face and sneered. "I'll assume, for your sake, my dear Sunny, you've returned with the Kelley children. Otherwise, I don't know why you'd return, knowing red walls would be in your future."

Sunny stood tall and firm, his hands clasped in front of him at his waist. "I don't have the Kelley children—"

Edgar growled; his finger in Sunny's face joined the others to form a fist.

"However," Sunny continued, "I have good news."

"This had better be the best damn news to ever tickle my ears."

"I've confirmed; the kids don't know."

Edgar relaxed his hand and placed it on Sunny's cheek. "And how have you reached this conclusion?"

"I've had discussions with everyone the kids conversed with from here to San Diego. There's been no mention of our ... undertaking. I am confident. As your trusted Emissary, I promise they do not know."

Edgar patted Sunny's cheek, turned back toward the door to the room, and raised his hands above his head. "Hallelujah!"

"And, I have even better news."

He lowered his hands. "You're spoiling me, Sunny. What could be better?"

"The last of your troubles, Lelah Kelley,"—he swallowed—"is dead."

Edgar eyed Sunny from over his shoulder. His fingers moved as if they were pulling the information shared from the air. He slowly turned, promptly moved toward Sunny, and urged, "How can you be certain the Kelley Matriarch has left the earthly plane?"

Sunny's lips pressed into a thin line, leaning close to Edgar's face. "I found her cold body."

"The proof? The head?"

"Delivered to your room."

Edgar's eyes widened as a devilish grin slowly stretched across his face. He clasped his hands over his mouth as a fit of chuckles overtook him. He performed an awkward, high-stepping movement as if he wanted to dance but was tempering his glee.

An interrupting cry from the room stilled his celebration. Not a cry from the woman. Not a cry of pain. But a high-pitched, tremulous wail—an announcement of birth into the world.

Edgard turned from Sunny, approached the room, and gently placed a palm against the door. "I will satisfy him with long life, and accord him my salvation. Let us rejoice at the birth of another blood donor. And may we live for an eternity on earth as in Heaven."